CANDY IN
CAPTIVITY

By the same author:

THE ACADEMY
CONDUCT UNBECOMING

CANDY IN CAPTIVITY

Arabella Knight

This book is a work of fiction.
In real life, make sure you practise safe sex.

First published in 1996 by
Nexus
332 Ladbroke Grove
London W10 5AH

Copyright © Arabella Knight 1996

Typeset by TW Typesetting, Plymouth, Devon

Printed and bound by
BPC Paperbacks Ltd, Aylesbury, Bucks

ISBN 0 352 33078 3

Chapter One

Salt spray stung her lips as the lumbering ferry shouldered through a swell of grey sea. Flickering her tongue out, Candy winced as she tasted the harsh tang mingled with the sticky sweetness of her smudged YSL Nouveau Rouge No. 9 lipstick. The ferry rolled and pitched once more as the heaving waves rose up and collapsed back into creamy spume. Candy staggered as her spiked Manolo Blahnik high heels skidded on the slippery deck of the *Puffin* – now almost four hours out of Oban and nosing doggedly westwards into the wide Atlantic. The two-man crew shrugged off their discomfort with the benefit of oilskins and nips of neat malt. Candy Brompton, shivering in her clinging Cesare Paciotti two-piece, suffered miserably. The biting wind that flattened the smoke belching out of the tall funnel whipped up her blonde hair. She blinked as the razor-cut wisps lashed her stinging cheeks. Gripping the wet handrail, the sole passenger gritted her teeth and braved the fierce spray.

It would be worth it. Worth it all. She had hired the ferry at Oban after a flight up from London. She was heading for the Isle of Oaigg – and a lucrative property venture. An unguarded fax in her office had caught her alert eye. The Laird of Oaigg was dead and his castle was up for sale. Candy Brompton remembered some Dutch businessmen she was cultivating. By flying up from London on the red-eye and commandeering the *Puffin* she could wrap up the deal within 48 hours – telling her office she had to visit a sick aunt to cover her sudden absence. A rich, sick aunt, of course. Candy moved in circles where only money, or the prospect of money, mattered. When she pulled off the deal, by cutting out her company and cheating them of the fat commission, she stood to gain a cool eighteen thousand. Eighteen thousand four hundred, to be precise. Candy Brompton was precise. She always carried a pocket calculator inside her Gabriela Ligenza stitched satchel that bounced against her ripely rounded thigh.

The *Puffin* slewed north eastwards, and in the early morning sunlight of a summer day, Candy saw a speck of land on the brilliant line of the horizon. Thirty minutes later a sour-smelling mouth bellowed into her ear that they had arrived. The wind whipped the words away from the crewman's lips but Candy knew that she had reached her goal. She almost lost the heel of her left shoe in an ungainly disembarkment and was left alone on a forlorn wooden jetty as the *Puffin* departed, trailing a plume of sooty black smoke from her funnel.

So this was Oaigg, she mused. Bleak and isolated. On the edge of the western world. Still, she grinned, those Dutchmen knew what they wanted. Turning her slender back to the sea, she trudged across slippery shingle towards a ribbon of rutted road that rose up into a dense fir plantation.

Fir trees? Funny. The map she had briefly glimpsed had shown Oaigg to be treeless. Perhaps the late laird had joined the recent fir-tree City tax dodge. The castle would be a mile inland. She started to walk. Above her, screaming gulls wheeled and swooped. Despite her excitement, she felt tired. Coffee and a hot bath would be good, she thought. She shivered deliciously at the thought of hot, scented water lapping at her rounded, shining breasts. Then, down to some brisk business with the agent for the sale. No. Factor. That's what they called them up here. An important detail. She knew the importance of details.

Turning a corner, she saw a castle looming up straight ahead. A stern granite pile which managed to remain gloomy and forbidding despite the golden sunshine. The white flint chippings of the drive crunched beneath her as she approached the imposing front entrance. The huge oak door was ajar. Candy paused. Should she ring? Or just go straight in? Her businesswoman's instinct told her to go straight in – the element of surprise was always useful in negotiation. Inside the vast entrance hall, her slightly battered high heels sank silently into a rich Moldavian carpet. Generations of careful polishing gleamed at her from the dark furniture. Beyond the vast hall, Candy counted eight doorways. Slightly overawed, she clutched her satchel strap and strode towards one. Beyond the door she found herself in a large library. Hundreds – no, thousands of leatherbound books lined the long walls from floorboards to lofty ceiling all around her. A desk and chair occupied the space immediately in front of a stained-glass window. Candy gazed up at the picture of a bear and three mastiffs depicted in purples, reds, greens and golds. The heraldic bear, she noticed, had a little red and white collar which sparkled in the sunlight.

Voices approached. Two young women in earnest conversation. Other property brokers? Rivals? Candy did not want to be at any disadvantage in her negotiations. She slipped behind a full-length tapestry just as the two young women entered. From her hiding place, Candy saw the lithe, beautiful girls, dressed scantily in tight, white vests and bottom-shaping shorts, quickly arrange a dozen chairs in three semicircle rows – four in each row – before the imposing desk.

'The Wise One will want a chair here for punishments after sentencing, won't she?' the tall, raven-haired girl asked.

'Yes, Chloe,' the other girl replied, her breasts bouncing softly as she straightened up.

Chloe arranged the wooden chair alongside the desk. The vivid colours of the stained-glass window dappled the scrubbed pine. Candy swallowed silently in her hiding place, her belly tightened slightly as her curiosity was tinctured with fearful apprehension.

'They're coming,' Chloe whispered urgently. 'Quick. Get the cane.'

The other girl, a heavily breasted brunette, scampered to

3

the desk and rattled a drawer. From its depths she extracted a 34-inch yellow bamboo cane and placed it almost reverentially on the top of the desk. Lengthways. It gleamed in the sunlight.

'Stand by your chairs,' an imperious voice barked.

Ten young women, similarly dressed in the figure-revealing uniform of crisp cotton vests and tight little shorts, filed into the library and stood silently by their appointed chairs.

'Be seated,' came the curt command.

Behind the tapestry at the back of the library, Candy watched as all twelve nubile beauties guided their plump bottoms down on to the hard chairs. Watched – as flesh kissed wood in silence.

'The communal court is now in session,' announced a superb, athletic specimen in a yellow and black tracksuit as she strode into the silent library. The brushed cotton clung to her lascivious curves like a second skin. The bosom joggled within its soft bondage. Candy watched as this saturnine beauty of some three and thirty summers languidly sat down at her desk and folded her arms.

'Stand up the accusers,' she invited solemnly.

Two girls rose up from their chairs.

'Annette? Whom do you accuse?'

'Emily,' Annette, the heavily breasted brunette, murmured huskily.

'The charge being?'

'Selfishness. She always takes an early morning bath and never leaves any hot water.'

'Sit down, Annette. Emily?'

Emily rose, her head of copper-red hair tossed back defiantly.

'Is this true?'

'No, Wise One.'

'And yet I seem to recall that we have spoken of this matter before. Did you take an early bath yesterday?'

'Yes, Wise One.'

'Did you in fact take all the hot water?'

'I don't think so,' the girl replied, shaking her copper hair thoughtfully.

'Did you take a bath this morning?'

'Yes, Wise One,' murmured Emily.

'Before the others on your landing?'

'I don't – I'm not sure.'

'Did you leave sufficient hot water for the others?'

Silence.

'Four strokes. To be administered by your accuser. Next.'

The second accuser rose up to her feet and spoke distinctly. 'I accuse Madelaine.'

'What is the nature and substance of your accusation, Samantha?' the Wise One enquired in an even tone.

'She was greedy at supper last night. I was late and there was nothing left for me.'

'Sit down, Samantha. Madelaine?'

A willowy blonde responded to the summons.

'Is this true? Did you leave nothing for Samantha to eat?'

'Yes, it is true, Wise One,' the lissome blonde mumbled penitently.

'Very well. You will receive two strokes. And then,' the Wise One paused, examining the bamboo cane that glinted before her, 'you will administer two strokes to Samantha. We do, of course, discourage greed, but we do not encourage slackness or indeed bad manners here. Being late for supper is ample evidence of both. Two strokes for Samantha. Be seated.'

Candy could see from the rows of nodding heads that the young women approved of the Wise One's deliberations and even-handed decision to have both accuser and accused punished.

'We have one more matter for the communal court to consider,' the august woman seated at the desk purred in a voice softly potent with menace.

An uneasy silence settled on the girls. The air crackled with the static of anxious expectation. Candy felt the pulse at her throat quicken.

'Two hundred cigarettes have been taken from the stores. We agreed, did we not, that one packet for those that required cigarettes would be sufficient?'

5

The cool tone, the dry, legal precision of the language and the solemn nature of the charge all combined to hold the assembled girls in thrall. Some nodded their memory of such an agreement. Candy studied them a little more closely, estimating their ages to be between a coquettish eighteen and her own youthful twenty-three.

'Stand up, Clare.'

The accused obeyed, protesting her innocence unconvincingly.

'Silence, girl. I find your protests unseemly. You are fully aware of the rules here. Did you take the cigarettes?'

Clare shook her head vehemently.

'Did you take the cigarettes, Clare?'

'No,' came the sullen reply.

'Clare. I know perfectly well that you like menthol cigarettes. Two hundred have disappeared from our communal stores. If you wanted more you only had to ask.'

'But I didn't,' replied Clare, blushing pinkly in her sudden outburst of defiance. 'Look.' She held up a packet of filter tips and waved them in triumph. 'See?' she crowed smugly. 'These are not menthol.'

Candy glanced at the Wise One to see the effect of this proof of innocence. The Wise One remained unperturbed. Almost serene.

'No, they are not menthol cigarettes,' the Wise One agreed pleasantly.

Clare smirked.

'They are exactly the same brand that went missing. Did I say menthol? How remiss of me. Thank you, Clare. Guilty.'

'But – I didn't mean – I'm sorry – I only took them because . . .' Clare whined frantically.

'You know the rules perfectly well by now, my girl. The cigarettes we can of course overlook. But your deceit is an offence, indeed an affront, to the entire community. Group punishment. Be seated.'

Clare, pale and silent, slumped down heavily into her chair.

'There being no other matters for the communal court to consider, we will commence with the punishments.'

6

Candy gripped the thick curtain of tapestry as the first pair of girls rose and stepped forward towards the desk. Annette, who had accused Emily of hogging all the hot water, stretched across the desk and picked up the yellow bamboo cane. Emily bowed down and placed her hands, fingers splayed out symmetrically, on to the seat of the scrubbed pine chair positioned alongside the desk for the punishments. Candy saw Emily's buttocks, plumply rounded in their cotton shorts, bulge invitingly as they were offered up submissively to the cane. Annette paused to examine the tip of the whippy bamboo for several delicious moments before suddenly flexing her wrist. The living length of supple wood swished twice as she thrummed the empty air with the cruel cane. Two silent paces brought the lithe, beautiful punisher close up to the left thigh of the passive, bending Emily – now positioned and pertly poised for her imminent pain.

'Four strokes,' pronounced the Wise One.

The tip of the cane rose up into the sunlight and quivered. Annette slowly lowered the whippy wood until it lay firmly pressed against the clenched hemispheres of Emily's proffered bottom. The bamboo indented the curve of the cotton-sheathed cheeks imperceptibly as Annette took a single step backwards to stand, her long legs now slightly apart, at arm's – and cane's – length away. The cane flickered and swept upwards, eagerly. The library was silent and still. Even the distant black-capped gulls wheeling and diving in the bright sunshine softened their mewling cries.

Swish. The spellbinding silence was sliced apart as the cane swooped down and struck the double domes of firm buttock flesh smartly, witheringly, with a savage swipe. Emily gasped audibly. Swish. Again, the cane whipped down to lash the bulging, soft cheeks with a searing, searching cut.

Dry-mouthed and wide-eyed, Candy stared in astonished fascination as the punishment proceeded. Her knuckles whitened as her fists clenched in response to each swipe of the bamboo cane across the upturned bottom.

Swish. The third stroke brought Emily's head up in a jerk. As the white neck of the punished girl craned and arched for a split second, her hair flounced wildly. Candy saw the ravished cheeks quiver in their sudden torment. Swish. The fourth stroke whipped the rounded bottom swiftly and surely, bringing the punished girl up on to her tiptoes in sweet anguish.

'Thank you, Annette,' the Wise One said softly. 'I am sure you will have plenty of hot water for bathing henceforth. Be seated.'

Annette replaced the silent cane lengthways down on the surface of the desk. To Candy's utter surprise, both girls – punisher and punished – returned to their seats hand in hand.

'Samantha, Madelaine. The communal court deems that you are both at fault. Two strokes apiece.'

Madelaine took the cane and offered it to Samantha. It was taken in silence. Madelaine bent over the punishment chair – Candy could have sworn the girl wiggled her rump teasingly, tauntingly, as she positioned herself for the coming strokes.

Crack. Samantha delivered the first swiping cut with enthusiastic vigour. The cane sliced down to swish the upturned buttocks with a geometrical exactitude, bisecting Madelaine's shuddering globes precisely. Crack. The second stroke fell, biting into the bunched cheeks along and exactly across the line of the first. Madelaine squealed softly, her left foot fluttering up from the floor – the white ankle sock pawing the empty air. In silence, the two girls exchanged roles and positions – the punisher now the punished. Candy found it almost impossible to swallow, her tongue had thickened in her dry mouth. A dread delight suffocated her. Never before had she witnessed such intimate, almost tender, punishment being dispensed. How different from those shivering occasions at her boarding school when naughty bottoms burned brightly – as red as the faces of the sullen schoolgirls. Candy remembered her own moments of discipline – being a wilful girl they were frequent – and her own sulky reluctance as she bared her

8

bottom for correction. How different it was here. How strange. For Candy, it was like being introduced to a new, heady cocktail. Four-parts fear mixed with a jigger of fascination.

Swish. Swish. Candy held her breath as Madelaine sliced the length of whippy wood down twice across Samantha's buttocks. The strokes were administered with a vicious tenderness. A savage joy. After the cane had been silently and respectfully placed down across the desk before the impassive figure of the Wise One, the two girls returned to their respective chairs – again, Candy noted in amazement – hand in hand.

'Clare,' the stern voice from behind the desk ordered. 'Step forward for a group punishment.'

Head bowed, the accused stood up and paced penitently towards the appointed spot. Candy watched, her heart racing, her eyes sparkling, as the Wise One rose silently and walked slowly around the desk. The lithe figure in the yellow tracksuit sat down on the punishment chair and nodded to the anxious Clare who stood, contrite and ashamed, her hands folded behind her. Candy saw the fingers – twisting in fearful expectation. Clare took three short paces forwards and eased herself down and across the lap of the seated woman. Candy felt a hot surge of pleasure awaken her sleeping loins – a moist warmth stirring deep down within her. Spellbound, she gazed from behind her screen of thick tapestry. To her mild alarm, she felt her nipples slowly thicken in their cool, silken bondage of her La Perla brassière. Already her panties were hot and damp. Blushing as she struggled to deny the meaning of this self-knowledge, she trembled and clutched the velvety curtain of tapestry tight.

'The severity of your offence merits and warrants a harsh punishment, Clare. I feel obliged to be very strict with you,' the Wise One said in an audible whisper. 'I believe I voice the will of the entire community when I propose that you receive and suffer your severe spanking bare bottomed.'

A subdued murmur of approval from the eleven seated

9

girls met this pronouncement. Candy luxuriated in the solemn words, thrilling to the cool, authoritative tone. Words so ponderous yet so potent. She shivered impatiently as the promise they concealed revealed itself to her hot imaginings. At the base of her aching belly, her warmth spread. Candy ran the tip of her tongue against the roof of her mouth as she pressed her soft thighs together with a firm squeeze. She gazed enraptured as the Wise One's slim, strong hands sought and found Clare's tight elastic waist band. Clare, unbidden, raised her thighs and bottom up submissively and lay, prone and meek, as the white shorts rode over her buttocks and eased down along the sweep of her luscious, clamped thighs. The elastic waist band snapped into her quivering flesh – hugging her trapped legs halfway down between the pillows of her soft bottom and the shadowed hollows behind her knees. The stricture pinned and trapped her into a passive, vulnerable immobility. Candy watched as the capable hands came to a silent rest, one carefully on top of the other, across the pliant, naked cheeks of Clare's bare bottom.

'You will arise and approach, one by one, to spank the bottom of this naughty girl. Please return to your place afterwards in silence.'

The first row rose in a ragged formation and the four girls slowly filed up towards the desk. Smack. The first girl in the punishment squad bent down, her breasts bulging within her white vest. Her slightly curved palm cracked down across the bare, ivory cheeks. Clare juddered as flesh met flesh in a stinging salute. The bare bottom blushed a becoming pink. Smack. The second girl had approached the buttocks and done her duty. Bending to administer the sharp spank, the punisher's rump had plumped to stretch her scanty shorts. Candy stifled her gasp of wonder. The harsh smack echoed in the austere library – leaving another faint, pinkish imprint on the bouncing buttocks. Smack. The third spank was a crisp caress. The reddening cheeks wobbled under its cruel impact. Smack. The fourth left the buttocks quivering, both cheeks now shining rubescently.

Clare was pinned down across and over the warm thighs

of the Wise One, who had placed one firm hand down across the nape of the penitent's neck and the other – flattened palm inwards – firmly against the clamped thighs just below the scorched, naked buttocks. Struggle and strive as she might, Clare could not escape the rain of pain.

Candy drank in every vivid detail greedily. The supine, helplessly passive girl, bare-bottomed and utterly vulnerable. The bite of the tight elastic encircling the naked, trembling thighs. The slender, strong hands that pinned and pinioned. The bare bottom. The soft, suffering cheeks. The pink, hot satin skin.

Smack. Smack. Smack. Ouch. Candy winced, but her eyes remained wide open. That last spank was very harsh. She felt her unbidden – unsuspected – excitement drip down freely against her stocking tops. Deep within her clamped thighs her Rose of Eve slowly unfurled its sticky petals under the fierce sun of her arousal. Her creamy thighs felt hot and moist as she parted them to ease the sweet torment of her pulsating pleasure. A spasm of feral joy flickered deep within her belly each time a hovering spanking hand swept down to sting the bare bottom below. Candy's fingers inched downwards to stroke and trace the contoured delta of her pubic mound – to dapple in the triangle of her tingling delight. Her fingers trembled as they brushed against the erect tip of her tiny sweet thorn.

Spread sensuously across the warm lap of her dominant judge and jury, the naked bottom of Clare squirmed and wriggled as her hot cheeks lay utterly exposed for the conclusion of her group punishment. From the back row, the remaining girls rose dutifully and filed forwards in graceful silence. Candy saw Clare's curved cheeks clench in fearful expectation.

Smack. The naked girl bucked and bounced within the firm, controlling restraint of the Wise One's pinioning hands. Clare's reddened buttocks were now ablaze and no doubt scalding in their fiery torment. Smack. Clare mewed plaintively as she strove to escape the spanking hands. Smack. Candy, her eyes fierce slits of concentration, focused hard on the naked buttocks seething in exquisite pain. She noticed how the sparkling colours thrown down from the stained-glass window flung a pattern of red and white from the bear's little collar across the voluptuous domes of the bare-bottomed punished girl. Smack. The speckled pattern of coloured light shivered as the spanked bottom wobbled beneath the swift chastising palm. Clare jerked her rump up in a reflex as the reverberating crack ignited her molten cheeks with burning flame.

Candy, her throat tightening, almost swooned. Steadying herself, she clutched the tapestry. It collapsed under her sudden weight, tumbling down and covering her struggles completely. High-pitched squeals of surprise and dismay filled the air, but rising clearly above the turmoil came the grim, calm voice of the Wise One.

'Seize him,' she thundered.

Clare dragged up her shorts and joined in the affray. Under the clinging weight of the heavy tapestry, Candy was helpless and imprisoned. She struggled in vain.

'It's a girl,' gasped several excited voices as many eager hands uncovered the squirming blonde.

'Bring her here,' commanded the Wise One sternly.

Candy, having inhaled copious amounts of dust from the collapsing tapestry, sneezed twice. Blinking, she was dragged to a spot two feet before the desk. The sunlight speared down through the stained-glass window directly into her eyes, denying her the chance to study her inquisitor.

'Who are you and what are you doing here?' the Wise One demanded. Despite the fierce grip of the girls who held her, Candy stood proudly defiant. She was a Brompton. The Bromptons never flinched.

'My name is Candy Brompton and I am here on Oaigg to buy this castle. I cannot name the principals I represent but they have funded me sufficiently to bid for the entire estate and all that is entailed by the late laird.'

The Wise One remained silent and sat, head bent down, running a fingertip along the length of yellow bamboo that rested on the desk before her. Candy's eyes followed the fingertip as it stroked the length of passive cane. Cane that had sung its cruel song not many moments before.

'I want –' Candy resumed briskly. A skilled negotiator, she promptly decided to dictate terms.

'Silence,' snapped the Wise One. 'Where is the camera?'

'A camera? I haven't gone one.'

'Tape recorder?'

Candy shook her head, startled by the abrupt questions.

'If you are a journalist you have come poorly equipped.'

'I told you, I'm here to buy Castle Oaigg,' Candy retorted hotly.

'So you are not a journalist?' came the measured response.

'No,' snapped Candy. 'I've come here to buy –'

'Castle Oaigg,' the Wise One intervened sharply. She paused and then looked down again at the yellow bamboo.

'Then you have come to the wrong island, Candy Brompton. This is the Isle of Orrag and this castle is most certainly not for sale.'

Candy, suddenly exhausted and bewildered, felt the floor rise up beneath her slightly buckling knees. Then the dreadful truth flooded her disbelieving mind – crashing over her like those heavy rollers that washed the prow of the *Puffin*, which had ferried her here in error. Oaigg. Orrag. She had commandeered the *Puffin* and her small crew at five in the morning and the hasty transaction was conducted against the noise of Oban – a busy, working port. Her Sloane vowels, her tiredness after the overnight trip, coupled with the crew's fondness for the odd dram had no doubt all contributed to the mistake. And when they had reached the island, the fierce wind had whipped the lilting Gaelic words out of the crewman's mouth. Oaigg. Orrag. Such a foolish blunder.

No stranger to the stress and strain of the London property jungle, Candy pulled herself together She felt the illustrious Brompton lineage surge up within her. She jerked her head back.

'There has been a stupid mistake,' she remarked. Her tone was brisk.

'Which has been made by you,' came the swift reply, in an even brisker tone.

13

Candy flashed a resentful glance at the Wise One. The Bromptons were not used to being bullied. Valour flowed through their veins.

'Trespass. Breaking and entering. Violating our privacy and invading our community,' continued her accuser.

Candy blushed and lowered her eyes. She had to acknowledge the charge.

'Yes, Candy Brompton. A stupid mistake.'

The words carried a hint of menace. Candy paled slightly but stiffened her resolve. She had been in tighter spots than this.

'I'd better telephone for a ferry. Or arrange for a helicopter to come and –' Candy said in a voice that had risen half an octave.

'Silence,' commanded the Wise One.

The tight grip on Candy's arms suddenly strengthened.

'Search her bag.'

The Gabriela Ligenza was seized and its contents spilled out across the desk. The golden bullet of the YSL Nouveau Rouge No. 9 lipstick rolled across the soft leather surface and came to rest, nuzzling the bamboo. Candy watched as her intimate things were examined. Her phial of Opium perfume. Credit cards. Keys to her BMW and her Docklands penthouse. Passport and driving licence. Then, yanked from her slim document wallet, a smudged xerox of the original Castle Oaigg fax – done in a twinkling under her bosses' greedy eyes – and the Dutchmen's banker's draft. The Wise One studied all this evidence meticulously before coming to a decision. Candy awaited the verdict. The Wise One flickered her large eyes. Verdict was pronounced.

'It appears that you have been telling the truth. You are not a journalist.'

'Of course I'm not,' Candy retorted hotly. Tired and frustrated at what could prove an expensive error – if she missed her chance of an early coup, the later open bidding could lose her Castle Oaigg and her fat commission – her customary short temper was close to exploding.

'What a very rude young woman you are,' whispered the

14

Wise One softly. It was the tone one would use to admonish a naughty child. 'Have you never been taken to task for your bad manners? Hmm? You crash in here, invade our privacy, spy on us. And,' the pause was measured, calculated. 'And yet I hear no hint of an apology.'

The implicit accusation hung heavily in the air between them. Candy shrugged and tossed her head back defiantly, flicking her golden mane impatiently. It would be a sign of weakness if she were to apologise now. And her sixth sense told her not to show any sign of weakness whatsoever to this shrewd, capable woman they called the Wise One. Don't weaken, Candy told herself. Stay cool. No apologies.

'May I use your telephone, please,' she said in a neutral voice.

The Wise One merely smiled imperceptibly as she neatly deflected the request. 'The scheduled ferry will call with our supplies in three weeks' time. You may return on it.'

'But you can't keep me here,' Candy cried, roughly freeing herself from the hands that gripped her so severely. 'I demand –'

'You demand absolutely nothing. In a few moments, you will be severely punished for spying on us.'

'No. You can't.'

'Then,' the Wise One continued implacably, 'then you will be taken to your room and remain here as our guest. And as our guest, you will observe – and strictly abide by – all our rules and regulations.'

'You can't do this,' Candy hissed vehemently. 'Let me go at once.'

'Go, by all means. Go. You are perfectly free to do so,' the Wise One suddenly smiled.

Candy frowned suspiciously. Turning, she walked slowly towards the library door. Obeying the Wise One's silent instructions, several young women stepped aside to let their captive pass unhindered. Candy felt the weight of the heavy brass door handle in her hand.

'Miss Brompton.' The voice from the desk was pleasant. A polite tone that veiled a smiling triumph.

15

'Yes?' Candy snapped, shouldering her satchel impatiently. 'What?'

'Can you swim?'

'Yes – no, a bit,' came the lame reply.

'I fear that a bit won't get you back as far as Oban.'

Candy sensed her doom closing in all around her. It pressed in on her like glass walls. Inexorably. She looked around the library. The throng of beautiful young women gazed back at her impassively.

'I'm sure you'd like a bath and some hot coffee after your overnight journey. Hmm?' This time the tone was conciliatory. Almost.

'Yes,' Candy nodded sullenly.

'Perhaps a little rest?' soothed her inquisitor.

'Of course,' came the ungracious retort.

'Very well,' pronounced the Wise One. 'Chloe, Samantha. See to it that our guest receives every comfort and consideration.'

Candy tossed her head back triumphantly. That's more like it, she thought. The Bromptons always get their way.

'After you have administered a punishment of four strokes.'

The words hit Candy like a splash of iced water in the face. She struggled but was easily overwhelmed. Chloe and Samantha efficiently stripped the dazed blonde down to her bare essentials of brassière, suspender belt, cotton panties and sheer stockings. Candy writhed in her near-naked shame.

'Across the desk with her,' instructed the Wise One.

Firm hands closed around Candy's wrists and as if in a slow-motion dream she witnessed herself being dragged down across the cool wood of the desk. In her lacy, under-wired cups, her rounded breasts spilled forward and bulged before squashing heavily, fleshily into the polished surface. Samantha tugged at Candy's unyielding wrists – straightening the helpless arms and then the full stretch of Candy's bending, supine body across the desk. Buttocks now upturned and utterly vulnerable, the spread-eagled blonde shivered in her mounting anguish.

16

Face pressed down into the wood, Candy burned with both anger and shame. The Wise One paced softly towards her prey and gently tapped the bunched cheeks. Candy's anger flared at this violation of her intimacy. The Wise One tapped her fingertips into the damp of the blonde's recent excitement. Candy's shame burned as her secret was discovered. The fingertips soothed the quivering buttocks.

'You are a rude girl. Ill-mannered and impertinent. A taste of discipline should correct your wilful ways. Four strokes.'

The punishment was meted out briskly, crisply and rapidly. Swish. Swipe. Chloe swept the supple length of whippy bamboo down across the bunched cheeks. Candy squealed. Swish. Swipe. Chloe's second stroke seared into the stretched cotton panties. The wriggling blonde bucked and jerked her tormented rump. Swish. Swipe. The third cut sharply across the shuddering cheeks, striping them red beneath their thin, white cotton protection. Candy squeaked her anguish and her outrage. Swish. Swipe. Down swooped the wood to seek out and stripe her defenceless upturned bottom with a fourth kiss of fire.

'Take her to the west wing. She may have a bath. See to her needs, Chloe,' the Wise One instructed softly. 'I will pay a visit within the hour.'

In a daze of shock and a haze of stinging pain, Candy followed Chloe along cool corridors and up two flights of stairs – the first of well-worn stone, the second of smoothly polished elm. In a sullen silence, the punished blonde followed Chloe into an airy bathroom. The door closed behind them, leaving them alone. It was spacious and brightly lit with a blue linoleum floor, a large, white porcelain bathtub and a full-length mirror. Golden sunlight flooded down from an oriel window. Chloe bent over to turn the twin brass taps on – her soft body breaking into the broad shaft of sunbeams. Steam quickly softened the air, clouding the full-length mirror with its warm breath. Chloe spoke softly.

'Let me undress you and bathe you. You are our guest now.'

17

Candy, still quivering with rage at the punishment her bottom had suffered, remained defiantly mute. Chloe gently insinuated her hands around the soft warmth of the sulky blonde and unclasped the taut La Perla brassière, allowing Candy's ripe breasts to spill and bounce as they tumbled free. Chloe's eyes widened with wonder at the splendidly heavy orbs of dancing flesh. Brushing her forearm against them as she bent forwards to ease the tight panties down, Chloe felt the nipples stiffen and peak. Candy blushed – almost as becomingly as her punished bottom. Next, nimble fingers unsnapped the suspender belt. It slithered over the proud swell of the thighs down to a passive surrender around the small feet. Chloe swept her firm palms down to unpeel the shimmering stockings.

'I will soothe your poor, hot bottom, Candy,' Chloe whispered huskily. 'Before you bathe.'

Slipping nimbly out of her own brief uniform, Chloe plucked up a yellow honeycombed sponge. She held it under the beaded brass cold tap. The sponge grew heavy as it swelled up within her grasp. Soon she was pressing the oozing sponge against the recently caned buttocks. Candy gasped softly and almost swooned at the delicious, healing touch. Kneeling, her shining eyes now only a few inches away from the four faint pink stripes that scored the creamy buttocks, Chloe pressed the cold sponge into the hot flesh once more. Candy rose up on her toes in response to the icy water as it sluiced over her bare bottom, trickling down across the hot, satin cheeks into a rivulet that found the shadowed valley of her dark cleft. Chloe pressed the sponge against the ravished rump once more, causing Candy to redouble her shivers of delight. The tiny rivulet splashed down from the clenched cheeks to spangle the smoothness of her naked, inner thighs.

Rage still burned deep in Candy's mind. Her anger at the discipline her bottom had been subjected to smouldered. It had not been just her soft cheeks which had suffered. So had her pride. The pride of the Bromptons. But Chloe's soothing ministrations cooled her lambent outrage and extinguished – for the time being - her burning resentment.

'That – that is so good,' murmured Candy with a deep sigh.

'Mmmm,' echoed Chloe, nodding her understanding. 'After the hot cane, the cooling water.'

Chloe's fingertips landed with butterfly lightness down on to the quivering surface of the faintly striped bottom. The cheeks clenched in a reflex of delicious expectation. Slowly, gently, soothingly, the punisher brushed the buttocks of the punished with a tender, healing touch. Candy's gasp melted into a shuddering sigh as her tense body loosened into supple submission. Deep down inside, the last hot embers of her glowing anger died. Unconsciously, instinctively, she thrust her bottom back into the fluttering fingertips, eager – hungry even – for their cool caress. Chloe inched her face closer still against the naked buttocks and, with her lips now almost kissing the four pink stripes where the cane had kissed the creamy cheeks, blew a cooling zephyr across the trembling surface of the swollen domes. Candy murmured dreamily. Slowly, the delight that had flickered when she had witnessed the hapless Clare's bare bottom being spanked rekindled – causing her pouting labial lips to tingle. Confusion troubled her. Already she understood her own warm stripes from the supple bamboo as being pleasantly painful. Sweetly sore. Could this be possible, she wondered. How could discipline be something to be desired? Mildly alarmed at her wanton thoughts, Candy retreated from them into the simple sensuality of Chloe's tenderness. Candy groaned as Chloe suddenly planted her wet rosebud mouth deep into the creamy, pliant flesh of the left buttock. It wobbled and joggled as she kissed it, lingeringly. Moaning aloud, Candy buckled at the knees and swayed – steadying herself at the last moment by thrusting her hands out behind her into Chloe's soft, raven hair.

'You must bathe now,' whispered the kneeling girl. 'Come.'

Rising slowly, Chloe brushed her bunched breasts against the blonde's bare buttocks. She hissed luxuriously as her hard nipples dragged against the twin domes of

19

heavy, satin flesh. The naked girls shared the same soft stab of raw pleasure – Candy gasping aloud her frank and utter joy. She turned, their eyes met. Belly grazing belly, breast squashed into breast, for nearly half a minute they drowned in their mutual delight. Then Chloe broke the weave of the spell that bound them by brushing Candy's outer thigh with a delicate sweep of her palm. A rippling spasm shivered down the length of the blonde's leg.

'Into the bath with you,' urged Chloe, playfully dominant as she imperiously tossed her raven hair. She lightly slapped Candy's bottom.

Obediently, Candy stepped over the side of the bath. Chloe watched the shadowed cleft between the recently caned cheeks widen as the naked blonde stepped gracefully into the scented water. Briskly, the raven-haired girl soaped and flannelled her passive captive. Tamed by the cane, and lulled by Chloe's soothing care, Candy surrendered completely. Fingers, soap and the searching flannel sought and found – frequently lingering – those secret, intimate fleshfolds usually explored alone. The bond of intimacy, undeclared but understood, was strengthened and deepened. It had begun with the dominant caning and was now blossoming with gentle aftercare.

'I didn't cane you too hard, did I?' Candy heard Chloe ask softly. Chloe listened to Candy's deliberate silence.

'It would have been worse if Samantha – or Emily – had striped you. They have a ruthless love for the cane. Samantha can be cruel with her cuts, and Emily's strokes are so severe,' Chloe shivered.

'It hurt,' Candy whispered. 'A little. I felt more shame than pain. But now . . .'

'But now?' Chloe encouraged.

'It all seems strangely wonderful.' Candy was surprised to hear herself utter this confession, and almost immediately regretted the frankness of her admission.

'Now let me dry you,' Chloe replied evenly, sensing the turmoil behind the confused blonde's eyes.

Candy lifted her shining nakedness up from the bath. Diamond droplets glistened on her white shoulders and across her bosom's trembling swell. Down in her nest of wispy, golden pubic hair, liquid pearls gathered. Chloe wrapped the naked bather in a large, white towel and patted and pressed with firm hands to dry the imprisoned breasts, belly and hips. Soon the flattened palms were caressing the ripe curves of the captive buttocks. Candy shuddered with pleasure. She shuddered again as a forefinger traced the outline of her pubic mound, and shuddered yet again – this time moaning softly – as Chloe returned to the joggling bottom with a fierce tenderness as she slowly squeezed and teased the cheeks apart. Candy's surge of delight all but choked in her dry throat. The probing fingers inched back towards the warm fleshfolds between her slightly parted thighs – and, within the bunched towelling – rubbed slowly, maddeningly slowly, at her opening sex. Chloe had a tantalising sureness of touch. It was also a touch of sweet dominance. Candy's labia quivered in their slippery warmth beneath the touch of sugared sovereignty. The naked blonde buckled slightly at the knees and threatened to topple. Chloe looked up in mild concern then steadied her captive's swaying hips between two firm palms. The white towel had slipped, abandoned, to the floor. Chloe rose up slowly against Candy's naked splendour. A single bead of water winked as it clung to the left nipple. Bending her head of raven hair, she greedily tongued the nipple. Soon her fierce lips had moulded themselves to suck the firm, pink peak. She sucked deeply. Candy mewed softly and swept her hands up to clutch her damp, blonde mane.

'I will powder you,' Chloe whispered huskily, mouthing the soft words into the milky white flesh of the quivering breast.

Beads of wet pleasure spilled freely down Candy's inner thighs. The tiny beads became a single stream as the talcum powder glided over each rounded buttock beneath Chloe's splayed fingers. The powder rose up in a fine cloud as it cascaded down over the mute blonde's shoulders and thighs. Candy smiled and, catching some of the stray, wanton talc, palmed her bosom. Fresh, wet heat oozed down

21

her inner thighs as she crushed down her rebellious nipples harshly.

'You'll have to wear these. It's the rule.'

Chloe handed the naked blonde her prescribed uniform. Candy took the white cotton vest and eased it over her head. It hugged her shoulders. She dragged it down slowly to imprison her full breasts, leaving the peaking nipples erect and inviting beneath the stretch of cotton. Relishing the restriction around her bosom, Candy smoothed the crisp fabric down over her breasts and belly with a firm sweep of her hands.

'Shorts,' Chloe whispered, flicking them across before stepping back briskly to struggle into her own.

Unaccustomed to the scanty shorts, Candy approached them uncertainly. Raising her left leg and flexing it at the knee slightly, she stepped gingerly into them. Her buttocks bulged then relaxed again as she straightened up, snapping the shorts into her pubic mound. Such a tight fit. Tight, but so delicious. Despite her fierce pride and ungovernable spirit, Candy acknowledged the wonderful sensation of the bite of the fabric into the cleft between her buttocks. The wonderful sensation of the moulding and squeezing of each fleshy peach. Sighing blissfully, she adjusted the waistband, fingering the elastic a fraction, but only a fraction, so that the stretched seat still hugged and cupped her heavy cheeks deliciously. Candy sighed once more.

'I'll take you to your room. The Wise One will visit you shortly.' Chloe smiled.

The door closed softly behind Chloe leaving Candy alone in her room. It was a simple, spartan affair. White-washed stone walls, a polished wooden floor of mellow pine. Just like a nun's cell. Severe. Candy gazed at the austere, narrow bed. And then at the solitary chair. A narrow Norman window, betraying the age of the castle to Candy's expert eye, gave a glimpse of the ocean. A stretch of aquamarine veined with silver. All was silent except for the murmur of rollers spilling on to the shingle beach.

Candy slumped on to her bed. The events of the morning surged like an ebb tide in her tired mind. She flicked through the crowded images just as she would flick through an illustrated catalogue at a property auction. She had a well-trained mind. It was her habit to select and focus sharply on the items she meant to have. To her surprise and curiosity, it was Clare's bottom that emerged as the dominant image. The rounded, creamy cheeks spread across the Wise One's lap. Pale, ivory buttocks, passive and pliant. Soft, so soft. Bare and vulnerable as they awaited their pain. The spanking.

Candy swallowed and shivered pleasurably. The spanking. She murmured the words like a child having difficulty with a strange, new phrase. Golden thighs pressed together, the line of obedient girls filing up dutifully, pink palms alert and firm. Pink palms raised. The spanking. The ripe cheeks flattened under the harsh rain of stinging, spanking palms. The juddering, joggling buttocks, deepening in their blushes from rosy pink to indignant scarlet. The spanking. Clare's bare bottom. Suffering, suffering sweetly. Such a delicious pain.

Candy blinked the crimson from behind her eyes and eased herself slowly, languidly, along the silk eiderdown at full stretch. Her head sank back into the single, snow-white pillow. She focused intently on the delicious image of Clare's bottom. Bared and prepared, bunched and poised for punishment. Splaying her thighs wide, she dreamily ran her fingertips down across her fiercely prinked nipples that quivered beneath her cotton vest. Clare's bottom. As round and as pale as the midsummer moon that hovers on the trembling horizon. An orb of perfect cream. A sphere of splendour. Candy squirmed down into the eiderdown, wriggling her bottom into its surrendering softness. She closed her eyes, allowing the image to develop more clearly. Clare's naked cheeks. The soft, trembling cheeks. Swollen and heavy. Ripe and round. The dark, secret cleft. The dark secret revealing itself as the shadowed cleft opened slightly when Clare snuggled into the warm thighs of her dominant chastiser. The subtle swell of the proud curves. Clare's wobbling rump. Soft as satin. Patient as the penitent lay perfectly still. Utterly submissive.

Submissive. An alien notion for Candy, yet one which secretly thrilled her as it flitted across her consciousness. Candy scorned the timorously meek, and yet tiny tongues of pleasure licked her hungrily at the thought of the word: submissive. She raised her hips, easing her bottom from the bed beneath, and placed two straightened fingers between her upper thighs – guiding them surely down into the moist warmth of her delta. Clare's bottom. The image burned brightly behind Candy's clenched eyes. Her fingers, now welded together to form one single, fused extension of her trembling hand, rubbed faster. Harder. Faster and harder – with an increasing fierceness of fervid concentration. Her hot wetness surged into a quicksilver flood, soaking her tight cotton shorts. Suddenly, as she surrendered to her approaching climax, an unbidden memory drove its burning image into her consciousness. It was of her own – not Clare's – punishment. Candy shrank back, alarmed and ashamed, as the image glowed. The image of Samantha gripping her wrists as she had been dragged, all but naked, across the cool, hard surface of the polished desk. Then Chloe, legs slightly apart, fingering the tip of the flexed whippy wood.

Yes.

Candy's fingers scrabbled frantically at her wet flesh-folds.

Yes.

The quivering cane twinkling as it rose up slowly, potent with malice.

Yes.

Her pantied bottom straining as it squirmed helplessly below. Swish. The cane swooping down. The searing swipe. The stinging stroke. The line of fire across her upturned, suffering cheeks. Swish. Again, the hiss and the kiss of the cruel cane. The jerking bottom's rejection, and enforced acceptance, of the lingering, loving lash.

Yes.

Hot-faced and confused, Candy shuddered as a pulse of raw pleasure shot down from her belly to her weeping loins. Her tingling labia were almost on fire. She squashed the

24

open palm of her wet hand down into them, grinding flesh against flesh. Sweat pearls drenched her face as she hurtled into orgasm.

The door opened and the Wise One stepped into the bleak bedroom. Teetering helplessly on the edge of her climax, Candy could only gaze with dull, unfocused eyes, and manage a soft snarl, before lurching over on to her face and surrendering herself completely. Face flattened into the single white pillow, her breasts squashed mercilessly beneath her, Candy's entire body bucked and bounced as the shuddering implosion gripped, raked and ravished her. With a feral groan that melted plangently into a sweet, protracted moan, Candy sank sated and spent into her bed.

'Twenty-one minutes. I timed it exactly. From bathroom to bedroom. A little allowance for you to marshal your memories of the morning. I trust you had an entertaining time? I promised myself a glass of sherry if my calculations proved to be correct. Twenty-one minutes to the very second. I'm seldom mistaken. Tell me if I'm right,' the Wise One continued suavely. 'Your pleasure commenced with memories of Clare having her bare bottom spanked. Yes?'

Candy, bewildered, merely grunted thickly.

'But your real pleasure came with the memory of your own stripes, hmm? Yes. I'll wager that the memory of the cane across your own bottom brought the sweetest, darkest pleasures.'

Candy, recovering herself slowly, stared up blankly. She found it uncanny. Incredible, utterly incredible. To be analysed so exactly. To have her most intimate thoughts and actions predicted. Not only predicted, she suddenly remembered, but actually timed. To the very second. Candy burned with a sullen anger. She resented the Wise One's knowledge of her. And she hated the nature of that knowledge.

'Will you join me in a sherry? No? Coffee and scones, then.'

As if at a prearranged signal, the door opened and Samantha entered bearing a large tray. The Wise One rescued a glass of pale, dry sherry from the tray as it

25

approached the bed. Candy sat up and accepted a white mug of coffee and a plate heaped with fluffy fruit scones, split and generously buttered. Suddenly hungry, she devoured her late breakfast before sitting back, silently and meditatively sipping her coffee.

The Wise One placed Candy's satchel on her bed.

'I've contacted Oaigg and notified them,' she said quietly. 'And your London Office. I told them it was a sick aunt.'

Candy's eyes widened over the brim of her white mug in unconcealed amazement. She stopped herself just in time from actually saying thank you to this preternatural woman. Checking herself, she merely gazed back in what she vainly hoped was an aloof silence.

'You seem to have enjoyed watching the punishments.'

Candy blushed, remembering the Wise One's inquisitive fingertips at her moistened panties.

'And even more so your own little taste of the cane,' the Wise One continued in her pleasant, conversational tone. A tone which both intrigued and infuriated the listener. Candy wrestled with her bewilderment. The imperious woman could have been discussing the delicious scones she had just eaten – not the cruel stripes she had earlier endured.

'Set fair, though the barometer is frail. We could have some pretty rough moments before the week is out.'

The Wise One had paced over to the narrow Norman window and was gazing out to sea. Her eyes reflected the brilliance of the cloudless sky.

Candy gulped. For the first time since leaving her boarding school – and her indomitable head of house, Miss Carthage – Candy had run up against a force to be reckoned with. More than her match, or equal, she had met her sovereign. The recent, intervening years in a ruthless, hectic climate of financial wheeling and dealing, office politics and cosmopolitan cut and thrust rolled away – peeling back to leave Candy a mere girl once more. A chastened and chastised girl. Vulnerable, unsure and not a little uncertain of herself.

26

Miss Carthage. Why had she popped into her mind? Candy frowned, battling to dismiss from her memory the unforgettable spanking in the dorm she had received over the knee of Miss Carthage. She flushed and buried her confusion in her mug of coffee.

'Your punishment was necessary. Your intrusion was both unwarranted and inexcusable. But you have been dealt with for that offence and the entire matter may be forgiven and forgotten. We pride ourselves here on Orrag in forgiving and forgetting. Once justice has been dispensed.'

'I'm to stay here?' Candy asked in a still, small voice. She must play for time, she calculated. Like a poker player with a weak hand. She must wait to see how the cards fall.

'Of course. The community welcomes you. And I think you will want to stay, if only out of curiosity. The ferry will return in three weeks. Until then, you are our guest.'

Candy remained silent, pretending to give these words some thought.

'You will of course abide by our few, simple rules. And obey all our regulations. On that point I must absolutely insist. Rules and regulations are essential, as are the severe punishments for those who wilfully transgress. It is important, indeed imperative, that you obey. Failure to do so will incur instant punishment. You see, Candy, discipline guides our minds and governs our bodies here on Orrag. Strict discipline.'

Candy's tongue thickened imperceptibly in her dry mouth with these words. Her pulse quickened and her heart hammered loudly. She tried to listen as the Wise One continued for several minutes, but her concentration wavered as the blood sang in her ears. She caught snatches of what was being said – the references to crisp canings, sore bottoms and penitent tears – but could really only follow the tone. A pleasantly polite, impeccably correct tone. But the message was chillingly lucid. Disobedience deserved discipline. The stubborn were spanked and the wilful were whipped.

Who was this woman? The one they acknowledged as

27

being so wise? The Wise One. She ruled Orrag with a velvet fist and an iron will. And what was the purpose of the community? A community, Candy realised, which fully embraced the values implicit in rigorous discipline and absolute obedience. Faraway from the prying gaze of the curious, these young women submitted themselves willingly and utterly to the constraints of their chosen lifestyle on the very last chunk of granite rock that marked the outer edge of civilisation.

But why? Why submit to the kiss of the fierce cane? The harsh humiliation of a blistering, bare-bottomed spanking? Candy struggled to deny the overwhelming curiosity which bubbled up inside her. The only task in hand was to escape, she admonished herself. Escape. Not to speculate as to why young, carefree women volunteered for this self-imposed exile. She must escape from Orrag back to London. London, where life for Candy was an endless whirl of fax machines, taxis, phones that never slept, Old Bond Street shopping – and a myriad of close friends whom she neither liked nor trusted. Yes. She was a creature of that hectic world and she wanted to return there. Here, under the cycle of the sun and with the relentless rhythms of the ocean, life was utterly different to anything she had ever known. Or imagined. Though tempted to uncover the secret of Orrag, Candy suddenly resolved that she could, and must, resist this particular temptation.

The Wise One's concluding words broke into Candy's stream of thought.

'Punctuality. And so if you observe those simple rules your bottom should not suffer many more punishing stripes.'

Candy shuddered. Many more? Surely she had meant to say any more. What simple rules? Candy dearly wished that she had been paying closer attention.

'But you will learn through close observation, humility and a greater degree of patience. Rare qualities, to be sure, but ones which are highly esteemed here on Orrag. Traditional, feminine virtues and qualities which we collectively endeavour to preserve and nurture. The cane soon seeks out and punishes vanity and selfishness. And I firmly believe that a spanked bottom is an excellent antidote to rudeness and pride.'

Candy lowered her head. Vanity, rudeness, selfishness and pride. Cardinal virtues in the cut-throat world she had inhabited only 24 hours ago. Corrupting vices to be severely dealt with here among the young women of Orrag.

'Do not judge us until you truly know us, Candy. And I think Chloe should be your guide and mentor for the first week. She will take care of all your needs.'

Candy looked up directly into the Wise One's eyes. Her gaze was met and mastered by a steady, unblinking stare. Candy lowered her eyes.

'Rest. Sleep if you can. We dine in a few hours. Lunch will be simple but satisfying. And you will find a fresh pair of shorts under your pillow.'

Candy flushed deeply, instantly remembering how the Wise One had entered the small, white-washed room to discover her in the violent paroxysm of a self-induced orgasm. She glanced down at the stain which had spread between her clamped thighs. Looking up at the slightest of sounds, she saw the door close behind the retreating figure of the Wise One.

Candy sighed and, curling up into a ball, drifted off into sleep. And in her sleep she had a dream. And in her dream she was back in the chilly dorm of Wensleydale House, her old boarding school. And in the cold dorm she recognised the half-familiar, half-forgotten row of iron-framed beds. On one of the narrow beds, face-down and bare-bottomed, Clare was being slowly caned by a lithe woman. Miss Carthage? Candy was sure it was she. Miss Carthage used to take them for early morning gym. Candy recognised the short, pleated navy-blue skirt. Yes, there, the hem was flapping against the creamy thighs just below the curve of the splendid buttocks. Flapping as the supple arm rose above to ply the whippy wood across the reddening bare bottom. And who else, Candy murmured in her dream, would be in the cold dorm of Wensleydale House, dressed in the trim, pert uniform of a gym mistress? It was in the rules. In the

29

rules and regulations. Only Miss Carthage could punish bare bottoms. It was definitely in the rules. Candy stirred in her troubled dream. The head girl and her prowling prefects could only slipper and spank the knickered bottoms of naughty schoolgirls in need of correction.

But in the coils of her dream, Candy grew confused. She murmured softly and squirmed. In her dream, the figure holding the quivering cane aloft over the bare, bunched buttocks paused and turned. Turned and beckoned to Candy. Candy trembled and moaned, rolling into her hard pillow. The tip of the cane was tapping the now vacant bed. It was Candy's turn. Candy's turn for punishment. But it was not the slightly weathered face of Miss Carthage that smiled at her with such sweet menace. It was the indomitable, the triumphant Wise One.

Stretched out, face down into her pillow, Candy shivered. Shivered with apprehension – despite the touch of the warm sun that fingered her through the narrow Norman window. In her dream she felt the magnetic will of the Wise One draw her towards the waiting bed. And punishment with the waiting cane. The Wise One was beckoning imperiously but it was the knowing smile that disturbed Candy. Then Candy was down across the bed, her bare bottom upturned for the imminent striping strokes. She felt the controlling hand of the Wise One alight on to her left shoulder. She felt the taloned fingers squeeze. Candy murmured a feeble protest and clenched her buttocks. Again, the firm hand on her shoulder squeezed and shook her gently. Candy woke. She blinked and opened her eyes. Chloe was shaking her shoulder. Candy sighed her soft relief. Chloe stood up.

'Come along. Time for lunch.'

Chapter Two

Lunch, as had been promised, was a simple but delicious meal. Candy sat next to Chloe at a long table covered with a spotless linen cloth. The Wise One sat at the head of the table, a small silver bell at her elbow. The silver bell tinkled, silencing the room immediately from an animated buzz to a hushed stillness. The assembled girls bowed their heads solemnly. Candy, unsure of what to do, looked up along the length of the table to be greeted with the Wise One's steady gaze. Blushing slightly, Candy lowered her eyes and slowly bowed her head. Smiling her grim satisfaction, the Wise One said grace. It was dedicated to Ceres, goddess of the pagan harvest. Candy listened to the strange, yet somehow familiar words but shrugged it all off as a simple eccentricity. The silver bell tinkled again, summoning lunch to the waiting table. It was carefully served by Madelaine, utterly naked except for a short white apron tied tightly around her slender waist – the deftly knotted bow draping down over the curve of her bare bottom. Candy found the grilled fish and salad, served with heavenly home-made bread, both appetising and comforting. Instead of her usual lunch of yoghurt and an interrupted espresso, she found herself leisurely consuming the delicately-cooked trout and dressed salad with relish. But the stabbing memory of her customary yoghurt and gulped espresso focused Candy's mind on the possibilities of escape. Fascinated as she was by Orrag, Candy quivered under the shadow of fear. Fear of the cut of the cane, fear of the indomitable Wise One. Yes, she consoled herself. She would give every outward appearance of accepting her fate – while inwardly, secretly, keeping escape at the top of her agenda.

'Sometimes we have lobster,' Chloe sighed wistfully.

Candy's calculating brain whirred softly. 'Fresh?' she managed in a vaguely attentive tone.

'Oh, yes. Going out on the boat to the pots is great fun,' Chloe whispered excitedly.

'I'm sure it is.'

Lobster pots. A boat. A chance to escape. Candy filed away the useful snippet and feigned interest in her salad, remarking on the crispness of the rocket.

Madelaine worked briskly and smiled brightly despite her menial tasks. Once, when she overlooked the pepper-mill when it was requested, she suffered a single slap across her naked left buttock. Candy watched surreptitiously as the uncomplaining girl continued to attend to the needs of the table with every evidence of charm and solicitude – her creamy bottom reddening all the time.

A blueberry crumble anointed with lazy custard followed. Then wedges of a mild Orkney cheese were presented with oat biscuits and dessert apples. Side dishes of soft fruits appeared on the soft, white linen cloth. Candy picked a handful of wild raspberries and dipped them fleetingly in the sugar bowl.

'Have we all finished?' the voice of the Wise One asked. It was a rhetorical question. Candy noticed that those who had not quickly did so – leaving only one girl nibbling at her apple. She placed the pippin down on her plate and swallowed almost guiltily.

'Good. You all know your allotted tasks and duties. Candy,' the Wise One continued. Candy looked up in surprise, not exactly anxious to be the centre of attention. 'Will you walk the south beach this afternoon and collect driftwood. It is excellent fuel for our kitchen. I'm afraid the Aga simply eats it up.'

Candy nodded. She knew that the request was not a suggestion but an instruction. She already understood the deep respect, a respect tinged with apprehension, the other girls held for the Wise One. Candy now shared their timid obedience, having no conscious wish to evoke the powerful woman's potent wrath.

'Good. That little matter is satisfactorily settled, then. There only remains the group punishment. Clare,' came the command in tones of stern velvet.

'Again?' whispered Candy.

'Three times, altogether. She gets it again after supper tonight as well,' Chloe whispered in reply.

Clare had risen and approached the Wise One. Already she was bending and stretching across the awaiting thighs. She obediently dipped her tummy and offered her bottom up as capable hands slipped her tiny shorts down to reveal her pert cheeks.

'One slap each. Step forward.'

One by one, the uniformed girls rose from their seats, approached the bare-bottomed Clare and administered a ringing spank across her exposed, upturned buttocks. Candy watched as Chloe rose up from her place at the table, scooped in her chair silently and paced softly over to where the Wise One pinioned the penitent across her warm lap.

Smack. Chloe stooped to spank the soft cheeks. They wobbled and bounced beneath the severe kiss of her hard palm. Candy swallowed and blinked. A gentle nod from the Wise One drew her up from her chair and slowly, al- most trance-like, towards Clare's bare bottom. A second nod from the Wise One signalled that Candy was expected to deliver a single smack to the naked cheeks that lay pass- ive and prone in their pain. Candy felt a large butterfly open its wings deep down within her belly. Her right hand felt heavy and peculiarly remote. She glanced at it as if it belonged to someone else. Suddenly she was standing be- fore the Wise One, her fingertips almost brushing the satin softness of the warm double domes upturned beneath them.

'As our guest you belong to the community. The group punishment is a duty extended to all here. Spank the girl. It is your obligation and her fitting punishment.'

Candy raised her arm and flexed it slightly at the elbow.

Palm cupped a fraction, then straightened, then drawn into a cruel curve, she swept her hand down swiftly.

Spank. Tiny electric sparks flashed across Candy's tightened nipples and scorched down into her belly as her palm cracked across the peach, perfect cheeks. A golden light exploded behind Candy's eyes as she felt her hand against Clare's juddering, naked flesh. And exploded again as she heard the harsh, echoing smack, and once more as she saw the soft cheeks wobbling after flattening beneath her burning spank. In a sweet daze of delight, Candy walked towards the door where Chloe was waiting.

'Your first spank?' Chloe enquired with evident interest.

'Mmm.'

'Glad it was Clare. She's got a lovely bottom. So spankable. Like mine,' Chloe smiled wantonly.

Candy blushed in her confusion of shyness and reluctant yet urgent curiosity.

Alone on the shingle beach which crunched beneath her feet, Candy paused in the act of stooping to pick up another length of grey driftwood. It was two o'clock. Three, perhaps. In her hectic London office, the fax would be chattering angrily. Striped shirts would be losing their earlier crispness and only the bad-tempered shouts of greed and impatience would be heard over the ever clamouring phones. Here, on Orrag, only the call of a solitary seagull could be heard over the plaintive sigh of the sea. Candy thrilled as the scudding foam from a tumbling wave sluiced her bare feet, shocking her small white toes with its icy touch. She squealed. Up in the sky, the seagull echoed her cry. She gazed out over the ocean, wondering if she would be able to manage a stolen boat single-handed back to Oban. The words of advice from the Wise One returned to haunt her.

'Stay with us, Candy. Stay and learn.'

'About life on Orrag?'

'No. About yourself.'

Candy scorned the suggestion. Why, only last month a tough team of staff appraisal consultants had given her top marks – for ruthlessness, aggressive negotiating and an achievement profile worthy of a polecat.

Laughter – a lascivious peal of lust – rose from undulating sand dunes to her immediate right. Cautiously, Candy approached the crest of the steep dune and crouched down to peer into the gulley beyond the wind-whipped crest. Down in the warm suntrap, sheltered from the wind, lay the two young women she knew from the morning's disciplining to be Annette, the heavily breasted brunette, and Madelaine, currently the maid who served the community on Orrag.

Annette was already naked, her creamy skin gleaming in the bright sunshine. Candy gazed down at the shadowed cleavage between the ripe breasts that rose proudly as the girl lay supine, her bottom squashed sensuously into the hot sand. The dark pubic patch between Annette's thighs glistened temptingly. Madelaine was kneeling as she peeled off her clinging vest. Crouching down, Candy watched closely as the vest rose up and swept over the blonde hair which, like Madelaine's firm, young breasts, shook loosely and lovely in a new-found freedom. Rising, Madelaine slowly and sensuously palmed down her shorts. Candy held her breath as the tight waistband rippled over the swell of the hips and the delicious curve of the heavy buttocks. Unfettered, legs slightly apart, Madelaine stood naked, splendid and superb beneath the benison of the golden sun.

Candy eased herself down silently until the entire length of her body lay pressed into the silver sand. Peering intently, she gazed enthralled as the blonde knelt down between the brunette's parted thighs and lowered her tousled mane of corn-gold hair on to the soft bosom below. A squeak of pure pleasure greeted Madelaine's lips as they connected with the peaking, straining nipples and connected, covered and consumed the quivering stubs of rubbery flesh. Annette threw her arms back behind her head and thrust her breasts upwards in happy submission to the questing mouth, lips and tongue of the blonde above. Candy stared spellbound as she saw Madelaine's wet tongue rasp the two nipples up into tiny peaks of painful pleasure.

Soon the tiny white teeth were teasing and tugging at the pink erections, drawing them up into miniature volcanoes of pleasurable pain. Annette flung her arms around the naked tormentress and dragged her down fiercely, crushing the blonde's face completely into her swollen bosom. Both the naked girls writhed and squirmed, pressing eagerly and hungrily into each other's soft warmth – Madelaine's flat belly dominating the brunette's sticky pubic mound. Blonde hair tangled with dark locks as their lips fused in a slow, searching kiss. Tongue tips flickered – languorously at first – then fenced with rapier speed and precision, darting and probing before finally exchanging mouths. Breast to breast, belly to belly, thigh welded to thigh, the blonde above and the brunette below, the two naked girls melted into one. Annette's hands sought and found the heavy buttocks above, cupping them lovingly, squeeze-teasing them tenderly then dragging their flesh slowly apart. Candy's throat tightened as she saw the darkly shadowed cleft yawn – and heard the feral grunt escape from the blonde's parted lips. Squirming sinuously, Madelaine escaped. She reared back momentarily before returning to bury her shining face deep down into the glistening pubic patch. With her hands now grasping and squeezing Annette's naked breasts, Madelaine fiercely tongued the brunette in a frenzy of furious licking. Candy saw the rounded, clenched buttocks jerk up from the bed of hot sand, pushing the hips – and what seethed between them – up into Madelaine's hungry mouth.

After a full seven and a half minutes of this silent, dedicated worship, Candy spotted the first tell-tale tremors of the approaching paroxysm flutter across Annette's milky belly. Then the tongued brunette was past the point of no return. All the signs of an imminent orgasm were there – to be read as clearly as any Sapphic verse penned by Aphrodite, infamous daughter of Eros. The large, unfocused, eyes that saw nothing but their own crimson joy. The gaping, slack mouth with the lust-swollen tongue to which speech was now denied. The arched neck. The fiercely prinked, berry-red nipples, quivering and erect in their sweet torment. The flattened belly. The ripples of shuddering pleasure down along the sheen of the thighs. Candy read these and many other ciphers in the *Book of Pleasure* and understood their meaning at once.

Madelaine covered the splayed, wet labia completely with her hot mouth, pushing her thick tongue up inside the warmth of the submissive brunette. Candy gasped as she saw the dominant blonde slip her hands underneath her captive victim to bury taloned fingers into each swollen, naked cheek of the fleshy buttocks. Squeezing hard, Madelaine ravished the pillows of pliant flesh, working them with a brutal tenderness before dragging them painfully apart. Annette screamed. Softly. She screamed again – her cry melting into a soft sob of suffering – before bucking violently as her orgasm swept over her like a blanket of living flame, ravishing her nakedness with its fingers of fire. The triumphant blonde was now sitting back, her buttocks squashed down into her heels. She surveyed the writhing Annette with a cruel satisfaction that clouded her otherwise affectionate eyes. Eyes in which there seemed to be neither pity nor mercy. Just the steady blaze of conquest. In that single moment, Candy herself saw and half understood the sweet, dark satisfactions of reigning supremely over another – another, tamed and tongued into total surrender. Candy saw, and struggled to understand, the bitter-sweet experiences of submission and its dominant sister, supremacy.

'Are you not both supposed to be at work?' the stern voice of the Wise One asked, breaking the ethereal silence and stillness of the warm afternoon sunshine.

Annette scrambled up to her knees – Candy saw the two circles of silver sand imprinted on her buttocks – while Madelaine rose hastily to stand, her head bowed meekly in shame.

'The work you do is important. Each of us has our appointed tasks. Mine is to ensure that you carry out yours. Come here, both of you. No. Do not bother to get dressed, Annette. I want you bare-bottomed.'

At these ominously delicious words, something warm

and sticky stirred deep inside Candy. Bare-bottomed. She licked her dry lips and swallowed in expectation.

'Kneel, both of you. Side by side. Closer. More. Closer together. That's better,' the Wise One briskly instructed – her tone one of easy, natural yet absolute authority. As she spoke, she fingered the thin black leather belt that hugged her lemon track suit.

Candy narrowed her eyes greedily and studied the two naked bottoms of the trembling girls as they crouched, kneeling down together hip to hip, thigh pressed against thigh. The four soft cheeks were bunched closely together in a mouth watering array of passive submission. The up-turned buttocks – two still covered with the fine, powdery sand – were shivering in their tremulous expectation. The Wise One knelt, unbuckling her thin leather belt slowly, casually almost, with her left hand. The buckle opened and she slid the belt off, wrapping it tightly three times around her right hand. Leaning over, her breasts pressing down to squash into Madelaine's bare bottom-cheeks, she stretched across and gently dusted sand from Annette's buttocks with her fingertips. Madelaine's cheeks quivered and slackened under the delicious weight of the warm bosom above them, her cleft widening. Annette clenched her cheeks at the touch of the sweeping fingertips. Rising, the Wise One flexed her right arm and snapped the leather belt twice. The crouching girls, heads pressed down into the soft sand, huddled closer in their shivering anxiety.

'I am going to whip your naughty bottoms as a punishment for shirking your duties. The work you leave undone has to be done by others. That is not a satisfactory state of affairs. When you suffer my strap, think of these three things. One –'

Swish, snap. The supple leather belt whistled down eagerly to lash and slice the four exposed cheeks – leaving them seared and scalded after the fierce hot kiss of pain.

'Laziness is unlovely. Two –'

Swish, crack. Again, the leather whipped across the naked, upturned buttocks. Again, leaving them blazing and jerking in their bouncing torment.

'Selfishness is ugly. Three –'

Swish, snap.

'Idleness is theft. Theft of another's time.'

Candy thrilled to the sight of the supple length of leather suddenly straightening out into a thin, cruel line of fire inches before sinking down on to the bunched domes of bare flesh, witheringly striping the vulnerable peachy cheeks. Each of the creamy, rounded hemispheres now bore three faint pink stripes as they swayed and quivered in the golden sunlight.

'Have you listened? Have you learned, Annette?' the Wise One demanded imperiously.

Candy had to strain to catch the barely audible whisper as the punished brunette submissively replied to her dominant inquisitor, softly repeating the three precepts.

'Good,' nodded the Wise One, her jade eyes now a deep aquamarine. The leather belt dangled limply from her right hand. Limp, but still potent with the menacing promise of further pain. 'Now kneel up. Up. No. Face each other.'

The naked girls scrabbled up to kneel and face one another, soon positioned – nose to nose, nipple to nipple. Candy squirmed deliciously as she swept her own hand up to cup and squeeze her left breast. It bulged within her excited grip, the soft, ripe flesh succumbing at once to her ruthless grasp.

'You have my permission to embrace for these stripes. We are dedicated to love here on Orrag. Even in punishment, there is love.' The speaker's tone, Candy noticed, had softened a fraction.

The kneeling, naked girls clasped each other in an intimate embrace, their bare bosoms squashed together and fused, their bare bottoms pert, plump and poised. Delightfully rounded and vulnerable. Poised and patient for their pain. Almost proudly penitent, Candy reflected. It was as if the swollen cheeks were eager to receive and display the mark of discipline the imminent lashes would confer.

Crack. Crack. The staccato bark broke the loud silence of the beach. In the distance, a ragged line of white seagulls peeled skywards. Candy, couched and tense, savoured every moment of the whipping. The Wise One had flicked the leather belt down – to the left and then to the right – in a twinkling. Candy gasped as both girls jerked into one another, their bottoms seething beneath the searing lash.

'Madelaine. Repeat the three precepts you have learned.'

'Laziness is unlovely,' the willowy blonde whispered into the wind.

Crack. Crack. Again, the lithe leather snapped twice, kissing the swelling curves of both bottoms passionately – striping them pink across their soft, creamy domes.

'Selfishness is ugly,' Madelaine moaned sweetly.

Crack. Crack. Candy pinched her nipple with furious delight as the thin line of leather whipped across the bare bottoms in swift and sure certitude. Unerringly, it sank into the supple, pliant flesh – biting deeply and devotedly into the scorched orbs of quivering satin.

'Good,' acknowledged the Wise One after Madelaine had completed her catechism. Re-threading the hot leather belt around her hips, the Wise One concluded her stern admonishment. 'You both seem to have learned your lesson well. I trust that you remember it and do not repeat these transgressions. Now, get dressed and go. Do not let me catch you shirking again.'

Candy watched the striped bottoms bulge as the two naked girls struggled into their uniform shorts. Gathering up their white vests, which they clutched to softly jiggling bosoms, they strode out of the dune and padded away in silence. The Wise One stood facing the retreating girls. Candy gazed in awe at the supple curves of firm flesh that rippled within the bondage of the lemon track suit. The narrow waist, the plump hips and the svelte thighs. Such a powerful figure, as sleek and as sinuous as a panther.

'You can come out of hiding now, Candy,' the Wise One, still with her back to the crouching girl, called out distinctly. Candy blushed and swallowed. Her heart thumped wildly. Would she too taste the leather lash? Rising slowly, she crested the dune and trod the crumbling sand down towards the Wise One.

'Although we observe and administer strict discipline

here on Orrag, we are equally dedicated to pleasure and love.' The Wise One turned and looked directly at Candy. 'There is a special pleasure in both dispensing, and receiving, punishment. Pain and pleasure are like lovers. Never far apart and ever eager to embrace. I see by your silence that you already have some understanding, but you still have much to learn. About yourself.' Candy looked down at her feet, avoiding the searching gaze of those piercing jade eyes.

'There is Chloe. She will conduct you through some of our activity workshops this afternoon. Look and learn, Candy. There is much here for you. I'm sure there will be. And three weeks is too long to spend in wanton idleness.'

'I'll work,' Candy blurted, the memory of the two girls' painful lesson still vivid in her mind. She shivered slightly as her eye was briefly dazzled by the golden buckle of the leather belt as it winked in a flash of sunlight.

'I am so glad to hear it, my dear,' the Wise One smiled indulgently. Then she called aloud to Chloe, beckoning with an imperious wave. The raven-haired girl approached at a gentle trot, her generous bosom softly bouncing.

'Take Candy to our workshops. Take her to see the Aphrodite first, then proceed to the Amazon.'

First Ceres, the pagan goddess of plenty, of the ripe harvest. Now, thought Candy, Aphrodite the goddess of beauty and a reference to the Amazons – fabled for their athletic prowess and nubile, physical supremacy in conquest. The young women of Orrag clearly regarded the pantheon of pagan goddesses as a source of inspiration.

Back inside Castle Orrag, Chloe led Candy upstairs and through a large, oak-panelled door. Inside the room, all was as black as a moonless night. Candy stood expectantly, straining to see in the inky darkness. Suddenly, blindingly, a bluish-white light flashed. Again. And yet again. Four times the brilliant flash stuttered for a split second – vividly illuminating a superb nude spread across a pool of crimson, shimmering velvet. It was Emily, the plump-buttocked coppery redhead. She was being photographed by Samantha who crouched intently behind her camera.

'The Wise One insists we all spend some of our time here in the Aphrodite workshop. By surrendering ourselves up to the camera, we can more fully appreciate the potent power of feminine beauty. Samantha is so gifted behind the lens. Quite wonderful.'

'Shut up,' Emily snapped at Chloe. 'Don't interrupt,' she added in a petulant, waspish tone. 'Samantha is working on me.'

'Take a break,' Samantha sighed, rising from behind the tripod and shrugging resignedly at her difficult model.

Emily, pouting, stretched herself sinuously as strip lighting flickered on. Blinking, Candy adjusted her eyes to the sudden glare. All around the brightly-lit studio lay velvet couches, onyx plinths and other exotic props. Nets and lobster pots adorned the furthest wall. Candy counted five pots. One had been painted yellow. The secret filing cabinet in her mind yawned open silently. Under lobster pots she filed a memo. The boat. And with the boat came escape. Candy computed the information. Silently, the drawer in her mind slid shut.

'I'm putting a photographic essay together entitled *The Loves of Sappho*. But it isn't working out,' Samantha grimaced. Lowering her voice into a conspiratorial whisper, she added that a certain redheaded ego was proving too large even for 35mm film. Chloe and Candy giggled and nodded their immediate understanding. Emily flashed them both a suspicious, dangerous look – her copper-flame hair shining beneath the harsh neon above.

'Sappho ensnared her lovers with her overwhelming beauty, didn't she?' Candy murmured, half-remembering some forbidden bedtime reading in the dorm at Wensleydale House. How she would have been severely slippered on her bottom if that book had ever been confiscated by any of the prowling prefects.

'Mmm. I think so,' agreed Samantha, totally absorbed in her task of getting an accurate focal length.

'Then why not use that old fishing net? Don't you see? Wrapped around the naked model.'

'You mean have the subject struggle as she is ensnared

42

in the net, the symbol of Sappho's beauty?' Chloe chimed in.

'Exactly,' Candy nodded.

'D'you know, I think I'll give that a whirl. Smashing idea,' Samantha grinned. 'Come on, Emily. This time, I want you –'

'I'm not having that smelly old net next to my skin,' Emily snapped. 'Take me on a bed of silk with my breasts oiled.'

Samantha shook her head sadly.

'Hurry up,' hectored the impatient redhead. 'Do you want me like this? Hmm? Or how about this way? With my bottom . . .' she purred, coquettishly nuzzling her breasts down on to the pool of slinky velvet, offering up her superb buttocks to the dark, unblinking eye of the camera.

'Would you?' Samantha smiled invitingly at Candy, ignoring Emily completely.

'Me? Candy gasped.

'I want to try that idea with the net before it goes cold. Emily,' the photographer turned to her difficult model, 'that'll do for today. Better go along to the herb garden. They need help with the weeding.'

Still naked, but clutching her regulation vest and shorts angrily, Emily stamped out of the studio, slamming the door behind her.

'Be careful,' Chloe whispered. 'She is jealous. Beautiful, yes. But jealous and cruel.'

Candy silently voiced her relief that, by escaping in the boat as soon as possible, she would also escape the cruel attentions of Emily, cane a-quiver.

'Ready?' smiled Samantha.

Candy, undressed by Chloe, yielded to the stiff net. It enmeshed her completely, dividing into diamonds her bunched breasts, white thighs and bare, rounded buttocks. The harsh net captured and enslaved her nakedness in its fierce bondage. Arranged and splayed across a bed of more loosely-piled netting, Candy writhed and wriggled within the strictures of the stretched rope web. Samantha unclipped her camera from its tripod and encircled the netted,

43

naked girl – snapping eagerly, hungrily. In her absolute bondage Candy suddenly felt free. Yes, she suddenly realised. Free. Free from her fax, her phone, her punishing schedules and crowded diary. Free from the brutal, busy City which devoured her daily. Coltish, she rolled and twisted, thrilling to the click-snap of the whirring shutter, surrendering every intimate secret of her soft nudity to the single, implacable eye of the all-seeing lens. It was an orgy of exhibitionism – her willingness fuelled by a buried desire she dared not even name.

'Bend your head down. Bow down. Good. That's good. Now, struggle. Kick out and thresh. That's great.'

Candy obeyed – loosening the bridle of City sobriety in a frenzy of freedom. Crouching down, raking the naked, netted girl before her with the camera, Samantha coaxed and bullied her model, sweetly urging then harshly commanding Candy into postures of utter abandonment. Straddling the squirming blonde, Samantha dominantly snapped her greedy fill. Chloe gazed spellbound as the two young women, photographer and photographed, entered into their private world of narcissism and voyeurism. Dropping down on to one knee, Samantha switched over to automatic mode, sweeping the lens along the flesh that writhed as the latticed rope bit into it. She exhausted her film.

'Wait. Wait,' Samantha shouted excitedly, stabbing her finger down. 'Don't move.' She dashed across the studio, scooped up another loaded camera and flitted back. Sinking to her knees, she straddled her prey and started snapping.

'Chloe,' she called out urgently. 'Chloe. Get my cane. It's over there, on the table. Quickly. Stripe Candy's bottom. I want some good reaction shots.'

Chloe, cane in hand, was kneeling alongside Candy in an inkling.

'Go on. Cane her hard,' Samantha urged. 'Stripe her cheeks.'

Swish. The cane whipped down across the netted buttocks. Candy squealed. The camera drank in every nuance of her sudden suffering – the flared nostrils, wide, sparkling eyes and the twisted lips. Swish. Once more, the whippy wood sliced the rope-latticed cheeks, savagely slicing their bulging curves. Once more, the camera captured the anguish frozen for a fraction of a second on Candy's suffering face.

'Another.'

Swish. Chloe tamed the jerking bottom with a scorching swipe. Candy yelped, her punished buttocks bucking in exquisite pain. The wriggling blonde's beautiful mouth opened into a silent circle – the scarlet lips fully stretched. Suddenly the door burst wide open and Emily stormed in.

'Stop,' she stamped. 'Stop. What about me? I want to do these shots. I want –'

'Be quiet, Emily.'

'She's only –' the fiery redhead hissed.

'She's perfect,' Samantha purred. 'Another, Chloe.'

Swish. The living bamboo flickered and sliced down swiftly to bite the rope-imprisoned buttocks, rocketing Candy into a wanton paroxysm of naked writhing. Emily was utterly ignored. None of the three girls, photographer, caner or the caned, even noticed as she stamped out of the studio once more, slamming the door angrily behind her. None of them glimpsed the redhead's sullen face seething with a frown of fury.

Behind the double doors of the Amazon workshop Candy followed Chloe into an airy, well-equipped gym.

'It's used every day. We all love to keep fit,' Chloe explained. Candy gazed around her, taking in the hi-tech gear, the polished wall bars and squat, leather-backed vaulting horses. There were five girls working out. All were naked, their soft bodies glistening with exertion. At their head, the Wise One was briskly putting them through some tough paces. Chloe peeled off her vest and shorts and joined in.

'Running on the spot,' commanded the Wise One, giving her silver whistle a shrill blast.

The nude squad obeyed instantly, lightly pounding the

45

polished floor as they drummed their bare feet up and down. Candy slipped silently over to a square of coarse matting and sank down, pressing her bottom into its prickly surface. Squirming as her recently-striped cheeks kissed the matting, she made herself comfortable, her chin now resting gently on her drawn-up knees. From the many delights of the naked girls – elbows angled, breasts bouncing, buttocks bunching tightly – Candy shifted her gaze to the single vision of splendour. Superbly breasted and firm-thighed, the Wise One stood, arms on hips, legs apart, facing her group of naked gymnasts. Nominally covered – or rather revealed – by her one-piece, sheer black mesh bodystocking, she swept her hand up and back through her short, cropped head of silver-blonde hair. Candy swallowed as she sensed the lithe grace and potent strength of the tall jade-eyed woman. Jade? Or less smokey, Candy thought. Lapis Lazuli, perhaps. And how gorgeously the fit, supple body gleamed in its deep tan of honey-amber – severely contrasting with the stretchy black mesh fabric. A tantalising covering that buckled and bulged, giving way to the swell of bosom, hip and bottom. She was, Candy marvelled, at the peak of her beauty and prowess. And would remain so for many more years.

Suddenly, a stab of jealousy wounded Candy. She wished desperately to be in that golden decade – thirtyish to forty something – the full summer of ripe womanhood. Yet Candy knew that there was an indomitable will and an iron resolve within the supple grace, behind the magnetic smile. A will that had already imposed itself on Candy's own. She saw in the Wise One a character in full possession of that key to absolute authority – ruthless charm. Candy had been seasoned by her years in the City, in the rat race of the property world – honing and stiffening her survival instincts. But she knew and feared the Wise One's powerful charisma and supreme sovereignty.

'Join us, Candy. This is a community. We rather like to function as a unit. No singletons or loners, my girl. Strip and get weaving,' the warm, resonant voice echoed.

Was there a challenge – a mocking challenge – in the

invitation? Slightly nettled by the mildly ironic tone, Candy needed no second bidding. Peeling off her vest and treading out of her tight shorts, she skipped over to a space just behind Chloe. She'd show the Wise One what a Brompton could do.

'Squat thrusts. A dozen,' came the exhortation. The tiny silver whistle, poised between the full, sensuous lips, trembled as it spoke once more with a shrill blast.

Candy sank down, her soft buttocks tremulously perching over her ankles. In front, Chloe's plump bottom swayed as its cheeks bulged. So magnificent. So tempting. Heavy curved spheres of satin. Soft and pliant. Candy's eyes burned into the delicious, parted cleft and Chloe's earlier words echoed musically in her brain. *A lovely bottom. So spankable. So is mine.* A lovely bottom. Candy watched closely as it rose and fell before her, shimmering and wobbling temptingly as Chloe executed her prescribed exercise diligently. A lovely bottom. The creamy flesh straining and spreading slightly as it sank back down. The smooth curves just kissing the polished gym floor. Candy was mesmerised by the dark, yawning cleft. By the rounded, bunched glory of the swollen cheeks. So spankable. Candy swallowed and closed her eyes, swiftly surrendering to the fierce desire to ease the naked Chloe across her own bare thighs and palm the upturned bottom with slow, circular sweeps of flesh upon flesh – then pausing to intimately appraise, examine and inspect the naked cheeks – before the spanking. She shivered at the word. The spanking. The cheek-flattening, buttock-reddening spanking. And Candy sensed that as that ecstasy unfolded, Chloe's juddering nakedness would weigh deliciously across her lap beneath the raised, dominant spanking hand. And Candy would hear Chloe, in her hot, sweet anguish, gasp and squeal before moaning her whispered surrender. After the strict spanking, Candy would squash her naked bosom down into the crimson cheeks before easing back to gaze dominantly, tenderly and supremely down on the hot bottom. This, Candy realised, snapping out of the reverie, was true power. Not the power of money, but the triumph of the flesh. Candy had nibbled at it in her imaginings – now she hungered for more. She opened her eyes but the images burned brightly in her mind. She had failed to exorcise Chloe's beguiling words. *A lovely bottom. So spankable. So is mine.* Those words continued to sing their seductive siren song.

She closed her eyes tightly again. She must escape. Get away from Orrag. Soon. No. She would stay on Orrag. Stay to savour its many possibilities of pleasure. The turmoil took hold of her spinning brain. She struggled to untangle her conflicting desires. Escape. There was a boat. A boat could mean escape. That was what Candy's logical mind yearned for, even if her buried desires betrayed her.

Candy's nipples stirred and ached longingly. Opening her eyes, she glimpsed Chloe kneeling down on one leg and gazing over her right shoulder as she examined her heel. Their eyes met. Absolute knowledge and understanding flashed from one naked girl to the other. Chloe smiled slowly and sweetly, lowering her eyes demurely. Rising up on to her feet, she thrust out her buttocks provocatively, coquettishly, before teasingly wiping her palms deliberately against the softest, roundest parts of her cheeks – parting then splaying them in a wicked gesture of both pert invitation and meek submission to Candy's longings and desires.

'Emily. Just in time. Come along and join in. We're just about to tackle a few press-ups.'

The double doors slapped softly as Emily entered the gym. Ignoring Candy, the tempestuous redhead eased her sinuous nakedness alongside Chloe. Briefly, imperceptibly, their creamy thighs grazed. Chloe, Candy noticed, inched away. Emily flexed her muscled buttocks and remained poised on her splayed fingers and toes.

'Emily is our reigning champion. Let's see how safe her record is this afternoon. Commence.'

Another taunting challenge? Candy certainly thought so. She flexed her sinews and concentrated grimly. The Bromptons never could resist a challenge. The piercing whistle shrilled. Candy closed her eyes and slipped away into the tingling realms of physical exertion – as blissfully as if it were a foaming bubble bath. She focused on her sensual body – its feel, its suppleness, its obedience to her will. Rhythmically she powered herself up and down, her strong hands spread against the polished wooden floor. A mildly burning sensation stole like a blush from her arched neck to a spot just between her shoulders. It spread, the delicious ache now burning her forearms and wrists. But she was determined to meet the unspoken challenge implicit in the Wise One's words.

'Good. Carry on. Concentrate. Keep going,' the Wise One urged.

Candy opened her eyes. All round her, the rest of the naked girls were lying spent across the wooden floor – or were curled up in their soft nakedness and gazing intently at her. Only Emily was continuing with the slow, powerful press-ups. It was a battle between the two of them now. Brompton honour was at stake.

'Seventeen apiece. Excellent. Concentrate, the pair of you. Keep going,' the Wise One hissed in a warm whisper tinged with an unmistakable trace of excitement.

Emily powered on, as did Candy, pumping her bare body up and down in seemingly effortless thrusts.

Candy gazed up briefly and shivered slightly as she saw the jade-eyed, silver-blonde standing, legs apart, a mere eighteen inches from the spot where her own blonde hair and perspiring forehead repeatedly kissed the polished wood. Glancing up, Candy saw the superb breasts bulging within their tight, black mesh bodystocking. The same stretchy mesh would be cupping and squeezing the athletic, trim buttocks. The Wise One smiled down, her jade eyes shining with a magnetism that thrilled Candy. The smile became warmer, encouraging. Candy felt a deep delight dragging its invisible fingernails along her exposed spine and up across her vulnerable, satin rump. The sheer will-power of the Wise One surged into Candy, suffusing her turgid, flagging limbs with a determined resolution to battle on against the searing pain.

'Twenty-eight. Twenty-nine. Keep going. Keep going.'

Increasingly heavy arms, increasingly tired arms, carried

Candy beyond the count of 32. Her loosely spilling breasts pressed down heavily then bulged momentarily before instantly regaining their pendulous perfection as she thrust her arms up again.

Closing her eyes, Candy surrendered utterly to the image of her supine, fully stretched-out nakedness being intimately scrutinised by the dominant Wise One. Her buttocks rose up tremulously – up to the sovereign lips which burned in Candy's imagination. Down came the kissed cheeks – now pinioned under the imperious heel of the gently cruel Wise One. Up rose her bare bottom – up to the longed-for smack of the Wise One's firm hand. Candy trembled in her dark, secret joy. The idea of the firm, dominant foot pressing her down into the hard floor. The image of the incisive, sharp spank. Delicious pangs haunted her molten mind. Candy almost swooned as delight and exhaustion flooded her aching body. She powered herself up – slowly now – on quivering arms, then down once more, her gently weeping pubic mound leaving a sticky teardrop on the polished wood.

'Thirty-six.'

In front of her, Emily collapsed with a feral groan. She rolled over and sighed her surrender – beaten utterly by the punishing press-ups. Her sweet moan filled the eerie silence of the gym. She did not rise, but sprawled her nakedness across the wooden floor, exhausted.

Candy, her labia freely trickling the wet warmth of arousal, offered her bare bottom up to the Wise One's lips, tongue and hovering hand – her spanking hand – three more times before collapsing in a heap of burning flesh. Triumph. She had kept the Brompton name good.

'Excellent, Candy. You have equalled, but not beaten, Emily's record. Well done. I believe you had it in you and you did not prove me wrong. I am seldom wrong.'

Alchemically, such is the charisma of the dominant who rule with ruthless resolve. Candy's achievement was instantly understood by all to be the Wise One's own. And Candy could not deny that it was in fact true. Her triumph could only have happened in the presence of the jade-eyed, silver-blonde goddess. At that precise moment, if Candy's head had been garlanded with laurels, the sweaty *victrix ludorum* would have placed them in a humble tribute at the feet of the Wise One.

'Well done, Candy,' murmured the Wise One softly.

Candy, every inch of her naked body rebelling in its hot pain, lay face down on the floor. From her sweetly aching woman's wound, the tiny river of excitation flowed. She clamped her thighs, suddenly horrified that the cause of her wetness should stoop down and discover it. Surreptitiously, Candy inched her hand, palm down, between her belly and the wooden floor. Furtively, she smeared her juices dry.

'Shower. Then tea. Quickly now,' came the crisp command.

The nude squad of gymnasts rose obediently and scampered across in a huddle of girlish nakedness towards the showers. In the silent, deserted gym, the lithe instructress fingered the band of her black bodystocking where it bit into the divide between her buttocks. Her inquisitive fingers strayed to her pubic mound, easing the stretch of black net where it had snuggled a little too intimately in between her moist fleshfolds. Having fingered the fabric, she knelt down, dipping her extended forefinger into a tiny puddle which marked the spot where Candy's hot loins had repeatedly bruised the polished wood. Raising her wet fingertip up to her nostril, the Wise One sniffed. A slow smile spread across her face. And in her jade eyes, the deeper light of understanding.

Chloe and Candy were slow entering the showers. Intuitively, they found each other despite the fog of steam. They collided with a soft bump of bosoms under a shared cascade of hot water. They pressed close as the fierce sluice shattered into ten thousand diamonds on their naked shoulders, arms and rumps. Candy bent her face down and licked the droplets from Chloe's arched neck. Soon they were soaping each other with a vigorous tenderness,

51

cupping curded breasts and smoothly palming tightened buttocks. Candy pressed her slippery nakedness up against the cold white tiles at the edge of the shower, spreading her glistening legs apart to allow Chloe's single, straightened finger into her aching wetness. The approaching fingertip paused to tease and worry the wet pubic curls before parting and probing the velvety labia – inching slowly, gently but implacably upwards beyond.

'I want your bottom,' Candy moaned thickly, huskily. And then her voice sobbed brokenly as her frank admission was repeated. It was a full and utter confession of her paramount desire. Chloe smiled and nodded her understanding. Candy – who had up until now expended all her energies in the accumulation of mere money – had denied herself the more primitive pleasures of her own, and others', carnality. Chloe saw this and understood. She smiled. Emboldened, Candy poured forth her deepest longings.

'I want your bottom, Chloe. I want it. I want to hold you, tight. And to kiss you. Then spank you, and kiss your hot bottom. I want your bottom. To pleasure, to dominate, to own. Please . . .' she curdled in an ecstatic whimper.

Chloe, a year older but half a lifetime wiser than the quivering blonde, murmured her promise of consent.

'Tonight. Come to me tonight. You may have your wish. I will give you my bottom, surrender it up to you completely. And you may do with me what you will. Punish me and pleasure me tonight.'

From her nearby cubicle, the sulking Emily – who held long cherished designs on Chloe's bottom which were yet to come to fruition – snarled silently as she savagely towelled her bouncing breasts.

'I may be late for supper,' Chloe whispered. 'I have some small repairs to carry out on our boat. A paint job. She's seaworthy.'

'Oh, the lobster boat?' Candy asked, towelling her buttocks.

'Mmm. But I'll be back in time. The boathouse isn't far away.'

Emily listened intently from her hiding place. Her eyes narrowed. Her primitive sense caught the unnatural air of careful negligence in Candy's feigned disinterest.

'Can I join you, in the boathouse?'

'No need. I won't be late. It's only a quarter of a mile down the beach. Tucked in behind the outcrop.'

Emily craned eagerly to eavesdrop. She slipped and almost thudded into the wooden partition. She broke her fall with her soft towel, deadening the sound.

'But . . .' Candy insisted, her heart racing excitedly. Then she slammed on the brakes. Chloe must not suspect her. She must not seem too curious. Too eager.

'What?' asked Chloe, drying her toes.

'I'll miss you,' Candy sighed.

Chloe grinned.

Candy sank down in a panting heap on the cool, night sands. She had sprinted all the way from the castle, leaving the assembled community preparing for supper. She had calculated her chances, her every move, in her escape bid. By the time they missed her, she would be heading back towards Oban. Under the mantle of the night. Yes. There it was, just as Chloe had fleetingly mentioned. The boathouse. Tucked in against the rugged outcrop. Candy crept stealthily towards the door. All was silent. All was still. She cringed as the unoiled hinges of the opening doors squeaked. Taking a deep breath to steady her pounding heart, she stole into the musty gloom.

'Got you,' snarled Emily.

Candy squealed her alarm and struggled as the heavy netting enmeshed her threshing limbs. But it was useless to struggle. Trapped and helpless, Candy was dragged back along the moonlit beach by the triumphant Emily. Once, when she stumbled, her legs entwined by the clinging snare, Emily stood gloatingly astride her.

'I knew you'd try for the boat. Now you're for it,' she snarled, jerking at the net with a cruel yank. 'But thanks for the idea.'

Candy, who had ceased her futile writhing, looked up

sorrowfully. Chloe would be so disappointed, she thought. And Emily triumphant. And as for the Wise One – Candy clenched her buttocks and shivered.

'Idea?' she murmured, uncomprehending.

'This afternoon. Sappho and the net. I remember my Greek myths. Wasn't it Zeus who let his daughter marry Hephaestus, the lame god who worked as a blacksmith on Olympus?'

Candy remained silent. This was no time, she felt, for a chapter from the Greek myths.

'And he suspected her of deceiving him so he worked all day in his forge and that night he caught her being unfaithful with Ares – caught them in a bronze net,' she burbled brightly. 'Get up,' she added darkly. 'I want to see you get your stripes.'

Despite the dire threat, Candy struggled to conceal her smile. For she knew her Greek myths well. And the errant wife, daughter of Zeus, netted in the amorous arms of Ares was none other than Aphrodite. The most beautiful goddess of them all.

In the silence of the supper room, all eyes gazed on the captive. Stripped of the net and her scanty uniform, Candy stood naked and ashamed. An impromptu communal court was conducted. Opinion had ebbed and flowed. Not with regard to the verdict – guilty – but concerning the punishment. The nature and severity of Candy's punishment. Some suggested the cane; others argued for a group punishment. Bare-bottomed. Emily sat cat-like throughout the discourse, basking in the warm congratulations she had received for her enterprise. At last, she rose to speak.

'I suggest we make her maid.'

Candy twisted her fingers behind her back. No. Not that. They couldn't. They mustn't.

'It will instil the necessary discipline the girl so clearly lacks.' Emily spoke persuasively. Orrag was convinced. It looked on as Candy's nakedness was scantily covered by a white apron.

Then, having firmly tied the bow and draped it down

over the curve of Candy's bottom, the Wise One spoke. 'For Candy's benefit, I will go over the ground rules. Being the maid is something of an apprenticeship. In this menial role, you will serve and pleasure the community. You will obey every order. It is an act of surrender – submitting to every wish, command and desire. Serve the community well, Candy, and it will, in time, accept you into its folds. Remember, it is a privilege to serve. But fail to do so, and punishment is swift and certain. As maid, your bottom is anyone's. It belongs completely to the community.'

Candy felt the Wise One's fingers brush against her white apron. She flinched slightly.

'Wear your badge of office with pride, girl. Be sure that it is always kept spotlessly clean. Should I ever catch you in a soiled apron, I will personally cane your bottom.'

Candy gazed down miserably at her feet. Never before had she felt so vulnerable, so forlorn. As if to emphasise her reddening shame, the tiny apron barely covered her waist and upper thighs.

'You may commence to clear away the supper dishes,' the Wise One commanded.

The floppy bow tied tightly behind her, tapped her naked bottom as she walked along the table to begin collecting the supper plates. She approached Chloe and gazed away, ashamed. But to her surprise, Chloe smiled softly.

'Chin up. It isn't that bad. I had loads of fun. Loads,' Chloe whispered encouragingly, patting Candy's soft bottom affectionately.

'Can I still see you later tonight?' Candy faltered.

Chloe grinned and winked.

Candy's spirits rose. There was, after all, Chloe. Chloe's sweetly murmured promises in the shower earlier on. Candy felt a flood of expectation surge up inside her. Chloe.

'Oh, Candy,' Emily called, as if suddenly remembering some unimportant trifle.

Candy looked up and blushed. Emily paused at the dining room door, her slim hand cupping and squeezing the brass handle. Emily smiled.

'Come directly to my room the minute you finish your duties here, will you? I will require your services as maid tonight.' Tossing her ravishing copper hair, Emily departed.

Candy's nervous fingers twiddled with her apron hem. A vague sense of unease chilled her heart and tightened her throat. Emily's words hung like a potent threat in the air. 'I will require your services as maid tonight.'

Emily. The athletic, jealous redhead. Those powerful thighs. Those blazing eyes. Those sleek, strong hands. Tonight. Candy was to be Emily's to command, discipline and control. At will.

Chapter Three

Emily's room was plainly furnished. The style was austere, the comfort minimal. Though it was large, there was nothing other than a single cot bed, a plain pear-wood chair, a sink and a chest of drawers. Beyond a cascade of white muslin, the dark night sighed through the open sash window, rippling the thin curtain with its warm breath.

Candy trod the small rug nervously, kitten-like, with her bare feet as Emily splashed her face with cold water and, pointedly ignoring her maid, buried her face in a towel. In the oppressive silence, Candy's dark imaginings grew more fearful. But she was determined not to let Emily gain sovereign control. After her failed escape bid, Candy knew that she was doomed for a spell of captive servitude here on Orrag. She also knew that she must not allow Emily to break her, or life on Orrag would be intolerable.

Emily threw the towel down on to the floor and spoke casually over her shoulder, ordering the maid to strip naked. Candy obeyed, remembering the rule. The maid must be obedient at all times. She must do nothing to annoy or enflame the copper-haired beauty. To displease, disobey or revolt would lead to immediate and harsh bare-bottomed punishment. 'Your bottom belongs to the community.' Those were the very words used by the Wise One. They sang their disturbing song in Candy's ears, but fired by the pride of the Bromptons she was determined to succeed in her role as maid. For her, failure was foreign to her policy. Her policy being always to win. She peeled off her tight vest and plucked at the white bow of her tiny, starched apron. She was utterly naked within seconds. Utterly naked, her white body gleaming, her rounded breasts rising and falling gently as she struggled to stay calm.

'I will be attending a special ceremony soon. It is no concern of yours what that ceremony is,' Emily remarked.

Candy's interest was automatic. Was this the inner secret of Orrag? Did the ceremony hold the key? She was sure that beneath the calm, disciplined surface of the community there lurked a deeper, darker purpose.

'So I need to be prepared. You will shave me, maid. Proceed,' Emily commanded, slipping out of her shorts and standing, thighs splayed, by the small, white sink.

Her heart beating rapidly, Candy stepped forward.

'Kneel. Everything is there,' Emily gestured.

Candy knelt, her reluctant submission to the bullying redhead now complete. In the sink, the shaving foam and tiny razor were waiting. Cautiously, Candy dipped her fingers into the warm water and dappled them against Emily's coiled, coppery pubic hair. It was delicious to feel, having the quality of coarse silk to the touch. Candy, slightly emboldened, splashed a cupped handful of warm water on to the pubic fuzz and gently patted the wetness with her bunched knuckles. The shadow of fear slipped from her. This was a humiliating task, certainly, but Candy chose to experience it as exotic and hauntingly beautiful. And much easier to submit to than the hot stripe of the cane. Emily gasped aloud as her pubis was gently knuckled, and spread her thighs even wider apart. Who is in control now? The sudden thought flickered behind the kneeling maid's deepening indigo eyes. Consoled by the perspective, Candy – who had never seen, who had never touched another so intimately – pressed her palm firmly against the proffered pubic mound. Her nipples stirred lazily, thickening imperceptibly as her breasts grazed Emily's thighs. But they did not thicken into full, ripe erectness – subdued still by her unease and trepidation. Squirting the living foam into her open palm, Candy dabbed it carefully into the softness of the coppery nest, working the creamy froth in with her fingertips. Above her, breasts swaying sensuously, Emily moaned aloud. Still wary of the tempestuous redhead,

Candy denied the rising heat of kindled pleasure that burned deep down at the base of her belly, but despite her anxiety – perhaps in part because of it – her nipples now rose up stiffly from the curved sheen of her swollen breasts. Candy shuddered at her own evidence of arousal. It was strange and disturbing to respond to submission. But the excitement was there – unbidden, unsuspected, yet undeniable. Just as when the strictures of Chloe's tightening net and the cane's kisses had thrilled her, Candy was now discovering new pleasures in an appetite for the possibilities of pain.

Shrugging off these teasing thoughts, Candy focused on the task in hand. Leaning forward to work the foam well into the pubic patch, her erect nipples prinked against Emily's warm thighs once more. The redhead grunted her pleasure and grasped the cropped blonde firmly within her taloned left hand. Candy – utterly dominated – blinked and looked directly into the cruel, green eyes that glittered above her.

'Shave me, bitch,' came the steely command.

Candy's sticky labia fluttered like a butterfly. She shrank from the dominant hand that controlled her but the clenched fingers squeezed tighter still. Candy's subjugation was complete. And with her knowledge of it came the first sticky dewdrop from her pouting fleshfolds down below. Confused, Candy picked up the tiny razor and paused. Then, with a tenderness normally reserved for her own intimate parts, she fingered the foaming delta, stretching the sensitive flesh and spreading it slightly between two firm fingertips. She drew the razor down in a short, delicate stroke. Beneath the sweep of the blade, the white foam curled and disappeared like snow before a spade, leaving a track of glistening skin. Working with the precision of a watchmaker, Candy plied the razor with intimate accuracy. Soon the entire pubic area was cleanly shaved, leaving the pink skin like a peeled pomegranate. Candy almost swooned with delight as she rinsed the naked flesh carefully and patted it dry with a fistful of the soft, fluffy towel.

'Mirror,' demanded Emily, snapping her fingers.

Candy held a small looking glass at the base of the dominant redhead's belly then lowered it to her thighs. Emily glanced down but gave no sign of satisfaction. Candy watched her tormentor's heavy breasts wobble and softly undulate.

'Lick me.'

Candy gulped and looked up, uncomprehending.

'You had your chance to rinse me properly. And you failed, maid. Lick me.'

Candy shut her eyes and pressed her face into the warm flesh between Emily's rounded thighs. Slowly, the maid's tongue flickered out and tasted the faint trace of soapy foam. A stronger tang – the fig juice of female arousal – flooded Candy's senses as her tongue-tip probed. Emily, her head tossed back, her labia wet from the attentions they had received, slowly dripped her honey directly on to Candy's quivering tongue.

'Harder. Lick me harder, bitch. I command you. Do it.'

Candy buried her face deeper into Emily, working her thickened tongue furiously against the velvety flesh.

'Enter me,' moaned the shuddering redhead, now standing with her generous buttocks spread apart against the white sink and offering her open womanhood to the kneeling maid. Candy obeyed. Who is submitting to whom? Again, the seditious thought glimmered on the horizon of her mind. A savage tug from the taloned fingers that clenched her blonde mane immediately reminded Candy who it was who dominated – and exactly whom she dominated. But the enigma continued to haunt her inner consciousness. Who reigned supreme during delicious discipline, she wondered? The spanker or the spanked?

Closing her eyes tight, she forced her tongue in between the slick, slippery labia then upwards into the muscled warmth beyond. Emily arched up on her toes, grinding the base of her belly against Candy's face. The minutes dragged their heavy feet through the treacle of time that slowly congealed around the naked couple. Suspended in the arrested progress of the moment, Candy lost herself utterly within Emily's pungent wetness. The intense cloak of silence that enveloped dominator and dominated was only disturbed by the sounds of the kneeling girl's liquid lapping. A tremor fluttered down from Emily's belly to her shuddering thighs. Candy at first sensed – then palpably felt – the gathering storm within. The lithe redhead slumped slightly and groaned. Reaching down, she blindly pushed the blonde away from her weeping sex. To Candy's surprise, and pang of fleeting disappointment, the tormentress seemed to be denying herself satisfaction. The satisfaction of orgasmic delight. Why? Why tantalise and tease the body only to deny it the ultimate release it burned for? Puzzled, Candy withdrew, licking her lips and savouring the taste of the redhead's hot juices.

'Oil me,' her tormentor hissed.

Candy looked up, her wet face shining. The shaven girl pointed to a small phial close at hand. Candy, still kneeling, shuffled across to the table and picked up the thin pencil of glass carefully. Inside, the amber unction glistened. The phial felt warm as it rested in her open palm. It was cedar and almond lotion – warm, sticky and perfumed. Opening the phial by removing the stopper with her teeth, Candy fingered the sticky fluid gently into the area of freshly shaved skin, spreading the soothing balm into every creased fleshfold. Emily thrust herself forwards, eager for the probing, questing touch. Swiftly turning, she presented her naked buttocks to the kneeling blonde. Candy gazed up at the quivering, creamy globes. The redhead's taloned fingers flew back to her buttocks and, gripping each fleshy cheek, pulled them apart fiercely. The cleft between yawned revealing the dark anal whorl within.

'Oil me,' repeated Emily savagely.

Candy's glistening fingertip, oozing the aromatic unction, probed between the curves of satin flesh and entered the warm, shadowed valley. Emily groaned drunkenly, her voice thick with the ichor of hot lust, as the length of oiled finger slipped directly into her tightness. Easing the straightened digit out, Candy rapidly worked it back into the supple flesh – withdrawing and returning with speed – until the deliberate pumping motion changed from one of measured calculation to abandoned frenzy. Emily squealed and clenched her buttocks, instantly imprisoning the oiled finger in between the heavy flesh of her plump cheeks. Candy dragged her finger out and remained kneeling in silence as, yet again, the dominant redhead fought and struggled to repress and deny her savage climax. Candy watched the clenched cheeks dimple as they spasmed to contain the hot lava flow that threatened to drench her clamped thighs. Emily grunted and then shivered as if in an ague. Her flame-coloured hair flounced as she turned, a demonic light burning behind her eyes.

'Stand up, bitch.' The words were snarled.

Candy rose up with alacrity, her heart a-flutter.

'Turn around. Give me your bottom.'

The command was imperious, absolute. Candy obeyed in demure silence. Cruel hands gripped her naked buttocks, squeezingly exploring their pliant weight before painfully spreading the cheeks wide apart. The blonde shuddered anxiously as she sensed Emily kneeling down behind her to inspect and intimately examine her naked bottom. Candy held her breath – the intense perusal seemed to take an age – flinching slightly as she felt the warmth of Emily's breath against her bare domes. Then the redhead's stern voice fractured the loud silence. They were words Candy froze on hearing. Words she had dreaded.

'You are to be punished, maid. Go to the bed and kneel. You have neither served nor pleased me properly. Maids that displease are punished.'

Punished.

Candy felt the cruel fingers of fear pluck at her stiff nipples. She stirred with dark longings and rude imaginings.

Punished.

To kneel, head bowed, bottom bared. For what? The hot spanking hand? Or the searing stripe? Strap or cane? Fearful images tumbled through the jumble of Candy's spinning thoughts. All she could be sure of was the redhead's spiteful fury and her certain pain to come.

Trembling slightly – her earlier poise now crumbling –

Candy trod the floor across to the foot of the bed as directed. She sank down submissively on to her knees, wishing her bottom was not so rounded, so large and so inviting. In matters of passion and pleasure, such buttocks were a blessing. In punishment and pain, such a bottom was a betrayal. She bunched her Judas cheeks fearfully. Still mindful of her Brompton lineage, she resolved to take her stripes with equanimity – determined to deny her tormentress any satisfaction. There would, Candy resolved, steeling herself, be no teardrops of sorrow or squeals of suffering to gladden Emily's jealous heart.

'Stretch out and hold the bedposts,' Emily instructed as she sauntered over to the bed, stooped, and lifted up the mattress. Candy's eyes widened as she watched the kneeling redhead withdraw a length of clouded bamboo cane. It was, she vaguely recognised from her jaunts to the botanical gardens, a rare species of Thai bambusa, culled from the remote rain forests that clung to the cloud-capped mountains of Jang. The sharp frosts bleached the bamboo of its customary yellow, rendering it opaque, a pale colourless shade of pain. She gulped softly as she counted off the 26 inches of supple malevolence, then closed her eyes – only to find the cruel image haunting her retina. She squeezed the image away – only to send the burning icon to her brain. Etched there in raw fear, the vision of the whippy wood glowed. Blinking the spectre from her thoughts, the troubled blonde reached out and clasped the wooden bedposts. The gesture lifted her bare cheeks up a fraction – poising them perfectly for her punishment. She shivered. She was now kneeling, she realised, arms outstretched, head bowed, bare-bottomed, positioned for the whipping. Not even the bravery of the Bromptons could extinguish the dark flame of fear that flickered within her deep-blue eyes. She shivered again – as if her soft nakedness had suddenly been exposed to a sly draught of icy wind. But it was in her heart and in her mind that the cold chill resided, where the fingers of fear touched.

The tip of the quivering cane alighted on her left shoulder. It was beginning. Her moment of doom had come upon her. She gripped the bedposts and clenched her bare cheeks tightly. The cane stroked the entire length of her outstretched arm.

'So. You have strength in these arms, maid?' the jealous redhead whispered in a feral sneer. 'Enough for about forty press-ups, I hope.'

Remembering the episode in the gym, Candy swallowed hard.

'I am going to cane your bottom, maid. That will be my privilege. And then you will give me a private performance. Show me how many press-ups you can do. We'll try for forty, I think. You. Me. And my cane.'

The cane sharply tapped the curve of the kneeling blonde's pert buttocks.

'And that will be my pleasure,' Emily purred.

Swish, swipe. The length of wood cut swiftly down to sear and scald the bare bottom. Candy winced as the cane lashed her naked flesh, biting into the bunched domes of cream. Swish, swipe. Again, the cane spoke softly – no more than a sinister whisper – striping the cusp of the pliant cheeks with a thin red line. Swish, swipe. Swish, swipe. Two more cruel cuts kissed the trembling buttocks, leaving them hot and quivering, and blushing deeply in their burning shame. Candy squirmed, her damp palms slipping as they grasped the wooden bedposts. She looked deep into her scarlet pain – and beyond. Beyond the pain, she focused hard on the possibilities of pleasure. Of denying Emily her cruel satisfaction. And later on, the pleasures of Chloe. Madelaine, perhaps. And Annette. Orrag had more to offer Candy than her present misery, she reasoned. And out of her reason grew a grim resolve. A Brompton courage.

But Emily had not exhausted her Pandora's box of suffering. Not yet. She thrummed the empty air with a harsh swipe of the bamboo.

'Down on the floor, bitch. I want forty press-ups and with the help of this,' she swished the length of clouded cane again, 'forty I shall get.'

Candy shuddered as the taunting, cruel words mocked

her. Stretching her naked breasts and belly down on to the hard bedroom floor, she eased her buttocks up and squashed her bosom heavily into the polished wood. Powering herself up on her splayed hands, she quickly achieved four, six, eight press-ups. Emily knelt down slowly at right angles to the naked blonde in her thrall and gazed hungrily at the faintly striped clenched buttocks as they rose up and sank down before her. With a smile of grim malice, Emily quivered the length of cane above the bare bottom. With each successive upward thrust, the rounded crown of the twin domes softly kissed the potent threat. It was a cruel reminder, an ominous memento. Candy shivered each time her buttocks brushed the hovering bamboo.

Twenty-three, twenty-four, twenty-five. Painful press-ups performed beneath the waiting whippy wood. Emily's fingers closed tightly around the cane. She raised it up. It hung in the empty air above the outstretched nude – tremulously supreme above the slowly rising, slowly descending naked rump.

Crack. The cane sliced down right across the proffered peaches, striping the satin cheeks harshly. Candy mewled and wriggled.

'Come along, bitch. You can do it. Only nine more.'

Crack. Another brisk, swiping cut stroked the naked blonde's bottom. The recipient of the harsh punishment squeaked in anguish, her bare buttocks bouncing in a reflex of hot torment.

The door burst open. It was Chloe. 'Cut that out, you bully.'

Her crisp command froze the quivering cane in the air above the striped bottom.

'Get out,' blurted Emily in a shrill of anger.

'No. Candy is your maid, not your plaything. You cruel bitch, I knew you'd be . . .'

But Chloe never completed her angry words. Emily, nude and glistening, sprang up to grapple with the tall, raven-haired intruder. Chloe's normally affectionate grey eyes clouded instantly into slits of cold steel. She grasped the redhead's wrists and the two lithe beauties, one briefly clad in her tight uniform of vest and skimpy shorts, the other oiled and naked, swayed as they were locked into their fierce clinch. Despite her brave efforts, Chloe was mastered and subdued by the strength and cunning of the feral redhead, who forced her rival down on to the floor. To emphasise her sudden conquest, Emily planted her naked foot on to the buttocks of the quelled Chloe, pinning her firmly in defeat.

'Stupid fool. You know the rules and you've broken them. If I reported this to the Wise One, you'd be whipped soundly,' hissed Emily as, panting slightly, she bent down to straddle her foe, splaying her oiled, shaven delta across the soft buttocks. Chloe twisted her neck and gazed up resentfully at the triumphant redhead.

'The Wise One would . . .' Chloe began.

'Double your stripes if she knew you'd helped that bitch to escape. How else did she know where to find the boat? I heard you tell her in the showers.'

Chloe sank her face down into the floor.

'I will give you a choice. You can be caned by me, now. Or risk the mercy of a communal court after breakfast. Choose.'

A tense silence settled over the victor and her vanquished.

'Cane me now,' Chloe whispered softly in a voice broken by the weight of her doom.

Candy looked across at her friend and protectress who had risked the promise of pain in her vain effort to snatch her from the cruel attentions of the jealous redhead.

'So be it. Get across the bed. Shorts off,' Emily barked.

Chloe moved towards the waiting bed, her tight white shorts abandoned on the polished floor behind her.

'And you,' Emily snapped, pointing the tip of the cane at Candy. 'Across the bed.'

The two naked girls eased across the bed, offering up their bare bottoms to the whim of the whippy wood. Both knew, as they shivered under the shadow of the cane, that to rebel – to overpower Emily – would only incur harsher, more public punishment later. Chloe feared the extra stripes her disclosure of the boat would bring. Candy feared failure as a maid.

Swish. The cane quickened, sweeping down eagerly, gleefully, across the upturned buttocks, slicing into their shuddering creaminess with a ruthless delight. Both the naked girls hissed their sudden pang of anguish into the duvet. Swish. Burying their fingers and faces into the softness beneath them, the caned girls moaned deeply as their hot rumps jerked and writhed. Swish. Another thin, pink stripe laced the four soft, white flesh domes, leaving the bare cheeks stinging and a-quiver.

Emily grunted softly as her free hand fingered her freshly shaven flesh. Swish. Candy's breasts burgeoned as they squashed into the fluffy duvet. Her small hand sought and found Chloe's as the two bare-bottomed girls wriggled and squirmed. The blonde squeezed her raven-haired protectress affectionately, encouragingly.

Other hands were busy too. As one hand wielded the supple bamboo, so efficiently and effectively, the other hand of the cruel redhead fingered her oiled labia furiously. Emily could no longer resist her implacable dark desires. Swish. Swish. The naked bottoms bounced beneath the withering strokes of the slicing cane. Emily, eyes now tightly shut, sensed her twice denied climax bubbling and boiling just beyond her trembling fingertips. Swish. Both girls moaned their exquisite suffering as the cane kissed their blushing cheeks with fierce affection. Candy felt the girl beside her shudder as she received the lash, then felt the raven hair flounce as Chloe's head tossed in torment.

Silence. And in the stillness, the cane became tame. The caner sagged at her knees, buckling under the ravishing paroxysm as it exploded within her hot flesh. Her shining eyes raked the punished bottoms of the caned victims. Up on tiptoe she teetered, her lips parted in a victorious snarl of cruel triumph. The scorched cheeks – striped and passive in their molten fire – were her trophies. She staggered back, pressing her bottom against the cold, hard sink. Gasping, Emily lowered her copper-crowned head down and shuddered as her hot quicksilver – the juice of her joy – spilled down her inner thighs.

Candy, wide-eyed and wondering, sensed her tormentor's silent ecstasy. Peering cautiously back over her bare shoulder she glimpsed the cruel redhead clasping and squeezing her ripe and rounded breasts as she ruthlessly milked the ebbing orgasm for the last drops of dying delight. As her tumult melted softly, Emily was rendered slack mouthed and spent, the abandoned cane mute at her curled toes.

The seconds passed in absolute silence.

'Maid,' ordered the redhead slowly, in a thick voice. 'Come here. Kneel down and lick me clean.'

Candy, her striped bottom rippling as she scampered, approached and knelt before the dominant, naked redhead. Reaching out across for the white, fluffy towel, she started to soak a corner of it under the warm water. With it, she would wipe the redhead's sticky labia, dabbing away the film of milky silk from the soft, pink pouting lips.

'No. Not with that,' Emily snarled, her hand knocking the towel down on to the floor. 'Use your tongue.'

Candy's eyes flickered up anxiously.

'Tongue me, bitch,' whispered the cruel, nude girl huskily.

Candy closed her eyes and, craning her neck, parted her lips so that her wet, pink tongue could stretch to its fullest length. Inching closer, her nostrils flared as they sensed the feral tang of excitement.

On her bed of suffering, her clenched buttocks still ablaze, Chloe closed her eyes. And whimpered.

Breakfast, served by Candy with demure diligence, was coming to a close. Candy was attentive with the teapot.

'You have learned much already, I am sure,' the Wise One murmured as she eyed the faint stripes on Candy's bare bottom. 'No tea, thanks. Being a bondmaiden can be so . . .' she paused to dab her lips with her napkin, 'instructive. One learns so much. About oneself.'

Candy gazed back, nursing the teapot against her palm.

She smiled as she acknowledged the tribute and then, head bowed, moved along the line of seated breakfasters. Annette detained her progress, requesting the presence of the maid in her room afterwards. The summons was issued in a softly gentle tone. A pleasurable bidding.

Candy approached the bedroom with foreboding. It was a bright morning. The sun sang in the sky – its golden notes filling the long corridor as Candy trod the steps towards the bedroom door with a clouded mind. What lay behind the door? More shame? Further pain?

After closing the door softly behind her, Candy's heart skipped a couple of beats as the buxom girl strode over to her bed and lifted up her mattress. Candy swallowed as she glimpsed the length of yellow cane lying there menacingly. Annette reached beyond the cane and extracted several lengths of cord and an eight-inch, polished ivory dildo. Candy's dry lips parted as her fumbling fingers fiddled with the white bow of her crisp maid's apron gracing the upper, outer curve of her bare bottom.

'The last maid had a very gentle touch. Very gentle. I hope you'll be firmer with me,' the buxom brunette said brightly.

Candy's eyes widened with slow understanding. Annette was not going to enjoy Candy – Candy was here to pleasure Annette.

'In fact, you may be strict. As strict and as severe as you like,' continued the brunette in a velvety, low voice oozing with submissive, anxious pleading.

Strict and severe. The words echoed in Candy's ears. She repeated them to herself, savouring them as she would the bouquet of an expensive wine. Annette was gazing directly into the blonde's eyes. Candy returned the gaze, then slowly, and in silence, nodded her understanding.

'Take off your clothes, Annette,' Candy commanded, slipping into her role smoothly and easily – already feeling a tiny flicker of delight deep down within.

Annette struggled out of her vest. Candy studied the large, loose breasts appreciatively as they bounced softly.

'Shorts,' murmured Candy.

69

Annette stooped to ease off her tight cotton shorts. Again, the bunched breasts bulged.

'Stand up straight.'

Annette obeyed promptly, arrowing her arms down along her thighs, the palms of her hands inwards against her golden flesh. Candy slipped off her tiny white apron and stood directly behind the quivering brunette. Both girls shivered deliciously as Candy's blonde pubic fuzz grazed Annette's rounded rump cheeks.

'Discipline', Candy whispered softly into Annette's ear, 'is dispensed in many ways. There are many faces behind the stern mask of punishment.'

Annette gasped softly. 'Yes,' she nodded vigorously. 'That's perfect. That's exactly what I . . .'

'Silence,' hissed Candy – now completely in control – relishing her role. 'You have tasted the fruit of pain,' she continued in a curdling whisper, rasping her thumbnail across the bare buttocks before her in an echo of a cruel cane's stripe, causing them to tighten in a reflexive clench. 'Now, Annette, you are ready to taste rarer fruits. I shall crush the bittersweet juice of discipline to your lips.'

A broken moan escaped from Annette's lips. She half turned, her eyes bright and sparkling, but before she could speak, Candy placed her forefinger against the trembling lips in a commanding gesture for absolute silence.

'On the bed. Face down,' the maid ordered her mistress.

The voluptuous brunette bent, her cleft widening as she mounted the narrow mattress. Candy ran her thumbnail gently up, and then back down, the entire length of Annette's nakedness. The supine nude sighed sweetly. A sigh of utter pleasure. When prone and passive on the bed, face down as instructed, Candy arranged the girl for her taste of strict bondage. Gazing down, she examined the heavily-breasted brunette in her impatient state, noting keenly the quivering buttocks that dimpled – and dimpled once more as the bare cheeks clenched in anticipation. Slowly, Candy picked up the smooth dildo. It lay potent and gleaming in the palm of her left hand. Tentatively, Candy stroked the length of ivory with the tip of her forefinger. She closed her hand immediately, gripping the firm phallus in a clasp of delight, squeezing hard as if it might escape. On her bed of passive longing, Annette whimpered anxiously. Candy tapped the upturned buttocks smartly in a gesture of admonishment and firm authority. Annette, relishing the dominant touch, squirmed and gurgled in sheer delight. The brunette's buttocks were now almost welded together, so fiercely was she clenching them. Candy bent forward and, placing her finger and thumb on each cheek, spread the soft flesh apart – revealing once more the tempting, shadowed cleft. Annette groaned softly.

'Surrender your bottom,' Candy whispered vehemently.

Thrilled by the sugared venom of the command, Annette dipped her tummy and offered her buttocks up in complete surrender.

'More,' Candy purred. 'Give me your bottom. Utterly.'

Annette's submission was absolute. With her cleft now yawning deeply, the twin domes hovered above the bed. Candy smiled, acknowledging her triumph. And the smile was as subtle, as wicked, as the smile she once greeted a chattering fax signalling another coup in the money markets. Candy was surrendering to the seduction of the flesh. Where bullion once tempted, now it was the beckoning of bare buttocks that captured her interest. The City girl with a yen to make a mark now yearned to administer hot stripes. She had redefined the meaning of liquidity.

Placing the length of polished ivory between the supplicant cheeks, Candy smiled again as she saw the buttocks clench tightly – to imprison it longingly. Leaving the dildo snuggling in the warm, dark cleft, Candy took up the four short lengths of waxed cord and rose up from the bed. Taking the left ankle first, and then the right, she firmly bound Annette's naked feet to each corner of the bed. The muscles in the willing victim's thighs rippled as her splayed legs strained in their strict torment. Running her thumb-tip up the silken skin of the right leg – up over and across the slight wobble of the pliant buttock – and then along the entirety of the brunette's dimpled spine, Candy brought her hand to rest lightly but firmly on the

71

softness of Annette's right shoulder. Annette nuzzled her hard white pillow urgently. The pungent perfume of her free-flowing arousal pricked the air with a dark sweetness. Candy's nostrils narrowed in concentration as they focused on a scent something like that of ripe mulberries combined with the musk of sweating medlars oozing stickily under a merciless sun. The rank fragrance of split figs was there too. She closed her eyes and savoured the perfumed air. There was no more elusive – yet instantly recognisable – odour she realised, than the liquid musk of seeping female arousal. Candy smiled as she mediated briefly upon this solemn truth. No shimmering Persian orchard, or secret oriental spice grove, ever yielded such provocative pleasures as the smooth lust-honey weeping from the fissured comb clamped between the thighs of every female. Candy inhaled slowly and then exhaled deeply.

The left wrist. How pale, how vulnerable. It did not resist the deep bite of the waxed cord. It did not struggle as it was tied to the bedpost. The right wrist went willingly to its firm bondage. It too accepted obediently being lashed to the wood.

'Tied, tamed and tempting,' snarled Candy sweetly like a silken panther in a troubled dream.

Annette squirmed, despite her taut bondage. Her silvery labia bubbled – the wetness soon tiny dewdrops against her inner thighs. Candy's slightly trembling fingers found the dildo and gently removed from where it had snuggled between the warm cheeks. Expectation tremored along the length of Annette's spread-eagled nakedness. The tip of the dildo glinted as it rose up in an arc, alighting on the white nape of the exposed neck – just below the tumble of dark hair. Annette ground her face, open-mouthed, eyes tightly shut, into the hard pillow. The dildo traced its firm ivory finger along the nude's supple spine. She sighed softly, arching her back up to greet it – her buttocks straining and bulging in their swollen eagerness. Candy guided the rounded tip of the pale horn down into the shadowed flesh between the heavy cheeks, pressing firmly into the sticky cleft. Annette groaned – the carnal, vixen cry of brute lust.

Dry-mouthed, thick-nippled and soaking wet from the thrill of exercising such supreme control. Candy inched the dildo further down towards the glistening labia. The polished nub dragged against the wet silk of the fleshfolds, already opening wide with their smile of welcome. Slowly, deliberately, the shaft was stroked against the soft velvet flesh-curtains which trembled in the pulsing breeze of arousal.

'No, no,' Annette hissed, her voice almost choking with urgent desire. 'No. Not there. There is only for the ceremony. I can't . . . you mustn't . . .' The brunette writhed as she pleaded her prohibition.

Candy frowned. The ceremony. Only for the ceremony. She gazed down meditatively at what Annette had called 'there'. Intrigued, Candy's mind wandered. Could this be the same ceremony Emily had been shaved and oiled for? Emily too had fought to deny – unsuccessfully – her arousal and inevitable climax. Why did these girls tempt and test themselves to the utter limits of self-denial and self-control? The ceremony. What was this secret ritual which held the beautiful, disciplined young womanhood of Orrag in its thrall? Candy was determined to discover the secrets this odd community clasped to its bosom.

Blinking away her thoughts, Candy switched her attention back to the bound, naked brunette stretched out on her bed of bondage. The tip of the ivory dildo winked with the wetness of Annette's sticky excitement. Candy wiped it twice against her thigh, and frowned. Frowned at the challenge before her. She had been bidden as bondmaiden, to pleasure the naked Annette, but for some reason, clearly linked to the impending ceremony, penetration of the customary orifice was proscribed. So? How to pleasure the nude in her sweet strictures? Candy tapped her chin pensively with the tip of the ivory phallus. In the throbbing turmoil of the City, where she was just one more sleek barracuda among the sharks, Candy had played a slippery, versatile and highly inventive role. Surely her powers of flexible creativity would not desert her now, here in these remote waters on the edge of the infinite ocean.

Taking Annette's thick mop of shining hair in the clutches of her clenched white fingers, the loving tormentor dragged the head of the lovingly tormented back, exposing the pale face, the carmine lips. Applying the quivering dildo gently but firmly, Candy teasingly traced the outline of Annette's lips, using the dildo like a lipstick. The bound brunette shivered with delight and eagerly licked the slim shaft from stem to tip with her pink tongue. Annette squealed as Candy tightened her grip on the dark hair, teased the head back a little further, and tamed the flickering tongue with the firm ivory. Annette squealed again. Inserting the dildo into the gaping mouth, Candy spanked her free hand down across the bunched cheeks of the writhing girl. Twice. Then snatched back the shaft of ivory. The brunette's strong perfume of response stabbed Candy's nostrils. Another sinuous twist of her wrist completely tamed the brunette, leaving Candy completely in control. Gently stroking the phallus, she introduced it against the roof of Annette's mouth – the slow strokes becoming maddeningly tormenting, fiercely delicious. In her taut cordage, the subjugated nude wriggled and squirmed, squashing her heavy breasts into the hard mattress. Candy continued to probe her happy victim's mouth, wielding the dildo deftly as it penetrated the wet flesh deeply, dominatingly. Annette trembled – her nipples now erect and painfully swollen – on the outer edges of orgasm. Easing the shining dildo back across the flattened, tamed tongue, Candy swiftly withdrew it and immediately rubbed its hard length against the jiggling right breast, enflaming to new peaks of pleasure the engorged, berry-ripe nipple. Annette almost snapped her tight bonds as she thrashed and spasmed – crushing her breast downward to trap and enslave the demon phallus. Candy dragged the dildo away – slowly – taking pains to both pleasure and punish the exposed nipple.

The disciplined delights were highly controlled, carefully calculated and adroitly administered. Bucking and bouncing in her waxed cords, the writhing brunette howled aloud. The dildo alighted once more along the exquisitely dimpled spine. Slowly, so tantalisingly slowly, it scored the satin skin near the domes of the jerking buttocks. Candy herself was now very hot and wet between her glistening thighs where a prickling fire flickered and danced. Between her tight fingers, in her sure and certain grip, the dildo probed the dark cleft, pausing briefly to nuzzle the tight sphincter.

'Yes,' moaned Annette. 'There,' she beseeched.

Slowly, four centimetres at a time, Candy eased the cool phallus up into the warmth beyond.

A loud silence settled over the two naked young women, sealing them into their very private realms of illicit pleasure. Tenderly, but in supreme and absolute control, Candy eased the shining length of ivory in, then withdrew it very slightly, then reinserted it – guiding it up between the clenched buttocks more insistently. Further, deeper. Annette gasped. Rhythmically pumping the dildo, Candy concentrated on her pleasurable task. As maiden, she had to serve – and please. Pleasure the naked girl who had surrendered herself up to the sweetly fierce cords of bondage which bit softly into her struggling wrists and ankles. Pleasure her. Yes. The fluttering surface of the tight satin cheeks signalled the molten collapse which predicated the approaching maelstrom. Pleasure her. Yes. Candy pumped the ivory dildo faster. Ruthlessly, savagely, tenderly. Yes. Annette sank her white teeth into the whiter pillow. Yes. Candy grinned a grim smile of triumph – her little goose was almost . . .

Annette shrieked a wanton wail. The entire length of the naked brunette stiffened, arched, spasmed then collapsed as the implacable orgasm crushed her within its clenched fist of delight. Waves of raw pleasure engulfed and exploded as they surged across and within the bound brunette on her bed, welling once more like tiny tsunami from her belly's depths. It swept upwards to her breasts and tightening throat – and downwards to her molten core. Candy pinned Annette down by the nape of her neck at the very peak of her climax – rendering her utterly subjugated, entirely dominated, at the crucial moment. The conquered surrendered to her conqueror the empire of her senses, the realms of her ravished flesh. And for both victor and vanquished the struggle was sweet – with the juice of submission scalding Candy's inner thighs as she straddled the nude Annette. Candy pinioned the nape more firmly as the shuddering brunette's lithe limbs absorbed the dying ripples of her quivering implosion. The sensation of total domination caused Candy to feel her own floodgates straining as her surging lava flow within threatened to burst. Quickly slipping off the bed of bondage, she then positioned her splayed wet labia against the corner of the mattress. Gripping the edges, she thrust her pubis into the dense softness. Again, the downward sweep. Again, and yet again. At the fifth thrust of flesh against fabric, she achieved and surrendered to her own orgasm. Clutching the edge of the bed with her outstretched arms, she rode the wild storm within for several timeless moments before collapsing, shattered and spent, on to the cool floor.

Later, as the sun climbed effortlessly across its stretch of infinite azure, the silence of the bedroom was broken by a soft rustling. Candy was rummaging for a leather belt. The clink of the brass buckle told Annette that the belt had been located. On her bed, in her strict constraining bondage, the anxious nude twitched expectantly.

'And what have you learned this morning?' the Wise One murmured as Candy served her at the lunch table.

'So much,' whispered Candy, keeping her eyes downcast.

'There is more. So much more. Wine,' came the command.

Candy poured carefully.

'That Oaigg deal. Bidding for the late laird's estate. Was it very important?'

Candy's hand trembled slightly but she did not spill a drop of the chilled Chablis. 'Vital.'

'Vital?'

'Or so I thought. Then.'

'I believe Madelaine is anxious to be served by you after lunch.'

Candy could not completely conceal the flicker of interest in her eyes.

'There are, of course, certain means of communication open to you. To contact Oaigg. If it is vital.'

Candy surprised herself as she heard herself reply. 'I must see to Madelaine.' The words of response were spoken instantly, with simple candour.

The Wise One lowered her eyes and sipped delicately at the pale wine; nodded and savoured the delicious moment as it surrendered to her lips.

Candy attended Madelaine at the predetermined spot – under the scented pine trees at the edge of the sun-scorched sands. It was a little later than agreed. The lengthening shadows attested to the passage of the hours.

'Spank me. Spank me slowly as the sun sets,' Madelaine whispered in her wanton, elfin-like voice.

Candy certainly felt equal to the occasion, and rose to the challenge with both eager anticipation and warm enthusiasm. Of all the dark pleasures she had prepared, served up and sampled herself – the intimate spanking of a young woman's bare, proffered bottom proved to be the most delicious. Almost, Candy thought as she peeled down the white shorts of her willing victim, as delicious as being lovingly spanked oneself.

'Tell me how naughty I've been. How I deserve to be spanked,' Madelaine pleaded in a liquid whisper. 'Be cross with me,' she whimpered.

Candy maintained an ominous silence as she bared and prepared the girl across her lap. Firmly trapping Madelaine's feet under her own left foot, she slowly drew the penitent's hands fast together to pinion them against the small of her warm, naked back. Satisfied that the tamed nude was suitably poised and positioned for her punishment, Candy broke the soft silence with softer words.

'You have been a very naughty young lady, haven't you?'

Despite the gentle tone, the question was posed in a strict voice of stern authority.

'Yes,' whispered Madelaine excitedly as she squirmed.

Tenderly, Candy swept the upturned buttocks with a brief butterfly kiss of tremulous fingertips. Madelaine jerked her bare bottom up to greet the touch. Candy stayed the eager flesh with a firm palm. Madelaine moaned.

'Can you tell me, Madelaine, what happens to young ladies who have been very, very naughty?'

'They are punished,' came the answer in a sudden rush.

'And can you tell me, Madelaine, in what manner are they punished?'

'They are spanked,' she gurgled happily.

'And can you tell me, Madelaine, exactly how are they spanked?'

'Hard. Hard, on the bottom. On the bare bottom.'

'Thank you, Madelaine. I am going to punish you. I am going to spank you,' Candy crooned, smoothing the ripely rounded left buttock with her fingertips. 'On your bottom. On your bare bottom. Firmly. Very firmly, on your bare bottom.'

As the carefully modulated words came forth, Madelaine jammed her thighs together. Her cheeks wobbled a trifle in excited anticipation. Candy fingered them softly, gently. Spread across the warm lap, Madelaine sighed sweetly – and spasmed.

'The spanking will commence soon,' Candy continued in the dry, prim tones of a solicitor reading from a turgid tome. Madelaine thrilled to the cool, detached authority of her punisher's voice. The strict syllables alone were enough to make her sticky with delight. 'You are to remain absolutely still during your chastisement. No wriggling, no squirming. Do I make myself perfectly clear?'

'Yes,' gasped the bare-bottomed girl happily.

'Still and silent. No squeals of protest. Is that perfectly plain?'

'Yes.'

'Very well,' Candy continued. 'But first, a short treatise in praise of the bottom. The bare bottom.'

Candy drew her smooth palm firmly across the tight surface of the quivering, fleshy cheeks.

'The bottom, or buttocks. Crafted by nature to both attract and suffer – indeed, one could say excite and endure – many forms of suffering. Sweet suffering. A pleasurable pain which they incite and incur. The bottom, when bared, can be striped by the cane, kissed by the whip or stroked by the belt. All severe but satisfactory forms of corporal punishment.' Candy tapped the clenched domes as if to emphasise her words. She felt the length of Madelaine's nakedness tense and shiver deliciously across her lap. 'But the most intimate, the most delightful and the most memorable discipline – for both the punisher and the punished – is spanking.'

'Spanking,' echoed Madelaine in a thick throated whimper. 'Yes.'

'Spanking,' continued Candy in a tone of cool serenity, 'is flesh upon flesh. The curved palm was most certainly designed by nature in her wanton wisdom to be received by the curved cheek of the bare bottom.' Candy paused, raising then lowering her spanking hand, bringing it to rest across the upturned rump. 'How perfectly my palm fits and matches your bottom, Madelaine. Feel the perfection of nature.'

Madelaine responded with a delighted mewling as Candy illustrated her lecture with a slightly cupped palm across the creamy domes – one by one.

'The perfection of nature,' murmured Candy, thrilling to her task.

'Mmm,' echoed her penitent happily.

Taking up a thick fold of flesh between her pincered finger and thumb, she gently tweaked and tugged – working the rubbery buttock as a potter works the smooth, pliant clay. Obedient clay that can be moulded at will. Dragging the cheek outwards, Candy marvelled as the cleft darkened and deepened in its revealing yawn. Madelaine bucked, rocking forwards gently as she gasped with renewed pleasure.

'Still and silent. You will remain still and silent while I spank your bare, naughty bottom.'

Madelaine nodded vigorously and settled down warmly across Candy's thighs.

Smack. Five white seagulls scattered as they rose in surprise at the sound of the sharp spank. Smack. The harsh hand squashed down the shuddering crown of the perfect hemisphere of flesh as it spanked the left cheek hard. Smack. The right cheek flattened and quivered under the severe blow. A blush of flamingo pink crept across the swell of creamy flesh. Smack. The fourth – the sharpest slap so far – caused Madelaine to clench her punished cheeks tightly. Candy smiled. Smack. Smack. Smack.

Leisurely, unhurriedly, slower than the pulse beat of a sleeping lover who had filled her cup full from the deep well of Lesbos, the spanking continued at a strict, measured tempo. Candy felt Madelaine's heart flutter excitedly behind the naked breast squashing into her warm thigh.

Smack. Smack. How potently exquisite to feel one's flesh connect so intimately, yet so severely, with the flesh of a naked young woman. Candy gazed almost tenderly at the proffered bunched cheeks she was punishing with gentle violence, with fierce affection.

Smack. Smack. How delicious to control and punish such a beautiful, naked bottom. How perfect the bare, cheek peaches were. How taut, how rounded. And how becomingly they blushed. Smack. Smack. The surging swell of supremacy, of delicious dominance, flickered its furious flame deep within the punisher's inner being. Smack. Smack. The quickening tumble towards absolute surrender, into sweet submission, ignited and burned brightly in the crimson realms of the punished's molten core. Smack. Smack. The clenched domes wobbled in their sweet spasm of sharp pleasure and pleasing pain. Smack. Smack. Again, and yet again, the crisp kiss of hot hand to hotter cheeks.

Candy was addressing the outer curves, dedicating her swift, sharp slaps to their rounded, swelling glory. Smack. Smack. Smack. Imperceptibly but implacably, Candy wielded her gentle strength as she gripped Madelaine by the nape of her neck, pinning her willing victim into utter subjugation. The naked girl fluttered her fingers pitifully as her crimson buttocks bounced and jerked in a pathetic bid to escape the blistering spanks. To no avail. Candy turned her lethal, unerring attention to the lower curved quarters of the bare, upturned bottom – the ultrasensitive, velvety soft area of vulnerable flesh just above the invisible crease of the upper thigh. Smack. Smack. The crisp cracks withered the softly suffering cheeks, scorching them with scarlet fire. But they were not the savage blows of anger, or the brute blows of the bully. They were sensitively, lovingly measured and judged, if deliberate, applications of a firm hand to the almost buttery flesh.

Candy was getting wet. Madelaine was getting wetter. The punisher's seeping sex oozed its slow treacle. The punished's raw arousal flowed like molten gold through her pouting portals of Eve. Smack. Smack. Smack. Madelaine jerked her reddening rump in an ecstasy of anguish beneath the triple echo of hot delight.

'Keep perfectly still,' Candy admonished severely, steadying the squirming bottom with the palm of her still spanking hand. 'You have been very, very naughty and must be stingingly punished. Keep silent and absolutely still.' Candy insinuated a waspish note into her voice as she continued to admonish the bare-bottomed girl. 'Now give me your bottom. I want it up. Up, big and round.'

Jerking her buttocks up obediently, and bunching her cheeks as instructed, Madelaine made sweet moans. Smack. Smack. The blushing peaches now burned red. Smack. Smack.

Under a purple nightfall, the waves rose and fell sonorously beyond the shore, heaving and sighing like maidens suffering love's gentle wound for the very first time. Smack. Smack.

'Please ...' shuddered Madelaine, arching up her scorched bottom in a yearning despair.

Smack. Smack.

'Yes,' she muttered thickly, clamping her glistening thighs. 'Yes.'

Smack. Smack. Smack.

Suddenly, the naked, punished girl wriggled free from her firm subjugation and, struggling, rose up to embrace her loving chastiser. Squatting her hot cheeks fiercely down into Candy's lap she wrapped her lithe legs around her punisher's waist. Bosom to bosom, they clung in their close embrace. With Madelaine's scalded bottom splayed down across her thighs. Candy felt her joyful victim's hot wet slit pulsing against her lower belly.

'Wonderful,' half sighed, half sobbed Madelaine, burying her face into Candy's soft shoulder. 'You were wonderful.'

Her spasms climaxed into a sudden jerking shudder – and then the spanked girl came against the flesh of her sweet, strict discipliner. To her astonishment, Candy came too.

Long moments later, still clutching each other with intense delight, they both rolled over and sprawled into the cooling sands.

82

Chapter Four

The evening of the ceremony was heralded by a spectacular sunset. Far out to the distant horizon, the sun submitted to the azure sea in a silent surrender of red and gold.

In her onerous duty as bondmaiden, Candy had been consigned to the kitchen – strictly prohibited from attending the esoteric ritual. Strictly prohibited by the Wise One.

'Although you are settling into the rules, routine and regime of our community with remarkable speed, Candy, you must remember that you are only passing through. A brief visitor to Orrag,' the dominant, jade-eyed beauty had purred reasonably. 'The ceremony is reserved for those completely dedicated to our aims and goals.'

So, mused Candy, biting her lower lip sulkily. I was right. The ceremony holds the key to Orrag.

Spank. A swift slap across the swell of her left buttock – delivered like a flash of lightning by the ever watchful Wise One – broke into Candy's reflections with a burst of scalding scarlet.

'No sulking, maid. You are not to visit us during our ceremony. That is my decision and it is final. And remember – a maid who sulks is a maid who will suffer,' came the ominous admonishment, emphasised by a sternly wagging finger from the very spanking hand which had just ravished her rump.

The exclusion made Candy all the more eagerly determined to attend. She had a stubborn streak skin-deep beneath her gloss of cultured refinement, her sleek patina of civilised allure. The Bromptons were thoroughbreds. Candy was a mustang – born to buck the bridle, bred to scorn the whip. Even though she knew she was putting her bottom at the risk of dire consequences if her forbidden presence should be detected, she was determined to be at the ceremony come hell or hot bottom. In a typically chattering, unguarded moment, Chloe had let slip the time and the venue. Candy had pretended to let the slip go by unnoticed. And so, of course, Chloe failed to notice her slip. Seven o'clock. In the temple of Venus.

And so, at twelve and a half minutes before the appointed hour, Candy was there, secreted in the former billiard room behind a huge cabinet of gleaming walnut. Soon the tiny, golden hands of a carriage clock stretched to touch the hour and a shrill chime tinkled. Winchester chimes. Candy grinned. Her Aunt Lucille had just such a clock with Winchester chimes. How hale and hearty Aunt Lucille kept herself – never a day's ill health since Candy's childhood. Ting. Ting. Ting. Candy counted the concluding chimes and shrank back into the shadows. The room was illuminated by flickering candlelight only. In the centre, a huge four-poster bed had been prepared earlier with a covering of rippling crimson sheets. Sheets as soft as sin and smoother than a virgin's inner thigh. Before the dying chimes had faded, the double doors swept open silently admitting the girls of Orrag. Candy watched breathlessly as the line of utterly naked girls filed quietly into the Temple of Venus to form a phalanx of flesh around the four-poster bed. A full two minutes of tense expectancy elapsed before the approaching soft footfalls signalled the arrival of the Wise One and her two attendants. They too were stripped and sensuously oiled, but wore face masks of thinly beaten gold leaf. Candy could see the glint of the trembling candlelight in the eyes that gazed through the gold. The fragile light lapped among the subtle shadows of their nakedness, gently emphasising the swell of the bosom, the curve of the thigh.

'Prepare the bed,' instructed the Wise One in a voice of warm honey.

Two young women stepped forward and stood by the edge of the bed, opposing one another across the crimson silk between them.

84

'Proceed,' ordered the Wise One, her golden mask flashing as it caught the tiny points of light.

Candy could not quite identify the girl who lay down, arms and legs slightly splayed, her buttocks heavy, on the wine-dark silk. But it was Annette who climbed up on to the passive girl below, turning as she did so to arrange herself face down into the dark delta – lowering her own parted thighs firmly into the pale, upturned face. Stretched out, the two naked young women mouthed and sucked one another. Candy thrilled to the soft lapping as Annette buried her face hungrily in the thighs beneath her. Her naked buttocks rippled in reflexive spasms as her subjugated victim repaid her in exactly the same coinage. Annette stretched out and pinioned the ankles of the girl she straddled and licked so searchingly – only to shudder and moan as her own ankles were gripped fiercely and the hidden tongue at the base of her taut belly worked busily, furiously, into her milky depths. Candy gazed in spellbound silence as the two gleaming figures suddenly stiffened in a frozen paroxysm before shuddering in their mutual climax. Annette slumped down, her flattened belly squashing into the rounded, soft, bare breasts beneath. Slowly, the two girls eased themselves up and out of their hot, wet union.

Swift hands dragged at the rippling sheets and held them up aloft to the candlelight. Candy glimpsed the dark stains where pure pleasure had wept openly – spilling its tears of raw delight. The Wise One, remote and omnipotent behind her mask of thinly beaten gold, examined the dark, wet stains and nodded – her long fingers lightly brushing the patches of liquefied lust.

'You have prepared the bed well. It is anointed. Venus has been honoured. Let the ceremony commence.'

The two handmaidens sank on to their knees at either side of her lithe, supple thighs. Candy watched intently as a leather harness was produced and wrapped firmly around her naked loins. Sinuous hands fluttered and tugged at the short leather straps which were fastened tightly across the rounded buttocks. Candy's tongue thickened within her dry mouth as she saw the fleshy cheeks bulge within the straps – each heavily ripe, swollen buttock threatening to burst in its strict bondage. The leather seemed to sink into each perfectly rounded cheek with a savage tenderness. Candy blinked and licked her dry, thick lips. The two naked, kneeling handmaidens were raising a white dildo horn up to the base of the Wise One's belly. Fitting it securely into a socket in the harness which graced her pubis, they twisted it firmly until it stood in a proud erection. The tip of the slightly curved phallus shone in the flickering candlelight. Candy tried to swallow but could not, so dry and tight was her throat.

'Take your positions,' the Wise One ordered.

Her handmaidens, heads bowed, soft bosoms bouncing gently, padded across to the head of the four-poster bed and stood on either side of the swathe of stained silk. The Wise One turned to the assembled girls.

'Our purpose, as you know, here on Orrag is to grow strong, to become more effective and to prepare for positions of power and command. For thousands of years, the secret of woman's triumph and prowess has been guarded by the ancients – Juno, Aphrodite, Ceres, Minerva and Venus. We have revived those secrets and here, on Orrag, where we pay homage to the Ancients, we learn to prepare for positions of power and the supreme exercise of self-control. Former members of our small community now run multinational operations, international institutions and media empires: key commercial and political posts, all held by successful women. Women from Orrag. You too can achieve much, control many, once you have acquired the skills and the wisdom. The secret of the Ancients bequeathed to us by the Vestal Virgins. Self-control. Self-discipline.'

The secret. Candy knew, as she trembled in the darkness, that she was on the brink of discovering the true nature and purpose of life on Orrag.

'To control. And to have absolute command and sovereignty is the rightful role of womankind. It befits us. It is our proper function. But first, a woman must be able to control her own body. Subjugate her will. Once she has these checked within the tight reins of self-discipline, she can rule over anything, be mistress over anyone. Most of you have been here as part of our community long enough now. The time has come to test you. Tonight, I will select and put to the test one of you whom I think is ready. Ready, perhaps. Perhaps not. We shall see. If successful, the chosen one will be invited to assume a directorship in a Paris-based museum of contemporary art.'

An excited murmur rippled through the ranks of naked girls.

'The museum board would normally wish to appoint a bearded, middle-aged academic man. That is the tradition to which they have regrettably become enslaved. Word of Orrag has reached them. They have learned of our outstanding reputation and they are anxious to appoint one of our number.'

The ripple grew to an excited buzz. In the darkness made visible by candlelight, soft bottoms joggled.

'The ceremony. Upon being selected, the chosen girl will submit to me.'

Candy saw the phallus quiver as it nodded ponderously in the vacant air. The Wise One changed her weight to the other foot. Her buttocks bulged. The phallus bobbed slowly once again.

'I will pleasure her here on this bed before you all. But she must endure without enjoyment, denying by sheer willpower and the exercise of absolute self-control, any capitulation to climax. I will light a certain fire within her. She must quench – not kindle and be consumed by – those special flames.'

A feral moan passed swiftly across the lips of the assembled. They had heard and they had understood.

'I will now call upon the chosen one. Step forward . . .'

Emily, tossing her fiery red hair, stepped forward.

'Clare,' the Wise One whispered.

Candy saw the scowl of fury darken Emily's disappointment. The spiteful redhead flashed resentment – pure hatred – at the Wise One.

'Annette, Emily. You may bear the votive lamps.'

Little brass boat lamps were lit and offered to Annette and Emily who, cradling them carefully, formed a guard of honour at the foot of the bed. Clare slid up on to the bed and remained, head bowed, on her hands and knees, her shining rump thrust up behind her. The Wise One mounted the bed, her weight dimpling the taut silk. Kneeling upright directly behind Clare, she swayed her hips slightly, causing her phallus to brush the curve of the proffered buttocks. Clare gasped and clenched the sheet between her gripping fingers. The length of gleaming ivory nudged the soft peach of the left cheek, then the blunt tip of the shaft found the furrow of the cleft – and gently settled in the shadowed warmth. For a full minute the dominant figure in the thin golden mask seemed to be taming the kneeling nude – pressing the potent length of ivory between the upturned buttocks. Eight inches of polished ivory, Candy marvelled, her nipples thick and tingling. It appeared to the watching girl that the dildo formed a link between the warm bodies, bridging belly to bottom and fusing the flesh into one.

Lowering herself gently, so that the finger of ivory stroked slowly and firmly along the cleft and then down into the moistening labia below, the Wise One crushed her loose breasts heavily against Clare's bare bottom. She then guided her searching fingertips between the splayed thighs to find the weeping fig: the widening, dew-soaked fruit of Eve awakened. Candy watched the sure touch of the strong fingers prise apart the sticky labia of the kneeling girl. The inquisitive tip of the dildo quivered as it paused, poised and potent, before inching inwards. Slowly. Exquisitely. Clare whimpered as she accepted the initial strict strokes of penetration. The Wise One straightened herself up suddenly, jerking her hips forward and ramming home the firm phallus. Clare groaned sweetly and Candy saw her shoulders tense as she absorbed the probing shaft. Clenching her glistening buttocks within their taut bondage of fiercely criss-crossed leather straps, the Wise One pounded her thighs powerfully into Clare's bottom, thrusting home the cruel sword into its slippery sheath. The rhythmic pumping of flesh into flesh drew shining pearls from Clare's wet wound, but she gripped the crimson sheets determinedly – fighting to resist and deny the swell and surge of her rapidly amassing liquid response. Clouds of lust dappled and darkened the wide sky of her large eyes. She gazed out into the soft darkness, unseeing and unfocused, bearing the vacant stare of the possessed.

Candy bit her knuckles as she watched, wide-eyed and breathless, in case her grunts of savage joy betrayed her forbidden presence. How could Clare not succumb, crumble and collapse under the delicious burden, the overwhelming weight of such fierce and absolute pleasure? Peering in disbelief, she trembled. She herself, a mere witness, was already wet between her tightly-clamped thigh-flesh.

The Wise One jerked furiously, the buried shaft now a white blur. She was like a priapic swan dominating a latter-day Leda within its snowy glory. Grasping and mastering Clare's slippery buttocks between her strong hands, the golden-masked tormentress launched into a frenzied paroxysm of heaving thrusts, driving the ivory finger deeper and deeper into the sweetly suffering girl. Candy sensed that Clare was now only a few seconds away from her climax. All the signs were there. Soon the thin, primal scream of delight would confirm the girl's surrender to her natural desires – at the same time signalling loudly her failure to exercise self-control. The museum would have to seek its new director elsewhere. Clare was by no means ready, it seemed, to control or assume command.

Five, four, three. Candy counted the slow seconds, her eyes fierce slits of avid concentration. On the bed, in her hot delight, Clare was shuddering, a-quiver from nipple to rump. Two. One. Now. The Wise One pistoned the phallus ruthlessly. Warm milk dripped freely down both the naked women's thighs. Candy gulped as a low, liquid cry of longing poured from Clare's lips. She cried out her climax long and loud.

A sudden movement caught Candy's eye. The mere flicker of a shadow's shadow, but enough to alert her sixth sense to danger. Emily, her pale face a study of frustrated fury, had briefly dipped her boat lamp, deliberately spilling a little of the burning oil on the rippling silk. A yellow tongue, shimmering within an eerily blue haze, licked hungrily at the shining fabric. Three short seconds later, it blossomed into a ball of orange. Emily's eyes blazed with cruel, mocking triumph. And soon, Candy realised instantly, the bed would blaze more brightly. Several of the girls squealed their alarm.

'Look out,' cried Candy, dashing through the darkness towards the four-poster bed. More cries of dismay bruised the air. On the bed, Clare, frozen within the paroxysms of her orgasm, looked up, her face a blank – her features bleached by savage lust. The Wise One swiftly turned her golden mask towards Candy, her eyes glittering furiously at the interruption. In a split second, they flickered down, saw the flames and widened. Candy stretched out and unceremoniously pushed the pleasurer and the pleasured off the bed. Locked into each other – welded by the deeply buried dildo – they rolled, clasped together, down on to the floor. The impact drove the shaft upwards and inwards, rocketing Clare into the jerking abandonment of a renewed climax. Screaming her sweet agony, she pounded her rump into the sweat-spangled thighs that rode her.

Candy snatched up the blistering sheet and quickly rolled it up into a tight ball, extinguishing the circle of flames. An acrid stench hung heavily – along with the stunned silence of the assembled girls – in the darkened air.

'I'm sorry,' Candy blurted out, lowering her eyes as they met the furious gaze of the Wise One.

The ominous silence ensued as Candy squeezed the rolled up satin sheet between nervous, contrite fingers. The flesh on her bottom goosepimpled with anxiety, fearing the punishment to come. Despite her quick-thinking and fast reactions, she knew that she would be asked awkward questions. Awkward questions which would have to be answered. And when words lapsed into silence, then the cane would speak.

'What are you doing here?' the Wise One demanded, drawing herself up to her full, majestic height.

'Watching. Watching the ceremony,' Candy managed to murmur.

'Did I not specifically forbid you from entering this room?'

'You did.'

'And you dared to disobey my direct order?'

'Yes, but you see, I . . .'

'You concealed yourself in here with the clear intention of spying?'

'No – yes. That is . . .'

'You dared to –'

'I only wanted . . .'

The questions were crisp and searching. The answers were lame and stumbling.

'Annette,' the Wise One said, turning to the wide-eyed girl. 'You will remain with me. The rest of you,' she continued, 'will all depart. The ceremony is over. Candy. Kneel down. You must be punished. Severely.'

Candy, trembling, faltered uncertainly.

'Kneel,' thundered the Wise One.

The subdued girls filed out of the room in silence, several stragglers scampering at the Wise One's final, stern injunction. Annette busied herself, snuffing out the candles between her moistened finger and thumb before clicking on the electric light. It blazed harshly after the soft candlelight. Candy peeped timorously at the Wise One who stood, legs parted, as Annette approached and, bending gently, carefuly removed the phallus together with its leather harness. Working swiftly and quietly, she unbuckled the straps and relieved her mistress of the ceremonial apparatus. Unburdened, the Wise One raised her hands to her face and removed the mask. Her cropped blonde hair sparkled under the bright light above as she shook her head free.

'Arrange her over the bed and prepare her for her punishment,' came the stern command. 'I will use the leather strap, not the cane,' the Wise One added softly. 'Prepare her.'

Annette nodded obediently and stole silently towards the kneeling figure of Candy.

'Up,' Annette ordered.

Candy rose, shivering in her anguish.

'Across the bed.'

Candy obeyed, quivering in her fear.

'Bring me the leather,' hissed the Wise One in a tone as soft as a bishop's blasphemy.

Stretched across the centre of the four-poster bed, her squashed bosom kissing the wetness of earlier events, Candy closed her eyes tightly and moaned silently. Her nipples stiffened as they grazed the damp patches on the crushed crimson – then stiffened more severely as her brain decoded the memory and the meaning of the sticky sheets.

Candy's anxiety was exquisite. A sensual fear laced with the silken skein of delicious dread. Her bare bottom was thrust out superbly behind her – poised, passive and penitent for her impending punishment and pain. In the tumult of her mind, Candy was already imagining the lethal leather barking down angrily across her naked, upturned cheeks. Crack. Crack. Again, again and yet again, the supple strip of dead hide would snap and stripe her living flesh. Again, again and yet again, her bare bottom would be blazed by painful flames, licked by tormenting tongues. Candy shuddered. Severity – together with her attendant maidens Sorrow and Suffering, the pagan daughters of Punishment – would soon be visiting her silken peaches to pay full homage to them, bruising the vulnerable fruits with demon delight.

The leather. The supple leather. The pain. The scarlet pain. Candy curled her toes up in clenched expectation. Soon the length of hide would whistle down. Whistle down and crack across her bunched cheeks. Crack down – and bite. Soon.

'This is the instrument of discipline. Taste.'

Candy opened her eyes fearfully. Annette was pressing the coiled strap to her dry lips. As instructed, Candy gave the leather a rasping lick, her quivering tongue shy and hesitant.

'Taste, and remember.'

The leather strap was removed. Candy closed her eyes

and moistened her lips. The tang of the hide haunted her. It was primitive. Savage. And yet that very savageness, primitive and raw, was not entirely displeasing. Candy was a complex creature. Civilised yet primal. Cultured yet carnal. The sensation stirred the mustang, the wild colt, within her. She suddenly glimpsed the possibilities of punishment – how sweet the severity, how soft the pain. Being whipped by the Wise One held forth the promise of savage joy, she suddenly acknowledged. Marvelling at this seditious truth, Candy shivered. A whimper troubled her throat.

'Legs together,' barked Annette, now astride behind her, arranging and preparing the naked penitent for her punishing stripes.

Candy sighed softly as she pressed her inner thighs closely, tightly, together. Her bare buttocks bunched beautifully – rendering the taut flesh a-quiver.

'She is ready,' whispered Annette huskily. 'She awaits the lash.'

'You have done well,' murmured the Wise One. 'And now you may withdraw. I will chastise the girl alone.'

Annette obeyed, withdrawing silently. The heavy doors closed and clicked shut behind her, firmly sealing Candy into her realm of doom. The Wise One knelt down briefly at the edge of the bed and draped the soft, heavy leather across the tremulous cheeks. It hugged them with a fierce affection before hanging limp beside the curve of her pale thighs. Candy flinched, the reflex of her anguish rippling her milky flanks. Rising up slowly, the Wise One stood, a little to one side, gazing down steadily, almost serenely, at the rounded rump she would soon ravish.

'Bad girl. Such wicked disobedience. It saddens me to meet such wilfulness but gladdens me to punish it. You were warned, Candy Brompton, warned – but you disobeyed. You disobeyed and now must pay the full penalty. And the penalty is?'

'Pain,' mumbled Candy thickly, her soft lips mouthing her response into the crimson sheet.

'Pain,' echoed the Wise One with a dark tenderness suffusing her velvet voice. 'Pain.'

Candy shivered and bunched her buttocks tightly together. The cleft between them was now a severely creased fleshfold. The leather strap rose and fell in keeping with the heaving swell of her shining domes of rounded, creamy flesh. The weight of it maddened her – teasing her with the potent threat of delicious torment.

'In a little while, I will gather up the leather and administer the punishment. You are to receive twenty, I repeat twenty, strokes.'

Candy, her small fists clenching and unclenching, whimpered softly.

'Twenty strokes. But the whipping will not be brief. I shall linger, and you shall . . .'

Suffer, thought Candy. Suffer. By the eighth stroke her poor little bare bottom would surely be ablaze. By the eleventh, most certainly molten. But what lay ahead – beyond – at the end of her tunnel of torment? Would she be wet by the thirteenth? Could she climax at the sixteenth lash of leather across naked rump?

Candy was a wild colt. Born to run free of harness, rope and crop. But like many creatures of the wild, deep down in her half-glimpsed, half-understood consciousness, she sensed a dark, liquorice desire. She longed to be in the thrall of that which she most resisted – discipline. She desired to drown in the deep pool she vehemently avoided – domination. She yearned and burned for the rigorous pangs of a very special pleasure – punishment. Coming to Orrag had been Candy Brompton's pilgrimage. A journey to wisdom and self-knowledge. And Candy knew, with a full knowledge that kindled a sweet fear, a sugared dread, that there was one – and only one – living soul on the face of the broad, wide world who embodied this inner turmoil, who personified this bittersweet conflict: the Wise One. The Wise One – who was about to administer a severe whipping. The Wise One, before whom she now knelt, passive and prone in her naked vulnerability, her bottom bared for the leather lash. Candy pressed her soft thighs together fiercely and moaned.

'But first I will sit down for a short while and think.

Meditate upon your punishment. You too, I fear, must kneel and think, Candy. Meditate upon your pain. I shall savour what you must suffer – that is the essential difference which both separates and unites the punisher and the punished. The whipper,' she soothed softly, 'and the whipped. Together we will anticipate that which you alone must suffer – pain. But remember, Candy, that punishment without purpose or meaning is pointless. You must understand your errors and acknowledge them for what they are. Then, and only then, submit your bare bottom up to the penance of my strokes. Reflect well upon these things, Candy. Reflect, while I relight the candles and soften the lights.'

A match scratched. Six candles flickered. Click. The harsh neon lights died in an instant. In the stuttering shadows of the candlelight, Candy pressed her face down into the firm surface of the bed beneath her and contemplated. Contemplated her foolishness and wilfulness. The foolishness and wilfulness which had brought her, naked and kneeling, buttocks bared for punishment, to this bed of pain and shame.

Why? She had known that to disobey the strict, clear instructions meant harsh and instant retribution. So why? Why? Was she stubborn or was she stupid? Wilful or wanton? What demon had driven her into spy upon the ceremony, to trespass upon its secrets? Curiosity or contempt for the constraints of obedience? She was intelligent, capable. A little ruthless, perhaps, in her competence. Her London desk – envied by many, feared by more – attested to that. She had commanded a huge salary, doubling it with commission from dubious deals within a year of leaving Wensleydale House. So what exactly was it – what flaw in her not-yet-formed character had helped to make the wrong decision; the decision to enter the forbidden room? Enter the forbidden room, and flirt with the real risk of severe chastisement. These thoughts weighed heavily on Candy's mind as six-and-a-half slow minutes dragged by. The potent, passive leather weighed equally heavily draped across her bare bottom as the 390 slower seconds of anxious torment congealed into a timeless purgatory.

'The moment has come,' the Wise One whispered. 'The moment has come.' Beneath the quiet solemnity, Candy caught the flicker of excitement. 'Twenty strokes.'

Candy sensed the series of soft movements in the air behind her as the lithe, jade-eyed nude stooped to gather up the length of supple leather in her slim, strong hand.

'Twenty,' she repeated, almost affectionately, slowly threading the entire length of the dark hide between a firm pincer of straightened forefinger and rigid thumb.

A ripple of apprehension dimpled Candy's spine in the gently illumined darkness.

Crack. The scorching blow was swift and cruel, scalding the jerking spheres of soft flesh accurately, mercilessly. Candy gasped aloud as the leather striped her peaches – biting into their velvety ripeness, searing their satin swell with a blaze of pain.

'You have spirit, Candy. Great spirit,' the punisher mused aloud as she palmed the buttocks of the punished. 'But spirit should be checked. Rein it in, girl. When the spirit bolts, the consequences can be dire and –' crack. A flick of the wrist made the leather bark as it striped the plump, pink rump once more. '– painful.'

The whipped girl jerked her scalded moons in a spasm of exquisite anguish. The whipper leaned forward and steadied her rump, checking and stilling their quivering with a cool hand placed palm inwards against the tight curves of punished silk.

'And you have imagination, Candy. Imagination. But imagination can, and indeed will, run riot if not bridled. Curb your wild, wanton imaginings, girl. If you fail to do so, you will, I fear, suffer many penalties and much –' Crack. The strap spoke again, with evil eloquence. The clenched cheeks reddened. '– discomfort and distress.'

The next stroke followed immediately, snapping down across the crown of the shimmering buttocks. It seared the suffering girl's inner being with molten gold, gilding the scarlet shadows of her mind. Her bare bottom bucked and bounced as she writhed – twisting and wriggling in her hot torment. Then again, the cool, dominant touch of her tormentress: the firm hand of the chastiser on the bottom of the chastised – steadying and stilling. The punished rump ceased its quivering beneath the thrilling touch of the five splayed fingertips that pinioned and pinned. Then again, the stern voice, the dominant tone of the whipper – quelling the rebellious mind of the whipped.

'And you have determination, Candy. Determination. Be sure that it does not become mere stubbornness. The stubborn often have to be persuaded. And persuasion, my girl, can often be most –' Crack. Candy writhed under the hot lash. '– pitiless.'

Dropping the length of leather, the Wise One knelt and cupped the hot fleshy globes between her taloned fingers. Candy squirmed at this fresh torment but the grip was firm. Firm and sure. Lowering her glowing face down towards the hot, imprisoned cheeks, the punisher dribbled a silvery spindle of cool saliva. It sparkled down in a twisted rope of translucence, then softly splashed the scalded swell of the disciplined buttocks. Within her tight clasp, the Wise One felt the bare bottom quiver as the cooling balm trickled down into the valley of the cleft. Tracing its progress with the tip of her finger, she gently probed the ribbon of velvet within the cleft, rocketing the dominated cheeks into fresh jerks. Candy moaned like the evening breeze shivering an ancient elm. The probing finger sought and found the tight rosebud whorl of the sticky sphincter. Candy tensed and held her breath within her bursting lungs. A rush of riotous blood sang loudly in her ears as dark longings burned in her heart. The teasing fingernail scratched at the puckered flesh of the whorl, worrying it tantalisingly. Candy felt the petals of a strange orchid – as rare as it was delicate – brush against the inner walls of her belly as it opened up in sensitive response. The blunt fingertip probed further, delving darkly, deliciously. The warm, firm flesh yielded, admitting it into the depths of the inferno beyond. Candy, squirming and mewling, felt completely mastered, utterly subjugated. Never before had her mind, her body, her will – her very essence – been so completely conquered, so thoroughly dominated. She trembled on the brink of self-knowledge. And in that instant of slow dawning, a fresh longing leaped up like a flickering flame. A longing to torment her tormentor. A yearning to please her pleasurer. A desire to seduce her seducer. It was a pure affirmation of resistance. A primal power struggle. Willing to luxuriate in and enjoy her submission and subjugation, Candy suddenly – instinctively – wanted to balance the erotic equation; if not gaining the upper hand then at least attempting to raise up her own in a gesture of defiance. A Brompton to the very marrow of her bone, she decided to turn the tide. So, slowly, imperceptibly, she fought back. With the artful guile and subtle skill of the most accomplished, perfumed whore. The lizard-like eyes of the Wise One widened slightly as she felt her finger held within the tightening grip of the tensed, innermost muscle. Frowning a fraction, she attempted to withdraw it. The finger remained trapped within the fierce, relentless grip. Silently fuming, she struggled and tugged, but Candy's artful wiles and sinuous flesh kept the imprisoned finger tight within her warm thrall. A feral growl curdled deep in the Wise One's throat.

'Let go,' she hissed, instantly regretting this lapse of control, this slip of the mask of dominance. For she knew well and feared even more the possibility of shattering the spell she had woven around the mind and body of her happy victim.

A dark vision of mischievous triumph danced in Candy's eyes.

'You will suffer now. Truly, you will suffer,' rasped the Wise One, blinking away her fury.

No, mused Candy. You will suffer. For I will make you want that which you would whip. For I will make you pant for that which you would punish. For I will make you lust for that which you would lash.

The Wise One dragged her hot finger out of the hotter flesh and scrabbled for the abandoned strap. Her fingers found it, closing around the leather firmly. Crack. Crack. It snapped down across the swollen cheeks in a double splutter of fury, scorching each taut globe and striping the heavy peaches with faint red reminders of its brief but blistering presence. Candy, biting her lower lip ruefully, raised her punished rump and swayed it teasingly, invitingly. The dark cleft yawned wickedly, causing the Wise One to smother her snarl of lust.

Crack. Crack. Candy sinuously waggled her bare, striped bottom, raising it up defiantly in a promise of proffered plenty. In frank prelude to pleasure. The Wise One swallowed her confusion with a muted whimper and snatched the length of quivering leather up to shoulder height. Her sweat spangled breasts bounced slightly, then settled into a soft wobble, as she tightened her grip on the cruel hide. Wider and wider yawned Candy's deliberately inviting cleft. Down below, an emerging bubble of honey oozed from her sticky hive. The wet labia glistened in the candlelight. The leather lingered aloft in a hesitant pause. Every second's delay was a minute of sweet victory for Candy – confirming that she had pinned the Wise One between the polarities of pleasure and pain. To punish or to possess? Would the Wise One, Candy wondered darkly, weaken and succumb? Would she, who had not moments before conducted the ceremony so sternly, be tempted? Could Candy make her punisher submit to the higher authority of lust? The leather remained aloft. Candy hugged her triumph – however frail, fragile and fleeting it might prove to be – like a sweet thorn in her bosom. She thrilled to the idea of tempting and seducing the stern, green-eyed dominatrix. Like a siren, she would try to lure this proud craft away from the narrows of rigid resolve into the depths of surrender. The leather quivered aloft. Candy pressed her knees together, squeezing them tightly, and dipped her flat tummy down. Her bare buttocks rose, looming large, luscious and luminous in the pale candlelight. The Wise One drew in her breath with a sharp rasp.

Crack. Crack. Crack. The transient weakness passed – its passage marked harshly by the crisp sound of the punishing hide across the bunched buttocks. Candy hissed her anguish – an anguish deepened by her failure and disappointment. She had failed to tempt the Wise One. Failed

to seduce the jade-eyed blonde from her prime purpose –
punishment. Candy clutched to the meagre comfort that at
least she had arrested the leather and stayed the lash a
little. Her bottom now fully ablaze, she held on to these
facts as tightly as she gripped her bed of pain. Crack.
Stretched out now in utter and abject submission to the
strap, Candy writhed under the searching swipe.

'That is all the punishment I propose to give you,' the
Wise One murmured as she knelt closer, squashing her
heavy breasts into the hot bottom before her. 'Despite your
wilful disobedience, your presence at the ceremony proved
to be fortuitous. Let us call it a *felix culpa.*'

A happy mistake. A lucky transgression. Candy's Latin
was quite sound. It had been severely slippered into her at
Wensleydale House – a boarding school which prided itself
in instilling a good grasp of syntax and lexis among its
girls, no matter how painful the lesson might be. Indeed,
for Candy, the dative meant discipline, the ablative meant
angst. So it was with almost mechanical ease that she
translated the Wise One's words. *Felix culpa.* A fortunate
fault.

'Yes,' continued the Wise One, fingering the warm
leather absently. 'A *felix culpa.* Your quick thinking,
prompt action and generosity of spirit undoubtedly averted
a grave misfortune. Do not think that I am ungrateful or
unwilling to acknowledge what you so bravely did.'

'I'm sorry I disobeyed you. I really had no right to.'

'You are blessed,' the Wise One interrupted imperiously,
'with spirit, imagination and a boldness which sadly outrun
your judgement and restraint. You lack self-discipline,
Candy. That is all. Develop and nurture self-control and
your life will be a rich and a rewarding one. Let me help
you.'

'Help me?' murmured Candy into the mattress.

In the candlelight, the Wise One was rebuckling the
leather harness around her wide hips. Grunting softly, she
tugged at the supple straps, fastening them securely around
each swollen cheek of her imprisoned buttocks. Candy decoded the soft sounds – and the honey flowed more thickly

from her disturbed comb. A sudden thickening of her tongue denied further speech. Her tummy tensed and tightened.

'I will teach you to exercise self-discipline and self-control. I fear it may take many lessons. Sometimes painful lessons, but it will be worthwhile. You are, I believe, a pupil of both promise and potential. We shall see. Bottom up,' soothed the supple blonde as she returned to the bed, knelt and straddled Candy's upturned buttocks. 'Up,' she purred. 'Surrender it to me.'

Candy gasped as she felt the cool tip of the ivory dildo nudging firmly against the scalded silk of her recently ravished left cheek. Easing herself fluidly into a slightly more dominant position, the Wise One placed her left hand across the nape of Candy's neck – and parted the weeping labia beneath the hot bottom with the scissored fingers of her free right hand. The dildo nudged, then slid through, the sticky fleshfolds. Candy clenched herself as she accepted the smooth shaft, shuddering as the firm phallus swept up inside her. Her sweet moan became a groan as the Wise One drew her left hand – fingernails inwards – down the length of the dimpled spine. The hand came to rest at the curve of the left buttock. The sticky fingers of the right hand alighted alongside it. Both cheeks were now captive. Captive and enthralled.

The dominant hips closed in further against Candy's trapped thighs, driving the dildo in deeper. And then deeper still. After squeezing the punished buttocks with a gentle severity, the Wise One leaned forward, sliding her palms up against Candy's belly to clasp and crush the bulging breasts. Her supple fingers isolated each berry-hard nipple and tormented it intensely. Crying out like a lonely gull, Candy bucked and threshed in response.

'Deny it. Fight it. Try,' hissed the strict tutor into the pupil's thick mane of cropped blonde hair. 'Try.'

The urgent whispers ceased as she thrust her powerful loins into the passive flesh before her. Pinned beneath the hard belly of her bewitching mistress, Candy's soft buttocks joggled.

101

'Self-discipline, my girl. That is what you must aspire to. Absolute self-control. That is what you must acquire.'

Candy – already quite molten in body, mind and spirit from the attentive leather strap – buried her face in the hard mattress. Determined to attain the calm, serene pinnacle of denial and discipline, she strove to escape the hot, turbulent depths her sweetly savaged body now writhed in. The sinuous muscles of the Wise One's thighs rippled as she hammered the probing ivory shaft deeper and faster into Candy's tight, wet warmth.

'Deny it, Candy Brompton. Be sovereign over yourself,' hissed the Wise One. 'Deny.'

Candy – her breasts bursting with sweet agony within the crushing grip of her tormentress – sensed the heaving waves of orgasm welling up within her. Then they were rolling in heavily, creaming, foaming and tumbling as they crashed. They were, for the ravished girl, unstoppable – their progress inexorable, their power implacable.

'Try harder, Candy. Try harder,' rasped the Wise One savagely, now riding her bareback colt with all the fury of a demon Valkerie astride her stallion.

Candy screamed softly as she shuddered, froze and collapsed – her innermost being dissolving into hot molten gold. Spread-eagled across the wide bed, her flattened face pressed into the mattress and her arms outstretched in utter surrender, Candy hovered helplessly over her orgasmic maelstrom. With the hammering heartbeat and the racing, throbbing pulse of a wild thing, she trembled on the absolute edge of consciousness. The base of her belly collapsed – hurtling Candy down in a headlong spinning tumble; she was coming.

A silent hand of cards was slowly dealt out from the pack held in Time's closed fist. Meaning lost all significance, and significance lost all manner of sense.

'Not yet,' murmured the Wise One with a plangent sigh. 'Not yet.' She eased the phallus out slowly. It sprang upwards, smearing the fleshy buttocks with Candy's wetness, making the bunched cheeks glisten brightly. The Wise One dried the ivory against the swell of Candy's outer thigh.

The splayed girl groaned deeply as she felt the kiss of her own inner juices.

'We will have many, many more lessons. I will teach you. You will learn. But now, bed. I have more work to do tonight.'

'Work?' Candy echoed thickly.

'Emily has to be attended to,' came the soft reply.

Emily. Candy smiled. She closed her eyes and sighed blissfully.

'You did not betray her, I notice. She betrayed herself. I know what she did with her lamp. Emily,' the Wise One whispered, 'needs to become more intimately acquainted with my cane. I shall see to it soon.'

The Wise One knew. The Wise One was going to pay the spiteful redhead a nocturnal visit. Visit the cruel girl – cane a-quiver. Candy hugged her breasts with delight.

'Go to Chloe. Let her soothe your punished bottom. She has such a healing, gentle touch.' With these soothing words, she stroked the bottom her leather had lashed. It was a touch of tremulous, almost tender affection. 'And now I must go and teach Emily the error of her wilful ways. I will bring my whippy cane. Bamboo, I find, is such an eloquent instrument. It stings so sweetly even as it sings.'

Candy left the room in silence, closing the two solid doors behind her. Although they clicked, they did not remain firmly shut but swung silently ajar. Pausing in the dimly lit corridor, she turned and padded softly back towards the doors, her arm outstretched to grasp the dull brass handle. As her fingertips brushed the heavy metal, they froze. Grunts of carnal arousal were coming from the room she had just vacated. It was the Wise One, she suddenly realised, lost in the oblivion of self-pleasuring. Candy's eyes widened excitedly. Could it be true? Had her seductive provocation worked? Had she been successful in her efforts to tantalise and torment the cool, self-disciplined Mistress of Orrag?

Through the narrow gap Candy glimpsed the sight of the Wise One, naked and legs astride. She stood with her glistening buttocks to the doors. The leather belt, still warm from whipping Candy's bare bottom, was being swiftly dragged between the parted thighs, hugging the flesh of the exposed labia. Like a nude bather towelling herself intimately after a secret dip in the secluded pool, the Wise One was plying the strip of hide busily. Candy's eyes sparkled as she drank in the scene. The silver-blonde head, tossed back in an arc of ecstasy. The taut shoulders and sinuous spine. The tensed, rippling buttocks. The firmly splayed legs. One arm before, the other behind, with the stretched leather connecting the fists – the Wise One was lovingly punishing her innermost fleshfolds. The ripe, rounded buttocks tensed even tighter as a low grunt escaped from unseen lips. The climax was imminent, threatening to spill like the warmth of a sudden summer thunderstorm. Grinning her secret delight, Candy withdrew and softly stole away.

'Which is her room? I'm not sure. This one?'

'Yes,' Chloe nodded. 'Be careful,' she urged.

'I will. But I want to hear her getting what's coming.'

'I really don't think we should be doing this, Candy.'

'Remember what she gave us?' Candy hissed sharply. 'Come on.'

Candy and Chloe tiptoed towards the securely closed door of Emily's bedroom. Holding their breath they both strained as they listened intently. From within came the stern tones of a dominant voice admonishing a sullen, unrepentant culprit.

'But it was an accident,' they heard Emily whine.

Candy thrilled to the frisson of fear that rippled through the rising protests of the accused.

'Silence,' snapped the accuser. 'You surely cannot be as stupid as you are spiteful. I would be failing in my duty if I did not cane you most severely. Failing in my duty to you and in my duty to the community here on Orrag.'

'I couldn't help it,' snivelled Emily.

'Then perhaps after your punishment you will exercise more care and caution in the future. I sincerely trust so, for your bottom's sake. Now bend over that chair.'

The listeners at the door heard the faint squeak as the chair scraped the polished wooden floor.

'Legs together,' instructed the Wise One brusquely. 'Bend right over.'

Candy reached out and clasped Chloe's hands. She squeezed them affectionately. Chloe returned the gesture, her mounting excitement fully palpable.

'Feet together, Emily. Come along, girl.'

Outside the door, in the coolness of the corridor, the listeners shivered pleasurably. Silently, they turned towards, then into one another. Lips to lips. Bosom to bosom. Thigh to thigh.

'Bend over. Right over, I said. Give me your bottom.' The voice of the Wise One was becoming a trifle waspish with impatience.

Candy cupped Chloe's soft buttocks in her hands. Chloe grasped and gripped Candy's with feverish fingers.

'No. I want it bigger. Rounder. Head down, Emily. Thighs together. Tighter, that's better. You know full well how to present yourself to my cane.'

Candy dragged her lower lip slowly across Chloe's ripe, sweet mouth.

'No squealing. And double punishment if you squirm during your dozen. Understand?'

The stern voice of admonishment thrilled the girls as they nuzzled in their furtive ecstasy.

Swish. A softly muted thrumm of hissing bamboo sliced the silence of the night. They heard Emily suppress her whimper as the cruel wood bit into her upturned cheeks. Candy gently chewed on Chloe's lower lip – taking the soft flesh into her own mouth – and squeezed the cupped, captive buttocks with fierce gentleness. Swish. Again, unseen but understood, the telltale sound of punishment: the sweep of the cane slicing down to sear and stripe with scarlet pain. Candy's tongue slipped into Chloe's mouth in a hot, wet fusion of urgent celebration. Chloe signalled her response by dragging Candy's heavy buttocks apart. Swish. Inside the room, the punisher stroked and striped the punished methodically, intimately, accurately, ruthlessly and precisely. The Wise One was a witch with the whippy cane. She could conjure red and pink stripes across the creamiest of rumps in an inkling. And indeed red lines of fire now blazed the clenched creamy cheeks that awaited the cane's kiss in mute anguish and passive penitence.

Outside, the two girls hugged and kissed, delighting in the sweet sorrows of Emily. Swish. The fourth cut. Swish. Then, the fifth. Delicious. Each striping stroke set ablaze the upturned cheeks, scalding their tight, creamy flesh. Each soft sound signalled another flicker of the cane, another thin flame of fire. Candy now squeezed Chloe's bottom in time to the punishing strokes. Swish. Swish. Swish. Dropping down on to their knees, the eavesdroppers leaned heavily into each other, their breasts bruisingly fused. They were enraptured by Emily's unseen but none the less severe chastisement. Swish. Swish. Chloe clenched her fingers in a double reflex, gripping Candy's taut cheeks, in an echo to each whispered stroke of the cane. Swish. Swish.

'Come. Leave her to her pain. I want to – I must . . .'

'I know,' Candy grinned. 'So do I.'

They scampered back to Chloe's room, keeping the flame of arousal between their moistened thighs alive with the fuel of memory and imaginings: the flickering cane, the slicing cut, the withering stroke, the anguished jerking of the reddening rump and the flash of mute suffering across Emily's pouting scowl. The Wise One's cool, august authority. Her unerring aim. Those supple arms, so strong and capable. Another stroke, and immediately, the flick of the fiery redhead's hair, flouncing in a spasm of torment. The icy commands of the punisher. The hot liquid eyes of the punished.

Inside Chloe's room, they tumbled down on to the waiting bed. Eager fingers swiftly sought and found each other's hot wetness. Dappling in the dark shadows, frantic fingertips forced sticky flesh wide – and then wider – apart. Candy nipped and tweaked Chloe's tiny pink gland and teased it into erection. Chloe returned the gesture, easing out and capturing Candy's little tip of tissue.

'She got twelve. The bitch got twelve. Let's recount,' murmured Candy, almost tipsily, into Chloe's warm hair.

'One. Two. Three ...' Together, their voices chiming sweetly in unholy unison, the outstretched girls softly recounted the successive strokes – recreating and relishing Emily's misery. The copy was as sweet as the original. Together, belly to sweating belly and thigh to fluttering thigh, their hands moved slowly but surely. Together, drowning in the hypnotic cadences of their recreated joy, they counted. 'Four. Five. Six ...' whispering huskily as they tugged at their quivering love thorns. 'Seven,' they convulsed, the two syllables congealing with the dark delight of the moment. Their stiffened nipples rebelled. Soft was their suffering, sweet was their pain. 'Eight,' they moaned, slurring the vowel as they grew drunker on the liquor of lust.

'Nine ...' they gasped, their thighs rippling and tensing. Firm flanks fluttered. Ripe, tight buttocks clenched, expectantly. 'Ten, eleven ...' they sighed softly, eyes now tightly closed. 'Twelve.'

Their wet mouths closed together. With a synchronised tweaking tug, their finger and thumb pincers squeezed hard. Two liquid grunts followed – as both naked girls came – melting away into the violent calm of wanton carnality.

Chapter Five

Dawn rose and gathered up her sister Night's fragile mantle of cloud, revealing the third sister, Sky, stark and naked. Sky blushed deeply in crimson and scarlet, as she so often does when thus discovered early on a summer morning. Her chaste blushes bathed the crisp linen spread across the breakfast table, suffusing it with pink. Candy paused as she studied the effect, the twelve heavy silver forks forgotten in her left hand. Her eyes narrowed a fraction as she thought of Emily's bottom – and the severe stripes of the whippy bamboo. The soft whiteness of the bare bottom. The pink glow – after the cane had spoken.

Breakfast. The maid set about her business briskly, trying hard to concentrate on her duties. Bustle. There was toast to be made. Eggs to cook. Coffee to prepare. Much to do, and Candy was a little late.

'I'll make the coffee. Is the marmalade out?'

'No, not yet,' Candy shrugged.

Chloe grinned and returned to the kitchen where two large kettles bubbled on the Aga, their clouds of steam moistening her breasts. Chloe fingered her damp vest, plucking at the clinging cotton and easing it away from her peeping nipples. As the kettles sang in shrill harmony, she stretched up for the coffee pots.

'They're coming,' Candy called in from the breakfast room.

'Nearly ready,' Chloe laughed. 'Don't panic.'

Candy stood quietly in a corner of the room, by a tall, blue glazed vase. The vase, a late Japanese Tang piece, was decorated with figurines of honey-gold. Diminutive Kobi priestesses, sinuously and sensuously entwined as they celebrated the rites of pleasure. Tiny red frogs looked on, wide-eyed, at their lubricious sport, as did an amazed silver moon hovering above. Candy loved the little red frogs. The vase was filled with chocolate-dark bullrushes. One of the dried heads drooped drunkenly, brushing and tickling Candy's soft shoulder. The young women of Orrag filed into the sunlit breakfast room, their smiling faces and girlish chatter just as bright and golden. Candy smiled shyly at each one. At Madelaine, the willowy blonde with the very generous mouth. At Annette, the heavily-breasted brunette whose pale hands, ever aflutter, never seemed to come to rest. At Samantha, the sallow-skinned beauty with the dark, mulberry eyes. Her buttocks, Candy noticed, were as firm as small melons, almost bursting out of the pert, white shorts. The laughing banter subsided as the girls dutifully approached their appointed places and sat down to breakfast.

Some places remained unoccupied. Candy frowned. Chloe, she knew, was in the kitchen, being an absolute brick by helping out with breakfast. An act of friendship which could well save the tardy maid a slapped bottom. But the empty places? Where was Emily? And Ruth? Ruth, the quiet, tall girl with the flowing length of chestnut hair. Candy's blonde mane flounced gently as she turned her bright-blue eyes to the doorway. A shadow darkened it as Emily appeared. Candy narrowed her eyes – eyes that clouded suddenly to a deepening violet. Emily was not dressed in her usual vest and shorts – a uniform which, Candy grudgingly acknowledged, displayed Emily's curves splendidly – but strode into the breakfast room in a tight, black track suit. Behind, similarly dressed, was the saturnine Ruth, her cruel red mouth firmly resolute. Emily positioned herself behind the Wise One's customary chair. Ruth, motioned to do so by an imperious hand, stood beside her. Candy prickled with apprehension. Something was wrong. Quite wrong. Emily wore a smug smile of satisfaction. She stood supreme. Supreme and triumphant.

'I have an important announcement to make.'

The girls buzzed softly with expectation.

'Silence,' barked Emily, tossing her copper-coloured hair dangerously.

Her command was instantly obeyed.

'The Wise One is indisposed and will be out of circulation for a while. According to her explicit instructions, I will assume command.'

Command? Candy's heart trembled at the vehemence of the word. She shivered as a murmur of disquiet rose from the assembled girls.

'I will assume complete command of Orrag until further notice.'

Candy caught the thin falsetto in Emily's strident tone as her voice rose a full octave in her effort to stamp her authority on the breakfast table. A hushed silence settled.

'Ruth has been deputised to be my assistant. You will all heed and obey her instructions. She has my full authority to punish any transgressors. Disobedience will not be tolerated. I propose to increase the range of severity of all punishments. I feel there has been laxity of late. From this moment, let discipline be the watchword and obedience be the rule.'

The girls lowered their heads in subdued silence.

'Serve the breakfast, maid,' Emily rasped, nodding curtly to Candy as she sat down.

Chloe appeared from the kitchen bearing four large silver coffee pots, two in each clenched hand. Glimpsing Emily, track-suited and in the Wise One's pride of place at the head of the breakfast table, her affectionate grey eyes widened.

'What is the meaning of this? Are you the maid?'

The waspish severity of Emily's tone stopped Chloe dead in her tracks. She looked around her, blankly.

'Well?' pressed Emily.

'I just thought I'd help.'

'Don't think, Chloe. Just obey. Ruth . . .' Emily added glancing over her shoulder.

The flowing length of chestnut hair rippled sinuously as Ruth moved like a shadow – silent without substance.

'Give Chloe four strokes with your cane. Bare-bottomed,' Emily instructed.

Chloe mumbled a protest but Ruth moved swiftly across the carpet and ordered the anxious coffee-bearer to bend over. The four silver pots wobbled precariously on the carpet but Chloe did not spill a single drop. Swift, strong hands snapped down her tiny shorts, bringing the elastic waistband to a squeezing circle a little above the bending, bare-bottomed girl's knees – biting into the soft thigh-flesh as it imprisoned and entrapped her. She shivered in her strict band of bondage, her upturned cheeks bared for the cane. Swish. The stinging wood flickered and cracked down against the proffered rump. Swish. Again, to Candy's distress – and Chloe's painful shame – the pencil-thin wood whipped the naked buttocks. Candy saw the gently swelling curves of her friend's silken cheeks rippling under the biting lash. Swish. A large teardrop glistened in the suffering girl's grey eye. She blinked – it sparkled on her cheek. A stab of pity bruised Candy's heart.

'Make the fourth unforgettable, Ruth,' snapped Emily from the head of the long, silent table as she feigned indifference to the proceedings and busied herself with her linen napkin, arranging it carefully and smoothing it firmly over her thighs.

Ruth steadied the tip of the cane against the upper quarter of the bending girl's left buttock, indenting the quadrant of the naked cheek slightly. Candy swallowed, her dry mouth awkward, her tongue feeling swollen and stupid. She was frozen between fear and fascination. Fearful that her beloved Chloe would suffer, fascinated by the ruthless efficiency of the crisp caning. The length of yellow bamboo jerked backwards and upwards. Ruth's bosom heaved, the fulsome breasts burgeoning. The quivering cane hovered in the sunbeams, glittering with bright menace. Swish. With a sparkling flash the whippy wood swooped. Swoosh – the eerie whistle broke the oppressive silence of the spellbound room. The harsh crack of punishing wood across penitent flesh snapped loudly as the cruel stroke striped the naked buttocks. Candy saw Chloe's white toes curl up in anguish, and in that dark moment the burning light of vengeance glowed deep in Candy's brain. Ruth would pay dearly for her cruelty.

'Proceed with breakfast.'

Emily's icy voice sounded crisply across the solemn surface of silent table. The sound of flapping napkins followed. Chloe dragged her tight shorts up over the swelling cheeks of her striped rump and sat down to breakfast, eyes lowered and head bowed in shame.

Candy sprang into action, deftly serving everyone within minutes. She shrank a little as she neared Ruth, but her vulnerable bottom – minimally shielded by the bowed strings of her scanty white apron – escaped the expected spank. Relieved, she returned with the toast to serve Emily. Approaching the black track-suited figure, Candy's heart fluttered. Emily ignored Candy, merely taking a small triangle of toast in silence. Candy sighed softly and turned to attend to the other breakfasters. Spank. A crimson flash exploded behind the maid's eyes as the severe smack scorched her bare left buttock.

'This toast is cold, maid. I expect warm toast. See to it at once or your bottom will be hot. Very hot.'

Candy blushed, her cheeks flushing angrily as she heard Ruth's barely suppressed giggle of glee. Not now, Candy bit her lip. Not now. Bide your time, my girl. Later. Retribution, like revenge, is best savoured cold. Under the guise of meek obedience, Candy supplied fresh hot toast in an instant.

As soon as Emily had completed her breakfast she drew the entire table to attention. Speaking in stern tones, she warned the assembled girls that the regime was going to be stricter, the punishments harsher.

'No workshops this morning. I'm putting you all on fatigues. Cleaning, digging and weeding – Ruth has drawn up the roster. I discussed these arrangements with the Wise One after supper last night.'

Liar, whispered Candy. Liar.

'All has been approved. Those who work hard and work well may earn the privilege of an afternoon workshop.'

'But I wanted to finish my –' Madelaine bleated.

112

'Silence. You seem to have some difficulty understanding what I say, Madelaine.'

'I only wanted to . . .' pouted Madelaine in a sulky sotto voce.

Candy saw the frown of fury cloud Emily's face.

'Ruth. Take this girl to her quarters and punish her at once.'

'Strap or cane?' Ruth replied softly.

'Spank her. Slowly and severely. Spank her hard until your hand is too hot to continue.'

Ruth escorted the pale-faced Madelaine to her appointed doom.

A chill wind arrowed keenly over the ocean and whipped across Orrag. It stung the bare-thighed work party toiling in the vegetable garden, mottling their flesh with pink and orange blotches. Cold fingers curled around the unyielding wooden handles of Dutch hoes and rakes. Ruth, cane a-quiver, strode between the labouring girls, strictly supervising their efforts with the heavy loam. The girls worked hard. The potent twitch of the ever present cane proved very inspiring. By late morning, almost a quarter of an acre had been tilled, the soil raised up into level beds ready for asparagus. Emily joined the workers and closely inspected their efforts.

'Well done, Ruth. These girls were going soft. Under my tougher regime I will stiffen them up and build both their bodies and their minds. Character is what I aim to strengthen. That, and discipline. Are you cold, girl?'

Annette, the heavily-breasted brunette, had snatched a moment's respite and had been surreptitiously blowing on her fingers – now quite numbed by the unseasonable chill. She looked up guiltily, dropping her hoe in alarm.

'Give me your cane,' Emily said softly. 'I think she needs warming up.'

Annette stooped to pick up her implement. Emily snatched the cane from Ruth and swished it across the proffered buttocks with a flicker. The bending girl squealed and straightened up at once.

113

'Pick it up,' Emily ordered crisply.

Annette, her face knitted anxiously, obeyed.

'Hold it above your head. Arms up. Higher.'

The hoe rose up at full arm's stretch.

'Running on the spot, commence,' barked Emily.

Annette's heavy breasts bounced invitingly, their swollen ripeness jiggling deliciously beneath the cotton vest's imprisoning bondage. Swish, swipe. The bamboo snapped across Annette's buttocks. She tumbled slightly but recovered and resumed her running. Swish, swipe. Again, the cane lightly whipped her tightened cheeks.

'Anyone else here feeling chilly?' Emily drawled laconically.

The only audible response to the mocking enquiry was Ruth's gurgled titter. The girls immediately redoubled their efforts with the heavy loam, heads bent down, legs splayed and thigh muscles rippling.

'Good. Carry on, Ruth. And do not hesitate to use this,' Emily purred, returning the length of glinting bamboo to the eagerly outstretched hand of her deputy.

When Candy had been ordered to sweep the entire ground floor she naturally assumed that a broom would be provided. It was not. Emily, with Ruth grinning slyly in attendance, had pointed to a small yellow plastic handbrush and dustpan.

'On your knees. Work.' Turning away from the kneeling maid, Emily spoke to Ruth in a more excited tone. 'I have something to attend to. Upstairs.'

Candy thought she caught a certain emphasis, significance perhaps, in the words. Especially the last one. Upstairs.

'The maid will be kneeling at her work,' Emily remarked over her shoulder as she departed. 'A very convenient position should it prove necessary for you to chastise her.'

Time passed. Satisfied that Candy was working hard, Ruth went out to supervise the gardeners. Candy worked diligently, laboriously, squatting to her task like one of the little red frogs frozen in time on the frieze of the Tang vase.

The steady, rhythmical sweeping lulled her into an hypnotic reverie. She wiped her perspiring brow with the back of her hand and sat back. The long corridor was empty. She was all alone. She settled softly, her full buttocks squashed down on her heels. A week ago, she mused ruefully, she was totally and blissfully unaware of yellow plastic dustpans and their equally hateful brushes.

A week ago. Her office in London, like her converted warehouse loft in trendy Wapping, always spotless. Somebody – who it was Candy was not quite sure – came in to clean and tidy when Candy was not there. And after a frantic day at work Candy swept off leaving her office in chaos. A riotous tangle. The next day it would be pristine. She would return to it to find it exactly as she expected it to be. Not a single paper clip out of place. It had been such a cossetted, orderly life. A week ago. In London. In London, where whatever passions lurked deep down in Candy's psyche they remained undisturbed, unsuspected and unexpressed. But since her *felix culpa* – she smiled at the Wise One's ironic epithet – her fortunate mistake which had delivered her to Orrag, those undeclared passions and longings had surfaced and found tongue.

To punish.

To hold a soft bottom tightly in one's thrall. To palm the passive cheeks, thumbing the shy cleft deftly as one thoroughly and intimately inspected and examined the creamy cheeks. Creamy cheeks, tightly bunched, of a bare bottom poised and passive – patiently impatient for punishment and pain.

Punishment.

The fluttering hand, palm down, rising and falling, spanking the beautifully curved buttocks. The sharp, echoing smack. The rippling thrill of flesh upon flesh. The sudden clenching of the savaged cheeks, the spasm of hot satin in anguish. The pink sheen of scalded silk blazing into a blistered crimson. The slight, deliberate pause, with hot hand hovering above the fearful buttocks below, or, better still, pressed down firm and flat, squashing the scorched cheeks to quell and calm their quivering. Yes.

How delicious it had been to discover the dark, sweet delights of spanking. And how darker, sweeter, still to be spanked.

To ease slowly over the warm, soft thighs of the dominant one. To offer up one's bare bottom in utter and absolute submission. To surrender – ceding sovereignty of one's bare buttocks – and suffer the imperious rule and dominion of another. Another – the Wise One.

Yes. But where was the Wise One? What was going on? Candy snapped out of her reverie and tried to resolve the disquiet in her troubled mind. Where indeed was the Wise One? Ill? Indisposed? Why had no doctor been summoned? Why had no one been allowed to see her, tend to her needs? And why had Emily – after her disgraceful behaviour at the ceremony – been deputised to replace her?

'That warmed her up. They'll be digging hard for the next hour or so. Bring it to me. I'll be up there, waiting.'

The voice of Emily, returning from her brisk sojourn in the asparagus beds, where Annette had just been so severely warmed against the chill wind, broke into Candy's turbulent thoughts. The speakers – Emily and Ruth – were unseen but not unheard.

Upstairs. Of course. The Wise One was upstairs – but Emily's tone, the all too easy air of authority, the sneering satisfaction, alerted Candy. All was not quite right. Silently setting aside her dustpan and brush, she rose up and softly stole along the corridor. Emily, closely followed by the sychophantic weasel Ruth, was ascending the narrow staircase. Yes, Candy frowned. Something was surely amiss. Candy knew for certain that the Wise One's room lay at the head of the other, broader staircase – the wide wooden stairs that rose up from the well of the spacious entrance hall. Watching, she saw Emily continue onward, skipping up two stairs at a time, towards the disued attic. Ruth turned and walked down along the first-floor landing, towards the former library where the ceremony had been held last night. Candy pressed herself flat against the cool wall, her bare bottom flinching as it kissed the cold plaster. Which way should she go? Follow Emily? Or turn left, along the first-floor landing to see what Ruth was up to? Shrugging off the distinct possibility of a sound whipping if discovered, but resolved to discover what was going on, Candy skipped silently onward and upward, carefully stalking Emily.

Up in the neglected, dusty reaches of the attic, forlorn with cobwebs and yesteryear's dried dust, Emily unpocketed a small iron key and inserted it into a rusty keyhole. Candy heard the scraping and grating. The door, its paint dull and peeling, swung inwards with a groan. Emily entered the room, the door creaked slowly and closed behind her. Her heart pounding, Candy remained secreted in a shadowed alcove. She flattened herself into the shallow depths as Ruth appeared up the narrow staircase, the harness from the ceremony trailing in her left hand, the short leather straps tapping against her outer thigh. Ruth headed straight towards the door through which Emily had passed only moments before. Candy was just inching cautiously out of her recess when the door suddenly sprang open.

'Stupid fool,' Emily snarled.

'It must have dropped out. I'm sorry,' Ruth whined. 'I'll go back and look.'

'Wait,' snapped Emily. 'I'll come with you. Four eyes are better than two in a search. Come along.'

The two young women descended the staircase, heads bowed as they carefully searched. Of course, Candy realised. The dildo. They were looking for the ivory phallus. It had become detached from the leather harness somewhere on the stairs. Fear and curiosity waged battle royal within Candy's brain. Fear won several fierce skirmishes, but curiosity won the day. Determined to know the secret beyond the door with the peeling paint and groaning hinges, she tiptoed forwards. In the dank gloom, lit by a single, low-watt naked light bulb, Candy spied the cot bed. On it was a pale-blue mattress. On the mattress, spread-eagled and face down – tightly bound by the wrists and ankles to the four corners of the iron bed frame – lay the Wise One. She was gagged and blindfolded. Her pale nakedness glowing softly in the gloom. Faint red stripes across her beautiful, upturned buttocks attested to some recent suffering, some searching punishment. Cane strokes. Candy suspected. Emily, no doubt, Candy reflected. Voices rose up the stairs. Footsteps followed. With her retreat cut off, Candy slipped silently under the bed and held her breath, shivering in the darkness.

Candy heard the harness jingle. Emily grunted softly twice: once as she fastened the straps tightly around her hips and loins, again as she screwed the dildo firmly into place.

'Unbuckle your belt. Give the bitch a warm up then I'll ride her.'

Candy froze, horrified, as she heard these words. Heard, and fully understood, their dark meaning. Several moments of ominous silence ensued. What was happening? What were they doing?

Crack. Candy heard the belt snap down across the bared bottom on the bed above. Simultaneously, she felt the mattress buckle slightly as the spread-eagled Wise One, receiving the full force of the searing lash, bucked and jerked in her bondage. Crack. Candy ducked instinctively as the mattress bulged into a convex – absorbing the reflex spasm and shudder of the whipped woman lying on it. Crack.

'That will do for now. Move aside, Ruth. I've been waiting for this moment.'

Candy, her eyes tightly shut, decoded the soft sounds. The creak of the iron bed frame. The soft squeak of the bed springs. A pause. Muffled movements. A quick gasp. A slow, triumphant snarl, carnal and cruel. The heavy bouncing weight above. More rhythmical squeaking of the bed springs. Emily was riding the Wise One, the dildo deeply penetrating the trussed, spread-eagled captive.

What should she do? What could she do? Even Chloe, lithe and limber, had proved no match for the athletic Emily. And there would be Ruth to tackle as well. Futile to try anything. No. Better to wait. Candy realised that, despite her anguish, there was nothing else for it but to wait.

'I can't believe it,' Emily panted. 'She hasn't twitched a

muscle. I'm deep inside her yet she's still completely dry. Impossible. The bitch has a will of iron. I must break her. Give her a few more stripes with your belt.'

Candy heard Emily ease back from her perch of dominion – saw the mattress bulge as it sagged beneath the cruel girl's shifted weight – and then watched as Ruth's feet approached the side of the bed. The feet rose up slightly, twice. Twice, the belt snapped down across the bare buttocks. Twice, Candy could have sworn she heard soft groans. Soft, gagged moans of suffering. Were they Emily's moans of satisfaction? Or her victim's grunts of pain? Candy trembled in her impotent rage.

Silence followed the brief whipping. Then a grunt, smothered by a long sigh. Then the rhythmic joggling resumed above on the bed of shame. Again, the bed springs raised their thin voices in protest. Soon, Emily was panting, her breath coming in stifled sobs. Candy strained to listen, transfixed. A pause. The pause became a silence.

'Still nothing. She's as cool as an ice cube and just as unmelting.'

Spank. Candy flinched, wincing. Emily had just fiercely slapped the bare buttocks displayed before her – no doubt trapped between her scissored thighs. She harshly smacked the helpless cheeks beneath her hovering hand. Spank. Spank.

'We'd better get back downstairs and show the flag. I'll have two or three of them punished after lunch. It doesn't really matter who we whip. Fear is the important thing. Fear instils obedience. A couple of severe punishments should keep them quiet and in line. As for you, bitch . . .' Spank. Spank. 'I've arranged for some pals of mine to come across and collect you. They've got their own boat and are due at two-thirty. When all the girls are hard at work in the gardens, we get you aboard. I'm taking over here.' Spank. Spank. 'You are finished.'

With these words of contempt, Emily clambered off the bed and, before Candy could work out what was happening, the room was suddenly in darkness and a loud click at the door told her that she was locked in.

119

'Don't be alarmed. It's only me,' Candy whispered.

'Hmm?' grunted the Wise One through her tight gag.

Candy, emerging from beneath the bed, crept softly over towards where the light switch should be. Her hand pawed the smooth plaster in the darkness. Nothing. She swept her palm in a broad, circular sweep on both sides of the doorframe but failed to find the expected switch. Damn, she fumed. It was on the external wall. This would have been a servant's room, candlelit no doubt, in the days when wenches wore mob caps and suffered their master's riding crop. Oil lamps would have illuminated later bouts of the lordship's leisurely pleasure. Electricity probably came just before the Great War. In that sultry Edwardian summer, when the canny laird would have insisted that the switch to such a room be located outside, heaven help the bottom of the naughty parlourmaid found wasting the wattage. All alone in the remote attic room, her thin cotton shift scant protection – and so easily raised – for her soft cheeks across the angry laird's knee for a spanking. Perhaps more.

'Let me. Here,' whispered Candy, loosening the blindfold and casting it aside before untying the tight gag, her blind fingers working intuitively in the gloom.

'Thanks,' gasped the Wise One. 'But how . . .'

'She led me to you. I knew something was wrong. Oh, your poor bottom. Let me see,' Candy murmured.

The Wise One sighed as Candy lowered her face down over the scalded buttocks, her sweet lips hovering less than half an inch from them. She blew a soothing breeze across the punished domes. They quivered and clenched tightly. She planted soft, lingering kisses. The hot flesh rippled and tensed. She licked each hot peach, lingeringly, longingly. The taut hillocks softened and relaxed, submitting serenely to the healing care.

'She came down to breakfast, with Ruth in tow,' Candy continued, panting slightly as she untied the spread-eagled nude's hands and feet from their stern cords of bondage.

'It just didn't seem right, Emily taking your place. And she's been dreadful. Bullying and punishing nearly everyone,' Candy rattled, her tone rising in feverish excitement.

120

'Shush,' the Wise One soothed, rubbing her left wrist with her free right hand.

'Sorry,' whispered Candy, apologetically. 'I'm just so furious. Did she . . .' Candy hesitated. 'Did she?' her voice faltered.

'She failed,' came the cool reply. 'She failed to break me, just as she failed in her brief spell of stolen leadership. Emily has failed utterly. They came before dawn,' the Wise One continued almost conversationally. 'I was asleep. You can guess the rest.'

'But why?'

'Power. Revenge. Discontent. Stupidity. Emily was not one of Orrag's successes. She failed to grasp our principles or accept our guiding spirit. She's jealous, selfish and cruel. She has all the qualities Orrag despairs of. I punished her last night.'

Candy blushed but remained silent.

'I told her she would have to go. All of this was her somewhat childish act of revenge.'

Candy listened in the darkness as the Wise One recounted her story, quickly and simply, with sadness rather than rancour. Emily had planned to usurp her, take her place and, having maligned and discredited the Wise One in her enforced absence, take over as undisputed Mistress of Orrag.

'She is not unintelligent but she is clever and cunning. She calculated that if she ruled with a fist of steel she might just pull it off.'

'What now? We're locked in,' Candy sighed.

'First, I must thank you. Come here.'

In the darkness, the two embraced. Candy was surprised at the tenderness, the gentle warmth of the deep embrace. She felt the Wise One's lips kiss, then linger, on her own.

'We will take our chance when they return,' she said, the stern resolve of her tone startling Candy.

'No. Not that way. It would be unseemly. You must not let them rob you of your natural authority and dignity.'

'Dignity? That went a little earlier,' came the thoughtful, slightly hushed response.

'Perhaps. But only you know that. For the sake of the girls, for the sake of Orrag, you must return in triumph, unruffled and in control. Calm and serene, that is how you must be when taking back command from Emily. And you didn't lose your dignity,' Candy added hotly. 'Or anything else. I was here. I overheard everything, remember.'

'When this is all over and Emily is banished, I will reward you well, Candy.'

'Look. That window.'

'It'll be barred.'

'Not necessarily. This wasn't a nursery and we're too high for burglars.'

'And too high for you to risk your neck, young lady,' replied the Wise One, her voice warm with affection for the gallant young blonde.

But Candy had already prised the stiff casement open. A shaft of bright light, and a gust of fresh air, swept into the dull, dank attic. The Wise One shivered and huddled her nakedness into a ball for warmth.

'I'll make my way down. You follow. There's a ledge, then use the ivy as far as the bathroom below us. There's a large oriel window and its open. O.K.?'

'O.K.' came the shivering echo.

'Lunch was not served to my complete satisfaction. Six strokes for the maid,' Emily announced to the communal court she had summoned immediately after coffee had been completed. 'To be administered by Chloe.'

A cruel touch, that. Pure malice. Candy gazed steadily at the stained-glass window. She counted the tiny red and white stripes in the bear's collar. Emily, eager to stamp her authority on the girls of Orrag, warmed to her task.

Authority, Candy mused. What did Shakespeare say? Dressed in a little brief authority. How brief Emily's stolen authority would prove to be. How grossly she squandered and abused it. Candy recounted the thin red stripes on the heraldic bear's collar. Red against white. The colours of sharp discipline, the shades of severe punishment.

'Next,' Emily shrilled, having just ordered the whipping

of two more blameless girls, 'there is the pressing matter of –'

'Your departure,' thundered the Wise One, imperious and quite splendid at the door.

Ruth gasped aloud and rose, wide-eyed and fearful. Emily paled, her hand fluttering vaguely at her throat.

'Seize them both and gag them,' Candy cried, pointing to the cowering bullies. She had mentally planned for this moment. She knew it was essential to silence the rebels and deny them the chance of revealing the indignities endured by the Wise One in the attic.

The girls of Orrag whooped as they rose up and executed Candy's strict instructions with willing alacrity. Rope was used on the struggling traitors once they had been spanked and gagged into submission. Tight knots were tied, the waxed cords biting lovingly into the passive flesh. Annette paid close attention to Emily's strictures while Madelaine lingered over Ruth's writhing torment.

'There has been a little test. Something of an experiment. It was not successful, both Emily and Ruth have failed,' the Wise One said calmly. 'Their departure has been arranged. I decline to give particulars or details,' she shook her head imperiously at several of the girl's eager faces. 'Their bags and belongings are packed. They leave within the half hour. See to it that nothing remains. I want no trace of them here on Orrag. I banish them, and with them goes disloyalty and cruelty. You may punish them if it is your pleasure so to do.'

A cheer broke out from the assembled girls. The brief but bitter reign of Emily was over. That is all they wanted to know and rejoice over.

'A souvenir of Orrag will speed them into exile,' Candy announced, returning from a minute's absence with an armful of whippy canes. 'We will see them to their boat in style. Take your canes.'

Emily and Ruth wriggled and squirmed as Chloe deftly bared their bottoms.

'There's a boat coming in,' Madelaine cried out.

'Get their bags down to the jetty. They'll follow shortly.'

The Wise One looked on, arms folded, a contented smile on her impassive face, as Candy lined up the young women of Orrag in a ragged guard of dishonour. Canes a-quiver, the impatient girls trod the ground beneath them, anxious for revenge.

'When I command you to do so, you will walk, not run, towards the jetty. Do you understand? If you disobey, I will march you back and we will do it again, and again, until we get it exactly right.'

Emily suppressed a savage snarl. Ruth merely shivered in her miserable expectation. Despite the cold wind, the sun was bright. The raised canes twinkled, glistening with potent malice.

'Proceed,' barked Candy.

Bare-bottomed, gagged and fearful, the two girls hobbled slowly away from the august portals of Castle Orrag down towards the wave-worn jetty. As they passed through the line of waiting girls, the eager canes flickered and swished, striping them unerringly and stingingly.

Ruth stumbled – a slice from Annette caught her suddenly bunched cheeks with a searing swipe. Candy plodded softly behind, driving the two penitents as a pagan goatgirl once drove her flock. Her own cane twitched feverishly, but Candy quelled its impetuous quiver. Not yet, she soothed, not yet.

Swish, slice. Crack, swipe. Candy suddenly grinned, realising what was happening. The young vixens of Orrag were tasting the sweet fruits of revenge. Standing in line, they were dutifully caning the pair of bare bottoms – but Candy noticed that, having administered the strokes, the punishers were skipping along the shining shingle only to reappear further along the line, to revisit the suffering rumps with renewed vigour. Swish, swipe. Crack, slice.

'Keep going,' Candy ordered crisply. Between her hot thighs, a trickle of moist arousal betrayed her keen excitement. Before her, a cane's length away, the two reddening bottoms swayed invitingly as they passed through the forest of living wood.

Swish, slash. Crack, swipe. They neared the jetty. The air

was heavy with the salt tang of dried seaweed – reminding Candy of the bitter tears of shame. Madelaine and Chloe had placed the bags and cases on the swelling deck of a powerful launch.

'Change of plan,' Candy called out cheerfully. Above, the seagulls wheeled and dived. 'Emily and her companion are leaving,' she called above the seagulls' screams.

The two women at the wheel of the launch simply stared, open-mouthed and aghast.

'Little leaving ceremony we're putting on. Nearly done,' she laughed breezily.

The launch, caught by a rolling wave, rose and nudged the jetty.

'Halt,' commanded Candy sternly.

Sullen and sore, the two bare-bottomed girls shuffled to a standstill.

'Bend over.'

Reluctantly, they obeyed, presenting their striped cheeks up for the final rain of fire.

'Six apiece,' Candy said to Chloe, offering her the bare bottoms.

The girls of Orrag had scampered up to form an appreciative semicircle. They gazed at the bending, punished buttocks in raptured silence, their canes shouldered in a mute salute.

'I have only two things to say to you both before your final strokes,' Candy said in a low, calm voice as she steadied and joined together the shivering cheeks with the tip of her cane. 'Learn to value loyalty and renounce treachery. Chloe,' she turned, her golden mane whipping in the chill wind. 'Do your duty.'

Swish. Chloe's cane kissed the bare bottoms – pressed together cheek to cheek – savagely. Emily's eyes widened in anguish. Ruth's shut tight with pain. Swish, swipe. The supple bamboo licked the reddened cheeks hungrily. Emily's nostrils flared above her tight gag. Swish, crack. Ruth twisted her fingers as if moulding invisible clay in the empty air behind her, her hot buttocks clenched in their seething torment. Swish. Chloe's cane sang sweetly yet again, searing the upturned buttocks with another crimson lash. Swish. The fifth, a withering slice, cracked harshly down into the rounded hillocks, cutting into the taut curves to bite and scald. Ruth tossed her head in exquisite anguish.

'Head down,' warned Chloe, tapping the flounced tresses ominously with a dominant touch of the cane tip.

Swish, swipe. The suffering girls almost buckled at the knee as the sixth stroke exploded across their blazing bottoms. Emily's rump was already on fire, the lambent flames licking her seared globes. Ruth's cheeks were scarlet – a perfect specimen of punished flesh.

The launch chugged and gurgled. The thrashed girls scampered aboard, red-bottomed and tearful. The engine coughed then spluttered into life, causing the encircling gulls to peel away in alarm. To the derisory cheer of those watching from the shores of Orrag, the rebellious miscreants – like Adam and Eve before them – were banished from their Eden cloaked in pain and shame.

Candy sought the cool, empty space of the gym after the warm work and crowded hours of her demanding day. The cavernous calm seemed exactly right. Here she felt she would find the peace and quiet so eagerly sought. A still point in her changing, spinning world. Alone among the scuffed leather, taut rope and polished wood of the deserted apparatus, she heard the faint echoes of squeaking pumps and pounding feet. She sniffed, inhaling the vague scent – now no stronger than a vanishing memory – of perspiring, nubile girls.

Slowly, she peeled off her vest, delighting in rather than denying, the delicious sensation of the soft cotton dragging against her pink, stubby nipples. Nipples already pebble round and hard. The vest removed, the full bosom swung freely in its sudden release. Candy steadied and stilled her joggling breasts with her firm palms, pressing them in against the soft fleshmounds perhaps a little fiercer than was strictly necessary. After relishing the delightful sensations, Candy teased her tight shorts down a few inches at a time, so that the faint chill of the cool air visited the plump hemispheres of her partially exposed buttocks softly, insidiously. Her fingertips, timorously emboldened, pushed the taut waistband down with a shy eagerness. It hugged the crown of her twin, creamy peaches firmly, almost jealously, as if intent on keeping sacred the secret of her dark cleft. Down came the waistband a little further to encircle and embrace the soft, silken skin of her upper thighs. A little further, and the delicious feeling of being imprisoned, fettered and immobile opened and juiced her pouting labia. The sticky fleshfolds parted like velvet under her probing finger. Candy closed her eyes and tossed her head back, arching her neck and flouncing her mane of golden hair. Her taut body rippled as her finger sought out her wet warmth.

'There you are.'

The gym doors flapped, the broad rubber trims slapping in applause as they swung back after admitting the Wise One. Candy blushed becomingly, the deepening damask suffusing her startled face.

'I was just . . . I thought, perhaps . . .' she blurted.

'Come here at once,' the Wise One whispered. 'No, do not bother with those.'

Candy let her vest and shorts, snatched up in haste, flutter back down to the floor. They lay at her feet in soft surrender.

'I have come to pleasure you, as promised. Not punish you,' the Wise One chuckled tenderly, taking the naked blonde in her soft, strong embrace and kissing away the flicker of fearful expectation.

Candy surrendered utterly to the delights to come. The Wise One – strict mistress of punishment – may prove to be an equally devout priestess of pleasure.

'No more words. No need to say anything. Let our tongues stay silent, though perhaps not absolutely still.'

No words were spoken. Sweet silence reigned supreme. But eye spoke eloquently to eye. Lips signalled urgent longings to lips. Tongues flickered their dark secret joy. The Wise One was the empress, Candy the slave. Yet it was the empress who served the slave – bringing to her the exotic fruits of desire and the rich, sweet wine of delight in the banquet of lust spread lavishly on the altar of Lesbos.

The feast unfolded, and no sweetmeat was overlooked. The Wise One made imaginative use of the facilities surrounding her in the deserted gym. She took Candy by the hand and approached the squat vaulting horse. Obeying her pleasurer, Candy eased herself up and settled face down across the smooth suede. Her bare breasts squashed heavily into the solid body of the horse, which she straddled and gripped tightly around the swollen belly with encircling arms. Her legs splayed, she offered up her naked bottom in total, happy submission. It was an utterly sensual surrender. The Wise One stood alongside the horse, her belly pressed into its cool flank. With her strong left hand she pinned the nude girl by the nape of her neck. Candy's lips crushed softly into the bruised leather skin. It tasted of dark, forbidden delights. Slowly, deliberately, the Wise One positioned her outstretched right hand – fingers straightened – across Candy's upturned buttocks, the palm gently but inexorably flattening the ripe cheeks as it kissed them then pressing down more firmly. The horse creaked slightly under the sudden weight of Candy's naked warmth. Candy sighed. The long, white fingers retracted slowly, squeezing the rounded cheek within its talons, pulling the cleft apart. The fingertips dipped into and then gently dappled the velvety cleft, drumming the ultra-sensitive ribbon of darkened skin steadily, rhythmically. Candy, with thickening groans curdling her throat, conjured up the image of a stallion pacing and pounding some distant moonlit sands along an unmapped shoreline. Pacing and pounding, pacing and pounding. The drumming hooves, the drumming hooves. Sweetly tormenting, mercilessly delicious. The dominant fingers drummed relentlessly, the beat of skin against skin maddeningly wanton. Curving her hand sharply at the wrist, the Wise One sank it lengthways into the warm divide between the gently wobbling cheeks. As it sank and settled, Candy willed her buttocks up a fraction to receive it. The fingers around the soft nape of her pinioned neck tensed and tightened imperceptibly.

Candy thrilled to the firm touch. The dominating touch. The touch of absolute authority. She held her tremulous breath within her fluttering bosom, and was soon quite liquid with longing, and quite wet with the lubrication of lust. The warm hand dividing her trembling buttocks slowly began a devilishly delicious sawing motion, rubbing deeply into and along the shadowed warmth within. Candy clenched her cheeks, bunching her buttocks tightly, but could not delay or deny the demonic delight. The hand slipped back and forth, its speed and pressure increasing. Soon it was skimming rapidly along the valley between the hillocks of wobbling flesh – inflaming and increasing the moist, sticky warmth oozing from the enthralled blonde. Faster, firmer. Faster still. Arching up her buttocks in abject surrender, Candy moaned sweetly. The Wise One acknowledged the moans by increasing the severity of her grip on the nape of Candy's neck, intensifying the severity of the disciplined pleasure. Candy rocketed in response – golden lava now flooding from the eruption between her thighs. Moments later, her pouting labia kissed the leather *adieu* as she slithered from her suede mount and slumped on the hard, polished floor below. As she curled up at the feet of the Wise One, giddy and reeling with delight, her sugar sovereign inspected the large wet patch on the plump stretch of hide.

Up on the wall bars, her naked body dangling face down towards the empty gym, Candy clung with gripping hands to the spar above. Her arms ached, deliciously. Her feet, prinked and slightly arched, pointed straight down to the floor five and a half feet below. Transfixed and suspended in utter naked splendour, Candy tremblingly awaited the sweet assault to come. It approached, cat-like, as one stern pleasurer slowly ascended, mounting the wall bars one by one. Candy squirmed. The pleasurer neared. Candy writhed, her molten imaginings spilling freely from her hot labia. Candy parted her legs a little. Then a little more. Soon the soft thighs were frankly splayed – offering the passive prey of her delta to the prowling predator: the jade-eyed huntress of warm, wet flesh. The Wise One inched closer, tongue swollen and a-quiver. From her perch of pleasurable pain, her burning arms and shoulders aching sweetly as they supported her soft, naked body, Candy glimpsed the cropped silver-blonde head of the Wise One rising up to pause, lips level with the swollen heaving bosom that hung in heavy splendour. Glancing down she saw the parted lips reveal a flash of tiny white teeth then close in and completely cover her quivering left nipple. Spangles of silvered scarlet splintered her brain as the strong lips sucked hard, fiercely punishing the erect bud with a savage tenderness. The hungry mouth worked busily at the breast, taking most of the creamy ripe flesh into its wet warmth. Hot honey spilled freely down Candy's inner thigh as the Wise One pleasured and rewarded her rescuer. Firm white teeth were now enclosing the other pink, stubby nipple, biting the swollen berry gently. Candy screamed a silent scream and urged her soft bosom into the tormenting mouth. Suspended and immobile up on the wall bars – as the Wise One had arranged and prepared her prior to the pleasuring – Candy felt perhaps for the very first time the true sweetness of submission, the sharp pleasures of helpless surrender, the dire delights of domination. Her breasts now burning with the soft flames that bathed them, Candy felt the firm, wet tongue of the Wise One trace down between her glistening cleavage, licking and lapping at the tremulous globes of heavy satin. Wickedly, the hard white belly of her tormentress deliberately brushed against her sticky labia, crushing the erect clitoris therein. Candy shivered on the dizzy edge of unconsciousness and gasped her sweet suffering in a melting, molten sigh. The tip of the hot tongue worked down her own belly, then further down to probe and tickle-touch the outer fringe of her blonde pubic thicket. Her labial curtains were already drawn wide apart. Her window was open. The tongue entered, its sinuous tip cautiously seeking the hot wetness within before teasing out, and taming, the sliver of erectile tissue.

Candy's squeal was electrifying. It curdled thickly in her throat, rising to a sudden shrillness as she climaxed – her inner muscles contracting and convulsing and her pounding hips hammering her bare bottom mercilessly into the hard wall bars behind.

Later, under the drumming stream of hot water, Candy offered up her ravished flesh to the raking fingers of the shower. Tiny pearls bespangled her shoulders. Hot diamonds of the splintered deluge danced between her proud, bare breasts. Silver rivulets sluiced the cusp of her ripe rump, arrowing directly down into her dark cleft. Her silken cheeks shone, the bare buttocks bunched tightly and quivering with delight. Slowly, rhythmically, the Wise One massaged the tablet of scented soap between her tightly compressed palms. It creamed instantly, surrendering its curds. She paused, momentarily, examining the bubbles that escaped through her splayed fingers. Candy shivered deliciously as expectation stroked her imagination. Her swollen bosom strained, eager for the soaping. The Wise One obliged, firmly foaming her captive nymph with a ruthless gentleness of palm to passive flesh. Generously, the bobbing breasts were lathered. Tenderly, the taut rump was soaped. Candy leaned forward, supporting herself with outstretched arms against the hard, white tiles – thrusting her buttocks out for the soaping hand, shuddering as a stray finger lingered between the heavy ripeness of the fleshy cheeks. Lingered and probed. Probed and entered – with a smooth, unresisted graceful glide.

Rinsed and gleaming, her nude body sparkling, Candy succumbed to the waiting embrace of the soft towel. Wrapped within – indeed trapped within – the tight fabric, she gladly endured the sweet strictures of the patting, rubbing, searching hands as they pummelled and squeezed, moulded and palmed her limbs. A gentle corner was raised to dab dry her arched neck. A fuller, firmer handful punishingly palmed her breasts. A severe sweep of the towel banished the gathering pearls on her shoulders, back and rounded buttocks. Busy hands brusquely towelled the tapering length of her splayed legs. Her soft thighs and swollen hips were not spared a vigorous scouring. Soon, only her golden

pubic wisps remained glistening. The Wise One slowly took
the towel and twisted it into a thin rope. Threading this
between the clamped thighs, she carefully dried the pubis.
The sensation was far from displeasing. Candy smiled her
wanton pleasure as the flames flickered once more down
below. Her sighs – soft sobs of joy – grew more urgent as
the Wise One roughly pumped the towel with her outstretched arms, dragging it rapidly back and forth between
Candy's clenched flanks. The soft material slightly scalded
the sticky fleshfolds. A loud gasp, dying into a low moan,
escaped Candy's lips. Her quivering body shuddered as,
behind her eyes, a snowstorm raged across the silvered
contours of her mindscape. The soft burning between her
tightly squeezed thighs spread upwards to her belly, bathing it with living fire. The towel was suddenly – almost
brutally – jerked away and thrown on to the wet tiles.
Candy cried out, mourning the loss. Roughly, in absolute
control, the Wise One gripped Candy by her shoulders and
span the naked nymph round. Forcing Candy down on to
her knees, the supreme dominatrix studied the raised buttocks of the dominated girl as they swayed in supplication.
Inch by inch, the Wise One lowered her delta down on to
the bare bottom. With fervent speed, she rasped her hot
wetness across the raised rear, causing Candy, her mind
ablaze with the searing understanding of the source of this
fresh thrill, to buckle and collapse under the imminence of
her orgasm.

Faster and firmer came the sweeping sticky intimacy as
flesh ground against flesh. Soon Candy's buttocks glistened
with the sparkle of the Wise One's weeping labia. Carnal
grunts punched the steam soaked air. Shivering and shuddering, Candy surrendered – broken like a wild colt under
the bridle and crop – to her fierce rider. Moments later, a
sweet screaming flooded the vast, deserted gym, drowning
the naked couple as they mutually paroxysmed into their
single whirlpool of wet, bubbling gold.

Chapter Six

The following day the sun burned down on Orrag, banishing the chill brought in on the earlier Atlantic breeze. Candy paused from the pleasure of her delicious lunch – a hearty salad served with thick slices of ham, a delectable breast of chicken and wafer-thin wisps of moist tongue – and watched as a late butterfly brushed the windowpane with its orange wing-tips. The sweeping of the velvet reminded Candy of the Wise One's eyelashes fluttering against her upturned, yearning face.

'Sweet chutney?' Madelaine murmured at her side, happy to be maid once more. She was bending forward, her bosom burgeoning.

Candy smiled and spooned the glistening relish from the dish before her. She turned slightly to watch the willowy blonde striding along the line of seated girls, the white bows of her knotted apron strings tap-tapping against the swell of her swaying bare bottom. Candy returned to her lunch. The chutney was subtle, spiced, yet succulently sweet. As sweet as the Wise One's lips which had crushed down upon her own. Sweeter than those same lips which had returned, moments later, anointed with the feral tang of Candy's wet excitement sucked deeply from between her trembling thighs.

A bee bumbled busily at the other windowpane. The brightly striped bee, symbol of honey. She closed her eyes and shivered deliciously. And remembered. Remembered how her own honey flowed freely when giving or receiving, administering or accepting, stripes. She remembered that with the honey came the sting. Candy opened her eyes. The honey and the sting. The treacle of warm pain spreading slowly across a bare, punished bottom. The sweetness of discipline. The sorrow of the stripes.

Looking up, she saw the Wise One selecting a soft peach. The fruit lay heavy in her outstretched palm. The Wise One seemed to weigh it – as if judging the fruit's perfection – as Candy knew she would weigh a ripe breast before pleasuring it or a fulsome buttock before punishing it. Candy's fingers gripped her bread roll. It crumbled instantly under her mounting excitement. Down at the head of the lunch table firm fingers were now enclosing the trapped peach. Squeezing the captive fruit gently, the fingers paused as if willing to bruise, but reluctant to blemish, the passive sphere of flesh within their grasp. Candy's mouth dried, her throat constricted slightly, and her nipples prinked as she watched the Wise One drag her thumbnail slowly along the furrow of the peach. Thumbing the cleft, the Wise One suddenly gazed directly, dominantly, into Candy's eyes. Instinctively, Candy clenched her buttocks. Glancing up shyly – curiosity banishing bashfulness – she watched the Wise One probe the imprisoned fruit, the peach now partly split and oozing, with deliberate strokes of her long, pink tongue. Candy, remembering how agile her tongue was, shuddered. A sudden liquid flutter troubled her sticky labia. The Wise One, smiling her sure and certain smile, fluttered her jade eyes and worked the fruit adroitly with her teeth, lips and tongue. The gathering storm within Candy's loins flickered and grumbled deep down at the base of her smooth belly. The peach devoured, the Wise One wiped her lips, slowly and carefully. Candy sighed audibly, unclamped her trembling thighs and absently fingered some wild strawberries set before her by the bare-bottomed maid.

'Cream?' whispered the warm, sweet breath of Madelaine in her ear, the full soft breasts brushing Candy's shoulders.

Candy's nipples stirred and thickened yet again as lunch on Orrag proceeded beneath the brazen zenith of the sun.

'Emily's behaviour has cast a dark shadow.'

Candy was walking slowly along the expanse of white

sands of the beautiful, unspoiled beach. Beside her, matching stride for rippling stride, was the Wise One. Occasionally, their golden flesh would briefly collide in a deliciously tingling graze.

The Wise One continued thinking aloud. 'We need to establish the old order. Get Orrag back to where we were. Before Emily.'

We. Candy, who had been listening attentively, did not properly hear the rest of the sentence. We? She thrilled inwardly at the inclusive pronoun. It proclaimed what she had already half sensed but had hardly dared to hope – the Wise One now regarded Candy as her unofficial assistant. Her role in first exposing and then expelling Emily and the sullen Ruth had of course been acknowledged and rewarded. Richly rewarded. Those liquid moments of weeping joy in the gym. And of course she was no longer maid. No longer bondmaiden, her bottom at the mercy of every cane's whim. To be walking along the warm, white sands under the midday sun sharing the Wise One's confidences, her innermost thoughts, electrified Candy.

'No real damage done, but do you think the girls will settle down again quickly?' The Wise One looked enquiringly at Candy.

'Of course they will. They are loyal, don't forget. Loyal and disciplined. You have them extremely well-trained.' Trained. Candy lingered on the word. 'Your special training offers them the direct route to self-advancement through discipline and control.'

'Discipline and self-control. Yes. And inner strength. The secret of the Ancients,' the Wise One said, nodding. 'You seem to both understand and approve of my methods.'

'I do,' gushed Candy unreservedly, suddenly blushing shyly.

'Yes, I believe you do. I had hoped it would be so from the moment I first saw you.'

'There is a slight problem. Samantha.'

'Samantha,' echoed the Wise One softly. 'I believe she played some part in Emily's rebellion.'

Candy nodded but added that Samantha's role had been a very minor one. 'And she hasn't been punished yet,' she remarked.

A silence ensued. They paced across the hot sands. Up above, a large white seabird harried the grey-capped gulls. The wheeling gulls cried as they tumbled out of the sky.

'I delegate the matter to you, Candy. Speak with her. If she merits punishment, administer it. Chastise her soundly. And see to it that she repents fully and absolutely. Yes,' nodded the Wise One emphatically. 'I leave the entire business, and Samantha's bottom, in your hands. Look. Up there. The large bird. Isn't that a storm petrel? Charming. Yes,' repeated the Wise One. 'In your capable hands.'

As instructed, Samantha was sitting on her bed in her Spartan room, waiting for Candy's arrival. Her beautiful face was somewhat pale and a sombre gravity had unseated and replaced its usual playful levity.

Samantha, it was widely known, had bold ambitions. She saw herself as a key player in the financial markets, leading a team of astute dealers and buyers. She aspired to command fear and respect not only in the City, but throughout the international financial community.

As the hot afternoon stretched towards, and then past, teatime, her immediate future was of more pressing concern. What would her fortune be? She shuddered to speculate. The would-be mistress of the money markets bit her lips apprehensively. Squashed firmly down on to her bed, her bottom tingled with anxious expectation.

Candy closed the door softly, but firmly, behind her as she entered the small bedroom. Samantha looked up quickly, her face sallow, her dark, mulberry eyes not a little fearful.

'I think you have something to say to me,' Candy said in an even, neutral tone. 'Something to confess, perhaps?'

Samantha glanced down at her hands which she had pressed, palms together, between her thighs.

'You will feel much better after you have confessed,' Candy urged gently.

Samantha hurled herself down on to her narrow bed, burying her face in her hands. Candy noted the ripe rump. Already it was upturned, the cheeks clenched, for the inevitable punishment to come.

'I didn't mean to. I didn't want to,' Samantha whimpered in a muffled, contrite rush. 'Emily made me.'

Candy strode over to the bed and sat down, nestling the heavy swell of her curved buttock against the penitent's bare thigh.

'I'm sure you're not a bad girl, Samantha. A little unwise, perhaps. A little foolish, certainly. But not wicked.'

'But I am wicked. I helped Emily.'

Clenching her upturned buttocks tightly, she buried her face into the white pillow and made a full and frank confession of her misdeeds. Candy listened in silence. The confession was not alarmingly serious, she judged – merely evidence of Samantha's serious misjudgement.

'Is that all, Samantha?' she catechised solemnly.

'Yes, honestly. Does it mean –' the sorrowful girl turned her tear-stained face up and gazed at Candy over the shoulder of the tight white vest. 'Does it mean I'll have to leave Orrag? What will the Wise One think of me? What will she do?'

'Nothing,' replied Candy in a cool, calm voice. 'The Wise One will not do anything.'

'Do you mean I won't be whipped?' gasped the girl.

Candy paused. Samantha gazed up, expectantly. Fragile hope lightened her deep-mulberry eyes. Candy arranged the anxious girl's arms down alongside her soft, warm body, leaving the curled fingers of the cupped hands against the golden skin of her rippling thighs. With a single movement of skilful grace, she peeled the taut shorts across the crown of the pliant cheeks and dragged the elastic waistband down to bite into the fleshy thighs below. The bare buttocks joggled with an imperceptible wobble as Samantha shivered. Candy rested her hand, palm dominantly down, across the exposed bottom, causing the penitent to clench her buttocks tightly as she moaned into the hard pillow.

'No,' Candy purred. 'The Wise One will not punish you, Samantha.'

The tensed buttocks slackened and relaxed.

'That duty falls to me.'

The creamy spheres tightened immediately, their flesh quite firm with fear.

'I shall have the pleasure of punishing you if and when I deem it necessary. But from what you have confessed to me so far,' Candy massaged the passive cheeks, flattening her hand down in slow, circular sweeps to crush the quivering fleshdomes, 'I believe you have done nothing that merits more than brief – but severe – chastisement.'

Samantha wriggled and squirmed at these words, her rump writhing provocatively. Candy quelled the buttocks with a single, sharp spank then instantly stilled the reddening bottom with a steadying touch of her dominating hand. The control was absolute. Samantha froze in her rigid submission.

'No, Samantha. You have been very foolish, but not wicked. The Wise One has authorised me to deal with you.'

'And the rest of the girls? Will they . . .?'

'They need never discover your foolish indiscretions. Once you have been punished, the entire matter may be forgotten.'

Candy's straightened index finger carefully traced the creamy slope of the inner buttock down the sweep of tight satin to the warmth of the tempting cleft.

'Punished?' whisper-whimpered the near-naked girl through trembling lips.

'I am going to consider your punishment very carefully, girl. I believe, and I do not doubt that you will concur, that a suitable and fitting punishment must be devised,' Candy pronounced, framing her words in the maddeningly elaborate formality of a Shires solicitor. 'I cannot be fully persuaded that mere stripes from a cane . . .' She illustrated her sentiment by scoring the bare bottom twice with a firm fingertip across the swell of the bunched cheeks before her. 'That mere stripes from a cane will suffice. No, Samantha. You are to remain here on your bed, exactly as you are, while I determine the nature of your punishment. Thank you for confessing your minor involvement with Emily. A transgression for which I am certain a penalty can and will be devised.'

Candy gazed down at the bare bottom. Whatever she determined – whatever Samantha's punishment was to be – the bare bottom would suffer. It was a slightly heavy bottom, fully fleshed, the cheeks peachy, pliant and ripe. Smooth spheres of flesh. Soft, creamy flesh. Creamy flesh that blushed delicately with the merest hint of pink. How that pink would darken to a deep damask under the spanking hand of retribution. How that creamy flesh would quiver under the keen slices of the swishing cane. It was indeed a delicious bottom, Candy mused as she palmed it firmly. A bottom that spoke with mute eloquence of its absolute fittingness to be chastised. It was, without doubt, a bottom fashioned by nature's cunning hand for the pleasure of pain. Cheeks to be cherished with cruel whippy wood. Buttocks that demanded the stinging homage of the spanking hand. A bottom, Candy reflected – struggling to resist the almost overwhelming temptation to kiss it sweetly and bite it lovingly – that begged to be blushed by bamboo.

The Pleiades shivered high above in the deep midnight sky. Candy gazed up, her blonde mane and white shoulders splayed loosely on the warm sands. She carefully counted the seven stars, straining somewhat to catch the plangent music of the heavenly spheres from the seven virginal sisters – fixed for eternity in the dark, velvety vaults above – shimmering in their yearning and sparkling as they pined. Cold, pristine virgins – mutely wailing for the warmth of Orion, the Hunter, or perhaps the fiercer heat of Apollo, the all devourer. Cool, chaste, unfingered and unbruised by the ardent planets that swirled around them, the seven stars trembled in the knowledge of their infinite, everlasting longing.

Despite the warm breath of the night breeze upon her nakedness, Candy shivered. Her upturned gaze swept the

arched heavens, her narrowed eyes peering into the impen-
etrable mantle of the deep void. The Plough stood stark,
splendidly glittering. Then she found Venus close to the
horizon. Even Venus looked a little lonely tonight. A tiny
cloud of melancholy threatened to settle over Candy, but
she shrugged it off at once. No cold abstinence for her, she
smiled secretly. She would be returning soon to Samantha's room. Candy stretched out luxuriously across the
sands, wriggling her bare buttocks down into the soft
warm beneath.

Samantha. Candy conjured up a graphic image of the
wretched girl sitting at her makeshift desk – head bowed,
chin in hand, her pale face a mask of anxious concentration. Candy chuckled. Even now the naughty little
miscreant would be softly easing the weight from one bare
buttock to the other on the seat of her hard wooden chair.
Candy smiled darkly, recalling with pride the punishment
she had devised for the girl with the sallow complexion and
the dark, mulberry eyes – eyes soon to glisten with sorrow.
Candy's gaze flickered up to slowly count the seven sisters
in the Pleiades once again. Seven. A prime number. Not
like nine. Candy's smile deepened. The nine muses. That
had been part of Samantha's punishment. To sit down and
write an essay on the nine muses, and how they had
fashioned, controlled and edified the minds of men
throughout the centuries. The essay would – like that of a
naughty schoolgirl's – contain minor errors. Red ink would
root them out. Red ink. How appropriate, Candy mused
as she shivered slightly with pleasurable anticipation, that
red ink would in turn mean punishment. Red ink on white
paper, red stripes on creamy flesh. Candy was sure that
Samantha's spelling was not her strong point. Girls with
such beautiful breasts paid scant attention to the diction-
ary. And as for the little minx's punctuation, Candy was
sure that it would be atrocious. Girls with bottoms so
superbly shaped usually had little grasp of the usage of the
semi-colon.

Candy's fingers found her nipples. She trailed her digits
across the stubby peaks languorously, nipping each tightly

swollen berry firmly before pausing to pleasure and torment the tiny tips of tumescent flesh. Darts of pure delight stabbed her belly softly – arrowing further down to sting her sticky labia. She spread her thighs wide, inching them open until her glistening pubis pulsed. The sea tumbled towards the beach, the waves shouldering one another as they surged and foamed, splashing their spume and glinting suds on to the moonlit beach. Tiny specks of the icy water spattered Candy's bare feet. She moaned, cupping and squeezing her proud breasts fiercely, thrilling to the rebellion of flesh as the bosom burgeoned within her grasp – trembling at the heaving swell of warmth beneath her punishing palms. The sea crashed towards the shore, flinging up a sparkling spray as it collapsed at Candy's feet, leaving her nakedness diamond-spangled. Candy gasped sharply with illicit pleasure. Her fluttering fingertips now skimmed the drum-tight belly and honey-dark inner thighs. The angry, swelling ocean lay spent and tamed at her feet, its curds eddying submissively around her ankles. Up above, the seven sisters twinkled forlornly in their chill, chaste void. The Pleiades. All seven of them. Seven. Would Samantha's bare bottom receive seven severe stripes? Possibly more. Samantha's bare bottom was as luscious and as luminous as the perfect sphere of the creamy moon above. Such a beautiful, pallid orb. So poised.

The rollers swished loudly on the neap tide as they lashed the shore. Candy listened, eyes closed, hearing instead the hiss and the swish of a punishing cane. She had her duty to perform, just as Samantha had her task to complete. Nine muses. Then, the red ink. For each error in the essay penned by the sulky penitent, a reddening stroke of the cane. Swish. Swish. Up above, the heavy, swollen moon hung poised in the dark void around it. Ripe, round and naked. Swish. Swish. The sea moaned its chorus of sweet pain, its endless hymn to discipline. Swish. Swish. Behind her closed eyes, Candy saw Samantha's bottom, poised in its passive perfection for its sure and certain punishment.

Punishment. Candy's fingers stole down into the tickle

of her golden pubic fringe to pucker her velvety flesh. Swish. Swish. She teased her labia. Swish. Swish. She toyed with her clitoris. The ocean urged her on. Up above, the shimmering lunar orb beckoned her, enflamed her, increased her wanton imaginings. Stripe me, stripe me. Swish, swish, the ocean whispered back.

A crashing roller split the night, spillings its spume in a living vein of silver up the beach. The icy waters sped unchecked, sluicing Candy's legs and upper thighs, instantly quenching the flickering fire that smouldered within her open sex. Squealing, she jack-knifed her knees up to her squashed breasts and rolled over, laughing with primitive joy. Another amorous wave rose up, only to collapse down as it spanked the sands in a fury of foam, its spent waters scudding up the beach to splash Candy's bottom. She squealed again and, scrambling to her feet, stumbled through the bubbling surge. On dry sand, she stood and shivered, her legs shaking. The brusque fingers of ice had suddenly cleared her mind, rinsing it of her delicious reverie. Her face set on the grim pleasures that awaited her, she turned her shining wet buttocks to the sea that had just kissed them and strode boldly back towards her uncompleted duties.

'But I'm sleepy. Come to bed, please.'

'No. Work to do. Punishment,' whispered Candy.

'Mm? Who?'

'Samantha. Come on, I'll need you.'

'Samantha?'

'She has a beautiful bottom. Have you ever . . .?'

'No,' Chloe replied breathlessly as she bounded out of her bed. 'But,' she grinned, 'I've always wanted to.'

'Come on then,' Candy urged. 'I'll spank. You can cane.'

They walked quickly, hand in hand, along the silent, deserted corridors to Samantha's bedroom. Chloe gave Candy's hand an excited squeeze as they approached the door. Candy returned the intimate gesture. The chase was on, the hunt was up, and the quarry was a soft, punishable bottom.

142

Inside the bedroom, they found Samantha exactly as Candy had pictured her – scantily clad in only a tight vest – and sitting pensively at her little wooden desk. Her naked thighs were clamped together; her long, bare legs were crossed and tucked away beneath her chair like a naughty schoolgirl suffering the miseries of detention, and contemplating harsher penalties to come. Candy noticed the inky blue stain clouding the miscreant's pale fingertips. Pages of spidery writing littered the desk top. Samantha looked up, her fingers fiddling nervously with the pen, her dark-mulberry eyes wide with apprehension. And in their depths was the knowledge that her fateful moment had come; her appointment with doom had arrived.

'I see that you have completed your task,' Candy observed, picking up the pages and scanning their contents. 'Let us hope for your bottom's sake that it is of a satisfactory nature.'

Candy sat down on the bed. Chloe stood beside her. Heads bowed, they both pored over the essay. From time to time, Candy's wrist flickered as the thin, red pen she grasped briskly underlined yet another error, yet another mistake. Samantha, hands folded behind her back as if subconsciously shielding her bare bottom from the fierce heat to come, watched and trembled as the scattering of red lines signalled her imminent pain.

'Not a bad effort. Not bad at all. In fact, a tolerable attempt, Samantha. You have, however, made several glaring mistakes.'

The irony of this double meaning was not entirely wasted on the anxious girl. She shivered slightly, grinding her left foot into the polished floor.

'Mistakes for which both Chloe and I will now punish you. Kneel.'

Samantha obeyed immediately and sank to her knees, wincing as they kissed the hard floor. Her white vest rode up over her hips, revealing the perfectly cupped buttocks that were about to be visited by hot hand and cool cane. Candy rose up from the bed, leaving two rounded depressions where her bottom had squashed the bedspread. She strode over towards the kneeling girl, the corrected essay in her right hand. In a low, steady voice – entirely free from rancour or anger – she slowly enumerated the mistakes she had discovered in the writing, being careful to distinguish between errors of syntax and errors of content.

'Do you concur with my findings?'

Samantha nodded in miserable silence.

'Very well,' Candy said as she returned to the bed and sat down, her soft bottom placed exactly in the spot it had occupied moments before. 'Come here, Samantha. Bend over my knee.'

The instruction was polite but stern. Samantha rose up, rubbed her knees gently and approached Candy. In a fluid, graceful motion, she eased herself across the seated girl's lap, snuggling her soft bosom against Candy's thigh and presenting her upturned, bare bottom for the delicious pain of punishment. Candy gently pushed the hem of the white vest away from the slender waist, fully revealing and exposing every inch of the naked buttocks. Bare and vulnerable, they shivered in expectation. Pausing to examine and inspect the soft, creamy domes, Candy cupped her palms and framed the captive, quivering cheeks, squeezing with a fierce tenderness.

'Chloe,' she whispered softly over the snowy domes, 'will you slip your hand beneath Samantha's mattress and retrieve her cane?' Candy felt the cupped rump flinch and spasm at her words.

Chloe dutifully knelt and rummaged silently for the length of whippy yellow wood. Looking up, she shrugged. 'No cane here,' she said in a voice of ill-disguised disappointment.

Candy sighed and shook her head sadly. 'Foolish girl. How foolish to try and hide your cane. Another mistake, Samantha. One which, I fear, will cost you an extra two strokes.' Again, the buttocks trembled in mute distress at the words. 'All in Orrag sleep with the cane beneath them. It is a symbol of their quest for advancement through discipline and control. Where is your cane, Samantha?' Candy asked softly but clearly. Silence, loud and all pervading, ensued. 'Samantha,' Candy warned. Still no response from the silent, squirming girl. Candy placed her right hand, palm down, across the bare-bottomed girl's slender waist, pinning her down in the punishment position. With her free left hand she nipped a generous fleshfold of soft, creamy buttock and, with a pinching, pulling motion, tightened her squeeze. Across the punisher's thighs, the punished writhed – her hips and upthrust rump swaying and jerking.

'No, don't,' squealed the captive.

'I will ask you only once more,' Candy crooned to the suffering fleshy buttock.

'Above the curtain rail,' gasped Samantha with a swift groan.

'That's better,' Candy purred, releasing her pincer of fingers and immediately rewarding the juddering cheeks with a resounding spank. Blushing a delicate pink, they wobbled under the sharp impact of the flattened palm. The spanker noted the spanked girl's feet rubbing together.

'Got it,' crowed Chloe triumphantly from the window, bringing down the 21 inches of supple bamboo from its futile hiding place.

'Will you be good enough to stand there? Yes, there. That's about right.' Candy nodded to the desired spot.

Chloe's small feet shuffled. She stood a foot and a half away from where Samantha lay stretched, bare-buttocked and prone, across the blonde's warm lap.

'Judge the distance,' Candy murmured.

The tip of the lowered cane alighted on the bare bottom, dimpling the soft satin swell. It fell just beyond the cleft. Chloe inched her feet forward a fraction, until the glistening length of cane lay fully across both pink hemispheres.

'Excellent,' hissed Candy, her voice now thickening with a note of delight.

Chloe whisked the cane up in a salute of acknowledgement as she stood smartly to attention, the erect bamboo a-quiver.

'I shall spank, then pause – allowing you to administer one stroke. That is how the punishment shall proceed. Agreed?'

Chloe nodded vigorously. 'Yes,' she curdled, eyeing the beautiful, bare bottom hungrily. 'Agreed.'

Spank. Spank. Two slaps rang out as Candy's hand swooped down, cracking the tightly clenched cheeks with searing, searching smacks. Samantha pressed her thighs together in response, clamping them tightly. Spank. Another scorcher scalded the taut domes across the crown of their glorious curves. Across her lap, Candy sensed the chastised girl jerk and bounce in a reflex of pain. Smack. The fourth sweeping swipe of the hot palm kissed the ripe roundness of the hotter satin flesh. Samantha moaned sweetly in her delicious agony.

'Chloe,' Candy invited, removing her spanking hand from the hot cheeks across which it lay resting, and instantly trapping and pinioning the bare-bottomed girl by the nape of her neck and the backs of her thighs. Nodding briefly, the spanker offered the bottom to the caner.

The cane sparkled as it flickered down, the stroke whispering its evil intent before biting into the proffered cheeks and striping them with a thin, faint red line. Samantha gurgled her squeal of torment – a sound as soft as that of a turtle dove made lazy by the evening sun.

Candy smoothly palmed the punished rump in silence for a full two and a half minutes, pausing only when the sighs below melted into a sibilant murmur – the murmur of pleasurable pain. Spank. Spank. Under the implacable palm, the luscious cheeks smarted and suffered. Spank. Again. Spank. And yet again. Candy felt the entire length of the captive girl across her thighs juddering and writhing in her sweet paroxysm of fiery delight. A firm, dominant hand touched and quelled the squirming buttocks. Stilled and steadied, the punished succumbed to utter submission.

'Keep still. Chloe is going to cane you once more.'

To Candy's mild surprise, the bare bottom inched upwards an imperceptible fraction as she felt the girl's slight weight ease up from her lap. Yes. The soft cheeks were straining eagerly to present themselves more fully, more completely, for the kiss of the cane. Was it an illusion? Surely not. No. The minx was definitely anxious to receive

146

the next cruel stroke. Swish. Chloe's cane spoke, interrupting Candy's reflections. It sliced the raised rump with a sweet savagery. The striped cheeks clenched and quivered. Candy felt a trickle of wet warmth seep down her naked thigh. Samantha was responding to her chastisement in liquid celebration. Spank. Spank. The tiny droplets of hot honey thickened as they splashed down. And there was no mistaking it now. Samantha was thrusting her bare bottom up in an undisguised display of keen appetite and sharp desire for the tender harshness of discipline. The pliant, poised cheeks – deep pink and striped an angrier crimson – felt quite hot to the touch of Candy's inquisitive fingers. The scorched satin dimpled beneath their probing stroke. Samantha sighed softly – the sound of sugared yearning.

Spank. Spank. Swish. Chloe, whose full breasts joggled deliciously as she administered each strict stroke, shouldered her cane then suddenly slipped the tip of it between her parted thighs. Tap-tapping rapidly, she teased and tormented the ultra-sensitive flesh of her pubis. Candy stared across the naked buttocks directly at the yellow tip of the bamboo stick, then flickered her gaze upwards, directly into Chloe's eyes, half-closed in concentration. Spank. At the sharp crack, Chloe opened her eyes wide and stared dreamily back into Candy's sparkling pools of untroubled blue. Spank. The harshly intimate slap of flesh across flesh, punishing palm to punished cheeks, seemed to snap Chloe out of her trance. She raised the quivering length of cane aloft. Trembling with supple whippiness, it hovered above the bare buttocks. Candy nodded. Swish. Samantha bucked and bounced like a rebellious colt as the wicked wood once more ignited her pliant, reddening domes. Candy arched her back and parted her rosebud lips, eager to receive and accept Chloe's questing mouth. They kissed. A slow, deep, lingering, satisfying kiss. Joy wept freely from Candy's wound as tongue-tips touched. During the languorous kiss, the last eleven inches of Chloe's cane lay firmly across the scalded buttocks of the punished girl, pressing down into the ravished flesh – taming and subduing utterly and completely. Candy's hot hand caressed the curve of the bunched cheeks just beyond the seamless juncture where upper thighs become a satin sweep. The punishers kissed again, exchanging their wet warmth from mouth to sweet mouth.

Prone, pinned and passive, Samantha wriggled expectantly. The punishers parted their lips and gazed down at the ravaged rump. Candy felt the open warmth and sticky wetness – an urgent treacling of arousal – of the disciplined girl turn her own thighs quite slippery. Gazing at the hot, bare bottom, she was suddenly possessed by a dark desire. She inclined her head a little. Chloe, mistakingly thinking this to be the signal for more hungry kissing, leaned down to lick Candy's slightly parted lips, but Candy bent her face fully down to bury it completely in the hot flesh below. Samantha howled her joy – Chloe, frowning, drew back, the knuckles whitening dangerously as jealousy fuelled her sudden fury. Oblivious to Chloe's anguished dismay, Candy pursued her instinctive desire with lips, tongue and tiny white teeth – sucking, licking, nibbling and biting the warm, soft hillocks of the chastised girl. Samantha struggled furiously in a paroxysm of frenzied delight and broke free, only to twist, turn and surrender utterly to her cruel punisher. Turning into Candy, belly to belly, she rubbed her wet sex into Candy's firm, milky flesh.

Chloe suppressed her snarl of chagrin as she stood and quivered, rigid in her rage of molten envy, staring as Samantha slipped down on to her knees, scarlet buttocks thrust out behind her, and buried her shining face deep into Candy's delta. Buried her shining face deep into Candy's source of sweet liquefaction to nuzzle and lap the soft, sticky fleshfolds and suck eagerly on the hot honey deep within the fissured comb. A soft, sibilant lapping – heard only when Lust guzzles greedily – filled the small room. Candy closed her darkening indigo eyes and clutched blindly, wildly at the kneeling penitent's hair, dragging the whipped one closer still, and then even closer, into the depths of her lambent flesh. Carnal grunts and liquid moans from the dominant and her dominated built up their invisible wall beyond which Chloe writhed in her exile of jealous loneliness. The length of yellow bamboo clattered to the floor, rattling on the polished wood, as it dropped from her lifeless fingers. Locked into their absolute ecstasy, an ecstasy now shuddering towards mutual climax, neither the pleasurer nor the pleasured heard or even noticed as Chloe ran stumbling from the room – tears of torment scalding her soft, grey eyes.

With the heat of climax still smouldering within her moistened loins, Candy skipped down along the cool, deserted corridor towards Chloe's bedroom. Her tiny teeth bit down apprehensively into the curve of her lower lip. How selfish and how foolish she had been to exclude poor Chloe. Exclude her and made her suffer and endure the sharp pangs of jealousy. But the temptation of the bunched cheeks had been too powerful, too seductive to resist. In the dizzying heat of the molten moment, Samantha's hot bottom had proved irresistible. And Candy had succumbed, and in doing so – she now realised – had banished poor, tearful Chloe to the wastelands of want, the exile of exclusion. As she scampered down the corridor, Candy resolved to make amends. She would seek Chloe's forgiveness and, accepted into the raven-haired girl's narrow bed, hold and hug the delightful, slim girl in the fiercest of embraces. Kisses would follow. She would slowly kiss those soft, grey eyes. Kiss those sweet red lips. Drag her mouth down the stretched white neck to the delicious bosom below. The soft, creamy bosom – gently awaiting its pleasure.

Chloe's breasts. Yes. Candy would take, and leisurely pleasure, each breast and slowly, lingeringly, subject each soft, warm pillowy mound of flesh to her caressing hands, her firm palms pressed inwards. Hot, eager lips would then delight the captive nipples, sucking and biting the tiny peaks of puckered flesh. Chloe would moan sweetly before loosening her trembling thighs, opening up and yielding their inner warmth and wetness to Candy's savagely tender attentions. Soon they would be reunited in their intimate, mutual joy. Candy was sure that the brief moment of jealous pain could be kissed away, soothed and healed with the licking and the lapping of her penitent tongue.

149

But when Candy stole into the darkened bedroom like a mouse into a midnight pantry, she found the narrow bed unruffled and empty. Like the room itself, the bed was unoccupied. In the stillness and the silence, Candy frowned. Her eyes narrowed and her beauty was swiftly clouded with anxiety. She left the empty room in silence and confusion. As she scuttled softly through the shadows of the sleeping house down towards the kitchen for a soothing glass of ice-cold milk, and perhaps a sinful slice of that wickedly delicious chocolate cake, Candy's mind was in a whirl. Poor, dear Chloe. Probably pacing up and down the seashore, the salt spray adding to her tears, the chill night adding to her shivering rage. Poor Chloe.

Furtive whisperings, muffled giggles and a soft squeal of frank pleasure stayed Candy's silent feet. Behind the slightly open kitchen door – the room was in darkness but it was a darkness made visible by the glow of the Aga – Candy could just make out the softly luminous figures of two kneeling, naked girls. Madelaine and Chloe. Belly to belly. Bosom to proud bosom, they knelt and embraced. Madelaine was tonguing Chloe deeply, clasping her captive by the buttocks and thrusting her piercing tongue deep into Chloe's wet mouth. Candy managed to suppress her gasp of angry surprise and pressed herself into the cold plaster of the hallway wall. Inside the kitchen, the furtive flesh-feast continued with appetites unabated. Like velvety panthers, the two naked girls performed their lustful rites with silken, sinuous grace. Candy inched her face towards the partly opened door and gazed into the kitchen. Madelaine was clenching an orange in her right hand. Candy watched as the gripping fingers relaxed and slowly opened, like the leaves of a lotus blossom. The orange rolled slightly and then settled gently in the centre of the upturned palm. Madelaine guided the orange up to Chloe's chin. Guiding the citrus carefully within her upstretched hand, she rolled it down the craning neck, down across the swell of the left breast, then down the white belly to the pubic fringe below.

Candy swallowed her feral snarl of anger as she watched, with resentful fascination, her nipples peaking painfully despite her fury as, with a subtle flick of her wrist, Madelaine rolled the fruit. With her palm supporting the orange tenderly, she rolled it slowly, very slowly, pressing the waxy skin on to the glistening labia. The trembling hand rocked back and forth as the heavy sphere from Seville bruised the velvet fleshfolds. Chloe hissed her savage joy aloud like a wild cat in a blizzard. The hand suddenly began to roll the orange more quickly. Faster. Faster still. Faster and firmer. Candy saw the sinews of Madelaine's wrist stiffen. Chloe tossed her head back, arching her white neck. Her shining raven hair cascaded down over her gleaming, naked shoulders. She squirmed and writhed, but Madelaine gathered up a dominating handful of the loose, cascading hair, totally controlling the captive she pleasured between her loins. Dry-mouthed, her pulses racing and with mounting excitement hammering at the doors of her wildly beating heart, Candy held her breath as she watched Chloe approach and then tumble headlong into her sudden, almost violent, climax. Madelaine hugged the naked, quivering girl as she orgasmed. The wet orange, dripping Chloe's inner juices, rolled forgotten across the flagstone floor towards the spot where Candy, still unseen and unobserved, trembled in the outer darkness. She stopped its progress with a firm, angry stab of her foot. The instant her bare toes touched the slippery fruit, a strangely powerful emotion swept like a sudden sheet of pain across her breasts, burning her peaked nipples. Jealousy. Jealousy and bitter anguish. The voyeuristic and undeniably pleasurable excitement of secretly spying on Madelaine's pleasuring of the kneeling, naked Chloe had frozen all emotion within Candy's heart and mind. But the sudden and unexpected connection with the wet rind of the heavy, slippery orange had ignited a pure, raw pain within her.

Jealousy. Now Candy was being crushed under its cruel heel – just as she had caused Chloe to suffer when succumbing utterly to Samantha's bare bottom. Now it was Candy's turn to feel the sharp stab of jealous torment, the soft wounding of frustrated desire.

In the shadows of the kitchen, Madelaine's wandering hand had found a cucumber. A thick, long, superb specimen. She wielded it expertly in the darkness, inserting it slowly and gently into Chloe's hot, wet core. An inch. Chloe sighed wistfully. Another inch. Another gasp. The third inch of the snub-nosed, probing cucumber was buried deeply between the splayed thighs. Chloe's whimpering grew deeper – then a silent snarl distorted her twisted lips when her tormentress cunningly turned the supple shaft within her warmth a full rotation. Chloe was ruthlessly rocketed into renewed buttock-bouncing writhing. Candy ogled the superb breasts dancing loose and lovely through tears of salt. Another cruel, deft twist of Madelaine's wrist paroxysmed her ravished victim who jerked her bare rump in a fresh frenzy as she straddled the thick shaft that sweetly impaled her. Candy felt her jealous pain spread slowly down from her sick heart to her cold belly. She shrunk inwardly from the cold heat of its icy flames.

Someone approached. Footfalls padded gently along the narrow, darkened corridor. Despite her almost choking fury, Candy's sixth sense – finely tuned to self-preservation after years of City life – alerted her to the approaching danger. She melted swiftly into the deepness of the surrounding shadows just in time to see the Wise One sweep past and walk down towards the library door. A loud carnal snuffle – a liquid grunt of implacable passion – stayed the Wise One in mid-stride. She turned swiftly and stole up towards the kitchen door. Candy cowered back into her cloak of protective darkness, the ripe roundness of her rump squashed anxiously up against the cold wall behind her as she flattened herself in fear of discovery. The hour was late, after all. Very late. And their presence unauthorised.

Harsh neon light responded instantly to the sharp click of a switch, bathing the naked, kneeling girls in a bright swathe of light that mercilessly fingered every shadowed curve, ruthlessly caressing every deep valley and cleft. The thick length of cucumber now fused and welded the midnight lovers – five inches of delicious blunt end buried between Chloe's wet, splayed thighs; three inches of the other end wrapped by Madelaine's shining, thick lips. They knelt, locked in their compact of lust. Candy risked another quick glimpse, peering beneath the swell of the Wise One's heavy buttocks, and noting with grim satisfaction the fear that widened the startled girls' eyes.

'Disgraceful conduct. You are in total breach of the agreed rules. You are behaving, or rather misbehaving, utterly abysmally. Up. Both of you. This instant,' snapped the Wise One angrily.

Candy shivered pleasurably. They were going to be disciplined. Harshly. And there would be no mercy, clemency or reprieve for their naked bottoms. Candy knew that the Wise One meant to be particularly tough in enforcing the strict letter of the law on Orrag. Emily's brief rebellion had been snuffed out, but in order to establish absolute control over her girls, the Wise One had openly resolved to be ruthless. Bottoms would be whipped. Tears would be shed – all for the good of the community.

Trembling in their shame and fear, the miscreant nudes rose up from the flagstone floor, heads bowed and eyes cast down demurely.

'You disappoint me. Both of you. You will have to be punished. We are here to acquire the discipline of self-control and yet I discover you indulging most flagrantly. Take that wooden spoon, Chloe, and administer six strokes to Madelaine who will now bend over and touch her toes.'

A firm finger of awakening pleasure strummed Candy's sticky labia at the sound of this harsh instruction.

'Instantly,' snapped the Wise One sternly.

The two naked girls woke out of their reverie of frozen fear, Chloe scooping up the long handled wooden spoon and Madelaine stooping, palms flat and turned inwards, fingers straightened and pointing directly downwards – brushing her fleshy thighs and then skimming her kneecaps as she strained to touch her tiny white toes. As the bending girl adopted the required position prescribed for her imminent punishment, her buttocks rose up into full view. Pale, shimmering, swollen and ripely rounded. Perfectly poised and presented, Candy observed, for the hot, savage attentions of the cruelly curved wooden spoon.

'Six,' whispered the dominant Mistress of Orrag in tones of venom.

How noble, it suddenly struck Candy. How noble and how true to her ideals the Wise One truly was. Who else would refuse to indulge in the delicious delights of exercising absolute sovereignty over these two naked maidens' bare bottoms – here, after midnight, in the quiet kitchen. Few, if any, could have done so. Few, if any, could resist the opportunity to wield the wooden spoon, cracking it down at leisure across the soft, creamy upturned cheeks. To swipe the fat spoon into the flesh of such perfect, naked peaches. Total control, superb punishment and absolute joy. But not the Wise One. No, Candy realised. The precepts of Orrag's rigorous training relied on self-control and self-discipline. The Wise One was demonstrating both to a remarkable degree. And how better to do so than to instruct the two transgressors to be the authors of each other's right and proper punishment.

'Six strokes,' repeated the Wise One.

The soft instruction interrupted Candy's reflections, forcing her to focus on the matter in hand. A wooden spoon. A bare, upturned bottom. Punishment. The conjunction of the first with the second led inevitably to the third. A wooden spoon hovering above naked, clenched cheeks. And over both hovered the crimson shadow of imminent suffering and sweet anguish. Swipe, crack. The rounded, perfectly sculpted spheres of taut flesh dimpled and depressed beneath the sudden stroke. Under the harsh neon light above, a pale pink blotch appeared against the milky satin of the ravished rump. Swipe, splat. Again, Chloe's unerring stroke scorched the upturned, naked cheeks with a fearsome thwack, causing Madelaine's beautiful bottom to quiver and dance in its split second of delicious agony. Swipe, crack. As pleasurable as Madelaine's swift, sharp chastisement was to glimpse and listen to, the thought of Chloe's punishment was for Candy sweeter still to contemplate. Soon Chloe would be bending.

Bending and shivering. Shivering and squirming as she waited for the swiping spoon's hot pain. Jealousy danced with goblin footsteps within the shadows of Candy's tormented brain as she breathlessly awaited the moment. The moment when Chloe's bare bottom would be softly bruised and warmly reddened. Punished, Candy smiled darkly, for her lustful pleasure. Those lustful pleasures which had brought such distress to Candy's jealous heart. Swipe, crack. Swipe, crack. Madelaine sighed her low sweet moan of suffering. Peering round the doorway – and glancing directly between the Wise One's parted, lithe legs – Candy saw the sixth stroke of the searing spoon bite into the bouncing cheeks. Swipe, splat. The peaches flattened under the final stroke of the prescribed punishment – already their soft flesh seethed with damson-dark blushes. Candy grinned.

'Now you, Madelaine. Up. And administer six severe strokes. Chloe, bend over please and give Madelaine your bare bottom to beat.'

Candy thrilled to the instruction. A silver bubble emerged from her glistening labia. The moment – that sweet moment – had arrived. Chloe placed the warm wooden spoon she had wielded to such deadly effect on to the kitchen table. Slowly, reluctantly, she stooped. Her pale almond buttocks, shimmering within their tight swathe of lovely satin skin, rose up, bare, beautiful but vulnerable. Candy gazed at them triumphantly. Suffer, my darling Chloe. Suffer. The words whirled in Candy's brain. But no sooner had she half-formed, half-uttered them, Candy instantly regretted them. Poor Chloe. Candy suddenly felt the stab of protective concern. Concern for the bare-bottomed beauty. For Candy now understood – having tasted the bitter fruit of jealousy on her own sour tongue – the anguish Chloe must have suffered when Candy had succumbed to Samantha's bare bottom upstairs. Candy fully and completely forgave Chloe just as she hoped that Chloe would in turn forgive her. Candy had betrayed Chloe and Chloe had betrayed Candy. They were honours even. Love all, as they say in tennis. Candy smiled ruefully at the phrase. Love all. Candy bit her lower lip. Please, oh please don't stripe and scorch poor Chloe's bottom. Please.

Swish, whack. The wooden spoon cracked harshly in the solemn silence of the midnight kitchen – the hard cherry-wood punishing the soft, defenceless flesh with a resonant splat. Candy gulped and blinked, her own taut buttocks shrinking in a reflex spasm of sympathy. How poor sweet Chloe's bare bottom must have suffered. Swipe, crack. Chloe's clenched cheeks danced in their flush of pink pain. Candy, all her senses alert to every nuance of the bending, bare-bottomed girl's exquisite torment, dug her nails into her palms. The savage revenge she had hoped for was now hurting her every bit as much as it was hurting Chloe. What was she to do? To intervene now would only complicate everything. Of course, she would sneak back upstairs and slip into Chloe's bed. In between Chloe's cool, white sheets. Soon, her hot bottom ablaze, Chloe would creep into her darkened bedroom, naked and ashamed. But Candy would be there, waiting. Yes. Candy would be there, slim and slender, warm and welcoming, between the stretch of the cool white sheets. Waiting to receive the tearful, quivering Chloe. Waiting, like the cool, white sheets around her soft, ripe body, to receive and soothe, comfort and ease Chloe's reddened cheeks. A little cold cream, gently applied with two fingertips in slow, widening circles across the hot, rounded domes. Across the swell of the hot cheeks of the ravished rump as Chloe lay face down – to soothe and balm the angry buttocks. Cold cream. Gently, sensually rubbed in against the pliant, wobbling flesh of the upturned bottom. Cold cream, hot flesh. Firm fingertips, passive cheeks. Soon the heat and the pain – along with the burning shame – would ebb and ease away. Kisses would surely ensue. Kisses – sweet, slow, searching and languorous. Of that, Candy could be certain. Of that, Candy would make certain. Nipples would bud and ripen boldly, thighs would shiver and part, slackening and spreading to yield their soft, warm centres. Fingers would exploringly probe – probe dark clefts deep between the heavy hills of creamy buttock flesh. Fingers would probe and penetrate

deep down into hot, shadowed clefts, then pierce the tight
warmth of the muscled sphincter beyond. Joy would delight them and delight would confuse them. Pleasure,
drunk frequently from the sweet cup of Lesbos, would
madden them into dizzy tipsiness and drive them headlong
into their dark sober frenzy.

Comforted – indeed, driven slightly to sweet distraction
by these and similar thoughts – Candy stole away from the
brightly lit kitchen and, dusting the flakes of plaster from
her bare bottom, scampered along the dim corridor then
up the uncarpeted stairs towards Chloe's bedroom. Leaving behind her the kitchen. The kitchen, harshly lit by the
all seeing neon eye above. The kitchen, where a wooden
spoon sliced down again, and again; and a sore bottom
suffered.

Chapter Seven

Her cascading shiver of golden hair tumbled loosely down to form a sensuous curtain around the pale face within as Madelaine, the willowy blonde, bent over promptly and touched her toes in order to receive her chastisement.

Swish. Candy's supple cane sliced down to bite the bared buttocks below. The punished cheeks blushed at the cruel cane's kiss. Candy raised the bamboo back up to shoulder height.

'Problems?' asked the Wise One in her soft, unhurried voice as she approached.

Candy looked up. Their eyes met above the trembling naked bottom between them. 'No. Just applying a firm hand to the tiller. Prevents drift,' she said brightly, her large, indigo eyes smiling.

Swish. The supple wood swept down in an inkling to crack sharply against the bunched cheeks. A thin pink stripe instantly attested to the accuracy and the severity of the stroke, as did Madelaine's curled toes scrunching the polished wooden floor below.

A firm hand on the tiller. The stern touch of authority. The magnificence of authority in firm control. Candy smiled as she twitched her cane with a menacing flick. She personified the swift and absolute assertion of dominance. The young women of Orrag needed it. Sorely. They needed the framework of discipline, the management of their bubbling passions, the good governance of their wilful exuberance.

'Madelaine was charged with the task of cleaning. On close inspection, it seems that she has been either unwilling or unable to discharge her duties satisfactorily. Six sharp reminders should settle the matter.'

'Excellent,' purred the Wise One. 'Have you seen Clare?'

Candy lowered the length of impatient bamboo down across the double domes of the upturned buttocks. Eager to execute its task, the cane quivered restively within her fierce grip. Madelaine shuddered and clenched her soft cheeks expectantly.

'Her failure at the ceremony the other night has left her somewhat disconsolate,' the Wise One murmured. 'I spoke with her briefly before lunch. She pleaded for extra training. Extra training to steel her and prepare her more fully for the rigours and demands of the ceremony. I suggested . . .'

At these words, Candy's eyes widened an imperceptible fraction. As she gazed directly, unblinkingly, into the Wise One's jade stare, a pulse quickened in her throat.

'Perhaps you might like to take Clare in hand. Train her in readiness for the next ceremony. Could you?'

Candy nodded vigorously.

'We are all running along so smoothly here now. Everything is back to how it should be. Discipline and obedience have been firmly restored,' the Wise One smiled. 'And it would be such a thrill if Clare was successful next time. Such a thrill for all the girls.'

Candy understood. The Wise One was delegating the most important of tasks here on Orrag to her. Tasks central to the philosophy and purpose of the community. She gripped the cane tightly in her mounting excitement, absently dragging it across the satin curves of Madelaine's naked bottom.

'I will continue here and complete this girl's punishment. Pass me the cane,' the Wise One almost whispered, so soft was her curdling tone. 'I see that this naughty young woman has already received . . .'

As Candy offered the cane across the upturned cheeks, she saw the Wise One firmly fingering the bare, punished bottom as she counted the faint, deepening stripes.

'Two. Very well. I will administer the remaining four

strokes. Thank you, Candy,' she said, accepting the cane. 'I believe you will find Clare out in the garden gathering the last of our blackcurrant crop. We tried soot on the roots in the spring to promote growth. Soot, being rich in carbon, accelerates the fruiting. Indeed, we have been blessed with a heavy harvest. The bushes seem quite swollen, the fruit extraordinarily ripe.'

Swish, crack. As Candy walked away, she shivered deliciously at the sharp snap-crack of the cane as Madelaine's bare-bottomed caning resumed. Swish, crack. Gently, almost reluctantly, closing the heavy wooden door on the sounds of the crisp correction proceeding apace, Candy strode out into the late summer sunshine. A whiff of early autumn, the subtle suggestion of over-ripe fruit and the trace of a chill night frost, lingered in the warmth of the splendid afternoon. She left the cinder path and turned into the rows of fruit bushes. As her soft thighs were teased affectionately by bending gooseberry bushes that parted to allowed her progress, the scented air of the kitchen garden assailed her. Candy sniffed happily. Lemon grass, lovage and the sharper tang of thyme mingled in her senses like a sweet melody – a melody embodied and emboldened with the deeper bass notes of parsley and mint. Down among the luxuriant blackcurrent bushes, Clare was bending dutifully and diligently to her appointed task. As Candy approached, she noted with pleasure the ripeness of the pliantly plump rump swelling generously within the tiny white cotton shorts. Each rounded, heavy buttock-cheek was perfectly moulded and delineated by the fierce swathe of the stretched fabric. The scanty shorts enhanced the swollen curves to sheer perfection. Candy struggled – and failed – to fight down, tame and quell the surge of sensual excitement and pleasurable anticipation which burgeoned within her bosom as she perused and intimately appreciated Clare's beautiful bottom.

Training. The word exploded softly inside Candy's head. She was to take Clare to a secluded spot and prepare the girl to withstand the rigours of the imminent ceremony. Training. To strictly yet sweetly discipline the girl so that all her liquid longings and urgent desires could be controlled, regulated and ultimately mastered. Training and discipline. Again, the soft echoes of the silently exploding words spilled their dark, delightful meaning behind Candy's dancing eyes. Training and discipline. To achieve and attain the desired state of self-control, Clare would have to taste the stings of discipline. Willingly, in total surrender, Clare would have to submit and subjugate herself to Candy's stern tutoring. Submit her beautiful, naked bottom to Candy's firm, controlling hand. The naked bottom offered up to the hand of the tutor who had a strict lesson to teach.

Clare rose up from her fruit gathering and surrendered herself instantly into Candy's close embrace. A tender kiss – the merest brushing of lips against soft, red lips – was exchanged. Clare blushed slightly, a delicate damask tinging her comely cheeks, and lowered her large eyes demurely.

'I will need a cane for your training. Can you select one for me?' Candy asked in a tone of barely suppressed urgency.

An utterly dominant touch – requiring the one to be whipped to select and secure the cane for the one who would do the whipping. It was the sweet paradox of sovereignty. The sharp pleasure of dominance. Candy smiled as she watched Clare, head bowed, busying herself among the blackcurrant bushes seeking a suitable length of bamboo – emerging moments later with a thin, 31-inch specimen of the springiest, whippiest wood.

'Come,' Candy beckoned.

Shouldering her cane, Candy followed obediently, a shadow of fearful apprehension clouding her large, clear eyes.

They walked in silence towards the pine trees. Now arm in arm, soft warm flesh linked to soft warm flesh, they strolled beneath the scented canopy of towering firs. A jay streaked up into the blue sky, startled by their approach. Rooks peeled away from the uppermost balcony of branches to wheel dizzily in the sudden sunlight, flapping their ragged black wings in mute protest until the two young women below had walked by, passing along further and deeper into the plantation. Not a word was spoken on their silent pilgrimage. Arm in arm, their golden thighs frequently brushing, the teacher and her eager pupil walked gracefully towards the heart of the pine forest. And as they walked, each carried an expectation of the long, slow, sun-drenched hours of the afternoon awaiting them. Long, slow, sun-drenched hours of sweet sorrows, fierce joys and carnal delights. Intense moments of hot intimacy. Long, slow hours during which flesh would dominate flesh, and during which will would subjugate will.

They reached a clearing, a natural glade of open space, down into which the sun punched its soft fist of shimmering gold. The ground beneath their naked feet was strewn with pine cones and thickly carpeted with a litter of prickling needles. A red squirrel quivered and froze before scampering aloft to safety as, in silence, both girls slowly peeled off their white vests and hip-hugging shorts to stand, happily unselfconscious and blissfully carefree, in naked splendour. The sun sought out and warmly caressed the shadows within their rippling curves and swelling contours.

'Put your shorts back on,' Candy instructed.

Frowning her puzzlement, but quick to obey the command, Clare bent down and scooped up her shorts. They were still warm from their recent embrace with her warmer flesh. Guiding her feet, then her long, shapely legs, into the skimpy cotton, Clare dragged them up tightly around her thighs. Candy watched with hungry eyes as Clare pulled up the shorts – watched the buttocks bulge invitingly, watched the cleft yawn deliciously, watched the thighs shimmer seductively. Soon the second skin was stretched across the upper flesh of the firm thighs, hugging and cupping the rounded buttocks – cupping and squeezing each cheek tightly within a fierce grasp. The seam found the deep cleft between the buttocks, dividing them delightfully as Clare released the snapping elastic waistband.

'Kneel,' commanded Candy in a thickening voice.

Clare's knees kissed the pungent pine needles as she obeyed. With her hands drawn together behind her back, resting passively against the upper swell of her buttocks, she looked up at Candy expectantly. Shifting her left knee slightly, she caused her bare breasts to joggle softly. Candy's belly tightened.

'Pleasure and pain,' the teacher told the kneeling student in a luscious whisper. 'That is the equation we have to balance this afternoon. Together. Together we will work hard to attain that goal. I will bring you pleasure and I will bring you pain. It is for you to balance the equation.'

Clare mewed her understanding in a plaintive whimper.

'Once you have mastered and controlled yourself, you will be able to master and control anything, anyone. You will succeed in the ceremony and then go on to succeed in that important post in . . . Paris?'

Clare nodded vigorously, her eyes shining excitedly. 'Teach me how,' she pleaded – her low tones as dark as chocolate, as sweet as oozing honey.

'Your lesson will be one of pleasurable pain. A painful pleasure, perhaps, but with that Paris post as your prize, well worth the learning.'

Up in the sibilant pines above, soft doves called to one another dreamily in the bright sunshine.

'Pleasure and pain,' continued Candy, stooping gracefully to pick up and firmly flex the supple length of bamboo cane. 'The slow fusion of discipline and delight. The sweetness of strict punishment fiercely binding the silken tresses of harsh pleasures. Together, we will', swish – the sparkling cane sliced the warm air with a seductive hiss,' balance the equation. The pleasurer and the punished, the punisher and the pleasured.'

Clare cupped and squeezed her breasts. An impatient pleading filled her large eyes with its burning, liquid longing. 'Please . . .' she moaned, the tone thickening into a curdled groan.

'Such a lesson must not, and shall not, be hurried, Clare. There can be no sudden rush to understanding. I am your teacher and will take pains', swish – Candy flickered the cane almost absently, 'to make sure that my teaching makes a lasting mark.' Again she thrummed the sunbeams, slicing the air with a venomous hiss.

Clare shivered, clamping her thighs together as she clenched her buttocks anxiously.

'A lasting mark,' mused Candy. 'A deep impression. Attend closely to your lesson, Clare, and you will pass the test. Now. Stand up. Up. Face that tree. That's right. Now, embrace it.'

Clare, having risen up and brushed the congealed pine needles from her smooth kneecaps, approached the appointed pine tree and, nestling closely into it, stretched out her encircling arms to embrace the rough bark.

'All the way round so that your fingers touch.'

Clare rose up on her toes to hug the girth of the pine, offering her hands and wrists to Candy who had moved to the other side of the tree trunk to receive them. They were bound together in a flash, the action drawing Clare's soft body even more closely into the harsh bark of the tree trunk. She moaned sweetly as her naked breasts – now fully squashed into the rough surface – suffered deliciously. Candy quickly paced around to where her willing victim stood, face pressed in against the pine, her bare bottom pertly poised. Thumbing the elastic waistband that hugged the swell of the bound girl's hips, Candy slowly peeled the white shorts down a fraction, exposing the upper quadrant, but no more, of the bunched cheeks. The warm sunshine played affectionately on the bare, silken flesh. With a soft, sweet sigh, Clare squirmed and wriggled expectantly, her arched left foot digging frantically into the soft pine needles below. Candy placed her flattened palm across the swell of the left cheek, then slowly dappled her fingertips down into the tight seam of the shorts. She sensed the captive cheeks bunch more tightly as she lightly fingered the cleft between them.

'I will begin with your bottom, Clare. Your bottom . . .' She cupped and squeezed the partially covered buttocks, noting their spasm of response within her firm, capable grasp. 'Your bottom,' echoed Candy. 'I will make it the

164

focus of my teaching and your learning. All knowledge and wisdom is held within the realm of this perfect orb.'

The cupped hands gripped and squeezed once more. Clare scrabbled up on tiptoe, offering her bare bottom in a gesture of utter and complete surrender to Candy's controlling hands. Hands which now competently unpeeled the shorts down to reveal slightly more than half of the plump, pliant cheeks within. The waistband bit into the deliciously quivering hemispheres, causing the upper curves to bulge and burgeon invitingly. Candy, accepting the invitation, slapped the soft bottom sharply. The hot cheeks wobbled a trifle in their sudden pain.

'This will be the source of your pleasure. Not the sole nor indeed the chief source of delight.'

Clare, striving within the strictures of her firm bondage, sighed.

'Though,' Candy added reflectively, squeezing the reddening buttocks, 'I shall see to it this afternoon that it becomes the fountain from which sweet sorrows flow.'

The bunched cheeks quivered and clenched.

'And now the lesson will begin. As your teacher, I will monitor your progress. Vigorously.'

Candy pulled the shorts fully down, revealing the entire glory of the shapely, curved buttocks to the golden sunshine. The heavy twin peaches joggled softly. Stooping, Candy gathered up a small fir cone, fingering the dry husk delicately as she held it in front of Clare.

'Observe this cone. It is dry. After fully initiating your body to the pleasurable potential of my mouth, my mouth on your nakedness, I will inspect this cone and examine it very carefully. If it remains dry, you shall be spared the cane. But be warned. If it is wet . . .' Candy gently grazed Clare's lips with the tip of the fir cone. 'If it is wet, you shall be soundly thrashed.' Candy used the cone once more, lipstick-like, against Clare's trembling lips. 'Remember. If it is wet, you will be whipped.'

Wet. Whipped. The words wove a spell of feverish delight that instantly bound the two naked young women together within a promise of dark joy. Tracing the tip of

the questing cone down between the soft swell of Clare's
buttocks, Candy carefully positioned it firmly into the
seam of the shorts so that the blunt tip nuzzled against the
partially unfurled pink labial petals. Then the tight cotton
fabric was dragged upwards over the heavy sweep of the
coquettish rump – the elastic waistband snapping back to
hug the hips of the bound girl who clung to her silent tree.

'These are the pleasures of the mouth, Clare. Delight in
them but be sure to deny them.'

The pale, sinuous shoulders, sunlight dappled, shrank
slightly as Candy's warm mouth neared. Her soft, sweet
breath brought a softer, sweeter zephyr to their tremulous
flesh. Lips pursed, Candy planted gentle kisses on the pliant skin. With her wet tongue-tip glistening as it flickered
and darted, Candy lapped at the bare nape of Clare's
bowed, exposed neck, then turned her amorous attentions
to each of the soft, snowdrop earlobes. Small white teeth
were soon nibbling eagerly at the exquisitely sensitive
pearls of milky flesh. Clare squealed her raw pleasure, the
shrieks frank and candidly carnal. With firmer, more
severely dominating strokes, the full length of the
thickened tongue now licked and lapped at the squirming
back – tracing the subtle secret shadows of the sinuous
spine. Deep, sucking kisses dragged the sweetly tormented
flesh – deep, ruthless kisses which delighted in the passive
flesh mercilessly. Clare was writhing in her strict bondage.
Prone, passive and utterly helpless, she suffered the demon
delights of the burning lips as they explored and claimed
her nakedness. Once more, the tiny white teeth of her cruel
benefactress nibbled and nipped – this time openly, fully
and unashamedly enjoying the fleshy buttocks bunched
within their tight cotton shorts. Candy closed her wide
mouth down over the quivering crown of each fulsome
cheek, pressing her tongue against the white cotton firmly
before sucking severely, kissing lingeringly and biting lovingly. Kneeling, she buried her entire face into the splayed
softness of the passive cheeks, as if meaning to drown in
the heaviness of the swollen, delicious flesh. As Candy
worked her mouth hungrily, busily, Clare – her right knee

166

pressed hard into her left leg – scrabbled her feet in an ecstasy of helplessness. Unseen, but sensed and understood by Candy, Clare's pale hands writhed – fingers stretched out straight in their exultation.

'Shall we see what progress our pupil has made? How well she is learning her lesson?'

Candy mouthed the thickly mumbled words into the suppleness of the left buttock. Clare almost swooned at the words she only half heard but all too fully understood. She shivered pleasurably, expectantly, but remained absolutely silent, as Candy, still kneeling, once more slowly peeled down the taut cotton shorts. Gently removing the fir cone from the shadowed warmth of Clare's pubis, Candy rose up and examined it closely, turning the tip in the sunlight to inspect it. It sparkled – the wet tip treacherously betraying the honey of Clare's hot, liquid response.

'Pass? Or fail?' queried Candy in a silken whisper, holding the tell-tale fir cone three-and-a-half measured inches before Clare's eyes.

'Fail,' mumbled Clare softly, her whisper as frail as sin.

Smack. The trapped buttocks – positioned perfectly for such a spanking punishment – bounced and reddened. Smack, spank. Candy's firm hand, palm flattened, scorched Clare's bare bottom with fiercely resounding slaps. Smack, smack, spank. Again, and yet again, with an almost hypnotic rhythm, sweeping flesh cracked down harshly to scald softer, suffering flesh. The swift, hot hand scorched the hotter cheeks – cheeks which wobbled in their anguish, cheeks which quivered as they suffered, cheeks which squirmed as they reddened. The spanking was severe. Severe as it was sweet, short and sharp. Candy bent down in the ensuing silence to kiss, then slowly lick, the hot, penitent flesh.

'That is how we shall continue our lesson. Learn from your pain, dear little Clare. Learn to exercise supreme self-control. You must strive to ensure that your self-control is absolute. As absolute as my control over you.'

Clare hissed a carnal sigh and rose up on her toes. In her strictures, her peaked nipples grazed against the harsh bark of the pine tree to which her nakedness was firmly tethered – instantly thickening and engorging painfully in their soft mounds of squashed, creamy bosom. Electrified by the sudden thrill, she hugged the bark fiercely, straining and striving to embrace the trunk with her clamped thighs.

Spank. Punished cheeks quivered anew. Reluctantly, the taut thighflesh loosened and the somewhat sullen maiden stood to attention, nipples crushed into the bark, thighs back together again in a symmetry of disciplined obedience. Smack, spank. Two swift slaps across her upthrust rump sharply reminded Clare that punishment was pleasure's reward. She whimpered and pawed the warm earth below, her hot bottom swaying deliciously in a futile bid to escape its inevitable sorrow.

Candy's swift fingers untied the cords that bound Clare's wrists together on the blind side of the erect pine. The freed fingers splayed and flexed before disappearing as Clare withdrew them thankfully. Candy paced around the tree to face Clare. Their eyes met – then their lips. Candy pressed down dominantly on to Clare's upturned, passive wet warmth. Gently but firmly propelling her pupil backwards into and against the pine tree, the teacher skipped around to the blind side to gather together and bind the helpless hands once more. This time, Candy chose to position the hands lower down against the trunk than before, with the soft palms pressed into one another. Pausing to savour and fully appreciate this perfect picture of passive submission, Candy reflected dreamily upon the sweetness of sovereignty and the delightfulness of domination, before pulling down and removing completely the white cotton shorts. They fluttered helplessly at Clare's treading feet – the ultimate symbol of surrender. Striding back to face once more the pinioned penitent – whose bosom was now thrust proudly out before her in pert splendour and whose spanked, sore bottom was now squashed into the cruel bark – Candy caught the sharp taste of power. It had a bittersweet tang with a smoothly seductive aftertaste. The pleasure of power. More intoxicating – here, now, in the sun-drenched pines – than the mere power of pleasure. Candy reached out and placed her upturned fingertips beneath Clare's chin. With the lightest of gestures she tilted Clare's face upwards and dominantly backwards – all the time gazing directly into the large anxious eyes.

'The spanking you received was just a taste. Nothing but a taste. A taste of the feast that awaits you. A feast of sweet suffering served up with this cane – the very cane you yourself selected from all others in the blackcurrant bushes. This is the cane.'

Snatching up the 31 inches of cruel whippy wood, Candy stepped backwards and traced the outline of Clare's luminous nakedness with the blunt tip of the bamboo cane. Pausing briefly at each nipple – which she worried intimately with the tip of the gleaming wood – Candy spoke in soft, unhurried words, lingeringly describing the precise, exact detail how many stripes Clare's bare bottom would probably receive. How many stripes, and how severe, how bitingly severe, each searching lash would be. Clare, once more straining up on her toes, whimpered her soft yearning. The naked girl wriggled – head back, her breasts thrust painfully forward, the pale thighs tightly clamped.

'Across your naked bottom. Do you understand?' Candy concluded her cruel catechism.

Clare nodded vehemently. Unseen, around the pine tree trunk, her bound hands flexed expectantly.

The probing, sweeping tip of the cane skimmed across and down the outer swell of Clare's ripe, left thigh, darting inwards unexpectedly to briefly scratch at the fuzz covering her luscious pubic plum, then traced, with a maddeningly controlled, dominant sweep, the entire inside length of her trembling left leg. Bound fast and tightly pinioned, her arms welded at her wrists behind her, Clare groaned a low, feral moan. Feverishly, she rubbed her spanked bottom into the rough bark – igniting it anew with fresh flames of lambent fire.

Candy stepped back, tossing the length of cane down on to the soft, pine-scented earth. Fighting down her own surging desires, she struggled valiantly to master and control the moment. The liquid, molten moment. The imminent moment – rapidly approaching on wings of burning silk. Implacable. Inevitable. The unique moment when she would utterly own, totally control and absolutely dominate the naked girl before her. She must not, Candy knew, move towards this moment too quickly. She must not, she knew, let the reins of power slip through her slightly trembling fingers – allowing the stallions of desire to bolt. Candy clenched her fists. She must remain calm. Calm, and in control. In control, and supremely in command.

Clare's eyes looked up beseechingly. Her bare breasts, full, soft and rounded, wobbled tremulously. Clare's hips swayed as she arched her rump into the bark behind. Candy swallowed – acknowledging the fluttering flicker deep down in her tightening belly. The moment had come.

'Close your eyes,' came the crisp command.

Clare obeyed instantly. Behind her obedient mantle of darkness, she trembled inwardly. But nothing happened. Nothing. Where? Her heart hammered the question. Where? And what? Tongue, finger or cane? She gasped her pleasurable surprise as she felt the teasing graze of the pine cone against her mouth. It slipped down to glide along the wet flesh of her lower lip. Applied and cunningly worked like a heavy gloss lipstick, the blunt tip of the pine cone dragged across the submissive lip. Clare offered her flesh to the firm stroke in a sultry pout. Down in her belly, butterflies softly beat their wings. The pine cone probed between her parted lips, taming and subduing her soft, pink tongue. The lightning in her belly flickered and forked downwards. She clamped her thighs firmly as if determined to deny any molten splashes – splashes of hot, delicious rain that teems during such a sudden summer storm between a young woman's thighs. The inquisitive cone teased the tender roof of her mouth – sending a shivering thrill throughout her entire bound, splayed nakedness. Even the berry-hard nipples quivered – prinked and painful in their swollen alertness. The storm within rumbled an ominous, grumbling roar. The tempest was still chained, but it was now more than merely a potent threat – it was a powerful, implacable inevitability. Clare groaned, knowing she would surely be whipped. And whipped soundly. Across her bare bottom.

The wicked little cone left her mouth sparkling with the awakened silvery juices of desire. She squirmed and writhed against the tree to which she was tied so firmly – squirming and writhing anew at the promise of harsh punishment should she be found dripping such sweet stickiness from her other, more secret mouth below. Her left nipple peaked and thickened painfully as the scales of the fir cone rasped against the bruised fruit. Again, and yet again, remorselessly and with a tender ruthlessness, the harsh cone rasped. Again, and yet again, the golden lights exploded behind her tightly shut eyes. A silken tremor troubled the milky satin of her belly. The firm sweep of her white belly, buckling under the shivers of pleasure. She gasped aloud, her vixen cry melting into a soft, sweet pagan curse of delight. Down below, in strict disobedience to her conscious will, the soft petals of her young womanhood parted and unfurled imperceptibly like a sleeping rose awakening at the first modest blush of approaching dawn. A single pearl of wet joy glistened. Sensing it, Clare shuddered. She was now certainly going to be whipped. Soundly. Whipped soundly across her naked bottom.

The probing cane left her nipple erect and painfully stiffened – the ripe breast itself now swollen and burgeoning in its sheen of engorged satin. Mutely, the breast pleaded for the attentions of a firm, demanding mouth, for the attentions of a firmer hand, and even fiercer fingers. As the quivering cane withdrew, the abandoned breast burned in delicious anguish. The tip of the shivering bamboo alighted upon the other nipple, addressing it instantly with a savage intimacy. Worrying the bud busily, ruthlessly, it departed at last – leaving the ravaged flesh-bud silently screaming for more.

Down in her shadowed delta, the thunderstorm of ecstasy exploded. Against her thighs, the hot rain splashed. It had come to pass. Now, Clare knew, the hotter stripes of the stroking, searching cane would rain down on her bare buttocks. Clare clamped her thighs together in a vain struggle to stem the liquid tumult within. In their cruel, lovingly lashed tight bondage, her helpless hands writhed in silent supplication. Would the whipping commence now? Or would fresh, delicious torments tantalise her flesh. Where? Breast, belly or thigh? Back to her mouth, or softer, more secret fleshfolds? Where would the cane tip alight to rasp and torment?

Clare grunted thickly as she felt the velvet fleshfolds between her thighs part to receive and accept the upward thrust, then a soft silence cloaked her sweet distress as her tormentress continued the gentle probing – easing not the expected cane tip but the blunt nose of the pine cone once more into her all too willing wet warmth.

Wet.

Clare knew that when extracted, the stiff petals of the cone would be wet. Wet and shining with her response.

Whipped.

Clare knew that when examined, the glint of her wetness would mean a whipping. A whipping from the cane she herself had selected with her own trembling hands. A whipping from the cane she herself had carried to this secluded spot amid the pungent pines. In this secluded spot amid the scented firs where she would, soon – perhaps only moments away – be bending. Bending bare-bottomed for her punishing stripes.

Eyes tightly closed, Clare awaited her doom. Candy would have examined the wet cone by now and no doubt tossed it aside. Soon she would be hastily unravelling the cords binding the pale, helpless wrists together. Candy would then bend down to scoop up the potent length of whippy cane. Instructions would follow in stern tones. Instructions, in stern tones, to bend over. To bend over and proffer her bare bottom up to the swishing cane.

A silence fell as gently as mist on an evening lakeside. Up in their sun-drenched canopy above, songbirds checked their sweet trilling – as if aware of the unfolding drama below. Candy, her sweet breath fluttering within her swollen bosom, trembled dizzily in the vortex of her sharpening desires. She was almost upon the pinnacle – the very peak – of supreme dominance. For the very first time ever she had ascended to the seat of absolute sovereignty, strad-dling the summit of supremacy. Tipsy with lambent delights, she suddenly spun around and nestled her soft nakedness into Clare's perspiring body, thrusting her white back into Clare's cushioning bosom and urgently squash-ing her tight, rounded buttocks into Clare's welcoming, weeping thighs. Delicious sensations raked the violet-eyed blonde, ensnaring her within their sinuous, velvety talons.

The dominatrix was now herself dominated by a burning desire and fierce torment. The ravisher was now herself being ravished by the proximity, the seductive intimacy, of warm, yielding flesh. Silk to silk they snuggled, fusing at bosom, belly and thighs. Fearful of these surging sensations – fearful lest she should succumb and lose her powerful, controlling mastery in a moment of carnal abandonment – Candy snar-led softly and ground the tightened cheeks of her pert rump into Clare's splayed thighs. The rounded peaches rasped their soft flesh-weight into the passive pubis in sweeping thrusts again and again as Candy blindly attempted to quell and control Clare's soft, naked seductiveness. The captive's squashed breasts burgeoned beneath her oppressor's body, the prinked, hot nipples almost burning the satin skin of Candy's back. Against the superb curve of Candy's domina-ting buttocks, Clare's splayed, wet delta widened – anointing the blonde's cruel rump-thrusts with fresh honey-dew at each sweeping gyration. Trembling on the very brink of delirium, Candy clenched her fists and strove to fight down and deny those same sensations she was training Clare to abjure. Slowly, as she slumped back into her happy victim's bosom and thighs, she willed herself to regain the precarious heights of domination – the cool, unruffled, almost detached heights of disciplined sovereignty. It was but a mere temptation, a transient temptation which Candy rejected scornfully, for her not to grind her buttocks down against and into the weeping velvet labia of the bound, subjugated Clare. No. Candy denied herself that luscious luxury, knowing full well that darker delights were now imminent.

The shining wetness of her own rump meant a whipping for Clare's. A whipping. Candy swallowed thickly. Hot blood pulsed through her veins. Stumbling forwards, she wiped her sticky buttocks with firm, downward sweeps of palm to cheek – Clare's tell-tale excitement webbing her glistening fingers momentarily. She glanced over her shoulder at the bound, full-breasted girl. Clare had failed yet again. Clare was wet, an undeniable fact. Clare must be trained – punished, in fact. Punishment. An inevitable certainty. She paused, returned to the bound nude and dropped her hand into the secret warmth below the belly. Slowly removing her fingertips from between Clare's firmly clamped thighs, Candy held them aloft. They sparkled in the golden sunlight.

'You have not learned your lesson, Clare. I must untie you and cane your bottom.'

Clare could only offer a shudder in response. As the cords behind the pine tree loosened, she gathered her untied hands before her, gingerly rubbing and soothing her reddened wrists.

'Come. Over here,' Candy instructed, tapping the flat circle of a tree stump with the tip of her quivering cane.

Clare padded across the soft carpet of scented pine needles and dutifully approached the tree stump. Something indefinable in her naked obedience caused the expectant cane to flicker upwards. Alertly. Hungrily.

'Down. No, right across the stump. That's better. Raise your bottom up. More. Come along, Clare. Give me your bottom.'

Clare stretched herself, as instructed, completely across the flat expanse of wood. Her swollen breasts squashed down on to the pattern of concentric rings as she nestled into the punishment position. Bare buttocks offered up to the whippy cane, she waited, patient, passive and prone. The cane flickered upwards once more with a muscular, potent twitch – like a groom's erection stirring at the vision of the bride's maidenly nakedness emerging from her unpeeled satin basque. The thin wood felt alive in Candy's firmly clenched fist. Almost impatient. Perhaps, she mused,

174

it was the proffered swell of the blushing peaches that excited it. Perhaps, she wondered, it was the gorgeous valley of the cleft between the pliant domes it was its duty to stripe. Her grip on the cane tightened as she dismissed the wayward fancy, bending to kiss first the tip of the cane, and then – fleetingly – the bunched cheeks it longed to lash.

Candy tapped Clare's outer left thigh. Clare drew her long, shapely legs together in immediate response. The swell of her soft cheeks dimpled and wobbled slightly. Candy instantly quelled them with a smart tap. The creamy buttocks clenched expectantly – tightening even more after a second admonishing tap. A third touch of the quivering cane tip to the right ankle caused the lithe legs to tremble as both tiny white feet were drawn together – rendering Clare's cleft as seamless as a fervent nun's hands pressed in a prayer of pleading.

Swish. The cane flickered, sparkling brightly, and swept down to slice the perfectly rounded buttocks with a crisp, cruel stroke. Swish. Again, the bamboo sang its sinister song, thrumming softly as it split the sunlight before eagerly biting into the creamy upturned cheeks below with savage tenderness. Swish. The third stroke of the supple cane across the bare buttocks left a third faint crimson kiss. Swish. Clare hissed her sweet sigh of suffering as the length of whippy wood licked her satin cheeks intimately, searchingly, fiercely. She hugged her tree stump tightly – her ravished peach-cheeks bunching as they bucked and jerked, writhed and bounced in their pitiful attempt to escape. Swish. Another thin reddening stripe was added to the other cane-kisses.

Candy shouldered her cane and, arching her right foot, placed it firmly across the hot bottom – delighting in the feel of the scorched satin as she scrunched her toes. 'Place your fingertips there,' she murmured softly, briefly using her own straightened forefinger to tap Clare's exposed, oozing fig.

Tremulously, Clare eased her squashed breasts up from the tree stump and peeled her flattened tummy away. Fine sawdust clung lovingly to the curved profile of her soft, swelling nakedness. Tentatively, she obeyed Candy's instruction – probing the pubic fringe of her sex then gently dabbling the wet flesh of her labia with shy fingertips.

'Well?' Candy asked imperiously.

Clare gazed at her fingertips, studying their wet sheen. She nodded slowly.

'You have still to exercise complete self-discipline and self-control, Clare. That is why I must teach you. That is why you must be carefully and thoroughly trained. Trained with my cane. Train you through discipline to be disciplined. Do you understand?'

'Yes,' mumbled Clare softly. 'I understand. Train me. My bottom is yours.'

'Back across the tree stump. Stretch out. Good. Legs together. Bottom up. A little more. That's better.'

Swish, swipe. Clare's passive nakedness shivered – her hips and rump swaying sensously – as the cane whipped down across her scalded bottom. Candy watched the creamy, pink-striped cheeks jerk violently in a responsive spasm to the lash. Swish, stripe. The punished girl's fingers – tips still sparkling with her own wetness – splayed in their anguished reflex as Clare shivered under yet another deliciously sweet stinging stroke of the cane.

'Stay absolutely still.'

Having admonished the naked girl sternly, Candy poised the quivering cane slightly above, then immediately against, the soft nape of Clare's white neck. The shoulders tensed then trembled under the proximity of the whippy wood. Pausing briefly to establish absolute supremacy, the punisher dragged the cruel tip of the cane down along the naked length of the punished – indenting the soft furrow of the spine before gently tracing the silken swell of the buttocks. Tremors of imminent climax rippled along the length of the sensitive bamboo. Candy, sensing fully their gentle force and understanding their meaning, shook her blonde mane sadly. She recognised the signs of Clare's approaching orgasm and expressed her disappointment by depressing the bare, left buttock severely with the last nine inches of the yellow bamboo cane.

'Clare,' she warned, her stern tone redolent with foreboding.

The violence of the naked, outstretched girl's trembling increased. Her scalded rump shivered as Candy tapped it smartly with the flickering cane. The crimsoning dome of ravished flesh dimpled, but the ominous ripples of the approaching climax grew quite palpably into a tangible tremor.

'Clare,' Candy whispered softly, almost pleadingly. 'You must try to . . .'

Clare cried out softly, drowning Candy's imprecations. It was a long, low sweet moan of delicious anguish. Wriggling free, the orgasming nude rolled over on to her back and threshed spasmodically. Sawdust clung to her warm belly and soft bosom in a thick, yellow-orange coating. She drew her knees up in a jack-knife and crushed them into her bosom – the sudden gesture instantly displaying her hot, wet sex and her hotter, wounded bottom. She was climaxing – lost utterly in the realms of ravishment. Candy dug the pine needles with the tip of the cane, her eyes drawn back to gaze wonderingly as Clare, her tightly pressed knees crushing her breasts and spilling hot silver unashamedly from her parted thighs.

'Clare,' cried Candy furiously. Clare's failure was, she felt, her own failure. Failure to train the wanton girl. The tone of pure exasperation was unmistakable. 'Get back across that stump at once. At once, do you hear? Give me that naughty bottom. Immediately.'

The shrill command brought Clare across the stump of sawn pine once more. The cane rose up and hovered, twinkling its potent promise of pain in the afternoon sunshine. The long length of whippy wood sparkled as it quivered, trembling with the soft malice of its delicious threat.

'Sorry,' whimpered Clare, her voice somewhat dreamily distant and detached.

Candy gazed down. Gazed down and sighed ruefully. Sighed ruefully and shrugged with resignation. The cane dropped soundlessly on to the soft carpet of pungent pine needles. Raising her tiny white foot up, Candy placed it across the crimsoning bottom below. Clare squirmed and moaned. Candy, thighs parted, sought and found the focus of her own sweet burning torment. Sought and found with her fingers the warm, damp epicentre at the base of her belly. Excited fingers drew apart her sticky labia – fingers which had only moments before wielded the power and the pain of the bamboo cane.

The sun, now a pure ball of molten orange, dipped a fraction behind the ragged line of pine-tree tops. Darkening, smudged grey shadows stole silently into the deserted clearing, peopling the empty glade with phantoms. A red squirrel, sensing the approach of dusk's dark mantle, peered down from his perch high above. In the distance, against the purpling skyline, eleven black rooks clumsily flapped the last patrol, the final mile, of their busy day.

Her small foot pressed firmly into the quivering flesh of Clare's hot, subjugated rump – a pair of punished cheeks shivering in submission – Candy stood in triumph astride the whipped one. She, as chastiser, had tasted the possibilities of pleasure, and had relished the probabilities of pain, which Clare's bare bottom had promised. How delicious, how darkly disturbing and delightful the warm flesh felt as she repeatedly scrunched her tiny toes. Frantic fingertips now scrabbled at her own dribbling warmth. Candy braced herself, tossing her blonde mane back in ecstasy. Her fingertips now rubbing and probing, she closed her eyes tightly. The busy fingers found the inner wetness, and softly punished the hidden flesh. Candy trod down savagely into the hot rump and hissed a tuneless hymn to Lust as her hot honey flowed. Half a minute later, the red squirrel scampered away into the upper canopy as Candy squealed aloud – astride the naked girl below – as the fist of orgasm encircled her and squeezed. Pitter-pat, pitter-pat. Clare gasped as she felt the juice of Candy's climax spill and splash her hot punished buttocks. Straining beneath the pinioning foot, Clare proffered her whipped bottom up to the dripping pubis in a fresh ecstasy of yearning. Pitter-pat, splish, splash. Candy's molten joy fell like large summer raindrops upon the hot, parched earth – down on to her toes that pinioned the hot rump, and into the hotter cleft that yawned beneath the controlling ankle. Clare felt the wetness, screamed her delight, and rocketed into renewed paroxysms of forbidden carnality.

A butterfly fluttered by, silently beating its velvety wings as it zig-zagged through the warm, silent stillness of the shadowed glade. No more than a ghostly smudge of indigo against the deepening gold of the dying light, it hovered tremulously as it approached the pair of glistening, naked figures below. Fearing the fate of the kingfisher that once espied Sappho sporting sensuously among the nodding bullrushes along the banks of the river Omega – for which unintended crime he was condemned forever to skim the surface of all water for evermore – the butterfly shivered and glided silently out of the glade towards the darkness of the surrounding pines. It passed over Candy and her happy conquest as softly as a sunbeam.

'Kneel. No. On all fours.'

Clare, her hands gripping the needle-littered loam, knees and toes pressing down hard, obeyed. She glanced anxiously over her shoulder, her eyes widening with alarm. Her bare bottom, she feared, would now be searchingly, ruthlessly and thoroughly caned. A flicker of fear fleetingly rippled over the taut satin of her vulnerable cheeks.

'Head down. No. Further.'

To achieve her desire, cane tip a-quiver as it alighted, Candy pressed Clare's bowed head into the pine needles. The penitent buttocks rose up. Arching her naked leg, she straddled Clare, guiding her soft bottom down into the supine warmth beneath and between her thighs. Squeezing her knees together as if astride a wilful pony, Candy felt Clare's breasts – loose and lovely as they swung freely – bunch and burgeon fulsomely within the controlling pressure of her inner thighs. Clare gasped. So fierce was Candy's sweet dominance, her ripe bosom threatened to split like sun-swollen melons within their taut, shining flesh. With a gentle rocking motion, which caused her own bare bosom to bounce and joggle, Candy rode the naked girl beneath her – rubbing her oozing labia along the soft whiteness of Clare's warm spine. It was a delicious sensation, as well as a graceful enactment and realisation of pure dominance and sovereign supremacy. Within and between her clamped thighs, Candy could feel the shivers of raw pleasure quivering along Clare's nakedness – troubling the softly rounded hips and thighs. Reaching forward with her left hand, Candy grasped a controlling clutch of Clare's loose hair. Gathering it up, she now felt in absolute command as she dominated the subjugated nude. No set of supple leather reins could have supplied or equalled the complete control Candy now enjoyed. Eyes shut tight, Candy shook her golden mane blissfully – so powerful did she feel she could have straddled a stallion, or ridden the hot, dangerous fur of a tiger.

Clenching an even tighter fistful of Clare's hair, and tugging gently so as to raise the captive head back up in a curve of surrender, Candy stretched her index finger out behind her, but to her dismay could only reach far enough with her hand to spank the bare, bunched cheeks. Not far enough, she frowned, to finger the splayed fig. The solution to her quandry lay down at her feet – alongside her and the mount she straddled and rode. The cane. The answer, she realised with a flashing smile, lay in the cane. Scooping it up, she held it delicately between her fingers and thumb, then slid it lengthways between the dark cleft of the creamy buttocks with a mathematical precision. Clare hissed softly as the length of supple bamboo was inserted between her slightly clenched cheeks, slowly retrieved, and then guided down once more. Seven, eight, eleven times, with increasing vigour and rapidity, the supple whippy wood stroked the innermost velvet of Clare's exquisite cleft. She squealed, twice, then uttered a long, liquid moan of utter surrender – remaining obediently passive, however, in her total subjugation. Candy nimbly plied the quivering shaft of slender bamboo 23 more times – reducing Clare to a jelly of wanton expectation – before swinging the cane

aloft, changing her grip adroitly and teasing it down again
slowly. This time, inserting the blunt tip into the softness
of the kneeling girl's exposed fig. Discounting the glinting
honeydew of the slightly unfurled outer labia, Candy
probed more searchingly. The tip of the yellow cane, when
retrieved and scrutinised carefully, proved to be dry.
Candy inspected it closely, her eyes narrowed. They
widened as a soft light suffused her gaze of fierce concentration.

'Dry,' she whispered softly. 'Dry. You are learning, little
Clare. You are learning your lesson well. Look.'

Candy levelled the tip of the cane before Clare's eyes. A
shudder of relief greeted the dry wood. The trainer relaxed
her tight grip, the trained lowered her head in ease. Clare
celebrated her delight, shaking her hair wildly as she tossed
off the constraints of domination.

Smack. Candy's flattened palm swept down. The soft
cheeks suffered. Spank, spank. Clare mewed. Smack.
Candy rewarded her naked pupil not with an affectionate
pat but with a sharp staccato of spanks that instantly reddened the creamy curves behind.

'Stay perfectly still. The lesson continues,' Candy purred.

Sliding down over the upthrust rump of her shuddering
pupil, her sticky labia raking the sweep of Clare's spanked
bottom as she dismounted, Candy knelt down immediately
behind the anxious girl. Thigh to thigh, the teacher and her
passive, pensive student were indivisibly fused together.
Gripping each proffered buttock with her controlling
hands – palms centred at the cleft, fingers splayed to grip
the outer curves – Candy bent forward and gently blew her
warm breath along the furrow of the widened cleft. Clare
writhed, swaying her hips and dipping her tummy, but
Candy's grip was absolute. Tongue-tip outstretched,
Candy flickered it rapidly along and within the ultra-sensitive ribbon of shadowed flesh. Clare whimpered her delight
and thrust her bottom back eagerly. The dominant blonde
withdrew slightly and paused, only to return to overwhelm
and crush the shimmering cheeks with her breasts –

burying the bottom within her heavy bosom so that the hot peaches become smothered in her warm cream. Sheer delight ravished the kneeling girl's fluttering belly as she felt Candy's berry-hard nipples press into her naked rump. Candy girdled her captive with a sinuous encircling of her arms, and held the hot bottom tightly in her grasp. Clare struggled but was tamed. Golden moments passed. Then, slowly – teasingly slowly – with a maddeningly delicious peeling away of flesh from flesh, the heavy satin breasts eased away from the imprisoned cheeks. Clare moaned – her feral moan dissolving into a sigh of pleasure as her smooth buttocks wobbled under the downward thrust of Candy's rasping pubic fuzz. Then again, and yet again. The crisp thrill of the blonde-fringed pubis, followed by the palpable presence of the warm, sticky labia of her dominatrix. Clare, ablaze with searing pleasure, ground her buttocks fiercely into Candy.

Spank. The sweeping hand crisply cracked down across the thrusting cheeks. Clare swallowed her surprise, blinking away the scarlet explosion from the stern warning.

'Be still,' came the stern warning.

Clare pouted sulkily.

Spank. 'And don't sulk during disciplined training.'

Clare felt the blush of shame steal across her cheeks, as surely as the blush of pain stole across her buttocks.

'That's better, my girl,' Candy rasped. Her voice was very strict. Anxious to retain her total domination, she remained absolute in her resolve to dictate terms. That, she knew, was how a trainer trains. Spank. Spank. Spank. The punished bottom squirmed under the rain of smacks. That, smiled Candy to herself, is how a learner learns. Gripping the outer curves of the spanked bottom, Candy steadied it, then dragged her wet labia down against the luscious flesh. She shuddered as she felt the heat of the punished cheeks against her most sensitive part – shuddered, and almost swooned. Again, and again, and – remorselessly – yet again, her sticky petals of Eve's Rose swept against the captive cheeks. Her mastery of the bottom was supreme. Soon it glistened with her hot, wet excitation. Clare, abject and in utter surrender, could barely sob out her sighs of tormented delight.

Candy struggled to avoid a sudden orgasm. Tensing and disciplining her inner muscles, she struggled to deny the spasm. When her breath came more evenly, more naturally, she managed in as controlled a voice as her thick tongue would allow: 'I shall examine you shortly, Clare. I shall examine you intimately. If you are sticky, Clare, I will put you over my knee and spank you very, very severely,' Candy warned – her voice spindling the delicious threat like curdled honey.

Clare clenched her bare buttocks in response. A silent, but extremely eloquent, reply. Frantically, she struggled to deny the liquid bubblings which threatened to well up from her innermost cauldron.

The moment – the delicious, dreadful moment – for the inspection came. Candy thumbed Clare wide apart with a ruthless expertise and carefully examined her inner sanctum behind the velvety labia. Anxiety tightened Clare's throat and fear clenched her buttocks as Candy prodded and probed. As a dread delight peaked her nipples with sweet pain, anguish softly clawed Clare's milky belly with its spiked talons – tracing endless arabesques of suspense.

'Clare,' crooned Candy, her finger emerging quite dry. 'You have learned well. Dry, see? You have passed the training and can now exercise self-control and self-discipline. Oh, Clare,' she hugged the naked girl. 'I'm so proud, so very proud of you.'

Candy, so very proud of her own achievements as a trainer, could have hugged herself. Already, she basked in the anticipated esteem – and perhaps more – of the Wise One.

'You are an excellent teacher, Candy,' murmured Clare.

'And you an excellent pupil,' rejoined the blonde, rewarding her trainee with an affectionate kiss on each buttock. Clare, struggling with and against the far from tamed maelstrom within, groaned thickly.

'We had better make sure. For the ceremony,' Candy warbled happily. 'Oh I am so pleased, and so proud of you,

Clare. So very proud. You have acquired the eternal secret. The secret of the Ancients. All men, and most women, are henceforth at your command. Come, let us prove it. Let us test and prove this new found art.'

After a celebratory hug and many tender squeezes, Candy gently pushed Clare back down on to the warm ground. Clare gazed up, her dancing eyes now brimming with joy. Gathering up Clare's wrists, Candy pinned them down together into the carpet of pine needles with her left hand and gently guided the trembling fingertips of her free right hand down into the dark pubic fringe. There, the dancing, drumming fingertips dappled the silky warmth playfully, teasingly, tantalisingly. Easing her heavy breasts down into Clare's upturned face with ruthless, dominant tenderness, Candy squashed them firmly – impressing them for several suffocating moments – before dragging the hard, peaked nipples, rubbery and painfully erect, over the closed eyes and open lips below. All the time, the dancing fingertips never ceased their maddening, bewitching drumming across the swell of the pubis. Clare ground her soft, punished buttocks into the warm earth beneath as she concentrated hard to deny her welling desire.

Up in the pale violet of the gathering night, a late skylark tumbled its silvery notes of joyful song. It fell down to serenade the pleasurer and the pleasured below. Candy placed her soft, pillowy bosom directly against Clare's naked breasts. Their nipples grazed – Candy's thickened peaks rubbing exquisitely into Clare's prinked buds. The creamy flesh of the dominating breasts melted as they fused into the quivering mounds of the dominated. A delicious swoon threatened to sweep both naked girls away into the void on its molten wings. Golden wings streaked with scarlet, that cast no shadow. Wings that were form without substance, mere phantasms glimpsed by the tutored, inner eye.

Candy dragged herself back from the disintegrating brink of abandonment as she suddenly remembered her strict duty and stern responsibility and focused on the task in hand. Inserting a probing index finger gently, but mas-

terfully, up into Clare's secret warmth, she withdrew it and
held it aloft in the shadowed twilight. It was dry.

After rewarding her successful pupil with a slow, lingering kiss, Candy curled up and dozed. Out of the west, far
out over the limitless sea, the tired sun sank down slowly
and expired in a glimmering surrender to the silvery-grey
horizon. Deserting the darkening sky, the black rooks huddled together in the branches of the sleeping pines, their
long day done. Subscribing to the silence demanded by the
dusk, each and every songbird stilled the notes in their
throats. Only an awakening owl refused to acknowledge
the impending night. The owl rustled. Its mournful hooting
greeted the large moon which rose up in pale majesty
above its dark kingdom.

Candy slept deeply – sated and utterly spent after the
delicious rigours of her long, hot afternoon. Snuggling her
warm softness into her sleeping trainer, Clare remained
awake. Awake, wide-eyed and wet-lipped. The owl fluted
eerily once more. Clare shivered and rose up on one elbow,
her breasts grazed Candy's shoulders. In the moonlight,
her blonde hair strewn wantonly, Candy looked ravishing.
Peaceful now, Clare shuddered as she suddenly remember
the strict, stern trainer of the sunlight. The strict and stern
trainer who had administered such sweet, such severe punishment.

Clare looked around her at the unfamiliar darkness. The
clearing in the pinewood – her arena of pleasurable pain –
had changed. The sun-dappled spaces of the afternoon
where harsh pleasures and sweet pain had reigned were
now made strange by the inky darkness. Clare shivered and
tapped Candy's soft shoulder.

'Candy,' she murmured.

The blonde, drowning slowly in the depths of dream-
filled sleep, dreamed on. In her dream, Candy wiped her
perspiring brow. She was hot. Hot and thirsty. Punishment
was such warm work. Her arm weighed heavily – tired
after repeatedly swishing and swiping the thin rod across a
soft, naked bottom. Candy licked her lips. In her dream
she gazed lovingly at the pink-striped bottom as it

185

squirmed under the shadow of her hovering whippy cane. She licked her dry lips once again. Her dream continued. Her dream of punishing the naked cheeks with the whippiest of bamboo canes – canes plucked from currant bushes heavy with the burden of ripe, swollen fruit. Swollen fruit that threatened to blister and burst beneath the fierce heat of the scorching sun. Candy licked her hot, dry lips, and stirred in her sleep. In her sleep, she thirsted.

Clare rose up and knelt astride Candy's sleeping face. A single, brilliant moonbeam caught the devilish twinkle in her eye. Soft fingers sought and found her softer fleshfolds – parted them slowly, luxuriously, and then frenziedly scrabbled to unleash her pent up lust-fury. As she shuddered and approached her climax, the slow smile of sweet revenge spread like sin across a nunnery rooftop as it distorted Clare's pursed lips.

Candy stirred and moaned softly. In her sleep she burned, as hot as the bottom she dreamed of whipping. Her dry lips peeled apart. Astride the sleeping blonde, Clare grunted as she orgasmed. Like soft, spring rain, the happy tears of Clare's weeping wound splashed down to moisten and glisten Candy's parched, suffering lips. Her pink tongue tip peeped out to seek the liquid solace.

Up in its pine tree, the owl hooted sadly, twice. Two low, sweeter moans rose up from the darkness below in antiphonal reply. Perplexed, the wide-eyed owl blinked before launching into the darkness of the surrounding night on wings of silent velvet.

Chapter Eight

Chloe, her affectionate grey eyes reflecting the pink blush of dawn, tossed her hair in the moaning wind. The fine ends whipped Candy's soft cheeks, stinging them sharply. Candy laughed as she blinked wind-driven tears from her violet eyes and gasped as the blustery north-easter snatched both her words and her breath from her warm lips.

The laughing girls embraced – snuggling bosom to bosom, thigh to thigh – and exchanged more salt-lipped kisses and lingering squeezes. Their long night of Sapphic passion had brought them, sleepy and lazy, to the beach to watch the sun rise over the wave-tormented horizon. The sea was growing rougher by the minute, flecking the air around them with spume. The simmering surface of the ocean did not actually boil, as it would when in full spate, but seethed with a malevolent turbulence.

'Look. No, there,' Chloe pointed, her voice rising a full octave in an excited squeak. 'A boat.'

It was as she said. Candy saw the winking red and green lights as a small vessel, chugging at a steady ten to twelve knots, approached. Almost as if suddenly conscious of being spotted, the lights – including a small, bright white mast-head light – flickered and died.

'Funny. It's illegal to switch off navigation lights. Perhaps it's in some sort of trouble,' Chloe wondered aloud.

'Or perhaps they don't want to announce their arrival. The ferry isn't due, is it?' Candy asked quickly.

Chloe shook her head.

'What about the supply boat?'

187

'No,' Chloe shook her head once more. 'That's not due for another ... Look. It's coming inshore. They're going to land.'

Instinctively, the two young women crouched down in the wind-whipped sands.

'We'd better stay and watch. See what happens,' murmured Candy.

Four slow, cold minutes passed. Huddling together, their thighs welded for warmth, they watched and waited in silence as the strange boat neared, the blurred image of its silhouette growing clear as it inched towards them through the rough swell. The pink horizon glowed gold as the sun rose, bringing no warmth but only light with which it bathed the broken surface of the sea, drowning it in a swathe of pale lemon. The boat, now close to the island, left a clean, white wake behind it. The girls heard the engine gurgle, cough and expire. Powerless, the boat began to bob in the heaving water.

'It's Emily,' Candy hissed. 'I'm sure it's her. Look.'

She was not mistaken. The two crouching girls saw a beautiful figure – lithe and proud-breasted – standing in the point of the prow. The distance was just a little too far, still, to see the detail of the face. But there could be no mistaking the wind-tossed, coppery hair of the exiled redhead. The boat was now no more than a few minutes from bumping the wooden jetty. It nosed the swell in silence.

'She's back to make mischief. Stay here and keep watch, see what she's up to. I'll go and warn the others.'

Candy departed as silently as a shadow as she scampered through the dunes. Away from the beach she straightened up and ran back to the castle as fast as her long legs could carry her.

The girls, many nearly naked, more utterly so, thronged round Candy excitedly, pressing their shivering warmth into her as they clamoured for more details. Sleepy-eyed girls yawned and ruffled their unbrushed hair. Soft bosoms swayed and joggled. A stray hand lazily scratched at a plump, bare bottom.

'What is going on here? What is the meaning of this noise? Candy?' the Wise One demanded as she joined the hubbub.

So strict and stern was her tone that the stray hand absently scratching the plump rump automatically cupped and covered the velvety cheeks.

'It's Emily. She's back. In a boat, down at the jetty. And she's brought . . .'

'Two others. Reporters or a TV crew,' Chloe broke in breathlessly. 'A woman, a man, a video camera . . .' she panted, flushed and perspiring after her dash.

'They'll be struggling to unload at the jetty. That gives us just enough time. Thank goodness we have a contingency plan to hand,' the Wise One observed. 'You know the drill, girls. Operation Smokescreen. Action stations.'

The command, delivered in a calm, unruffled tone, emptied the hall in a twinkling of creamy thighs and pale, soft bottoms.

The rising, rippling laughter almost drowned the comfortable clink of cutlery and the reassuring sounds of plates and cups being put to full use by the table of prettily dressed young women. Pastel jumpers and designer jeans were highly favoured by the happy breakfasters. Generous, ripe bosoms hovered inches above the white table cloth. Mouth-watering, as were the delicious breakfasts below. Candy toyed with her blueberry yoghurt as she sat in her hastily borrowed lemon shirt and white, corduroy miniskirt. They were Chloe's who lounged decorously in a turquoise kimono. The Wise One, svelte and chic in slightly more severely cut casuals, ate lightly grilled kidneys with every evidence of relish as she sat among the bubbling girls.

The male reporter, introduced simply as David, leaned towards Emily, who sat under a cloud of sullen incomprehension, and whispered aloud. 'Where's this – what did you call her? Maid. The naked girl who serves everybody at table?'

Emily reddened and scowled.

'And you said,' the audible, whispered accusation con-

189

tinued, 'they all wore tiny white vests and tight shorts, like a sixth-former's gym uniform.'

His questions, hissed in a tone of rebuke, were interrupted – fielded and caught by the ever watchful, ever listening Wise One.

'No maid service here, I'm afraid,' she smiled brightly. 'And we are, as you see, too remote to attract domestics. All the girls pitch in. Do try some honey with your toast, David. It is from our own hives.'

Her voice spoke in cadences of casual ease, but her jade eyes never left Emily's frowning face. Breakfast, Candy knew, was going to be a minefield of such sticky moments, but, with Operation Smokescreen under way, they might just be able to spoil Emily's nasty little scheme of revenge.

'More coffee, David?' the Wise One suggested. 'You must forgive our chattering. Breakfast is always a bit of a merry picnic here,' she lied with surprising aplomb.

Candy smiled briefly as she sank her small, white teeth into a slice of wholemeal bread heavy with glistening gooseberry jam. Smiled briefly but deliciously at recent breakfasts she had witnessed at Orrag. The bare-bottomed maid service – her red cheeks wobbling after suffering public chastisement. And after breakfast – with the aroma of bacon and coffee still hanging in the crisp morning air – the community court. The community court and the communal punishments. Some picnic, Candy mused with rueful glee.

'You said – you promised us . . .' David hissed resentfully at Emily.

Blushing in her confusion and anger, Emily fought back tears of frustration. Across the busy breakfast table, the Wise One smiled encouragingly to Candy.

'I don't know what tall tales that young lady has been telling you, I'm sure,' the Wise One whispered softly into the ear of Charlotte, the female reporter from one of the smaller independent production companies. 'I'm very much afraid you may be in for a disappointment. We are just, as you can see, an ordinary business-skills training centre. Seminars for presentational skills. Job-seeking and job-getting workshops. Putting together a good c.v.'

190

'Oh, I see,' replied Charlotte faintly. 'That sort of training.'

'Our interview technique workshop is, I must admit, very good. These girls come here with dreadful ideas that a winning smile and a short skirt will get them much prized secretarial posts. But if you've finished breakfast, why not come and see for yourself? Bring your camera. Coming, David? Goodness, how exciting. Imagine our little enterprise here on Orrag being shown on television.'

Perfect, murmured Candy to herself as she listened to every word. Perfect. The two intrepid reporters rose, looked at one another swiftly, shrugged, and dutifully followed the Wise One. Moments later they were in the studio watching a very prim and proper Madelaine sitting demurely at a table being gently coached in the arts of posture and voice projection.

'And use more positive statements. Say "I can" my dear, not "I think I can", after all, they will want to know that you are able to operate their word processor.' Madelaine smiled and nodded.

As Candy caught up with the party of visitors she was just in time to hear the Wise One's bland commentary.

'So many succumb to the strain of an interview. Madelaine, for example, tends to speak too quickly. And look, she's doing it again. Twiddling with her hair.'

'Mmm, I see,' nodded the female reporter, bored beyond words.

Candy grinned. The studio, now a blameless workshop, had not 24 hours since hosted a hot photo session in which Madelaine, now playing the part of the demure, prattling interviewee, had wrestled lasciviously with a naked brunette. The pinfall and submission had been secured – Candy remembered vividly – with Madelaine squatting down on to the upturned face of her spread-eagled victim and easing her gorgeous buttocks on to the girl below. It was also, Candy shivered deliciously, the scene of her own torrid time before the camera, where, naked and tightly netted, she had been ruthlessly snapped and striped by camera and cane. Striped and snapped until she had climaxed loud and long.

191

'You must come and see our gym. Several of the girls work out there every morning at about this time,' the Wise One gushed, ever anxious to play the part of the accommodating hostess.

'Nothing very odd, or of much interest here,' Candy heard the male reporter murmur to his companion, who merely shrugged and grimaced.

We're going to make it, Candy thrilled. Fooled 'em.

In the gym, five of the community were discovered leaping and bouncing through a reasonably punishing aerobic dancercise. The type of wriggling and writhing going on from Ruislip to Rhyll at that very moment. The sonorous beat of an old Kool And the Gang hit made speech difficult.

'Very healthy, dancercise,' boomed the Wise One with grating heartiness.

The increasingly glum reporters, dragged across a choppy sea to uncover and expose the dark, delightful secrets of Orrag, stared at the lurid lycra-clad aerobics class as the girls stretched, pranced and pirouetted in uncertain time to the braying music. David and Charlotte stood and stared – both perusing the taut buttocks of the bending gymnasts with more than a professional eye. As they stared appreciatively, Candy carefully watched them. Watched and studied closely as the two reporters shrewdly appraised the leaping lovelies. Candy smiled secretively as she saw a responsive gleam in their gaze. How much harder would they ogle and stare if they could witness a typical Orrag work out in the gym. Ogle and stare at the Wise One, supple and nakedly superb, pushing the perspiring, breast-bouncing girls through their rigours.

'Where is Emily?' the Wise One enquired politely. 'Poor girl. Came to us somewhat depressed, I believe. And completely lacking in ambition. Left hurriedly. Found it all a little too competitive here, I presume. Sad case. Her company sent her here to sort her out. We waived the training fee. Not quite up to the mark. Bit of a daydreamer, and far too imaginative for the business world. Very creative mind, though.'

'We've noticed,' the reporters chimed in dull unison.

'I'll go and have a quiet word with her. What a nice gesture, though, for her to bring you both all the way here to make your little feature film. Will it make the network or just a regional spot?'

Game, set and match, Candy grinned. The Wise One really was a wizard. The two reporters, already convinced that Orrag had no secrets for them to discover, nodded their agreement as Emily had been explained away so convincingly, so effectively. But one false move, the merest slip, and the privacy of Orrag would be exposed to their, and others, relentless glare. Better make sure, Candy resolved. Better make sure. Phase two of their plan was about to commence. It was time to divert, and distract, them.

'I'll bring – David, isn't it? I'll bring David along to see our other facilities,' Candy announced brightly.

Reluctantly, David turned his gaze from the bulging bottoms before him and followed Candy out of the gym.

'Jolly good idea,' the Wise One nodded – giving Candy the briefest of conspiratorial winks.

'And this is a typical bedroom,' Candy said over her shoulder as she opened the door to her own room in a carefree manner. Panties, snow-white, scarlet and black, some mere wisps of lacey nothingness, lay strewn across the carpet. Honey bronze stockings draped sinuously across the unmade bed. A bra, tossed wantonly on to a rumpled pillow, presented its deep, empty cups up yearningly, as if impatient to be filled with soft, warm flesh. David fingered the collar of his shirt and coughed softly.

'I'm not sure whose room this is but it's in a bit of a state. Naughty, naughty, girl,' Candy tut-tutted as she bent down and fingered a pair of scarlet silk panties. 'Leaving her room like this. She really should be punished.'

'P-p-punished?' David echoed slowly, his voice thickening.

'Most certainly. A strict reminder would not go amiss. If her desk drawers and Filofax are as untidy and cluttered as this room,' Candy swept the scarlet panties over the chaos she had carefully prepared and artfully created earlier on, 'she'll never make it in project management. She clearly needs discipline. Our training places great importance on orderliness and neatness. We run seminars in systemic approaches to organisation. Yes, she deserves punishment,' Candy murmured gently. 'An extra hour pushing a Hoover would do no harm.'

'Oh, that sort of punishment,' replied the reporter, barely able to hide the note of disappointment in his voice.

Candy grinned fleetingly. No doubt Emily had lured them to Orrag with tales of strict discipline, accounts of crisp canings and sagas of slow, searching spankings. Noting the dejected tone, Candy stooped forward and scooped up a wayward nylon stocking.

'No, I'm afraid we are very ordinary here. Bit boring, sometimes. Not much for your camera here, David. Emily tell you otherwise? Hoping for a sensational scoop, eh?' Candy laughed at her own remarks – her bright laughter covering just how carefully she was counting every word. Words counted, and calculated, to convince the reporter that, despite Emily's betrayal, Orrag had nothing to hide.

'No. Well, yes. I suppose so,' David smiled sheepishly. 'Emily spun us a bit of a yarn, all right. Gave us the impression that this place was buzzing with action. A veritable hornets' nest.'

Hornets. The word seeped into Candy's brain. Hornets. Goodness, she thought swiftly, how they stung. Sharper than the slicing stroke of crop or cane. How dearly Candy would like to have Emily, here and now. To have Emily, bare-bottomed and bending. Bare-bottomed and bending to suffer the hornet's sting of swishing whippy bamboo.

'As you say,' Candy remarked mildly, 'Emily spun you both a bit of a yarn, and through here,' she continued in her best estate agent's tone, 'I think you'll find more of our facilities. The usual arrangements, baths and showers.'

They had paused in the corridor and Candy had, with careful negligence, thrown open an innocent pine-wood door. Through the door, and the swirl of steam beyond, they glimpsed the white-tiled walls of an airy, expansive

194

bathroom. The steam hung in a dense cloud as it shouldered the pale-blue ceiling above. The muffled sounds of splashing water and laughter were unmistakable. David, twiddling with his light meter absently, hesitated in the doorway.

'Do let me show you our oriel window. Tudor, we are led to imagine, though probably restored. I'd value your opinion.'

They never got as far as the oriel window of doubtful provenance. Two naked figures, plump, pink and glistening beneath the silver cascade of their shared shower detained them. The light meter, Candy noticed, dangled forgotten at David's side. He simply stared, wide-eyed. His mouth gaping open even wider.

'Oh dear, we seem to have interrupted their abolutions. This is Annette.' Candy motioned with her hand.

Annette, stretching up to squeeze her wet hair between her fingers, smiled. Her breasts rose up in a pert salute. David swallowed.

'And I believe you have already met Madelaine,' Candy added nonchalantly.

Yes. He had already met Madelaine. But not utterly naked. The nude nymph glanced over her shoulder and smiled. David flickered his eyes briefly up from her fulsome, bare buttocks, blinked, and lowered them to feast once more, the quicksilver droplets sparkling in her dark cleft mesmerising him completely.

'Why not have one yourself? A hot shower would rinse away the rigours of your early morning boat trip, David. I'm sure you'd enjoy a steamy sluicing. Game?' Candy invited smilingly. 'I must go and attend to your companion. See you later.'

David proved to be game. After securing giggled promises that his frolicsome escapade would be kept a strict secret, he stripped in an inkling and stepped under a steaming cascade. Annette slipped into his shower – carefully following the plan of battle agreed earlier – and attentively plied her tablet of creamy, sweetly scented soap. Neither seemed to mind the tight squeeze caused by the confined

space which ensured that at all times her soft, warm love-
liness was pressed tightly against the entire length of his
quivering nakedness. Guided by her firm but gentle hand,
the soap creamed the naked man's shoulders, spine and
clenched rump with its soft curds. He gasped and sighed
sweetly under the silken spell of her capable ministrations,
his manhood twitching as it thickened slightly, and stirred.
Annette, cunningly and artfully thrusting her satin breasts
into his glistening back, and rasping his buttocks with her
wet pubic thatch, soaped his chest slowly, being careful to
drag her fingernails over his nipples. She smiled as she
heard him moan through clenched teeth. Smiled again as
she glimpsed his throbbing potency engorge and rise,
straining in full erection. She smoothed her soap-creamed
palm against his hard belly, taking pains to brush the bobbing knout fleetingly – slithering her hand down suddenly
to massage tormentingly the tops of his muscled thighs.
David spread his feet apart on the shining tiles below –
eager and impatient for the touch of her hand between his
thighs. It did not come.

Annette, secretly grinning, sluiced his arched body with
ice-cold water and then guided him out of the shower.
Madelaine awaited with a large, white towel. Swathed in
its soft, cocooning warmth, David sat on a cork-topped
stool, his eyes mere slits of hunger, drinking in the scene
that unfolded before him. It was a deliberate, teasing,
taunting display. Annette submitted her shining flesh to
Madelaine's briskly competent towelled hands. She plied
the towel vigorously, causing Annette's breasts to wobble
deliciously and bounce delightfully. Soon the milky shoulders and full bosom were wiped dry of every single pearl
droplet. Annette's flattened belly was dried – as were her
ripe thighs and softly rounded buttocks. David's responsive bulge at the base of his belly betrayed his close perusal
of the intimate drying of the naked Annette. He continued
to gaze as, softly talcumed and gently aglow, it was her
turn to towel and powder the luscious Madelaine. The
bare-bottomed, lithe-limbed Madelaine. Annette stood behind the heavily-buttocked, willowy blonde, nestling her

breasts into the wet skin. Dragging the towel down, she dried the glistening cheeks slowly and thoroughly then insinuated the soft material in between the parted, expectant thighs. When every intimate inch of the naked girl had been dabbed dry, Annette turned her face to David.

'Come here. We had better make sure you are properly dried. It simply would not do if you caught a chill,' she purred.

David obeyed, squeezing himself between the two nudes. Standing on either side of him, trapping him firmly between their warm outer thighs, they dried his bottom briskly. He stood proudly naked, his hot erection jerking upwards. Annette roughly towelled between his buttocks as Madelaine tantalisingly palmed his balls with the savage softness of the white cotton. Eyes tightly shut, teeth clenched, he surrendered completely as two cool hands touched him – one across his eyes, denying him sight, the other silken hand enclosing his hot, thick shaft. And pumping.

Who? Was it the heavily breasted brunette or the large-bottomed blonde? Who? Who was so bewitchingly driving him towards the trembling brink of imminent climax, and sweet and certain liquid release. Which of them? The blonde, or the brunette? Burning to know – yet relishing the thrill of not knowing – the identity of his sweet tormentress, David stiffened and tensed. With a soft groan, he slumped to his knees, sliding down in slow surrender between the firm, warm thighs of his naked controllers, and emptied his hot joy in a spurting stream of fluid delight.

'Bad boy. Bad, bad, boy. Now look what you've done. All sticky and wet on the floor. And there, up on the tiles. And on my tummy.'

'And on my breasts, you wicked boy,' chimed in the other with mock severity.

'Bend over. Come along, over you go. I'm afraid I'm going to have to spank you,' the tone brooked no denial. 'Give me your bare bottom this instant.'

Annette's stern instructions echoed ominously in the airy bathroom. To his unutterable pleasure, David, already on his knees between the two naked beauties, pressed his face down into the cool linoleum and raised his clenched buttocks up – up in obedience for the stern ravishment to come. Up for the harsh pleasures of domination and discipline. Madelaine sat astride him, easing her heavy satin buttocks down upon his back in a gesture of supreme and absolute authority. David almost swooned as he felt the rasp of her pubic fuzz graze his naked flesh – and shivered uncontrollably as he caught a fleeting whiff of her musky, pungent feminine fragrance. The excited nude was so close, so warm, so dominant.

Spank, spank, spank. Like the stern words preceding them, the sharp smacks across his bottom echoed loudly. The severe pleasure of being slowly, intimately and leisurely spanked by the beautifully bosomed brunette – while being so firmly straddled by the full-buttocked blonde – gradually unfolded in his brain like a lotus flower. Like a large-petalled lotus flower that yearns for the heat of the blazing sun. Madelaine squeezed her fleshy thighs tightly to restrain and control his jerking, bucking response to the spank, spank, spank of Annette's crisply curved left hand. David shuddered beneath the splayed cheeks which pinioned him. Pinioned him so exquisitely, so implacably, so absolutely. Annette, perspiring slightly, palmed her bouncing breasts then knelt down alongside him in order to address his scalded bottom more efficiently, more effectively, with her hovering hand. Spank, spank, spank. Her hot palm swept down across his hotter, spanked cheeks – causing David to groan thickly in his delight. Annette paused to softly palm the flesh then gently hold the burning cheeks between her slim hands – steadying and controlling the captive, punished bottom. His belly tightened and his thickly muscled manhood sprang up in a salute to Lust. Steadying and stilling his quivering rump, Annette leaned forward. Her nipples – berry-hard and firmly peaked with pleasure – nuzzled the hot flesh of his buttocks. His erection twitched and strained in response. Spank, spank, spank. Leaning back, Annette unleashed a further staccato of crisp, telling smacks which blushed the clenched cheeks with scalding scarlet. Spank, spank, spank. Above him, the heavy buttocks riding him ruthlessly. Behind him, the breasts – dominating his hot bottom supremely. And all the time the seething pain. The searing, searching spanking. The sweet anguish of delicious female discipline.

Again, and yet again, with precision and unerring accuracy, the remorseless spanking administered by the brunette blazed across his defenceless bottom. David jerked and juddered as he suffered the sweet pains of punishment. Annette gripped the hot cheeks and slowly spread their crimson flesh apart, sinking her thumb-tips into the yawning cleft that divided them so exactly. Madelaine rose up on her long, lithe legs and stepped over the kneeling man's bowed head. Turning, the blonde knelt down to face him, cupping and squeezing her breasts. David peered up and gazed devotedly at her trembling bosom. The ripe melons swayed slightly as she let them bob free. His hot shaft strained eagerly up towards the heavy pillows of fleshy satin. Bending, Madelaine cupped her breasts again, this time gathering up the entire length of his hot, muscled stiffness into the soft warmth that enveloped it. Buried deep within the pillows of smooth flesh, the twitching shaft jerked excitedly. Spank, spank, spank. Madelaine squealed as she felt his hot release of molten joy squirting and splashing on to her breasts. David sobbed his delight as he groaned his orgasm through clenched teeth.

'I see that you enjoy being disciplined, David. I am so glad that I did not forget to bring this,' Candy, who had just returned to the bathroom, remarked casually. Swish. She sliced the air with a supple length of yellow bamboo cane. David looked up. Swish. She thrummed the whippy wood once more. A sparkle of lust glinted through the cloud of spent exhaustion veiling his unfocused eyes.

'Madelaine,' Candy commanded. 'Take him.'

Candy inserted her straightened forefinger into her mouth, sliding it smoothly between her red, wet lips. Madelaine nodded her understanding and immediately obeyed, lowering herself down on the floor to do so – squashing her shining breasts, still wet from his ejaculation, on to the cool lineoleum. Taking David fully into her mouth, her soft lips encircled and enclosed his manhood firmly, completely.

'Bottom up, David,' Candy rasped crisply, tapping his rump with the tip of the whippy cane.

David could not but obey. His reddened cheeks rose up.

'Twelve strokes,' continued Candy imperiously. 'You will', she purred softly, tracing the curve of his left buttock, 'climax on the final stroke. Trust me. I know.'

The willing victim's eyes widened wonderingly, then closed tightly shut as, swish, swipe, his bottom shivered beneath the fire of the first hot striping lash. Swish, swipe. Again, and then again, the supple wood sliced the air, whistled down and cut into the bunched buttocks. As the thin, red lines across his taut cheeks deepened into an angrier hue, Madelaine worked her lips and tongue busily, hungrily pleasuring the shaft in her mouth as the cane spoke softly and assuredly – vehemently whispering its cruel notes of sweet sorrow. She sensed his hot manhood thicken and engorge at the fifth stroke, felt it tremor and throb at the seventh slice and saw the eyes of the punished man drown in their own liquid ecstasy at the ninth. Swish, swipe. The tenth, a savage cut, whipped down across the scarlet cheeks. David groaned and shuddered. Candy rested the length of cool cane across the hot flesh.

'Not until the twelfth,' she admonished sternly. 'Understand?'

The trembling man nodded briskly. Swish, swipe. The thin rod bit into his bottom with tender savagery. Arching up in a reflex of dark delight, the punished man plunged himself deeper into Madelaine's warm, wet mouth. Her eyes grew wider with wonder. His pumping hips, jerking in delicious agony, drove his flesh-spear further in. Both the man and the girl – connected by his engorged shaft – shivered and sighed, so exquisite was their mutual joy.

'As I promised,' Candy hissed excitedly, 'you will climax on the next stroke.'

Swish.

'The twelfth.'

So sweetly searing was the ravishing lash that it caused

the caned man to explode inside Madelaine's tight mouth. His shout of release echoed like a gunshot against the white-tiled walls of the bathroom.

'How curious,' murmured Candy as she examined the tip of the bamboo cane affectionately. 'I wonder if that's why they call it the Glorious Twelfth?'

David lay outstretched, face down, on the bathroom floor. Madelaine gently trailed her finger-nails against his scalp and soothed his sweat-soaked temples as she laid his head gently across her naked lap. He stirred in response and kissed her flesh. Submissively. Devotedly. Madelaine looked up at both Annette and Candy. The three exchanged grins of triumphant glee. Annette, easing her nakedness down and curling up against David's pale thighs, bent her cat-like face close to his striped bottom and licked the punished cheeks. Licked and kissed. Kissed and soothed the angry, red stripes.

'I must return to our other guest,' Candy announced, shouldering her cane. 'I must see to it that she too is entertained.' She paused at the bathroom door and paused. Turning, she gazed down at the naked man. 'Castle Orrag has a long tradition of hospitality. A Stuart king was pleasured here. Treat David royally. Deny him nothing.'

Candy departed as quietly as she had arrived, leaving the two naked young women to soothe and delight their captive. He rolled over on the floor, arms and legs outstretched.

'Have you ever played trains?' Annette whispered silkily.

'Trains?' echoed David thickly, almost dreamily.

'Choo-choos. I'll be the loco, you can be the tender. Madelaine, you be the carriage behind.'

'Ooh, yes. Trains. I love trains. Being coupled up tightly is such fun.'

'Come on, David,' Annette said gleefully, wagging her bare bottom as she knelt with her back to him. 'Choo-choos.'

He took Annette, who knelt with her legs slightly apart, from behind, powering himself into her so hard that his belly fused into her flesh – his loins splayed firmly up

201

against the deliciously soft satin of her bottom. Her swelling cheeks rippled as they accepted his shaft. Madelaine, kneeling, shuffled up from behind to complete the train, squashing her breasts into him, one slim hand resting on his glistening shoulder, the other down between his thighs to locate – and gently, squeezingly control – his balls.

'Choo-choo,' gurgled Annette, inching forwards on her knees.

David followed, measure for measure, with Madelaine, pressing her hot pubis into his recently whipped buttocks, bringing up the rear.

'Choo-choo . . .'

The tight, rhythmical jerking of the leading girl's buttocks, into which David was deeply impaled, compelled him into fresh frenzies of delightful torment. Golden paroxysms of lust raked his nakedness as he shuffled along, his exquisite anguish brought to new peaks of unutterable joy as Madelaine followed closely, her breasts crushed into him as she feverishly palmed his balls.

'Choo-choo,' warbled the naked, kneeling girls in devilish unison, as they shuffled their soft bodies in strict synchronicity.

Trapped firmly between the wobbling bottom in front, and driven by the heavily breasted, ball-tormenting nude behind, David felt his very soul melt down in lambent ecstasy.

'Choo-choo . . .'

Annette shuffled towards the side of a deep, white porcelain bathtub, increasing her speed a fraction. The deliciously coupled-up man could only follow where she led. His heart was now hammering like a blacksmith's iron against the anvil of his ribcage.

'Signal's red,' squealed Annette happily as she deliberately collided into the cold edge of the bathtub – sensuously cushioning her shunt using her bosom as buffers. The shock of her peaked nipples kissing then crushing the cold porcelain thrust her hips back severely. David, slamming into her softness heavily, speared her deeply with his thick shaft. From behind, Madelaine squeezed his balls expertly.

'Choo-choo,' they crowed in exultation.

Annette maintained her gyrating imitation of an engine – forcing him to echo her slow, lascivious grinding – while behind, her blonde pubic rasp raking down against his caned bottom deliciously, Madelaine pumped his shaft feverishly.

'Signal's green,' cried Annette excitedly, suddenly curvetting around the edge of the bathtub and shuffling rapidly across the linoleum floor. Completely caught up in the fresh spasm of muscular rippling – Madelaine having guided him into Annette's tight warmth – David cried out aloud. And screamed softly again as he lunged forwards, gripping Annette's ripe breasts savagely, and exploded inside her.

Stillness, broken only by their combined panting, reigned supreme. Then a gently seductive murmur floated across the splayed, spent bodies.

'Can we play trains again? And can I be the engine?' Madelaine sighed sweetly.

David, dry-mouthed and exhausted, merely groaned his agreement.

The fierce sun had scorched away the earlier dank chill. Orrag sparkled brightly down below, its green glistening, its golden sands and grey shingle glinting.

At the rear of the granite castle Candy stalked the secret corners of the large, rambling garden. Charlotte, the other half of the TV investigation team lured to Orrag by the vengeful Emily, had been given the freedom of the place.

'Please explore freely. Go where you wish,' the Wise One had smiled.

But it was a carefully orchestrated freedom. Charlotte had been shadowed all morning – better still, her wandering had been fully anticipated. In the kitchen, in the laundry, in the various workshops, she discovered nothing but busy young women happily at work. Not a single stroke of the cane or whistling slice of belt or supple crop had caught her ear or eye. Soon, Charlotte was convinced that there was nothing to investigate on Orrag. Nothing sensational at all.

Candy tracked Charlotte to the gardens and found her ankle-deep in the luxuriant lavender beds. Watching her quarry closely, she noticed how intently Charlotte, the prim and proper career journalist – her beautiful body tightly buttoned up beneath severe designer chic – sniffed at a richly scented late tea rose. Candy saw the woman's eye-lashes flutter and smiled knowingly at the straining swell of the tightly bodiced bosom as flared nostrils drank in the nectar. Here, Candy understood, was dry tinder-wood crackling with repressed desire, a desire that had yet to be consumed by the flames of its own fierce burning. It was time, Candy resolved, that a lighted match was put to this brushwood. Time for the hungry flames to lick and burn.

'Have you seen all you need for your documentary?' she called across the nodding roses.

'No – yes,' Charlotte replied, shyly dropping the wet rose she had been glutting her sorrow with and shaking herself free from its seductive perfume. 'The fact is, I don't think there's a story here at all. Emily had rather painted a more – a more . . .'

'Vivid picture?' Candy helped the struggling reporter out of her predicament.

'Mm.'

Good. We've fooled 'em, Candy thought – concealing any visible display of the relief surging over her. Now, to make sure. To make absolutely certain.

'Why not come down to the gym. There's some equipment I'd love you to see. Olympic standard, we were told. Didn't have enough time earlier. All those girls . . .'

Girls. Candy watched Charlotte's eyes widen impercep-tibly, and caught the shadowy ghost of Sappho flicker across their veiled glint.

The doors swung open and flapped noisily behind them as Candy and Charlotte entered the cool, spacious gym. Faint traces of young womanhood haunted the air. Traces of perfume, exertion and arousal. A pleasing, teasing mem-ory of that morning's aerobic session. The gym was in utter darkness and all was quiet. A perfect stillness ruled the calm gloom. Candy reached out softly and flicked on a switch – the third in a row of four. Immediately, a single, searching spotlight flooded down, bathing the darkness below with a circular pool of light. Charlotte gasped aloud. In the realm of sudden light a four-legged vaulting horse straddled the polished wooden floor. Across the scuffed, shining black leather body of the apparatus, a beautiful bare bottom rose up to meet their arrested gaze.

Perfect, Candy grinned to herself. Her timing had been spot on.

'Who is there?' a disembodied voice asked, the speaker unseen, from the other side of the vaulting horse.

'It's only us,' Candy replied casually. 'Seems as though we've interrupted someone's private work out,' she whispered to Charlotte.

'It's a Scandinavian technique. Dancers do it, I am told. Good for the thighs and of course for the bottom,' explained the unseen speaker from behind the belly of the leather horse.

Charlotte gazed avidly at the rounded bare bottom, the trembling silken thighs and the svelte, tapering legs draped over the horse, the tiny toes prinked and pointing straight downwards as if under some strict discipline.

'Watch,' commanded the voice. It was an instruction, not an invitation.

Slowly, the loose, dangling legs stiffened and tensed. Feet arched and tiny toes curled then flexed straight, the pale, long legs gradually rose up until they were stretched out behind in perfect horizontal exactitude. Candy and Charlotte glimpsed the soft, creamy mounds of the bare, quivering buttocks just above the soles of the pale feet now facing them.

'Keeps the thighs trim,' announced the nude gymnast. Slowly, her legs parted. Tantalisingly slowly. But soon the cleft between the straining hillocks of taut flesh yawned invitingly. And then the dark fig – slightly moist and extremely succulent – revealed itself. At first, with a peeping temerity, then with a shy boldness.

Candy heard Charlotte swallow hard in the darkness

that surrounded them. Out in the gym, in the pool of piercing light, the legs were slowly drawn together. As they closed to a seamless fusion of lithe, shining flesh, tightly clamped and motionless, the soft buttocks beyond dimpled slightly.

'The secret lies in using only the thigh muscles,' the voice from the dark side of the vaulting horse confided silkily. The tone was one of pleasant intimacy. 'One must resist using one's hands or arms.'

Candy thrilled to the tension out of the matter-of-fact words spoken by the softly sensual nude. It suddenly reminded her of her Knightsbridge manicurist who ministered to her in the warm salon – pert in a crisp white nylon coat-dress with absolutely nothing worn underneath. The delicious clash of the clinically correct and the seductively naughty.

'Squeezing the thighs and bottom is permitted,' whispered the naked gymnast as if describing the taste of fruit forbidden. She illustrated her meaning. Her cleft becoming a severe crease.

Charlotte's hand flew up to flutter at her tightening throat in a sudden gesture of response and fussed silently with an amber pendant nestling against her milky skin. Candy sensed the nervous movement, and felt the swift charge of excitement the movement of hand to throat betrayed. And suddenly Candy knew. Knew that Charlotte was taking the first steps along the seductive path of enlightenment. Beyond enlightenment lay lambent pleasures – and sparkling pain, perhaps. The pleasures of pain. The sweet pains of pleasure. Candy knew and understood because she too had come to Orrag tightly buttoned – in both body and mind – buttoned up within the strictures of a busy, hectic career. Slowly, Candy had stumbled – frequently driven on by swishing stripes and scalding strokes – along her path towards self-knowledge. It was, she sensed, Charlotte's moment. And the moment was ripe. Just as Candy's own moment had been signalled by her glimpse of the bamboo cane in the library that eventful first morning on Orrag. The supple whippy cane which had been left, passive yet potent, lengthways along the desk in the sun-light. The same cane which Chloe had picked up, expertly flexed and swished, and sliced down across Candy's tight panties.

Blinking away her moist memories of that cane's fierce kiss, a kiss that had scored a faint red stripe across her clenched cheeks, Candy turned in the darkness and touched Charlotte's shoulder.

'Shall we join her?' she murmured.

Charlotte nodded silently, and then meekly, yet willing-ly, followed where Candy led. Out into the pool of light that bathed the leather horse.

'Have we time for a brisk work out before lunch?' Candy asked softly.

The bare bottom before them suddenly became a de-lightful delta – the plum-pubis dark and tempting – as the naked body twisted around, the fleshy buttocks now squashed into the polished hide. The Wise One slowly emerged, dragging herself upwards to a sitting posture. Belly, breasts and then the sensual shoulders and arched white neck. At last, the serene, dominant face. A face of strength, wisdom and beauty. A smiling face – the lips laconic in a haunting echo of the Giaconda. Candy ground her toes into the polished wooden floor – wishing Charlotte a thousand miles away.

'Yes, I think so. Charlotte most certainly. Leave her with me,' the Wise One purred. 'I'll gently put her through some not too punishing paces.'

Candy grinned, then frowned slightly – puzzled by the single, white cotton glove on the Wise One's right hand.

'You'll be needed in the kitchen, Candy,' the Wise One added gently as she gracefully swung her lissome legs down and slipped off the horse. How the heavy satin of the bosom rippled, Candy marvelled. And how deliciously the trim buttocks bunched as she swept down from her mount of warm, supple leather. Goodness, Candy thought, she really was quite a tease, quite an artful seductress. It was a new perspective on the Wise One, and it rendered Candy sticky and hot.

'Assist Charlotte,' the Wise One motioned with her hand.

'I'll help you slip out of these,' Candy smiled, reaching out to begin the delicate task of slowly unbuttoning their visitor.

Charlotte. Quietly feverish in her whirling expectations, her wild heart beating, her blood pulsing rapidly in her veins. As if in a dream, she surrendered happily to Candy's deft fingers. Soon she was standing, legs slightly parted, superb in her underwired brassière – her buttocks plump and bulging within taut silk panties. The brassière, a La Perla, was pale blue. The rosy cleavage wobbled slightly within its strictures. Candy eyed the panties – noting how the crotch bit lovingly into the pubis, noting too the dancing design of pale-blue lilies that embroidered the elasticated trim around Charlotte's slender waist. Tight, silk panties, with a high waistline – containing and controlling the torrid tensions within. How Candy's fingers itched to gently trace the swell of the pert cheeks, happy captives in silken bondage.

'We shall see how supple you are, my dear,' the Wise One declared.

Candy immediately caught that somewhat brisk, imperious note redolent with stern authority.

'We will no doubt see you later, at lunch, perhaps,' the Wise One spoke to Candy. 'Leave us now.'

Candy stole out of the circle of light into the darkness beyond and walked towards the rubber-trimmed doors. Reaching them, she pushed at their heavy weight. They flapped noisily, announcing her departure. Candy remained motionless in the gym. Surreptitiously, she tiptoed into the furthest, deepest shadows and, turning her face once more towards the vaulting horse in the swathe of bright light, sank down softly on to her knees to watch. To watch and savour the awakening of Charlotte. Watch, as Charlotte stood, her left hand plucking at her tight bra strap that bit into her swelling softness. Watch, as the Wise One silently tapped the polished leather back of the horse with her white gloved fingers.

208

'Up,' commanded the Wise One somewhat curtly, making the invitation a demand.

Candy, her thighs slightly parted, felt a warm liquid bubble moisten her pubic fringe. Her wide eyes narrowed into slits of hungry concentration as she drank in every vivid detail beneath the blazing spotlight. The splendid, nude figure of the Wise One. The mild menace of the shining leather horse. The bashful beauty, obedient and passive in her stunningly provocative undies. The mesmerising tap-tapping of the white gloved finger against the black leather. Candy's silvery bubble shivered and burst, splashing its wet warmth down into the secret flesh of her clamped thighs.

'Up,' repeated the Wise One. Superb, supreme in her sovereignty.

Charlotte trod the polished wooden floor nervously with her bare feet. She took the necessary three paces forwards and brought her trembling thighs to the horse. With a buttock-bunching upward thrust, she mounted the silent beast.

'Bend over. Bend right over.'

Breasts spilling loosely, despite the tight strictures of her underwired brassière, into a burgeoning bloom of creamy ripeness, Charlotte lowered her belly down over and across the leather, presenting – indeed offering submissively – her tightly pantied buttocks up to the Wise One. The cotton-gloved hand hovered briefly before descending to alight gently, fingertips splayed, on the taut hillock of the left cheek. Candy heard Charlotte gasp aloud.

'We don't need these,' the Wise One cooed soothingly as she thumbed the silk panties over the wobbling cheeks – peeling them apart from the satin skin. Gently at first, to expose the bunched glory of the fleshy mounds, then with a crueller, snatching jerk to drag them along the quivering thighs and down the lithe length of the supine legs. Charlotte squealed softly, her cry of ululated pleasure dying into the feral cadences of a thickening moan. Belly down on the leather of the horse, she lay bare-bottomed – trembling with expectation.

'Or this.'

The briskly competent white-gloved fingers plucked at the bra clasp. It yielded – the straps shrivelling as the heavy bosom fell free from its firm bondage. Candy saw the ghostly fluttering of silk as the La Perla sank silently to the floor, and swallowed with a little difficulty as she saw it curl up in silken surrender.

'That's much better,' purred the Wise One. 'Isn't it?' she added in a tone that denied denial.

'Mmm,' sighed Charlotte dreamily as she succumbed to the forefinger stroking the length of her furrowed spine, stopping to tap dominantly at the crease of her cleft. 'Mmm,' she echoed, her satin buttocks wobbling.

'Much better,' soothed the Wise One, inching her thighs apart and pressing down hard on the horse. 'Slip down and we'll see just what you can do.'

Charlotte slid back down, her bare feet rejoining the wooden floor. Candy noticed the reluctance with which the heavy breasts departed from the scuffed hide they adhered to so lovingly.

'Step back. About eight paces. Try a forward roll.'

Charlotte obeyed – walking backwards away from the horse which she still faced, as if spellbound. Candy drank in the sensual sway of the naked bottom, and shuddered. She shuddered again as Charlotte raised her left leg and limbered up by loosely shaking it, her left cheek bunched as taut as an orange. Candy struggled to suppress the whimper of desire that troubled her throat. Automatically, her teeth performed a silent biting motion, as if sinking into a peeled fruit. Then, the soft thumping of eager feet. The supple-thighed spring. Charlotte landed heavily on the other side of the horse, spreading her arms out to maintain her uncertain balance. In an instant, her nakedness was poised and still. Only the heavy bosom joggled. Candy noticed it immediately the nude turned into the pool of harsh light flooding down from the single spotlight above. The ripely rounded breasts were magnificent. Mouthwateringly so.

'Now try for a hand-spring,' the Wise One, tapping the leather silently, invited.

Again, the soft thumping of the bare feet punishing the polished wooden floor. Again, the supple flexing and thrusting of a disciplined body – arching, leaping. But – thump. The spring was misjudged. Something went awry. Charlotte landed, belly down, breasts crushed heavily beneath her, on the leather-backed horse.

'Now that wasn't very good, was it? Not very good at all,' the Wise One admonished in a chiding murmur, lingeringly stroking the splayed buttocks offered up submissively to her tightly-gloved hand. 'Try again. And do not disappoint me this time. I do so hate to be disappointed.'

Candy's mouth dried and her lust-thickened tongue became so swollen it threatened to choke her. She knew the signs. Excitedly, she read the signals. Punishment haunted the air. Or at least, for the moment, the velvet-venom threat of punishment. Like a bitter-sweet *frisson*, it charged the atmosphere – curdling it with its very own sharp electric tension. And it remained so, hanging heavily with a hint of sugared menace, long after the Wise One's words had melted into silence. The bare bottom spread across the shining leather seemed to acknowledge and fully appreciate the implicit threat. The cheeks clenched involuntarily and dimpled in an anxious reflex of apprehension before Charlotte scrambled down and scampered back into the outer darkness.

Another run – the softly padding feet – another spring, the clean limbs arrowing up into the blinding light towards the dark leather beast. Thump. Soft nakedness smacked the hard leather as Charlotte failed to clear the horse.

'Try again. Put your panties back on,' the Wise One instructed.

Candy watched as Charlotte, having enticingly stepped back into her silk panties, and fingered her cleft to ease the tight material, tried in vain once more to execute a handspring. Candy grinned as, once again, the near-naked girl lay sprawled across the hard leather horse.

'Not good. Not good at all, my girl. Perhaps these,' the Wise One was now examining the lace panties intimately, were a mistake. Let's slip them off again, shall we?'

The dominantly prinked white-gloved fingers insinuated themselves under the elastic waistband and slowly, very slowly, eased and peeled the second skin of silk away from the fulsome cheeks. Candy smiled as she saw Charlotte jerk her narrow hips upwards to assist their passage. Dragging the wispy panties down to the wriggling ankles, the Wise One swiftly whipped them away, leaving Charlotte prone, passive and meekly submissive in her utter nakedness. In utter nakedness, bottom up across the warm leather.

A sweet, violent surge burned down from Candy's belly to between her legs. A sweet, violent surge, which emerged as hot honey from her slightly pouting labia. Now, she urged silently. Now. Spank her now. Crimson those creamy cheeks. Do it, oh please do it. Now. Candy – only a week or so ago the epitome of the cool, efficient businesswoman – was now almost whimpering and silently pleading to witness another's bare bottom set ablaze. And Candy was not alone in her silent pleading. Pleading for punishment to commence – stern, sweet punishment. Across the increasingly sticky, warm leather, Charlotte imperceptibly inched her bare buttocks upwards in a mute supplication and absolute surrender. Spank me, spank me, she pleaded to herself. Spank me, spank me, she sobbed softly, squeezing her cheeks together and crushing her bosom fiercely into the thrilling hide of the horse.

'Are you acquainted with behavioural modification, Charlotte? I do of course refer to the reward-punishment model of motivation. Let me assure you that it is most effective. Highly satisfactory results frequently accrue from its application and implementation. Highly satisfactory. Just as a hypothesis,' the Wise One murmured softly.

It's here at last, Candy suddenly realised. The moment. The point of no return. From now on, only two can act out this unfolding drama. The punisher and the punished.

'Just as a hypothesis,' the Wise One continued, 'I would like to know which would spur you on the most. Reward or punishment? A harsh reward.' The Wise One lowered her head down and lovingly licked Charlotte's naked spine from the nape of her soft, white neck down to the gentle sweep of her swelling buttocks.

212

Charlotte squealed.

'Or a sweet punishment?'

The white glove stroked the curve of the left cheek then pinched the rubbery flesh with a fleeting nip.

Charlotte sighed.

'Well? I am waiting for your answer.'

'Punishment,' moaned Charlotte. 'Punishment.'

'How astute of you to choose so intelligently.'

In the outer darkness, Candy shuddered as she cupped and compressed her tormented, swollen breasts greedily.

'Punishment,' echoed the Wise One meditatively. 'And shall we dare to test our little theory? Hmm? Let me see,' she bantered suavely, fingering the bare buttocks with slow, circular sweeps of her dominantly prinked, gloved forefinger. 'If I were to whip your bottom with, let us say, your brassière. Would that motivate you sufficiently?'

'Yes,' curdled Charlotte thickly. 'Yes please,' she moaned.

Both Candy and the Wise One, one in the dark, the other bathed in light, struggled to suppress their knowing smiles.

'Remove my glove. No. Not like that. With your teeth.'

Charlotte obediently craned her neck and brushed the glove fingertips with her dry lips. Nipping elegantly, if a little hungrily, at the taut cotton with her tiny white teeth, she pulled at each rigid finger, slowly removing the glove from the outstretched hand. The glove from the hand which was to grasp and wield the brassière. The hand which was to wield the brassière with which she was about to have her bare bottom whipped. The brassière – cunningly crafted to mould and marshal her fulsome bosom – which was about to seethe and stripe her quivering rump. Her naked, creamy rump tingling with eager expectation.

The Wise One bent down and scooped up the La Perla bra. Charlotte, the white cotton glove still dangling from her clenched teeth, shifted her hips a fraction and pressed her belly firmly into the leather. Swish, swipe. The crisk stroke of the elasticated fabric scalded the bunched cheeks deliciously. The whipped girl kissed the leather to smother

her cry of tormented delight. Swish, swipe. Again, the slicing swipe, again, the burning kiss to the suffering cheeks, and the smothered yelp of sweet anguish muffled by lips pressed into the harsh tang of leather.

Candy, weeping freely now from her throbbing sex, saw the creamy buttocks flinch and jerk in spasmodic response to the hot pain. Swish, swipe. Swish, swipe. Remorselessly, relentlessly and rhythmically, the bare buttocks were whipped. Each stroke was scorchingly accurate, searchingly intimate. Deepening crimson blushed the creamy flesh of the clenched buttock-cheeks with the lambent hues of hot anguish. Charlotte wriggled and squirmed but there was no escaping the ruthless ravishment of her naked bottom. Swish, swipe. Swish, swipe. The crisp sound of the brassière scalding her soft, upturned cheeks. Candy knew that liquid pulses of an unknown, as yet unidentified, powerful pleasure would soon be searing through Charlotte's nakedness, flooding the whipped girl's veins with the warm, oozing ichor ordained by Lust to lubricate Delight. A molten, golden Delight. A Delight which was probably already dribbling from her tingling labia – labia which kissed the leather of the horse. Swish, swipe. Swish, swipe. Candy saw the raised hips grind, crushing the wet wound down into the hide. Swish, swipe. The tremulous buttocks inched up to meet and greet their scarlet pain. The stinging brassière swept down again and again – the sweat-glistening breasts of the whipper swinging freely in their loose, lascivious splendour as she plied the punishment to the bare rump.

In her deeply shadowed silence, Candy groaned softly. Within her, the pangs of jealous desire failed to dull or dampen the fires of fierce delight. Jealous desire fuelled by the sight and sounds of Charlotte's rounded, peachy bottom being so thoroughly striped. Trembling, Candy squeezed her inner thigh flesh tightly to staunch the threatening stream of molten arousal which promised to flood at any moment – flood her flesh and scald it with its seething flow. In her eyes, her jealousy sparkled hot tears.

At the horse, out in the harsh pool of light, the Wise One dropped the brassière and bent forward to scrutinise and inspect the whipped cheeks. They glowed a deep, rubescent pink, shining after the thorough punishment. She thumbed the deep cleft dominantly then softly palmed the quivering globes. Bending down even closer, she deliberately spilled her breasts on to the hot flesh. Charlotte screamed the scream of a wanton virgin feeling her first piercing pleasure-pain. She squealed again in frank, unbridled joy as the stiff nipples scored the hot satin of her rump.

'And so you see, Charlotte. Sweet discipline can often be a harsh pleasure, both to dispense and to receive. Don't you agree?'

'Yes,' whispered Charlotte hoarsely.

'And a great motivator. But we have no time to test our little theory. We shall never know if a whipped bottom would help you vault the horse. It will be our little secret. Won't it?'

Charlotte echoed her mumbled assent.

'Good. And now, for your reward, I shall take you for a soothing shower. Charlotte. Will you promise me one small thing?'

'Absolutely anything.'

'Do not speak of this to any other. I'm afraid the young ladies here on Orrag are all very prim and proper and would strongly disapprove were they ever to find out.'

The Wise One smothered Charlotte's whispered compliance with soft, deep kisses. On her mouth, lingeringly. On her shoulders, longingly. On her reddened cheeks, lovingly.

With a sharp intake of breath – a stab of wounding jealousy – Candy shrank back into her darkness at the sight of these kisses. Shrank back into her darkness as the Wise One kissed, and now licked, the whipped buttocks. She shrank back even further into her misery as the Wise One led Charlotte by the hand into the adjacent showers. As the neon strip lighting flickered on, Candy peered intently at the two naked bodies behind the marbled glass of the shower door. Blinking through her tears, she realised that behind the opaque glass, within the swirling steam, the two bodies would be welded together – the rasping pubic snatch of the punisher grinding into the shining wet bottom of the punished. Scented soap, then fingers, would soon find out and invade those shadowed, secret fleshfolds.

Driven by a blind anguish, Candy stumbled into the leather side of the horse in her bid to flee the gym. From the showers, a shrill cry signalled Charlotte's first climax. Candy steadied herself against the warm leather flank. The scuffed hide glinted under the spotlight above. Candy's curious fingers stroked the slippery spot where the whipped girl's pubis had wept for joy. Snarling, Candy snatched up the abandoned brassière. It felt warm in her hand. As was the white glove she seized and donned – thrilling, despite her jealous resentment, to the tight grip of the cotton. A second ethereal shriek announced Charlotte's further orgasm beneath the steaming water. Candy threaded the brassière between her open thighs and began to work it rapidly, back and forth as if drying herself, into her glistening innermost flesh. She gripped the strap firmly within her clenched, gloved fist. Faster. Faster. The flimsy, stretched brassière skimmed her opening labia. Her hot, jealous pangs melted under the new, burning sensation. Between her splayed thighs, flickering flames lapped at her punished wetness. A third cry, distantly haunting like a curlew braving a gale, echoed around the gym eerily. Charlotte's third scream of joy. Her third trembling, utter surrender to the Wise One's soft cruelty and fierce tenderness.

Blinding her ears to the cries of sweet carnality and deafening her eyes to the inner image of the Wise One devilishly pleasuring another, Candy plied the stretchy brassière furiously. Faster, faster still. Her white, clenched gloved fist now a mere blur.

Chapter Nine

The trembling tip of the thin cane dragged slowly down against Candy's lower, equally trembling, lip.

'Silence. Silence during punishment.'

'But you kissed her,' Candy mumbled stubbornly, her resentment distorted by the pressure of the cane against her bottom lip. 'You kissed her. And then you took her to the shower. I heard you.'

The bamboo sparkled as it swept up over the bending nude, froze and then descended to tap and address the bunched cheeks which already bore several pink stripes.

'Yes,' nodded the Wise One as she flickered the cane upwards.

Swish, swipe. The rod whistled down to severely stripe Candy's bare bottom. The punished blonde hissed her sweet torment.

'And you saw. Spying on me, mm?'

'No.' But Candy was not an accomplished liar.

Swish, swipe. Candy yelped slightly as yet again the whippy wood sliced down and bit into her crimsoning buttocks. Her cropped blonde mane flounced as she shuddered under the lash.

'Do not lie to me, Candy. What brought you to the disgraceful decision to remain inside the gym and spy. Well?' the Wise One demanded.

The caned nude remained silent, her blushing face almost as hot as the curve of her punished rump. The caner tapped the bare cheeks imperiously – causing them to dimple in a reflex of fear.

'Was it curiosity, perhaps?' mocked the Wise One.

'No,' snapped Candy. An injudicious response.

The living wood shivered and swooped. Swish, swipe. The peach cheeks suffered. Candy, naked and bending, instantly rued her hot retort. It had merited her an even hotter stripe. Swish, swipe. Another. The slicing stroke – unexpected – was swift and severe.

'Or could it have been jealousy, perhaps?' purred the teasing questioner.

'No. I don't know – yes,' Candy mumbled.

'So,' triumphed the Wise One. 'It was out of jealousy. But I was only doing my best for the interests of the community. Trying to protect Orrag itself.'

'You kissed her,' Candy accused implacably.

Swish, swipe. There was pain, certainly. But this time, the scalding stroke across her bare bottom was instantly followed by the fleeting brush of the punisher's wet lips against the hot bottom. Candy sighed luxuriously as the sweet mouth kissed her ravished cheeks. Dropping her cane, the Wise One stole softly around the bending blonde and positioned herself directly behind the striped buttocks. Slowly, with an increasingly harsh tenderness, she gripped and squeezed the rump she had just whipped. Candy moaned thickly. Clenching, weighing and then moulding the scorched flesh within her talon-like splayed fingers, the Wise One stood serenely sovereign over Candy. Her dominion softened slightly as she relaxed her punishing grip and gently palmed the striped spheres. Bending down once more, the punisher kissed the punished bottom.

'Yes. I kissed our inquisitive little visitor. But strictly in the line of duty. But when I kiss you, Candy Brompton . . .'

Candy squeezed her thighs together, thrilling to the sound of her full, formal name.

'When I kiss you, I do so out of . . .'

Say it, damn you, say it, Candy screamed silently. Say the word.

'Affection.' The Wise One whispered the word, fingering as she spoke the warm, sticky shadow of Candy's cleft. The creamy cheeks clenched to imprison and hold the dominant, intimate forefinger.

218

Yes, yes, yes. She said it. She said it, Candy's heart sang. Rising up to embrace her strict, sweet sovereign, Candy's blonde mane met the controlling touch of a flat palm. The firm hand quelled the naked girl and forced her back down into the bending posture – positioning her for more punishment.

'Down, Candy. You may not rise up yet.' The silken tones insinuated themselves into Candy's spinning brain. 'I may have cause and occasion to punish you a little more. There may well be further stripes for you.'

The Wise One scooped up the yellow bamboo cane and thrummed it twice. Candy swallowed as it sang its curdling notes of pleasure-pain.

'Further stripes for your bare bottom. Should I deem it necessary to administer them. I am not altogether convinced that you have been whipped soundly enough.'

Lowering her head, Candy meekly touched her toes, offering her bare buttocks up in absolute surrender to the caner and the cane. But further scalding stripes did not visit her cheeks. Only the butterfly sweep of the punisher's cool fingertips against the superbly rounded buttocks. The light brushing of skin against skin, at which the taut satin shivered.

'Affection,' murmured the Wise One. 'I have much of that for you. And more. Hopes and expectations. You came to me a wild thing, unruly and untamed. First I tamed you, now I rule you. And you were so rude, so undisciplined. Remember?'

'Yes,' whispered Candy, blushing at the memory of her former arrogance.

'With discipline, you have blossomed into something quite rare and wonderful. You have opened up from the tight bud you were into full bloom.'

Watered by the sweet tears of chastisement, Candy thought. And ripened in the heat of fierce joy.

'Our visitors have gone. I took them down to their boat after lunch. I am sure we will not hear from them again.'

'They went away satisfied.'

'There was room on the boat for you, Candy,' the Wise

One whispered, tracing the outline of the bare bottom with her cane.

'I wouldn't have gone. I don't want to go,' Candy replied simply.

'Yes, I know. And I hoped it would be so. There is much to be done here still. Already you have given much of yourself and accomplished much. All to your credit.'

'Thanks.' Candy, basking delightly in this warm praise, glowed happily.

'But jealousy . . .'

Swish, swipe. The cruel slice flashed down across the soft, unsuspecting bottom. A crimson rose opened behind Candy's tightly shut eyes. Across her hot cheeks, a second, redder rose slowly opened its petals of pain.

'Jealousy is an acid. An acid, Candy. It eats away at the heart of . . .'

Swish, swipe. Candy yelped.

'Affection.'

The sweet word, accompanied by the sharp slice, ignited Candy's inner being. The soft endearment, the severe stripe. A bitter-sweet paradox which almost caused Candy to orgasm.

'You must expunge it. Isolate it and send it into exile. It is an undisciplined emotion. One that spoils as it spreads its ugly shadow. No more jealousy. Understand?'

Candy remained silent.

'Do you understand?' The cane tapped the trembling buttocks as if emphasising the question.

'No more jealousy. I promise. I'll try,' the blonde whispered huskily.

'There are many young women here. On occasions, I have to deal with them. Intimately.'

Once again, the cane traced the outer swell of the firm buttocks.

'I understand,' Candy murmured.

'I am so glad that you do. Now come over here.'

They were in the Wise One's private chambers. A lemon carpet covered the oak floor, adding softness and light to the severity of the Spartan room. The furniture was scant but discreetly tasteful. Expensive pieces of late French Regency. Ornate, Candy reflected, rather than merely opulent, as she padded across to the large bed rubbing her hot, striped bottom ruefully. Naked and unashamed, she trod softly past the gleaming walnut desk – so carefully polished the warm wood glowed – spotting the telephones and the fax machine. She smiled to herself, having known all along that Orrag must have good communications. Thinking swiftly back to her arrival, she realised that she could have been off the island within a few hours.

Why had the Wise One been so keen for Candy to stay? What prescience had prompted her to persuade, or at least gently convince, Candy to remain? What had she glimpsed behind Candy's rude and arrogant façade? Candy suddenly burned to know. The Wise One had taken a risk on an assertive, greedy young businesswoman with the ethics of an alley-cat. Why?

'I saw myself. I saw myself in you, Candy. That is why I wanted you here on Orrag.'

How on earth? Yet again, the Wise One had astounded Candy by reading her mind intimately and accurately, and answering questions only half-formed and silently voiced. Candy blushed, slightly resenting, yet fully relishing, the vulnerable feeling of being so transparent to her mistress.

'I thought to myself: here is a canvas I can work on. I sensed I knew every nook and cranny. With discipline I could develop you. And look at the masterpiece that has emerged. Perfect. Although from time to time your flesh tones are too creamy. Need a little reddening.'

Candy's blushes deepened obligingly.

'Come here, Candy,' chuckled the Wise One, softly stroking the ivory duvet that covered the entire bed. 'Down on the bed with you. No, face down. Give me your bottom, you naughty little minx.'

Clamping her thighs tightly together at first, Candy slowly and luxuriously began to stretch out and spread her legs, and then her soft, supple arms, as she nestled into the duvet, spread-eagling her bottom up across its sweep of ivory satin.

221

Then, the cool benison, the soothing balm, visited her hot buttocks. She relaxed and loosened her clenched cheeks. They wobbled under the delicious ministrations. Three firm fingers, dripping cold cream, traced ever widening, healing circles of delight across the surface of the freshly whipped cheeks. Their shivering crowns dimpled beneath the gentle touch, and Candy sighed softly into the white pillow as her punished bottom submitted utterly to pure joy. The rounded, reddened buttocks quickly cooled beneath the circles of cold cream. Inching her hips up a fraction to meet the balm, the blonde moaned sensually. A stray, cold-creamed fingertip slipped down the shining, inner slope of the swollen left buttock, tracing its descent deliciously. Candy groaned deeply, clenching the silken duvet between her tightening fists. Groaned even more deeply as the fingertip paused to tap the bouncing left cheek imperiously – commanding it to soften and relax – before dipping down to stroke the entire length of the velvety cleft. As the cool unguent kissed the warm skin, Candy shuddered. Her hot, sticky sphincter tightened briefly, then opened up its rosebud to willingly receive the probing finger.

A deep, mutual sigh – their twin delight bound up and entwined into one plangent note of exquisite intensity – signalled the entry of the cool finger into the warmth it pierced and probed. Fused, the flesh of one within the other, the two young women on their bed of tenderness tumbled into a brief timelessness.

Outside, the hot sun pierced the earth, stirring its depths and summoning up the very juices of regeneration, vibrancy and life. Beyond the shining shingle and warm golden sands of Orrag's ribbon of beach, wave upon wave rose and collapsed, the very bosom of the dancing ocean heavy and swollen with liquid desires – desires that were inexorable, implacable; desires that neither the stern hand of nature herself nor the softer hand of time could tame and subdue.

Inside, in the seclusion of the Wise One's private chambers, Candy slowly surfaced from the deep, crimson pool she had slowly been sucked into. She slowly surfaced to hear her sweet mistress speaking.

'Orrag has a special purpose, Candy, and you have an important role to serve. A very important role. Womankind must once again assume its rightful sovereignty over this earth, a sovereignty they once enjoyed in ancient times – before the written word, before the time of ice. Before the flood itself. When all males bowed down and kissed the feet of the women who ruled them. Ruled them wisely, strictly and supremely. Look at what man has done with his squandered legacy. Two great wars in this century alone, with not a day's peace between the blood-letting. Hunger and fear still stalk the world. A world poisoned by stupidity and greed. And the waters, even the very air, are noxious. But by turning back to the wisdom of the female Ancients and by learning all their love we can ensure that young women begin to take control once more. Secure key posts, becoming policy shapers and decision makers. Orrag is a small beginning. A very small beginning. Perhaps we may fail. But we shall have tried. Here, the cream of intelligent and beautiful young womanhood learn to acquire the necessary self-discipline and rigorous self-control to fit them for their task and purpose. Who can rule others who cannot rule themselves? Tonight,' the Wise One lowered her voice to an excited whisper. 'Tonight, we will hold another ceremony. Tonight, we will put Clare to the ultimate test. Did you train her well, Candy? Did you do your duty for Orrag?'

'I think so,' murmured Candy dreamily.

'We shall see,' hissed the jade-eyed dominatrix, leaning forward to crush her breasts into Candy's soft, supine nakedness.

Candy and Chloe worked hard, bustling briskly in the dancing candlelight. Their oiled nakedness glistened as they bent down to their appointed tasks. Candy, unselfconsciously assuming a mantle of authority, gave directions and crisp orders – commands which Chloe increasingly resented. An air of constraint dulled their usual warmth and playfulness. Candy merely thought it was the tension of the forthcoming ceremony looming over them that caused the coolness. Chloe, still a little skittish and yet to be fully disciplined in the ways of Orrag, nursed a sullen, brooding disaffection for Candy's dominant authority. As they busied themselves, the dancing tiny points of flame from the carefully arrayed candles caught the soft swell of their thighs, the deep, shadowed cleavage between their loose, ripe breasts, and the darker delights at the base of their bellies. Instructed to prepare for the ceremony, they were anxious not to disappoint the young women of Orrag, or their stern leader. Disappointment for the girls would earn their disapproval which would rankle and bring shame. Displeasure from the Wise One would without question bring them pain.

By the time the double doors yawned open that evening to admit Madelaine, Clare, Annette, Samantha and the rest of Orrag's pert pulchritude, all was ready and in place. Soon the room was full with naked, expectant young women, who formed a disciplined semicircle around the imposing Tudor bed. Inching closer, they tightened their ranks, thighs brushing against shivering thighs as soft bottoms joggled. The Wise One swept in, her proud, beautiful face concealed behind the mask of thinly beaten gold. Her two naked handmaidens flanked her, walking two paces behind. With her she brought an air of solemnity which calmed the electric crackle of excitement charging the potent atmosphere. Naked feet shuffled and tiny toes scrunched into the deep carpet as the watching girls saw the leather harness being strapped tightly to the Wise One's loins – the supple thongs criss-crossed her fulsome buttocks and biting into her creamy cheeks as her handmaidens buckled and secured her. Next, the horn of gleaming ivory, the curved phallus of Aphrodite, was screwed into place firmly and lovingly by trembling hands. Once secure, it rose up in a glinting arc of delicious menace. All eyes were fixed on it. Most hearts were aflutter, many throats thickened, several labia softened and grew sticky in response.

'Prepare the bed,' commanded the Wise One. Her dominance absolute, her supremacy total.

As a reward for refurbishing and restoring the crimson-sheeted bed to its former glory, and repairing the damage done by Emily, Candy and Chloe were nominated for this highly desirable duty. The Wise One, drawing upon rites and rituals which reached back to Sappho, Minerva and Venus herself, always insisted that the ceremonial bed was lust-annointed before the main ceremony. Not with the sap of the sweet cedar or with the subtle oil of attar, but with the wet warmth of a ripened Eve's fig, ordained by nature's cunning to be sweeter than the oozing honeycomb and more pungent than a weeping damask rose.

Candy approached the bed of joy from the left-hand side, pausing to tread the carpet softly as her thighs brushed the cool, silken sheet. Chloe faced her across the pool of unblemished crimson, dimpling the taut stretch of silk with her fingertips, and then her knees, as she mounted. Their eyes met. The unspoken question hovered between them in a bruising silence. Who was to assume the dominant position? Which of them was to take the lead in the ensuing Sapphic rites?

Chloe, caught up in her whim of rebellious resentment, decided that she would go on top and ride Candy. Ride her ruthlessly – squeezing the blonde's bottom and breasts a little too harshly, paying her back for her bossy disposition. She pointed to the rippling expanse of silk and gazed challengingly into Candy's eyes. Her meaning was perfectly clear. Candy, unperturbed, gazed back unblinkingly. Slowly, Chloe's resolve crumbled. Her eyes flickered downwards and a burning blush spread across her face. A curt nod from the blonde brought Chloe to the sheet. Spread submissively, she awaited the kissing of skins as Candy herself mounted the bed and descended. Candy, smiling triumphantly, a smile kept strictly behind her deep-indigo eyes, turned to face the foot of the bed. It was expected that she would mount, grip Chloe's ankles and then slowly lower her face down on to the spread-eagled nude's pubis. But Candy was stung. Stung and smarting – she had caught the fleeting, rebellious glint in Chloe's eyes. She had sensed the brief flicker of insurrection. Chloe, she grimly determined, must be taught a lesson. A strict, stern lesson.

Facing the end of the bed, Candy gracefully eased her weight down on to Chloe, guiding her plump buttocks on to the startled, upturned face. Squatting upright, and settling her heavy cheeks, the blonde pressed her splayed buttocks directly on to the raven-haired girl's face. Candy shuddered as, sitting bolt upright, she felt Chloe's thick, muscular tongue enter her deeply, fiercely. An audible murmur escaped from the attendant, watching girls as they gazed hypnotically. On the bed, Candy drew her knees together, capturing and painfully squeezing Chloe's ripe breasts. Taking an erect, peaked nipple between each finger and thumb, Candy pleasingly, teasingly tormented and punished the helpless girl trapped between her firm thighs. Muffled groans of anguish were smothered by Candy's heavy bottom as Chloe felt the golden fire bathe her naked breasts. The pungent wetness of Candy's splayed secret flesh thrust down heavily on Chloe's face, filling her senses and flooding her soul, with its gentle harshness. The captive raven-haired girl could only respond with her vigorously devilish tongue. Candy started to ride – literally ride – Chloe, squashing her creamy buttocks firmly down on the smothered face, then, after easing them up imperceptibly, savagely bouncing them down yet again. From time to time, the blonde would slew wickedly sideways, grinding her softness across the slippery face below. Each time her cheeks kissed Chloe's flesh, Candy received the probing response of Chloe's erect, quivering tongue. Received it deep into her tight, wet warmth, where the thickened tongue-tip lapped her molten core. Candy felt her curtains of flesh stir and tremble – tremble as they rustled silently in the winds of her gathering lust storm.

Feverishly, worrying the peaked nipples in her cruel thrall, Candy bucked and bounced, pounding her heavy bottom down on the sweetly suffering Chloe. Around them, the candles flickered and danced as if buffeted by the shock waves of lust emanating from the bed of joy. Faster,

226

faster, her eyes now tightly shut – mere slits of fierce concentration – Candy ground her buttocks ruthlessly with a wild yet clinical precision into the wet, shining face beneath. A face wet with Candy's free flowing juices, a face shining with Chloe's own feveral arousal.

They climaxed – their ragged, feral wailing fusing into a paean of pleasure. Lips stretched wide, her white teeth bared in a snarl of carnal savagery, the rider arched her head back – tossing her golden mane in sheer abandonment – and, rippling her hips and thighs, swayed sinuously from buttock to buttock as the probing tongue of the ridden girl triggered Candy into orgasmic violence. At precisely the same moment, Chloe herself buckled and quivered as she surged into her own writhing, molten surrender.

Despite the august nature of the ceremony, despite the strict rules for silence which demanded to be obeyed, the circle of naked, huddling girls moaned softly as the two naked figures on the shimmering sheets – the subjugated below the supreme dominatrix above – came loudly.

'Examine the sheet,' the Wise One instructed a few moments later after silence returned to still the room. Her voice was charged with a febrile tension alien to her customary cool aloofness.

Willing hands, eager and prompt to obey, dragged at the crimson sheet and held it aloft. Two large dark stains of freshly spilled lust attested to Candy's triumph. Satisfied, the Wise One motioned for the bare bed to be remade.

In the flickering candlelight, Chloe, still trembling slightly, reached out and found Candy's hand. She squeezed it tentatively.

'I'm sorry,' she whispered huskily. 'I didn't mean to . . .'

'You will be,' Candy promised. 'I will deal with you later.'

'Punish me,' urged Chloe.

Candy suddenly grinned.

'Promise?' Chloe pressed.

'I promise. I am going to make things very hot for you. Very hot indeed.'

They squeezed and entwined their hands. Chloe's belly tremored, the thought of her midnight spanking quickly rocketing her into ripples of warm wet delight. She closed her eyes and fought to suppress the curdling moan welling up within her restricted throat.

Back at the bed, the ceremony unfolded. With her two attendants holding aloft the lamps, the Wise One approached the crimson-sheeted bed with measured steps. Her erect phallus attached to the harness strapped tightly around her buttocks nodded ponderously – a lazy salute to Aphrodite – as the Wise One, taut-buttocked and lithe as a panther, silently padded the carpet beneath her strong, naked feet.

'Closer,' she commanded, beckoning the handmaidens with the lamps.

The two obeyed, drawing towards the bed. A pool of golden light flooded the crimson as the lamps hovered above. They were small brass lamps, fashioned in the manner of Phoenician merchant boats plied by the Ancients to scour the uncharted seas in search of the rare purple dye – the dye the temple virgins stained their white robes with when darkly signifying their eventual passage into ripe womanhood.

'Clare,' summoned the face behind the golden mask.

All eyes turned to the naked girl, drinking in her pale face, her slender shoulders, the nervous flutter of the hands up to her gently bobbing bosom, and the delicious dimpling of her bottom as she approached the bed.

'Mount,' whispered the face behind the golden mask.

In full obeisance, the naked girl mounted the stained satin sheet which rippled beneath her warm weight. All watched as her pale face bowed down. All watched as the kneeling girl's round rump rose up. A beautiful, throat-tighteningly beautiful bottom. Each cheek peach-perfect, softly sculptured and delectable. Kneeling down upon the bed, the Wise One drew her oiled hips up closely to the raised, upturned rump before her. Soon her flesh hovered only inches from the taut surface of the curved buttocks. Candy saw the tip of the polished phallus flicker then wedge firmly into the deep cleft, nuzzling the tight rosebud sphincter. Clare gasped aloud.

'We are gathered here tonight to test this young woman's resolve. To witness how well she can summon up the discipline and strength of will to quell the flames I am about to ignite within her body. She must exercise absolute self-control. All of you watch, witness and learn. And as you watch, women of Orrag, will her to succeed. Her triumph is our triumph. Her success if Orrag's. Extinguish the candles. Let the ceremony commence.'

Candy turned and pinched out three candles within reach. As she sucked her hot fingertips, gently biting away the second skin of congealed wax which sealed her flesh, she returned her gaze to the bed. All around her, one by one, the remaining candles were quickly snuffed, rendering the two naked figures on the darkened pool of shadowed crimson luminously indistinct. As the last candle expired, all Candy could perceive by the tiny points of flickering lamplight were the thinly beaten gold mask, the gleaming slopes of the Wise One's bosom and the supple curves of Clare's fulsome rump. The mask receded a fraction. Candy deduced that the wearer was inching back slightly, away from the warm flesh of the kneeling sacrifice to Aphrodite. The curved dildo would have jerked upwards, she realised, its blunt tip tracing the outer curve of the quivering left buttock. Straining up on tiptoe, Candy glimpsed the brief flash of reflected light from the golden mask as the Wise One inched back into Clare's bottom – no doubt gripping the naked hips before guiding the erect ivory horn up in between the kneeling nude's soft thighs to pierce the sticky labia. Clare hissed out a loud moan. Candy had been right. She nodded as the cry confirmed her accuracy.

Beside her, Candy saw Chloe flutter her fingertips up to her slightly parted lips, then flutter them down to tentatively torment a swollen nipple. Returning her concentrated gaze to the eerily shadowed bed of joy, Candy assumed that Clare's soft gasping signalled the entry of Aphrodite's smooth rod up into her tight warmth. Damn this darkness, Candy muttered – intrigued, maddened and tantalised by the suggestive shadow play. Craving more intimate detail and a clearer, fuller knowledge of the drama unfolding before her in the velvety darkness, Candy strained her eyes. But the mantle of mystery remained, fully cloaking the naked beauties coupling on the now colourless crimson. Fully cloaking them as they writhed, locked into their dizzying lust. Darkness cloaked them in a fragile modesty as they sported on their bed of joy. Their bed of joy from which now whispered soft rustlings. The soft sound was so elusive, so bewitchingly elusive – the merest shadow of sound's substance.

The flickering boat lamps only served to confuse her, but then Candy suddenly remembered. If she could only accustom her eyes to the darkness, all would become clear. Despite her urgent desire to feast her eyes upon the darkened bed, she closed them tightly. Immediately, the kaleidoscope of soft sounds, silken murmurs and plangent sighs fell into place and made graphic sense. She identified the stern, strict and regular breathing of the Wise One – counterpointed by the gasps and grunts from the sweetly suffering Clare. Opening her eyes gradually, Candy smiled a wicked grin of triumph. Her scheme had worked. Candy was at heart a wheeler-dealer. A problem solver. She prided herself in getting difficulties sorted. She glimpsed, peering slightly, into the darkness. A darkness made visible now that her optic nerves had adjusted to it.

The two kneeling nudes revealed themselves in a smudged silhouette – one kneeling erect, her hands now above her head, the splayed fingers teasing the short strands of cropped hair in a soft ecstasy, the second, face squashed into the bed, thrusting her rump up into the hips and thighs behind. The Wise One's bottom – tightly crisscrossed by the taut leather straps securing the harness of hide – was undulating spasmodically and, from time to time, jerking forwards in a series of muscular thrusts. Clare, her features rendered indistinguishable by her lust-mask, absorbed each successive thrust, signalling her dark delight by snatching at the crimson sheet with taloned fingers. Yes. There. Candy could just make out tiny pinpoints of light dancing along the flexed knuckles. The Wise One's dominant hips were hammering into the naked buttocks fluently and fluidly – thrusting the cruel phallus deep up into the splayed thighs and beyond. Candy could now clearly discern the hard belly flattened into Clare's hot flesh.

Fresh grunts – deeper and more urgent – suddenly bruised the darkness. Candy knew and understood the sound, as did most of the dumbstruck girls standing beside her. They too stood up on tiptoe, many squeezing their ripe breasts, most strumming their sticky labia. Candy managed to do both as she craned to see Clare melt, succumb and dissolve, for she was sadly convinced by the sounds from the bed that Clare was about to climax. The grunts became more frequent, more carnal, rising in both pitch and intensity until they became mere bat squeaks of electric sexuality. Candy gripped her breasts fiercely in an automatic reflex of response, but a sadness and a sense of dull disappointment slowly numbed her. She dropped her hands – leaving her bosom proud and free – and lowered her head in dejection. Clare was manifestly failing, as the moaning from the bed clearly indicated. Inevitably, Clare would soon fail the supreme test. And in her failure would be seen Candy's failure. Failure to train and prepare Clare properly for the sweet rigours and cruel ravishment of the ceremony.

Rapid panting, punctuated by loud gasps, deafened the silence of the darkness. A pause. Then the coupled figures on the bed thrashed and writhed in their feral fusion. A soft scream. Candy saw the figures on the bed collapse into an amorphous heap of glistening nakedness. Heaving, sweating, intertwined nakedness.

Clare had succumbed.

'Light the candles,' the Wise One grunted – her voice thick and slow. No doubt from exhaustion and disappointment, Candy surmised.

The rekindled lights filled the room with their dancing, pale illumination. On the crimson bed, Clare lay spread-eagled, utterly spent. A smile – beatific, serene and sublime

– haunted her broad mouth. Just like a sensual sphinx, Candy thought. A flash of anger clouded Candy's eyes. Inflamed by Clare's playful smile, she instantly vowed to take the girl back to their secluded spot in the pine woods with ropes and a cane. Tied up tightly, bare-buttocked and bending, her naked cheeks pert and poised for the imminent stripes, Candy would train her pupil properly this time. Teach her a scalding, bottom-blazing lesson that would be etched in scarlet in her memory. Never to be forgotten.

'Girls,' the Wise One announced, sliding down from the bed gracefully.

Goodness, she looks utterly exhausted, Candy thought.

'Clare has', the voice dropped to a whisper 'succeeded.'

Joyful whoops of delight split the air as the naked assembly cheered Clare's success.

Success? But then who . . .? Who, Candy puzzled, had climaxed only a few moments ago? Someone had most certainly succumbed to the sweet ravishment of orgasm. Of that, Candy was absolutely certain. She frowned, then grinned as she saw the shining wet inner thighs of the Wise One. So rigorous had her thrusting been, she had brought herself to the pitch of ecstasy, and beyond. On the bed, cat-like and thoroughly contented, Clare rolled over on to her back and stretched out luxuriously. Splaying her legs widely, she revealed her dark Eve's fig, offering up the dry labia for inimate inspection. Candy approached the bed, her throat tightening, and bent down across the crimson sheet. Fingering the slightly swollen fleshfolds, she found them to be warm. But undeniably dry. Warm, and pulsing softly. But without trace of sticky arousal.

'Oh, Clare. You did it. You did it,' Candy gasped, scooping up her successful trainee and kissing her tenderly.

'She most certainly did,' murmured the Wise One, not a little ruefully. 'Artful little minx.'

Sighing softly, Clare wriggled down from her bed of triumph. Kneeling down, she silently kissed the Wise One's pale feet. Kissed them slowly and solemnly in tribute to her prowess. Clare remained, her sweat-soaked hair tumbling loosely around the naked ankles of the magnificent nude behind the thinly beaten mask of gold. The Wise One confirmed Clare's success once more, announcing in warm tones that a certain museum directorship in Paris was now most assuredly filled. All the girls applauded thunderously. To the dying echo of their cheer, Clare shuffled across the carpet on her knees and embraced Candy, clasping and clamping her strict trainer tightly around the hips and buttocks. Candy ruffled Clare's tousled tresses playfully – her hand freezing instantly as she felt hot lips implanted firmly, sweetly against her glistening pubis, her soft buttocks tensing alertly as she felt Clare's compressed mouth sucking and dragging at her warm labial folds. The kneeling girl launched hungrily into a silent but generous tribute to her stern disciplinarian, licking her deeply.

'Clare,' whispered the Wise One softly. 'I do not think you need express your gratitude and appreciation quite so . . . Clare? Clare, stop it at once. Cease this instant.'

But Clare, clutching Candy's soft, rounded bottom fiercely, was buried deep between the shuddering blonde's splayed thighs. Her tongue pink and busy as it searched the wet warmth of Candy's sex.

'Clare. Stop it. Get a cane, somebody. Anybody. Quickly,' the Wise One demanded. 'Stripe the girl.'

Willing hands sprang to obey and soon Clare's taut rump was seething under a soft rain of burning strokes, but they only drove her deeper into her increasingly frenzied fury of licking and lapping. Candy, hearing the swish of the caning and sensing the kiss of thin wood across bunched cheeks, threw her head back in an arch of ecstasy – tossing her golden mane as she approached her implacable paroxysm. As she felt the hot tongue probe deeply, and heard once more the subtle swish of the whippy cane, she teetered on the very edge of her orgasmic implosion.

The celebrations after the successful ceremony lasted almost until midnight. Chilled champagne flowed freely, as did music, excited laughter and happiness. The recent shadow that had darkened the sky above Orrag – Emily's insurrection and exile, her vendetta with the prying TV reporters – was banished by the heat of this happy moment. Recent troubles were forgotten as Clare's success was shared by all, and toasted in pink champagne, to remind her of her delicious discipline. As Candy sipped the sparkling wine, she closed her eyes and remembered how pink Clare's bare bottom had become beneath the towering pine trees.

'Memories?' murmured the Wise One.

'Mmm,' Candy sighed.

'You must be very, very proud of yourself,' the Wise One smiled as she guided Candy to a quieter corner. 'To you, and your training methods,' she whispered, raising up her tulip glass brimming with champagne.

'To Orrag. Its purpose, its philosophy, and its future,' replied Candy, echoing the salute.

They sipped their drinks meditatively.

'You are a wonderful acquisition to Orrag, Candy. You have certainly made your mark.'

Candy smiled her cat-like smile. Memories.

'Of course all of these girls will need training. For their ceremony.'

Candy gazed directly into the jade eyes. Enigmatic, opaque jade-green eyes gazed directly back.

'And when they too have succeeded, many more will follow them down to the pine woods. It could take many, many more months. Years, perhaps, until our work is done.'

Our work. Candy's fingers gripped her tulip glass excitedly. Many, many months. Years, perhaps. This was it. The formal request, the longed-for invitation to stay on Orrag. To stay on and train all these beautiful girls.

'I will stay here as long as I can serve you. As long as I am needed,' Candy replied softly.

'That will be for a long time, I trust. Especially after tonight, and my failure at the ceremony.'

Candy's eyes widened.

'You alone saw what happened to me. My happy shame,' the Wise One whispered.

Candy blushed slightly at the memory of the briefly glimpsed telltale signs of the Wise One's climax. The slippery sheen of the inner thighs. The wetness of the leather harness. Suddenly, the blonde grinned widely.

'Perhaps you would take me down to your secret spot in the pine wood. Take me to the pine trees and train me,' cooed the Wise One, a gentle note of pleading stealing into her voice.

The room swam around Candy, as if her large measure of chilled champagne had in fact been iced vodka. A large lump rose in her throat. This was, she knew, the supreme tribute. To have the Wise One begging to be stripped naked, then tightly bound, offering up her bare bottom for a leisurely dispensed vigorous disciplining.

'Yes,' Candy uttered huskily, her tongue suddenly quite swollen. 'Of course we will walk down among the pine trees. Together.'

'I shall go and bathe now. Be sure you come to my room when you have seen these girls safely to bed.'

Safely to bed.

Candy patrolled the deserted landings like a predatory prefect itching to spank a chubby-cheeked, sixth-form bottom. Her duties were sweet. She received, and returned, many deep kisses as she tucked in the sleepy, champagne-giddy girls of Orrag.

Up on the top landing, she approached the remaining bedrooms. She came to the door of Madelaine's Spartan cell. Inside, the light was already out. On the bed, in the darkness, a sinuous stirring of nakedness rustled the crisp linen sheets. Madelaine. The willowy blonde. Training Madelaine would be a great challenge, Candy reflected, closing the door silently behind her and stepping softly into the room. Madelaine. The apple-buttocked blonde. Yes, Candy mused. Training her would be very difficult. The girl was so excitable. Just how did one discipline and strictly train such a constantly moist daughter of Lust? In the darkness, Candy paused to consider her task. Perhaps if she tied Madelaine's hands together tightly with a pair of honey-bronze nylon stockings, then eased the naked, bound, girl over her warm lap, prepared for punishment. Yes. Finger her sticky labia, and all the time – arched above the bare bottom below – the threat of the spanking hand. The spanking hand, curved and hovering. Such a delicious threat seven inches above the swell of the bare cheeks. No, it would not be the cane or the strap, the paddle or the crop for the blonde's bare bottom. Candy was convinced that only a spanking would secure successful results with Madelaine. A slow, controlled, deliberate spanking. And the feet must be tied too, Candy suddenly realised. Crossed at the ankles and firmly bound with the other nylon stocking. Not only would that establish Candy's supreme dominant control but it would ensure that the soft buttocks bunched up beautifully. Ripe and round, bared for their sweet suffering. Goodness, Candy shuddered, how the severe spanking would redden and scald the blonde's bare bottom. Softly stabbed by the sudden thrill of hot anticipation, Candy could not resist risking the light. Her fingers found the switch despite the darkness. Beneath the yellow glare, Madelaine stirred and turned over on to her tummy. Her slim hands, Candy noted, grasped the pillow tightly; her beautiful face was pleasantly troubled by some delicious dream. Approaching silently, Candy drew down the single crisp sheet, revealing the sleeping blonde's sinuously curved spine and sumptuous bottom. Candy appraised the swollen cheeks, and shivered with delight. A trifle pert, and unarguably pliant. The girl's hips were perhaps a little fleshy and the buttocks a shade heavy and plumply fulsome.

Perfect for spanking. Such shapely cheeks. So ripe and rounded. Yes. Perfect, when poised and bared, for a slow, intimate spanking. The lotus blossom of desire unfurled deep within Candy's belly as she hungrily eyed the naked bottom, perusing the sweep of the curved contours and imagining the fleshy peaches jerking and bouncing under her spanking hand. So delicately blushed with a tincture of pink within the cream, how crimson they would flush when punished. And how scarlet would be Madelaine's sweet pain. How sweet, Candy sighed, would be the ravishment of firm palm across soft cheek. Again. Again. And yet again. Gently covering Madelaine with the cool sheet, Candy extinguished the light and tiptoed out of the bedroom. Extinguishing the light, but not her wet imaginings, as she left.

Annette was standing in front of her long cheval looking glass as Candy entered.

'Not in bed yet?' Candy queried.

'Thinking of the ceremony. It'll be my turn, soon. I'm not ready. I need to be trained. I need,' Annette's voice dropped to a husky whisper. 'I need to be disciplined.'

Candy gazed at the naked girl. Annette. The heavily breasted brunette. The heavily breasted brunette who was pleading, in curdling tones, to be trained. Who was whimpering to be trained and introduced to discipline. When Candy had entered the bedroom, Annette had been inspecting, and frankling admiring, her generous bosom. Cupping the superb breasts, she turned and faced her visitor.

'You will train me, won't you,' she urged, squeezing her trembling bosom fiercely.

Candy nodded then pointed to the empty bed.

'How will you train me?' Annette asked, looking back over her naked shoulder as she obediently climbed into her bed.

In silence, Candy studied the brunette's bare bottom. Shrewdly appraising the delightful rump, she speculated. It was a slender, athletic specimen. Suitable for the bite of the crop? Or better still, a thin leather belt. No. Of course. A strap. Yes. The sleak, firm contours of Annette's buttocks were perfect for the kiss of the hot hide, the caress of the stinging lash. Candy smiled at the narrow hips, small waist and supple thighs. How they would wriggle and writhe beneath the strap. But then again, Candy thought. Those breasts. Annette's swollen pride and fulsome glory. Candy vowed silently not to overlook the rich possibilities of the brunette's bosom. Of sweetly tormenting their creamy heaviness. Of sweetly tormenting those perfect orbs of shimmering pleasure. Orbs. Candy mouthed the word silently, twice, causing the invisible pulse in her pubis to quicken. How she would cup and kiss, palm and squeeze those gently dancing globes.

'How?' repeated Annette, snuggling sensuously down into the cool linen.

'Goodnight kiss?' Candy whispered, approaching the expectant brunette.

Annette nodded happily and sighed as she offered up her lips. Candy received the kiss. In reply, she inched down the crisp sheet and slowly, lingeringly, kissed each tremulous breast.

Next door, Samantha was discovered fingering herself. Candy entered the bedroom to witness the sallow, not exactly plump girl frenetically pleasuring herself as she lay, legs splayed, face and breasts squashed into her mattress. Both hands were trapped, and busy, down beyond the base of her belly. The pear-shaped buttocks, mellow cheeks devolving sensuously down from the slender waist, were framed by ripe hips and heavy thighs. They were, Candy reflected, fulsome cheeks – perfect for the hot lick and sharp stinging bite of the swishing cane. Indeed, buttocks destined for the bamboo. Yes, Candy considered judiciously. The yellow whippy wood would sear a memorable lesson across Samantha's pear-shaped bottom. Memorable. For both the caner and the caned.

Striding softly towards the bed, Candy smiled as Samantha strained over her shoulder and glanced up. The girl on the bed looked up with unfocused eyes – mere deep pools of clouded mulberry. Would they deepen or sparkle lightly when acknowledging the strokes of the striping cane? Samantha, slack-mouthed, her features drained to an expressionless blank by the gathering tumult within her, pleaded her desires.

'Stripe me. Quickly. Please,' she squealed, her voice distorted by her throat-thickening lust.

Bending, Candy slid her hand beneath the mattress and retrieved the cane. Brandishing it aloft, she thrummed the air with it twice – cutting and slicing the silence with crisp strokes of menace.

'Stripe my bottom. Please. Quickly, I'm coming . . .'

Candy levelled the length of glistening bamboo above the clenched cheeks, judging the distance. Too late. Suddenly, the fulsome buttocks bounced as the naked girl climaxed. Candy lowered the tip of the cane down on to, and then fully across, the superb cheeks. Gently, but firmly, she tamed, controlled and dominated the convulsing flesh. Dominance. Pure dominance. Samantha shrieked her sheer joy – crying out again as she melted within her blistering paroxysm.

'Stripe me – hard,' she hissed, offering up her clenched buttocks, submitting her bare bottom completely to the quivering bamboo.

Candy steadied the cane and suppressed the swollen cheeks with a gesture of supreme authority. Understanding the touch of the absolute rod, Samantha's thighs shivered as she writhed in a fresh orgasm. Inching her hips up in sinuous jerks for the stripes and strokes she yearned for, the naked girl emitted a plaintive squeal, fuelling her second climax all the more by beseeching – begging – for that which was to be sternly denied her. Tonight.

'Not now, Samantha,' Candy whispered, depressing the bamboo across the juddering crowns. 'Later. Later, I will stripe you. Thoroughly, expertly, intimately. But not now, not tonight.'

Her voice dropping to a tone of curdled honey, Candy traced the full sweep of the wobbling cheeks with the cool cane-tip, traced the shuddering contours of the creamy globes. She whispered soft and soothing words to the naked girl imploring her for pain. Soft and soothing words which assured Samantha that soon, in the pine woods, in a sunlit clearing in the pine woods, hot lashes would rain down across her naked buttocks.

And then, as Samantha mouthed obscenities into her white pillow, Candy bent down closer to examine the rump she promised to ravish. Prising the heavily fleshed cheeks apart, she lowered her face and lightly licked the length of the shadowed cleft. Licked the buried ribbon of velvet lightly, and lingeringly. Samantha screamed softly, bucking and bouncing her bare bottom in a renewed frenzy, and moaning sweetly in her aromatic torment. Candy pinched the left buttock with a nip of fierce tenderness, and mouthed her goodnight into Samantha's hair. The dark, mulberry eyes followed Candy to the door, drowning in their liquid longing for more.

And so, at last, to Chloe. Chloe – her final point of call. Naughty, rebellious little Chloe. Dear, sweet Chloe. Friend from the very first moment on Orrag. Those very first, deliciously painful, moments for Candy on Orrag. Brushing aside the fleeting memories, Candy resolved to be firm with Chloe. Strict and firm. Order and discipline, that was what Orrag demanded. Order and discipline. And that was what Candy would most certainly supply. Chloe had had the temerity to rebel at a solemn moment in the ceremony. For her naughtiness at the crimson bed, Chloe had been promised punishment. The moment had come. Chloe was to sample order and discpline.

Candy was determined not to be seduced by a smile, or a kiss. Or any one of several sensual fetching gestures Chloe was so adept at achieving with careful negligence. Candy knew well that the artful little minx was accomplished in the sinful skills of sweet distraction. She paused, her hand around the bedroom door handle, picturing how Chloe would wriggle out of a hot spot by fingering her gorgeous raven hair, or lazily adjusting a bra strap, or widening her large, grey affectionate eyes innocently. No. The hand tightened and turned the handle. Candy opened the bedroom door. She would be strict, stern and absolute in her determination to dispense discipline tonight.

Candy closed the door softly behind her and entered the darkened room. Switching on the light, she sensed the rhythmical breathing emanating from the prone figure beneath the white sheet.

'Are you awake?' Candy murmured.

The thighs beneath the sheet clamped themselves tightly together. The pretence of deep breathing – denoting a sleep that should not be disturbed – was sustained. Candy smiled knowingly and shook her head.

'Pity,' Candy sighed aloud. 'I wanted to share something with you. Something from the ceremony. Dearest Chloe.'

The bedclothes exploded into life. 'Have you got the dildo?' Chloe gasped, her wide eyes asparkle, springing up out of her bed, having been patently awake all the time.

'No,' thundered Candy. 'Just my anger. My anger at your behaviour earlier on. Disgraceful. I am here to punish you as promised.'

'S'not fair. I was sleeping,' Chloe protested, rubbing her eyes like a kitten does with its inverted paw. But Candy was not for seducing.

'You were wide awake. Lying will only incur a more severe spanking. Now come here. You deserve a hot bottom and a hot bottom you shall have. Come along. Bend over. Over my knee this instant.'

Meekly, Chloe surrendered her bare bottom up to its doom.

Spank. The first smack was playfully sharp.

Spank. the second was more sharply playful.

Spank, spank, spank. The ensuing smacks stung sharply, briskly crimsoning the softly pliant, shuddering domes. Chloe writhed and squirmed but Candy was deftly resolute. Spank, spank, spank. The curved palm swept down, the silent bedroom echoing each crisp kiss of hot hand to hotter curved cheek. The soft, bare bottom suffered. As Candy felt the first warm trickle of wet delight seep down on to her thighs from the labia of the spanked nude, she ruthlessly launched into a merciless staccato of nine scorching spanks. Chloe wailed her protest and kicked her little feet pitifully. Candy quickly pinned her captive down supremely, one hand firmly subjugating the nape of the neck, the other resting menacingly across the swell of the hot, bunched cheeks as she stayed and steadied the drumming heels of the punished girl with her own sovereign foot. Spank, spank, spank, spank. Bucking and jerking abjectly, Chloe buried her tear-stained face down into the cool sheet. Candy, rubbing the scarlet cheeks of the hot bottom affectionately, rolled the snuffling girl over and, bending down, gently licked and kissed the salt tears away.

* * *

'You wanted to see me?' Candy asked, somewhat shyly, at the Wise One's open door.

'Come with me,' replied the sterm mistress of Orrag, tossing aside the large white towel with which she was drying her nakedness after a luxuriously scented bath. 'I have a little present for you, Candy Brompton. Something in the way of a reward for all your efforts.'

Remaining luminously nude, the Wise One walked down along the cool, dark corridor. Candy followed, bewitched by the softly scented nakedness shimmering before her. At the foot of some uncarpeted stairs, the Wise One began a careful ascent up towards the remote attic above. The attic – Candy's heart skipped a beat as she suddenly remembered – where the jade-eyed dominatrix, the queen of Orrag, had been briefly held captive and subjected to enormities.

The familiar creek of the unoiled hinges brought the vivid memories flooding back. Memories of betrayal and rebellion. Candy beneath the narrow bed while up above, tied and trussed, the ruthless tormenting of the Wise One.

'In here. See?'

The single naked light bulb – Candy had remembered that the light switch was on the outer wall – showed Emily, copper hair tumbling down to her shoulders in neglected, uncombed tresses, sitting forlornly on the narrow bed. Naked. No, not quite, Candy realised. Emily wore a simple, short white vest. Nothing more. Emily looked up, sorrowfully. Her penitent gaze met Candy's stern stare. Emily lowered her eyes and fiddled absently with her fingers. It was a humble Emily that Candy gazed down on. Almost naked and thoroughly ashamed.

'Emily did not elect to return to the mainland with our uninvited guests,' the Wise One remarked.

Emily shrank back a little at the barbed irony of the statement. Uninvited guests – how much damage they could have caused.

'She was free to do so, were you not?'

Emily looked up and nodded.

'But she has chosen to remain. We have arrived, after much discussion, at an understanding. Emily is to remain

242

with us here on Orrag. Stay with us, and, in time, fully rejoin the community. As maid, of course, for many, many weeks of servitude and suffering. This is Emily's decision. It is her wish. Is that not so, my dear?'

'Yes,' mumbled Emily, looking up briefly. 'It is as you say, Wise One,' she whispered respectfully.

'But before Emily, our little stray sheep, can be returned fully to the fold, she must be rehabilitated. I of course can play no hand in her punishment.'

Candy nodded her agreement and understanding.

'That is a task for you, Candy. Do you feel able to discharge your duties?'

Emily raised her pale face up to Candy. 'P-punish me. Please,' she urged. 'I have been very, very wicked. Foolish, vain and wicked. I've earned my stripes.'

Stripes. Candy licked her lips. Licked her dry lips excitedly. So this was her gift from the Wise One. Stripes – the word exploded softly in her brain.

A little later, when Emily and Candy were alone in the remote attic, sinuous thoughts teased the blonde's imagination. Gazing out into the depths of the night beyond the casement window, she caught a glimpse of the sparkling, moon-kissed ocean. Such a vast expanse, she wondered. Such a vast expanse. And would Emily, the near-naked penitent now bending for her punishment have to journey and span an equally vast expanse of sharp pleasure and soft, sweet pain before her rehabilitation was complete? Taking a final glance at the ocean's glittering eternity, Candy narrowed her eyes and examined the shining length of her supple cane.

In time, her soft fingers found Emily's left cheek. The curve was taut, the buttock tensed and expectant. She patted it. Almost affectionately. Almost.

Stepping back a pace and a half, Candy raised her arm – flexed at the elbow, straightened at the narrow, strong wrist – and with it the 23 inches of whippy bamboo.

Outside, an owl hooted plaintively. Seconds later, after the whistling swish of the slicing cane, the owl's mournful cry was echoed by a sorrow-sob of pain.

NEW BOOKS

Coming up from Nexus and Black Lace

Lydia in the Bordello by Philippa Masters
July 1996   Price £4.99   ISBN: 0 352 33092 9
Lydia, now back in England from her African adventure, is concerned by the double standards inherent in Victorian society. She is also fascinated by Brighton's brazen working-girls. When the mysterious Lady Amberson asks her to help provide some very special entertainment at her private parties, Lydia is initially shocked, but realises that to refuse would be to be guilty of the hypocrisy she so despises.

Rue Marquis de Sade by Morgana Baron
July 1996   Price £4.99   ISBN: 0 352 33093 7
Charlotte's inborn lust and submissive, masochistic tendencies temper her fear and hatred of Veronica, her sadistic stepsister, with whom she will soon be reunited. The sisters' destination is Steinreich, a tiny principality with some very bizarre laws and customs. Veronica seems quite at home there, but Charlotte dreads to contemplate what she will have to endure, in order to claim her share of her father's legacy.

Annie's Further Education by Evelyn Culber
August 1996   Price £4.99   ISBN: 0 352 33096 1
Helped by some obliging and enthusiastic friends, servants and fellow members of the Flagellation Society, Annie establishes Redhand House Academy – an institution for women desiring disciplined education. Yet it is soon evident that success has gone to Annie's head, and that she, too, has some harsh lessons to learn before her own education is complete.

The Chaste Legacy by Susanna Hughes
August 1996   Price £4.99   ISBN: 0 352 33097 X
Shipwrecked in a storm, the beautiful Corinda Chaste finds herself the prisoner of Constantine Stephanikis, a Greek pirate. As he teaches her to satisfy even the most bizarre sexual tastes, she proves to be an eager and totally uninhibited pupil. She is, however, unaware that Stphanikis has other – more sinister – plans for her.

Forbidden Crusade by Juliet Hastings
July 1996   Price £4.99   ISBN: 0 352 33079 1
1186, the Holy Land. Forbidden to marry beneath her rank, Melisende, a virginal young nobelwoman, determines to use her cunning – and her sensual body – to seduce the chivalrous young man she loves. But will her resourcefulness and appetite for sexual pleasure allow her to survive imprisonment in the harem of a Saracen Emir?

Lord Wraxall's Fancy by Anna Lieff Saxby
July 1996   Price £4.99   ISBN: 0 352 33080 5
1702, Lady Celine Fortescue agrees to marry the debauched Lord Wraxall, on condition that he spares Liam, her lover, who has been wrongfully condemned. Wraxall reneges on his promise, and Celine resigns herself to a life of subjugation. Liam, however, escapes and, allies himself with the lustiest pirates in the Caribbean . . .

The Houseshare by Pat O'Brien
August 1996   Price £4.99   ISBN: 0 352 33094 5
When Rupe bares his most intimate desires over the Internet, he does not know that his electronic confidante is Tine, his landlady. With anonymity guaranteed, cybersexual encounters are limited only by the bounds of the imagination, but what will happen when Tine attempts to make the virtual real?

The King's Girl by Sylvie Ouellette
August 1996   Price £4.99   ISBN: 0 352 33095 3
The early 1600s. Under the care of the decadent Monsieur and Madame Lampron, Laure, a lusty, spirited young Frenchwoman, has learned much about darker pleasures. Sent to the newly established colony in North America, she tries – and fails – to behave as a good Catholic girl should, and is soon embarking on a series of wild sexual adventures.

NEXUS BACKLIST

All books are priced £4.99 unless another price is given. If a date
is supplied, the book in question will not be available until that
month in 1996.

CONTEMPORARY EROTICA

THE ACADEMY	Arabella Knight	
BOUND TO OBEY	Amananda Ware	Feb
BOUND TO SERVE	Amanda Ware	Sep
CANDY IN CAPTIVITY	Arabella Knight	Jun
CHALICE OF DELIGHTS	Katrina Young	Mar
THE CHASTE LEGACY	Susanna Hughes	Aug
CHRISTINA WISHED	Gene Craven	Apr
CONDUCT UNBECOMING	Arabella Knight	
CONTOURS OF DARKNESS	Marco Vassi	
DARK DESIRES	Maria del Rey	May
DIFFERENT STROKES	Sarah Veitch	
THE DOMINO TATTOO	Cyrian Amberlake	
THE DOMINO ENIGMA	Cyrian Amberlake	
THE DOMINO QUEEN	Cyrian Amberlake	
ELIANE	Stephen Ferris	
EMMA'S SECRET WORLD	Hilary James	
EMMA ENSLAVED	Hilary James	
EMMA'S SECRET DIARIES	Hilary James	
EMMA'S SUBMISSION	Hilary James	Oct
FALLEN ANGELS	Kendal Grahame	
THE FANTASIES OF JOSEPHINE SCOTT	Josephine Scott	
THE FINISHING SCHOOL	Stephen Ferris	May
THE GENTLE DEGENERATES	Marco Vassi	
HEART OF DESIRE	Maria del Rey	

HELEN A MODERN ODALISQUE	Larry Stern	
HIS MISTRESS'S VOICE	G. C. Scott	
HOUSE OF ANGELS	Yvonne Strickland	
HOUSE OF INTRIGUE	Yvonne Strickland	
HOUSE OF TEMPTATIONS	Yvonne Strickland	Oct
THE HOUSE OF MALDONA	Yolanda Celbridge	
THE ISLAND OF MALDONA	Yolanda Celbridge	Feb
THE ICE QUEEN	Stephen Ferris	
THE IMAGE	Jean de Berg	
THE INSTITUTE	Maria del Rey	
SISTERHOOD OF THE INSTITUTE	Maria del Rey	
JENNIFER'S INSTRUCTION	Cyrian Amberlake	
LETTERS TO CHLOE	Stefan Gerrard	
LINGERING LESSONS	Sarah Veitch	
A MATTER OF POSSESSION	G. C. Scott	
MELINDA AND THE MASTER	Susanna Hughes	
MELINDA AND ESMERALDA	Susanna Hughes	
MELINDA AND THE COUNTESS	Susanna Hughes	
MELINDA AND THE ROMAN	Susanna Hughes	
MELINDA AND SOPHIA	Susanna Hughes	
MIND BLOWER	Marco Vassi	
THE NEW STORY OF O	Anonymous	
OBSESSION	Maria del Rey	
ONE WEEK IN THE PRIVATE HOUSE	Esme Ombreux	
THE PALACE OF SWEETHEARTS	Delver Maddingley	
THE PALACE OF FANTASIES	Delver Maddingley	
THE PALACE OF HONEYMOONS	Delver Maddingley	
THE PALACE OF EROS	Delver Maddingley	
PARADISE BAY	Maria del Rey	
THE PASSIVE VOICE	G. C. Scott	
RUE MARQUIS DE SADE	Morgana Baron	Jul
THE SALINE SOLUTION	Marco Vassi	
SHERRIE	Evelyn Culber	
THE SPANISH SENSUALIST	Josephine Arno	
STEPHANIE	Susanna Hughes	
STEPHANIE'S CASTLE	Susanna Hughes	

STEPHANIE'S REVENGE	Susanna Hughes	
STEPHANIE'S DOMAIN	Susanna Hughes	
STEPHANIE'S TRIAL	Susanna Hughes	
STEPHANIE'S PLEASURE	Susanna Hughes	
THE TEACHING OF FAITH	Elizabeth Bruce	
FAITH IN THE STABLES	Elizabeth Bruce	Mar
THE TRAINING GROUNDS	Sarah Veitch	
UNDERWORLD	Maria del Rey	

EROTIC SCIENCE FICTION

ADVENTURES IN THE PLEASUREZONE	Delaney Silver	
RETURN TO THE PLEASUREZONE	Delaney Silver	
FANTASYWORLD	Larry Stern	

ANCIENT & FANTASY SETTINGS

THE CLOAK OF APHRODITE	Kendal Grahame	
DEMONIA	Kendal Grahame	
THE HANDMAIDENS	Aran Ashe	
THE SLAVE OF LIDIR	Aran Ashe	
THE DUNGEONS OF LIDIR	Aran Ashe	
THE FOREST OF BONDAGE	Aran Ashe	
PLEASURE ISLAND	Aran Ashe	
WITCH QUEEN OF VIXANIA	Morgana Baron	
SLAVE-MISTRESS OF VIXANIA	Morgana Baron	

EDWARDIAN, VICTORIAN & OLDER EROTICA

ANNIE	Evelyn Culber	
ANNIE AND THE SOCIETY	Evelyn Culber	
ANNIE'S FURTHER EDUCATION	Evelyn Culber	Aug
THE AWAKENING OF LYDIA	Philippa Masters	
LYDIA IN THE HAREM	Philippa Masters	
LYDIA IN THE BORDELLO	Philippa Masters	Jul
BEATRICE	Anonymous	
CHOOSING LOVERS FOR JUSTINE	Aran Ashe	
DEAR FANNY	Aran Ashe	

LURE OF THE MANOR	Barbra Baron	
RETURN TO THE MANOR	Barbra Baron	
MAN WITH A MAID 1	Anonymous	
MAN WITH A MAID 2	Anonymous	
MAN WITH A MAID 3	Anonymous	
MEMOIRS OF A CORNISH GOVERNESS	Yolanda Celbridge	
THE GOVERNESS AT ST AGATHA'S	Yolanda Celbridge	
THE GOVERNESS ABROAD	Yolanda Celbridge	Sep
PLEASING THEM	William Doughty	Apr
TERESA'S VOYAGE	Romany Vargas	

SAMPLERS & COLLECTIONS

NEW EROTICA 2	ed. Esme Ombreaux	
THE FIESTA LETTERS	ed. Chris Lloyd	

NON-FICTION

HOW TO DRIVE YOUR MAN WILD IN BED	Graham Masterton	
HOW TO DRIVE YOUR WOMAN WILD IN BED	Graham Masterton	
LETTERS TO LINZI	Linzi Drew	

Please send me the books I have ticked above.

Name ....

Address ....

....

....

.....................Post code ....

Send to: **Cash Sales, Nexus Books, 332 Ladbroke Grove, London W10 5AH.**

Please enclose a cheque or postal order, made payable to **Nexus Books,** to the value of the books you have ordered plus postage and packing costs as follows:

UK and BFPO – £1.00 for the first book, 50p for each subsequent book.

Overseas (including Republic of Ireland) – £2.00 for the first book, £1.00 for the second book, and 50p for each subsequent book.

If you would prefer to pay by VISA or ACCESS/MASTER-CARD, please write your card number and expiry date here:

....

Please allow up to 28 days for delivery.

Signature ....

Seltén, G. Over Zaken, Namen, Boeken, enz. (Winkler Prins),
London 1977-1983.

Please contact a number of bookshops, make particular to
Source Books, 6, the value of the Book you buy make it. This
range for our purpose as follows.

of Grand III (?) – 1700 for the first book: after fewer number
qualifies.

Or was (including Republic of Ireland) £7.00 to the first
book, £4.00 for the second and third and 5p for each subsequent
book.

If you would prefer to pay by VISA or ACCESS/MASTER-
CARD, please write your card number and expiry date.

Please allow up to 2 days for delivery.